SPARKLE

The Queerest Book You'll Ever Love

By Rob Rosen

To Kenny…
The best husband a guy could ever wish for!

PRAISE FOR SPARKLE

"The charm of this glorious read rests in Rosen's wit and sense of timing. The characters literally leap off the page as the story effortlessly unfolds and blossoms before your eyes... If you're looking for an uplifting gay romp of a read then look no further, as Sparkle is most definitely the queerest book you'll ever love." – GaydarNation

"Rosen spins a fresh and colorful tale with style and wit of which to be envious. Don't be surprised when you actually laugh aloud as he weaves this account of comedy, intrigue, and suspense. Rosen gives the reader a glimpse of Gay Life. And what fun it can be!" – StoneWall Society

"Sparkle is the epitome of why everyone should want to be a gay male – and gives the reader a complete blueprint on how to do it! My hope is that this book tops some lists this year. (Oprah, you listening, hon?)" – Quest Magazine

"Add a little alcohol, drugs, and sex, and the unpredictable kinds of people you're likely to find on the streets of Baghdad by the Bay, and you have one of the most unusual novels to come out of gay San Francisco in quite some time." – The Letter

"Rosen's writing is hip and provocative. His characters don't pull any punches and they don't mince words. The narrator's blunt manner is especially appealing as he describes his lurid coming of age with Sparkle as mentor and friend... Somewhere between Queer as Folk and Hedwig and the Angry Inch lies Sparkle, which may well be the queerest book you'll ever read." – X Factor

"This book has all the potential for becoming the next gay cult classic! Because if you read it, you're sure to love it and tell at least a half dozen friends to get their hands on it, too." – OurBookShelf

"Readers will find themselves laughing right out loud as Rosen's comfortable style pulls them into Sparkle and Secret's twisted lives... An absolute perfect way to take a San Francisco vacation without actually hopping on a plane." – The Texas Triangle

FOREWORD

Welcome to the 10th Anniversary Edition of *Sparkle: The Queerest Book You'll Ever Love*, reworked, reedited, and bigger, badder, bitchier than the original. This is the book that started it all for me, my first attempt at writing, launching me on the path that I'm still travelling gaily along today.

So, as a little background information before you start your journey into my characters' rather twisted lives, let's begin at the beginning. See, from the moment I read my first gay book, *The Best Little Boy in the World*, I've had this fondness for the coming out story. Only, back then, most books in this genre were rather on the sad side: bleak, tragic, 50's, 60's, 70's, 80's gay-life-depressing. And I wanted my first book to be anything but these things. I wanted it to be in-your-face, un-P.C., upbeat, and quirky. Meaning, it had to take place in San Francisco and definitely deep within The Castro.

All it took was for me to get my first home computer, and then I hit the ground running. Six months later, I had my book: *Sparkle*. Within a year, it was on the shelves, getting rave reviews, and I was doing readings up and down the California coast. See, I'd always wanted to be a writer, always knew I had it in me to be a writer, and, suddenly, my dreams had come true. Seriously, holding that book in my hands, with my name splashed across the cover, it was like, well, *magic*.

And it was just the start, too. Because one dream leads to another, and yet another.

Divas Las Vegas followed *Sparkle*, was nominated for a Lammy, and won the 2010 TLA Gaybie for Best Gay Fiction. *Hot Lava* followed closely on its heels. In between all this, I've written short stories for well over 150 anthologies and wrote erotica for 5+ years for *MEN, Freshmen*, and *[2]* Magazines. Twenty of my favorite stories from those magazines can be found in my collection, *Good & Hot*.

But *Sparkle* always holds a special place in my heart. Always has, always will. And, so, ten years later, I decided to do a bit of editing and get it back out there for you to enjoy. And now, for the first time, it's also available for all eReaders. Meaning, fingers crossed, it will find a whole new audience.

All that being said, dear friend, I hope *Sparkle* will hold a special place in your heart as well!

CHAPTER ONE
FROM QUEER TO ETERNITY

Honestly, I can't say that being at San Francisco General at two in the morning is any great surprise to me. I mean, I had a feeling this would happen someday. And though I can't say for sure who shot Sparkle, I'm sure he deserved it. My best guess is that it was probably some bitter trick. Of course, in my years of experience, when it comes to Sparkle, they're pretty much all bitter. Go figure. In any case, since I'm up and you're up, let's try to figure out who pumped that little, old bullet into my best friend's magnificent shaved chest.

Yes, yes, I know what you're thinking. *Poor, jealous Bruce, mocking Sparkle while he lies fragile at death's door.* Well, you haven't met Sparkle; this is, in fact, the perfect time to mock and deride. Fucker's dangerous as all hell when he's lucid. In other words, don't be so surprised that I'm making fun of the man while he lies there drooling, possibly in an irreversible coma. Ooh, doesn't that sound all melodramatic-like: irreversible coma. Such a soap-operie condition. Well, friend, that's Sparkle all over. One big-ass soap opera. Big enough for Susan Lucci to play him if this shit ever gets televised. (Don't worry; the names will be changed to protect the innocent. If there actually are any.)

Anyway, Sparkle and I are indeed best friends, as I mentioned back there. Have been for many these long years. The *how* you're soon going to learn; the *why* is a mystery of the ages. I mean, if you knew Sparkle, you'd wonder how he manages to have any friends at all, really. And, yet, he does. Scads of them. And *way* more enemies. See, there's a mascara-thin line between love and hate, and I've seen one dude after the next skip over said line. Well, I think you get the point. I mean, you

1

look pretty bright up there. But, just to make it perfectly clear, Sparkle is plain, old evil. (And mean, vindictive, cruel, plotting, snide, crude, and lewd.) And, suffice it to say, I love him with every fiber of my being. God help us all.

So here we are, very early in the morning, too early if you ask me, but here nonetheless. And since we have nothing better to do or, sadly, any*one*, I might as well fill you in on myself and my life with that drooling, comatose son of a bitch. Now, first comes first, but you might be surprised to learn that I didn't used to talk this way, or act this, or even look this way. I mean, I was just your average small-town, confused, slightly neurotic, somewhat cute, and very closeted kind of guy. As straight acting, looking, walking, and talking as you can possibly get.

By the way, don't you just hate that term: straight acting? I mean, as if. Who in their right minds would choose to *act* straight? Oh, but now I'm sounding like Sparkle. Guess he's worn off on me over the years. Anyway, back to the story.

See, I met him fresh out of college. I'd just earned my Bachelors degree in English Literature and was doing what any normal college graduate would be doing: I was waiting tables. The place was called Joe Joe's, the owners both being named Joe. How original, right? In any case, I absolutely hated that job, but at the time I had no idea what I could do with my degree. I mean, what was I thinking? When did Jane Austen ever open up any doors for anyone? In any case, that's where and when that into my life walked Sparkle. Well, sauntered, at any rate. Heck, cat-walked was more like it. (Dude could give Naomi Campbell some pointers.)

Joe Joe's was, as usual, packed for Sunday brunch. Normally, very few gay men ate there, but on Sunday, between ten and three, watch out. Every queer worth his weight in Pradas could be seen downing a mimosa and eating one of the dozen or so mediocre omelets they had on the menu. Honestly, the restaurant was nothing to write home about, but it was certainly the place to see and be seen, even with the bad location, absolutely no parking, and, at best, so-so food. It did, however, boast several mirror-covered walls, so the cruisabilty level was way high. Also, it had the slammingest jukebox ever, filled to the brim with the best tunes of the day. Music-wise, I was in rhinestone-studded heaven.

So there I was, twenty-one, fresh out of the proverbial closet, and knee deep in queer every Sunday. I hadn't even done *it* with a man yet and I was surrounded by testosterone-coated yumminess, with nary a shred of a clue of how to get me some. Or what to do should, *gulp*, that even happen. I mean, I might as well have been from a different planet as I had no idea what these boys were talking about half the time. Truthfully, I was quite in need of an unabridged Webster's Gay English Dictionary. (This being long before *Sex in the City*, it certainly would've come in handy. Oh, Samantha, where for art thou?)

I can remember that day like it was yesterday, by the way. Even after all the drugs and booze. I mean, please, I can't possibly have more than a few brain cells left, and a couple of those are about to forever blink out. But that day, that day I remember perfectly, and it still gives me the chills just thinking about it. Because that's the day I took my first baby gay steps into the man you see standing before you today. (Well, teetering, at any rate.)

It was close to eleven, with a minimum half-hour wait to get into the place. All my tables were crammed full as soon as the doors were open, and I hadn't caught a breath since. Thank God they made a mean cup of coffee or I have no idea how I could've made it through those awful Sundays. Thankfully, too, the music had been incredibly fierce that morning. Lots of techno and industrial dance stuff: Bizarre Inc., Lords of Acid, and, at that very moment, My Life with the Thrill Kill Kult's mega-hit, *Sex on Wheelz*. Just as the song started, in came a party of six. I'd seen this group before. All pretty, all buffed, and all tweeked out on one thing or another. Miraculously, they'd rarely slept the night before and still always seemed to look fabulous. Better living through chemistry, I figured. The only difference this time, however, was the stranger they soon had in their ranks.

He was, be still my heart (and hard-on), six feet tall, with short-cropped, jet-black hair, not quite a buzz-cut, steel-blue eyes, a slightly aquiline nose, studded ears, and an immaculately shaved goatee. And, of course, he donned a deep even tan on his perfectly complected skin. Like the rest of then, he had on a form fitting muscle tee, blue jeans, and black boots. The dude was thin and tight and too, too dreamy. He was called, as I was later to learn, *a clone*. But, no, friend, because if there where others like him out there, life would be unbearable for us ordinary folk. And, *gasp*, he was coming straight (directionally forward) toward me. *Kathump* went my heart again. *Kapow* went that bulge in my work slacks.

Breathe, Bruce, breathe, I thought. *He's just like any other of the queers in the place, just a little more, well, um, perfect.* Seriously perfect. Serious as a

3

heart attack. Or, as in our present case, a coma. (We can turn Susan's head to the side for those scenes, away from the camera. A body-double would be much cheaper, yes?)

In any case, then it happened: he opened his mouth and spoke and, you guessed it, his purse fell out. Oh, sure, he had perfect pearly whites (caps, I was later to find out), his breath was minty and sweet, his eyes, from up close, were shockingly blue and stunningly intense, and, right on up to the point where he asked me for a cup of coffee, I could've sworn that my feet weren't even touching the ground. There was only me and this man and the music. And life, dear friend, was really fucking good.

And then he spoke and the spell was broken. "Girl, if I don't get a cup of coffee in the next few minutes, I'm gonna drop the fuck right on over. And you don't want that on your conscience, do you, Precious?" Like I said, spell broken. Crushed. Stamped on and trampled to death.

"Sorry, sir, my section is full. If you'll wait just a minute, I'm sure the hostess can get you your coffee," I replied, icily, before turning away. Well, somewhat *chilly*, anyhow; I mean, he was still awfully pretty, if not rude and frightfully nelly. (Did I mention stunning? If not, he was. Stu-nning.)

But, as I turned to head on back to the world of the merely average, fate stepped in. Leapt in, really. Barged and pushed and shoved in. Because that's when he grabbed my arm and asked, "What's your name, Sugar?" Oh, I was quick on my feet that morning. My gayest gene kicked in and I answered in a deep, lush voice, "Secret, what's yours?" If you don't get that comeback, mid-nineties-dated as it now is, may I suggest you go out and purchase *Sexplosion* right this instant, 'cause that's a Grade-A, thinking on your feet answer in conjunction with the song that was playing at that very moment. And he got it, too, quick as wink, because his eyes twinkled and the slightest grin appeared on his devilishly handsome face, and he looked me deep in the eyes (here's where the chills start) and he said, "Secret, I think I'll wait until your section opens up a bit and you can get me that cup of coffee your pretty, little self." And he turned and sacheted back to his six beau-hunk friends, leaving me quite breathless and dizzy. As the saying goes, he rocked my world, which thereon out would forever be at a noticeable tilt.

And, yes, he and his friends did stand around until I had room for all of them. And while the hostess gave them all cups of coffee,

Dreamboat Andy waited until he was planted at a tight, little table meant for five and I poured him his steaming cup of java. It was to be the first of hundreds I was to serve him over the years and, needless to say, it was certainly the most memorable. Fateful, I'd go so far as to say.

Unfortunately for me, the restaurant stayed packed all the way through closing, and I only managed to catch snippets of the conversation emanating from the group of those beautiful seven men. Most of that consisted of who consumed what drugs and who went home with which trick: pretty standard stuff for Joe Joe's on a Sunday afternoon, sad to say. Still, I'd gotten quite used to it all by then, even though I had yet to experience any of it firsthand. Of course, whenever Mister Universe opened his mouth, I managed to be nearby to hear it. Naturally, there were no surprises there. He was the crudest, rudest, snippiest, and bitchiest of the bunch. It was rather heartbreaking, really. If this was what it was like to be gay and popular and desired, then this was not what I wanted. (I know, I know, stop rolling your eyes up there; it was *exactly* what I wanted, just not how I wanted to be in order to get there. I think that's one of those double-edged swords you hear talked about. Ouch. Band-Aid, please.)

Two hours later, apparently full and tiring from lack of sleep, the group started getting ready to leave. As for that, my feelings were divided. I mean, on the one hand, I was glad for this man to leave. He was truly one of the most arrogant and pretentious gay guys I'd ever served. On the other hand, well, you know what that hand is used for, right? Come on now, he was stunning, after all, and the thought that I might never see him again did kind of give me a pit in my stomach. Pathetic, I know, but, as I've said, I had little to no experience in the ways of gays. And here before me was my ideal, my prototype.

Then, as they got up to leave, guess who picked up the check? Yep, it was him. No wonder why they put up with him all morning, I figured. The other six staggered out the front door as he turned and came up to me with the cash. "Keep the change, Secret, and thanks for the coffee," he said, looking me dead in the eye. (Yikes, there go those damn chills again) "And if you don't have any plans this Saturday, I'm having a little get-together at my house at around ten. I wrote the address down on the check." He turned around one more time before walking out the door, winked, and added, "Ciao, Precious," and then promptly waved his goodbyes. *Boom, boom* went the pounding in my heart. And, no, the pounding lower down wasn't much less noticeable. P.S., he left me a fifty dollar tip. What a fucking morning.

The rest of the day went by in a coffee-egg-ketchup-splattered blur. Thank goodness I was swamped, and didn't have much time to think about what had just happened. But when I did, man, did it ever terrify the hell out of me. I mean, I was just invited to my first gay party by the most amazing looking man I'd ever seen, plus I was way more scared than happy at the prospect of mingling with this particular group of demigods. To be honest, I had absolutely nothing in common with them and couldn't even begin to imagine what I could add to the conversations once I got there.

Well, live and learn my mom used to say. (No, not really, but she deserves credit for something. Raising me was no picnic, after all.) So I decided to make the best of it and I turned my frown upside down. Glass half-full. Hopefully with something strong and gin-and-tonicy.

When I finally made it home, I had a chance to look at what was written on the check. Lo and behold, my man had a name: William Astan. It was several months later, while I was doing the Jumble puzzle in *The Examiner*, that I realized what you get when you jumbled his last name... figure it out yet?... it's Satan. Of course, by then it was way too late. Water under the Golden Gate Bridge. If I'd noticed this at the time I first read his name, would I have done anything differently? Nope. I must say, I have no regrets. It's been quite a memorable and educational experience, really, and too much has happened to ever turn back. So onward and upward, or some such thing. Full steam ahead! (And batten down the fucking hatches, for goodness sake.)

First thing was first, though: shopping for the big event. William had, after all, given me fifty bucks. That and the other hundred I made in tips that day made for a reasonably nice wad to spend on an outfit and a new haircut. I mean, how much could a tight tee and jeans cost, right? Fuck my rent, I figured. (Hey, I was only twenty-one. Naiveté came easily.) But then, who knew that designer tops went for a minimum of forty bucks and jeans double that? Of course, if I had nothing to say come Saturday night, at least I would look nice standing there. The haircut, however, was trickier business.

Since officially coming out, I really didn't have any gay friends. In college, as far as I knew, I didn't know any gay people. And do you think moving to San Francisco made it any easier? It was like being in France and not being able to speak French. I could admire the beautiful surroundings, but I couldn't communicate with the natives. Heck, I didn't even know where to begin.

Well, thank goodness, that's when Kiki swished into my life. Oh, and you must pronounce Kiki like you're a twelve-year-old girl on lots of caffeine. I don't know why, it just sounds better that way. Like screaming *yippy* with your hands flung in the air.

Kiki, you see, gave me my first haircut. I'd been in the city all of two months and was very nearly broke from having spent all my money on moving to San Francisco and paying first month's rent, last month's rent, and a down-payment on a studio apartment that just barely held me and my ratty, old futon. Still, I figured that a new coif would brighten my spirits, if not severely deplete my funds. Cut It Out, the salon, just happened to be down the street from where I lived, so I walked in, and, as luck would have it, Kiki had just had a last minute cancellation. And you know what it says in the Gay Bible, don't you? *And a dresser of hair shall lead them out of the darkness and onto the path of enlightenment.* So it is written, so it shall come to pass.

"Darlin', you must be new to this city, 'cause I haven't seen a do like that since about seventy-six or so. Don't you know, disco is dead, Sugar, and that hair of yours should've been buried right along with it." Those were Kiki's first words to me, I swear it. And, yes, I was terrified of him. No gay man had so much as touched me, and here was this little wisp of a queen suddenly running his hands all through my hair. I was mortified. Honestly, I wish I'd died right along with disco. (God rest its soul. Amen.) But I was there, so I made the best of it.

"Just do whatever you think looks best then," I said, giving him carte blanche.

"Hon, you just leave it all up to Kiki, and you'll be looking fine in no time." And he went on to trim off almost all of my fine, long, wavy, brown hair until I fairly looked like a newly radiated cancer patient. What was left was just a bit all around and a spiky clump on top. This was not what I would call *looking my best.* "Welcome to 1996, Honey," he said, when he was done.

Welcome to Army boot camp, I thought, but it came out as, "Looks great, thanks." He smiled and gladly took my twenty. Maybe no one would notice, I prayed. And I could cover up all my mirrors. And avoid looking at the back of spoons.

"Sweetie, since you're apparently new to Never, Never Land, what say you let this little Tinkerbelle take you out for a drink tonight? My treat. And I won't take no for an answer, so you may as well just nod and say okay." My brain was saying *NO!*, but my head was nodding yes. "And don't you worry your pretty, little head, Sugar, 'cause Kiki is very much the married housefrau." Well, thank goodness for small miracles, because if he had made a pass at me... well, I don't know what I would've done since no one *had* actually ever made a pass at me, but I'm sure I would've reacted badly. "Then it's settled; meet me at my place at nine," he commanded, while writing down his address.

I just kept nodding, having no idea what to say to the man that just completely butchered my hair and very nearly took my last twenty. Besides, I've always been told that whatever doesn't kill you can only make you stronger. This little experience should've made me the next Sylvester Stallone, circa *Rambo*, I figured.

Still, I must tell you, in all honesty, I was just a little excited about my first outing with another gay man. Even if it wasn't a date, and thank God this wasn't my first date, at least it was a step in the right direction. I mean, I really needed some help, any help, by that point. And who better to help a novice gay man than a hairdresser? It's like having the Pope teach you about being a good Catholic.

Okay, so let's continue our trip down Memory Lane, shall we? Kiki's place, as it turned out, was a lot lovelier and grander than what I was expecting from a mere hairdresser. (No offense to all the hairburners out there.) He lived in a charming Victorian just outside The Castro. It was blue and green with yellow shutters, with palm tress and magnolias out front, all surrounded by a white picket fence. And just within that fence was a perfectly tended garden that was fairly bursting with every color of the gay rainbow. The smell of jasmine wafted languidly up my nostrils as I approached the house. Honestly, it was enough to make a guy sick. If that guy was the jealous type. Which, of course, clearly I'm not.

Kiki answered the door with a grand flourish and promptly handed me a martini. "Darling, welcome, welcome to my *humble* abode," he said, while bowing deeply and gesturing with his hands to the rest of his home. Of course, in doing so, he was also managing to point out the rather large gentleman planted in the living room.

Noticing my stare, he introduced me to Larry, his partner. Now, I know you're not going to believe this, but I'd never met a gay couple before. I mean, yes, I had seen them, but I'd never actually *met* one. I was enthralled. Not to mention, I couldn't believe Kiki had been able to snag a husband. Yes, I had a lot to learn, but all in good time, friend. All in good time.

Kiki went over and sat next to Larry, leaving me a comfortable looking easy chair to rest my butt upon. So I sat down across from the both of them and scanned the rest of the place. It was very nice, actually. Maybe I had the hairdresser thing all wrong. Okay, well, not really, because, as it turned out, it was all Larry's. That is to say, *Doctor* Lawrence Goldstein. Kiki, by the way, wasn't even Kiki, but Myron Schwartz, who sat beaming next to his partner of (you're not going to believe this one) seven years. Myron's mom, apparently, was the proudest Jewish mother of a gay son in all of Manhattan. (No small feat, mind you, when you think about it, because, *hint*, there are a lot of gay Jewish men in New York City.)

They'd met at their synagogue. Larry was fresh out of Medical School and fresh *out*. And Myron was fresh out of beauty school, but not the least bit *fresh* out. Not by a long shot. Some people, from birth to death, are just obviously gay. And others, like myself and Larry, well, we just sort of grow into it. In other words, some of us have closet doors and some of us don't. Heck, Kiki didn't even have the hinges.

Officially, my new friend had come out years earlier when he was, as he put it, "deflowered by a neighbor at the ripe, old age of fourteen." Needless to say, I was envious of him. See, my neighbor growing up was, like, the hottest man on the block and he wasn't married or seen in the company of women, ever! I fantasized about that man endlessly, but to no avail. I guess he thought that doing it with the innocent, young neighbor boy wasn't worth a prison sentence. As if I'd ever tell anyone about it for him to get caught, right? In any case, at least someone made out okay, and it certainly didn't look like Kiki was any worse the wear. Well, except maybe for the blush he was wearing or the hair extensions. Still, looking back on it, if someone had offered me a two-story Victorian just outside The Castro, knowing what I know now, I'd have worn a dog collar and barked at the mailman to land such a cushy life. But hindsight is twenty/twenty, friend. Sucks, don't it?

Another quick martini later, Kiki was ushering me out the front door. He kissed Larry goodbye, while I politely shook his rather plump hand. And then we were off. And I was, believe it or not, really and truly happy. Here I was, twenty-one and ready to be gay. I was going to a gay bar, with my gay friend, who had a gay lover, and lived just outside the gayest place in the known universe. Honestly, I felt like

Mary Tyler Moore getting ready to through her hat up in the air. And I could turn the world on with something more than just a smile... probably... I hoped.

Of course, it was just a Monday night, when gay bars in San Francisco, apparently, were and still are not known to be very full. Then again, that was really for the best, because my joy quickly gave way to an acute case of stage fright. A gay bar quickly gave way to A GAY BAR! Before, I was just gay in my own head, something I knew I was, but had never actually acted upon. And now I was about to step foot inside a true gay bar, that was full (well, not empty, anyway) of gay men.

Kiki, noticing my obvious apprehension, quickly shoved me through the door and ordered us two more martinis. (To this day, just the sight of a green olive makes me immediately relaxed.) So here I was, in my first gay bar, drinking a very dry martini and feeling quite gay. By the way, did I mention the name of the bar? No, I guess not. It was Badlands. Ever been? Certainly not as tragic as the other bars in The Castro at the time. In fact, it had a certain ambiance to it. On a side note, did you ever notice that gay bars always have the butchest names? The Spike, The Stud, The Eagle, and even Badlands, all have these macho names and all are frequently full of affected queens drinking lite beers and white Russians. Kind of ironic, huh? But I generalize, grossly. Please forgive me; it's been a trying day.

In any case, looking around, I could've been in any bar in the world: license plates filled the walls, with antique over-head lamps from one end of the bar to the other, lots of wood benches, a pool table in the back, and cases of beer scattered throughout. Of course, the two guys in chaps making out just a few feet over from us made it a bit different. Yikes, two guys making out in public. I had a feeling I wasn't in Kansas anymore. Did I mention I was from Kansas, by the way? Topeka, born and raised. Sort of makes for a funny coincidence. You know, what with the whole Dorothy landing in Oz thing and all. Only, instead of Toto, I had Kiki.

Trying not to look around anymore, lest I should see something more dazing, I concentrated on my newfound-friend, who, three martinis later, was getting more fascinating by the minute. And it wasn't very long before he had me telling the whole story about meeting William and him inviting me to the party on Saturday. It certainly felt good telling someone about it, even if it was someone I'd just met that morning. And even if that someone was someone who just happened to have massacred their hair that morning. No matter, I had a gay compadre. It wasn't much, but it was a start.

"Oh, Honey, your first queer crush, how adorable," he teased, while I turned three shades of red. (Wait, I'm gay... they were scarlet, crimson, and rose. It's so great to be gay. And useful.) And he continued. "I remember my first crush. He was the captain of the varsity basketball team in high school. Jerome was his name. He was six and a half feet tall and as black as the blackest night sky. He also had the hugest fucking hands I'd ever seen. One could only imagine what he hid under those skimpy, yellow nylon shorts of his. Well, I mean, one had to imagine *for a time*, anyway." Kiki suddenly had the slightest impish grin on his adorable face.

"You didn't?" I gushed, in amazement and awe.

"Boo yeah, Sugar. Kiki saw the whole miserable, little, shriveled, barely cause to remember prick she'd ever seen. 'Course, I was only sixteen, so I had little to base it on. But I knew they came much, much, *much* bigger than that. And it was easy as pie getting in to see it, too," he said, while I slid in closer, not wanting to miss one delicious word. "See, I was walking home one night from my friend Tommy's house. We were watching *Chico and the Man,* and he was just standing there on the corner. Just standing there alone, not doing anything." My heart was suddenly racing as Kiki took a swig of his drink and continued with his tale. "Anyway, Jerome looks down at me and says, 'Faggot, why don't you suck my big, black dick?' And who was I, this runty, little Jewish kid to argue? So I said, 'sure'."

"You said *sure?*" I gasped. I mean, this kind of thing had never happened to me growing up. Well, maybe once in the men's bathroom at the Jiffy Mart, but that didn't count, because the guy was really old and fat and nasty, and I ran away for dear life.

"Sure, I said sure," Kiki replied, clearly lapping up the attention. "I'd wanted to do just that for the last six months, and there I was, being told to do it. I might be nelly, Honey, but I ain't stupid."

"And you just, you know, sucked it right there on the street corner?" I barely whispered.

"Well, of course not, silly." He grinned and tilted his head down. "We went behind the bushes. And that's when I saw it. But just barely. Because, as I mentioned, there wasn't really much to see." Kiki giggled and began talking like Jerome. "'Yeah, come on, faggot, suck that big, black dick,' he'd commanded; only, this time, it was more pleaded. And, naturally, I obeyed. But, all the while, I was thinking, well, it is black, but I don't know where he keeps getting this *big* thing from." Kiki was clearly loving his tale, or maybe it was that fourth martini. "'Yeah, bitch, suck that big dick,' Jerome moaned. 'You like that, big, black dick, don'tcha?' Okay, I had had enough of that shit, so I looked up from his sad attempt for a boner and I said, 'Jerome, could you, like, stop with the idle chit-chat, please. And while you're at it, maybe look up *big* in the dictionary; I think you have it confused with another word.' And, just for a second, he opened his eyes and looked down and he just stared at me. I don't know if it was disgust or disbelief, but he looked at me in the funniest way. And then he zipped up his pants and walked away, mumbling 'faggot' as he did so. End of story."

"That's it? That's the whole thing? Did you ever see him again? What happened to him?" Suddenly, I felt like Rona Barrett. (What ever happened to her, anyway?)

"Shit yeah. We were in the same school and all, but he never spoke to me ever again. Poor guy. I mean, you have to feel sorry for him. He's probably this total closet case living in this big, black macho world of his and he, like, not only can't ever come out to his friends and family, but even worse, *much* worse, he's got this little, itty, bitty black dick. Poor Jerome. I mean, look, I'm not much of nothing, but I'm here, I'm queer, and I'm going on my fifth martini. That's a hell of a lot better than Jerome's probably got going on. So here's to Jerome," Kiki proclaimed, lifting his glass up high.

"To Jerome!" I bellowed. "May his little black dick find happiness some day." We drunk to that.

Actually, we were drunk to that. And then Kiki taught me Gay Rule #1. He said, "Honey, always remember this, because it will get you far in this big, bad gay world of ours: the fantasy is *always* way better than the reality. And that's Gay Rule #1." I nodded and hoped that I'd never have a Jerome in my life. Or at least a little black dick in it. Kiki patted my head. "You know something, Bruce? I like you. You're okay. And your hair looks so much better," he told me, a smile spreading wide across his face.

I looked in the mirror behind the bar, and, you know, my hair did actually look quite nice. And that's when I knew that I was on my *last* martini. "Thanks, Kiki. You're right; it does look, um, better. And thanks for taking me to my first gay bar, even if we're just about the only ones in it," I told him, really and truly meaning it.

And Kiki looked me in the eyes and put his hands on my shoulders and blurted out, "Then kiss me, Bruce. Let me be your first gay kiss. Most guys are schmucks. You're better off having your first kiss be from a friend who won't treat you like shit and then dump you for the next better thing that comes along, right?"

Well, I thought about it for a split second, and it sounded good to me. Of course, my logic was a bit impaired by the drinks, but, I figured, it would be a lot easier doing it for the first time with a friend. And I was certainly ready for it. Twenty-one years ready, as a matter of fact. And Kiki *was* looking rather adorable sitting there. In other words, I did it. I leaned in real close to him, looked him deep in the eyes, and then I kissed him. I kissed him for a really long time, in fact. His lips were so soft and sweet, with just the slightest hint of vermouth, and, for that brief moment in time, everything else around me had ceased to exist. And I kept thinking to myself, *I'm kissing a man. I'm kissing a man. I'm kissing a man!* All with fireworks fairly bursting from behind my eyelids.

"S'how was 'at?" Kiki slurred, dreamily.

"Well, you just broke the first rule, because *that* lived right up to my fantasy," I replied, but didn't slur. In fact, I suddenly felt wide-awake and sober as all hell. That is until I got up to go pee; then I knew how drunk I really was. Suddenly, I was on a Tilt-A-Whirl.

It was quite a challenge, actually, to make it from the barstool to the john. And even when I finally did make it, I was ill-prepared for what I found: a trough. In other words, I had to pee in a drain next to another guy. Now, I wasn't normally pee shy, but I had, until just a few hours prior, never been to a gay bar or kissed another man before. Suddenly, I had to pee next to one. And, just as I was getting ready to go, the guy peeing next to me nodded and smiled. My heart started to race and then I really couldn't pee. I managed a smile and a nod and looked straight down. Damn, this wasn't good at all. I was just getting used to the whole adventure, and now a new obstacle was in my way.

Suddenly, I could sense him looking at me and I noticed that he wasn't peeing anymore. I don't know if it was the alcohol or the nerve that I acquired from kissing Kiki, but I looked over at him again, and, sure enough, he was looking straight at me. (Well, straight at me and down a bit.) And he was cute, too. Jeez, he was cute and young and nicely packaged, and getting nicer by the second. Just then, Kiki walked in and stood on the stranger's other side. Cutie-pie looked back down, I looked back down, and, rather quickly, all of us started peeing.

Truthfully, I didn't know if I was relieved or upset that Kiki broke the spell, but it didn't really matter; the moment was over. The three of us finished and made our exit. Kiki went first, then me, and then the stranger. And that's when the dude grabbed my ass. I turned and he winked at me and pursed his lips a little. I nodded and smiled, and the whole thing was over. He went left to sit on a bench, while we went right, back to our stools. In any case, by then, I was feeling shit-faced drunk, and Kiki looked pretty sloppy himself, so, perhaps, I figured, it was for the best. (Don't worry, this all has a point. Just be patient. Fate, you see, sometimes takes its own sweet time getting around to things. Apparently, my little world wasn't high on its priority list.)

"C'mon, let's get out of here; I think we've had enough for one night, and I have to work tomorrow," Kiki groaned. I was luckier; I didn't work on Mondays or Tuesdays, so I could sleep it off. Which was great, because I was pretty wiped out from all the excitement. Then I thought, if this was only Monday, what was I in for on Saturday night when I'd be surrounded by gay, attractive men? I gulped, feeling a sudden rush of adrenaline, and then, before I knew it, we were back at Kiki's.

"You might as well crash here," Kiki said, while opening the door. "We have a spare room upstairs, and you're lookin' pretty schnockered."

I had to admit, the thought of walking home was a bit daunting, and I certainly couldn't afford a cab. But I hardly new Kiki, all things considered, and felt a little hesitant. In any case, I'd barely managed an answer either way when he grabbed my arm and dragged me inside. "C'mon, it ain't safe for no pretty, little gay boy out here this late and this drunk," he said, and I agreed.

We walked up the stairs and Kiki pointed out my room for the evening, then his and Larry's room, and then the bathroom, should I need to pee or anything. Then he walked down the hall – well, stumbled was more like it – and I flopped down on my big, cozy bed, smiling all the while. So much had happened to me in the past few hours and I felt, just, so free. And then I fell sound asleep with my happy gay thoughts spinning around and around in my happy gay head. Or maybe it was the room that was spinning that way. Hard to tell. Whichever it was, I was on cloud nine.

Waking up, of course, was a different story entirely. Cloud thirty-seven, the gray one far to the back, was much less enjoyable.

Because *happy* had been replaced by nauseous sometime during the night. My head was pounding, my mouth was as dry as the Sahara, and I felt like I was going to puke. I looked at the clock by the bed and it was already ten o'clock the next morning. Thank God I didn't have to go to work, as there was no way I could be gracious and accommodating for eight solid hours; that was hard enough to do when I was stone-cold sober. Plus, I was having a difficult enough time just throwing myself out of the bed and going down the hallway to go to the bathroom. And I'd just remembered that I kissed Kiki the night before. *Ugh.* Then I was peeing like a racehorse and wondering how I was going to face Kiki or, worse, Larry, when I heard a knock on the door.

"You okay in there?" Larry asked, sounding concerned. God, I felt guilty. How could I have kissed a married man? Oh, how the mighty have fallen!

"Um, well, I'm fine. I'll be out in a sec," I answered, my voice cracking just a hair. Damn, damn, *damn* those martinis.

Larry was waiting outside the bathroom door when I finally stumbled out. He was already dressed for work and looking quite the professional. "Coffee, Bruce?" he asked.

"Yes, please," I replied, demurely. (What? It could happen.)

So I followed Doctor Larry downstairs to the kitchen, where he served me my coffee and a nice toasted bagel with cream cheese, and then he told me that Kiki had already left for the shop. Larry looked so happy and domestic spreading the cream cheese, and fuck if I didn't feel instantly horrible. I just stood there and sipped my coffee and tried to think of something to say to the man whose partner I had swapped spit with barely a few short hours earlier.

"Myron's a good kisser, huh?" he asked, and I nearly choked to death on my bagel.

"Um, er, um…" I was eloquent as ever. But, come on, I was in uncharted waters here.

"It's fine, Bruce; Myron told me everything. He was my first kiss, too." He sounded so calm. And I, of course, was at a loss. Larry merely sighed and grinned. "I let Myron sew his oats every so often, Bruce; and it was just a little kiss between two friends. Don't sweat it. He always comes home to Daddy, and that's what's important."

And then Larry proceeded to tell me the story of *Larry and Myron*. They'd met at Temple Beth Israel. Myron had caught Larry's eye from across the pew, which wasn't too difficult to do since he had

15

bright pink hair and about six earrings in his left ear. Larry caught Myron's attention, also, which wasn't all that difficult either, considering Larry had on the only Armani suit in the place. Their eyes locked, there was a slight nodding of heads, and when the service was over, *BAM!*, Larry and Myron were *Larry and Myron*. Ain't love grand? And here I am, years and years later now, with nothing to show for it but a barely used gym card, what surely must be the onset of an ulcer, and a best friend in a coma. Could be worse, though. (How, I haven't a clue, but let's just go with that for now.)

Myron was Larry's first and only, and, according to Larry, that was fine with him; he'd found what he was looking for and there was no need to look any further. The fact that he was desperately busy starting up his practice at the very beginning of their relationship surely had something to do with it, but, still, he loved Myron with all his heart, and Myron, clearly, felt the same, except for a few dalliances along the way. Modern gay romances were new to me, so, naturally, I was a bit skeptical. But I should've been paying better attention back then, because Larry and Myron are still together, while I just finished with boyfriend number one-seventy-six, or *Johnny the Needy*, as he is so lovingly called. (Well, maybe not *lovingly*.)

That morning had a profound affect on me, actually. It showed me that gay people could live happily ever after. In other words, I still have hope. Hope and about four more good years of my youth left before it all starts sliding down hill. Like an avalanche. Thank goodness for Clinique moisturizer and Aveda hair care products. I mean, I can still pass for someone in their early twenties. (In bar light, anyway.)

I walked Larry to work, and he told me that he hoped we'd get together soon. All in all, I was really glad to have met him at that point in my life, because the only gay men I was getting to see were at Joe Joe's, and they weren't exactly what I would call good gay role models. Good Betty Ford candidates, maybe. And here was Larry: rich, successful, and still deeply in love. If he and Kiki could make it, I sure as hell had a shot at it, right?

I said my goodbyes to Larry and headed on home. I was still feeling like crap, but I was thinking bright, shiny thoughts. I mean, I did handle myself pretty good the night before, and I figured that Saturday night shouldn't be a sweat. Fine, I sounded convincing, but I was still doubtful. I mean, one on one with Kiki was a snap, but Saturday night would be me solo and on alien turf. If I'd needed all those martinis the night before, what was I going to need to get by on

Saturday? (Okay, a hell of a lot, as it turned out, but you're gonna have to wait just a little bit longer before I get to that part. Don't you worry though; it's worth it.)

Luckily for me, my week was busy and I had little free time to fret. Between work and the gym (back then, I went quite often, really), I was always on the go. And what free time I had, I spent with Kiki or Kiki and Larry. See, I was getting my crash course in gay, which I sorely needed by that point. Though I was still having a hard time with my feminine pronouns, by Saturday afternoon I'd managed a *Miss Girl* without even thinking about it, had my second and third nights out at gay bars, had cruised a couple of guys and had them actually cruise me back, and, most importantly, my hair had started to grow back in a little and I looked less like a clown and more like a clone. (We all have our little goals in life, you know.) And, before I knew it, it was early Saturday evening and I, dear friend, was a nervous wreck. In Titanic proportions. Post-iceberg.

William's stunning, modern, new apartment complex was way up in Twin Peaks. No Victorian for Mister Perfect. It was concrete, chrome, glass, and wooden floors throughout. And (surprise, surprise) William had a flare for track lighting, the beautiful art and furniture perfectly lit. It was all, like him, stunning and pretentious. And the pièce de résistance was the front balcony, with its envious and expansive view of downtown San Francisco. My humble abode was looking more humble by the second and the lump in my throat was getting ever-lumpier, making it rather hard to swallow.

"Secret, so good of you to come." I could feel his hot breath on the back of my neck as butterflies took wing inside my stomach and nether regions. "Let me show you around." His arm was quickly wrapped in mine as he pulled me to the bar. Thank God, because I needed a good stiff one right about then, and I *was* talking about a drink for a change.

He made us both perfect gin and tonics and then quickly meandered his way around the apartment, introducing me to several people and pointing out several pieces of art that he thought I might like. I couldn't tell you what he said, or whom I met, or what he showed me; all, you see, was a belly-knotted blur. I'd been swept up by hurricane William and was going down for the count.

Our brief tour ended up, where else, but the bedroom. It was all done in natural woods and it was, surprisingly, quite cozy. Not at all what I was expecting. There were pictures all over the room, mostly of

William in beautiful and exotic settings. And speaking of beautiful and exotic, guess who had me pressed up against the back of the door in no time flat? (Take notes, Susan Lucci, because here's where the getting got good.)

"Secret, I've been thinking about you all week," he fairly moaned, those butterflies of mine growing big as bats all of a sudden. His eyes were mere millimeters from mine, and I could smell his alcohol-tinged, sweet breath on my face as he pulled me in tight, my heart, in a red-hot instant, beating faster than I thought medically advisable. Then, before I knew what hit me, his lips were pressed hard on mine. He kissed like an angel as he held me firmly against the door. And, yes, this was what I'd been imagining in my head for the past decade and whacking off to. When I opened my eyes, he was looking deep into them. Man, you've never seen orbs so blue and so clear in your entire life before. Meaning, I kissed him back, even harder and with more gusto than I'd ever thought possible. Then, just as fast as it all started, he pulled away from me and said, "Vicodin?"

Talk about a sudden turn of events, right? "Um, well, I don't know, I've never, um…" But he was already handing me the little capsule and wrapping my fingers around it. So I took it. I mean, seriously, this man could've told me to jump off the Bay Bridge right about then, and I would've done just that. Head first. So much for good judgment. Sorry, Mom. (Who will be played by Dame Judi Dench, with a Midwestern drawl. Seriously, it has Emmy written all over it.)

And then he looked at me and gave me a whimsical, little grin and mussed up my hair and told me that I was just the sweetest, little thing before he gave me a peck on the cheek. Then he opened the door and walked me out of his boudoir and back into reality. Just like that. I swear. And, yes, my mind was racing. I mean, I hadn't a clue what to think or to say by that point, so I just stood there and watched him walk away, his stellar ass swaying from side to side. Thank goodness I had my gin and tonic (and it was good gin) or I have no idea what I would've done. (Personally, I think alcohol consumption is severely underrated, thank you very much. I mean, when Mary Poppins was singing about a spoonful of sugar helping the medicine go down, I seriously doubt she was referring to a packet of Equal.)

So there I was, alone, not knowing a soul, hunkered down on a warm leather sofa, watching the festivities going on all around me. It wasn't much different than work, really. Same boys. Same conversations. And since no one else was sitting down, it was just me and my little, old drinkee. And then I started feeling rather relaxed and just a tad bit giddy. Oops, guess what Bruce forgot he had taken? In other words, it was Prescription City from there on out. Now, I don't condone drug taking (in excess), mind you, but let me tell you, I, for one, was feeling no pain.

And then, *plop*, guess who sat down right next to me? Yep, it was that cute little thing from Badlands, the one that was cruising me in the bathroom. Trough Man! See, there was that fate again, ramming its thumb up my bum, all lubed up and ready to go. (Took it long enough.)

"You had the biggest grin on your face just then, dude," he said. "You happy or what?"

"Well, uh, yes. Actually, I am." And, actually, I was.

"Name's Chuck. What's yours?" he asked as he handed me his cute, little, blond, furry hand. I took it and pumped it hard, both of us lingering there for just a second longer than was necessary before we let go. *Yu-fucking-um*, I was thinking. Me and my crotch both, somewhat numb though it now was.

Then we got to talking. Or at least Chuck got to talking. I was pretty zonked out there for a while. But I know I nodded at all the right times and smiled intermittently to let him know that I was interested. And I *was* interested. And not just because he was absolutely adorable and perky and sweet, but because he seemed smart and for real. He wasn't talking about drugs or boys or parties; he was telling me about his graduate studies in biochemistry, in fact. And he was telling me about his great new apartment. And he told me about his childhood and growing up in Alabama and about coming out to his parents when he was fourteen. Fourteen! And there I was, almost twenty-two, and my parents thought I was dating a girl named Laura (don't ask). And I just sat there and dreamily smiled and nodded. If this boy loved an appreciative audience, he had one in me, drugged and drunk though I might've been.

"Can I get you another drink, Bruce?" he asked, already getting up to get himself another one. I managed a nod, and he was off.

I sat there thinking of my good fortune. Did he remember me from the bathroom at Badlands? It was awfully dark in there, after all. In any case, who cared? I was just glad to have this second chance.

And so I sat there waiting. And waiting. And waiting some more. And still no Chuck. I mean, how long could it take to get a

19

couple of drinks, right? Even with the Vicodin in full-force, I became impatient and struggled off the couch to go take a look. And, let me tell you, gin and pills are not a good mix, because walking anywhere wasn't easy. But I was a man on a mission and managed to search from room to room for him. Sadly, he seemed to have up and vanished.

Damn, I thought, I couldn't believe I missed another opportunity. So pay attention up there, because here comes Gay Rule #2 (you should read this with an echo effect in the background for maximum impact): never, I repeat, *never* miss an opportunity when love (sex) may be at hand; you will surely regret it if you do. And regret makes you bitter, and bitterness causes frown lines, and before you know it you're a tired old drag queen performing for quarters on Polk Street. No foolin'. So be warned.

Then, miraculously, I heard his voice, and he sounded upset. I followed the noise to the one room I hadn't checked out yet: the kitchen. See, my gay sensibilities were still in their infancy, and I was unaware that the kitchen is always the focal point of any gay party. (No, that's not a gay rule. Not yet, anyway, but maybe someday it'll make the list. I'll let you know.)

I peeked into the room, and in the corner was Chuck, holding back another guy who was cursing and who had obviously been crying. Drama! The only thing I could make out was the other guy saying, "I'll kill him. I'll kill that lousy fuck." And other things along those lines. Chuck was trying to calm the other guy down by telling him how it wasn't worth it and that he should just leave and to count his blessings that he found out now instead of down the road. Man, Chuck was cute, even in emergency situations. Luckily, the booze was by the door, so I poured myself another gin and tonic and continued to watch the scene unfold.

It took Chuck another five minutes or so, but the other guy finally started to calm down and was getting ready to leave, when guess who should pop in for a drink? Yup, it was our old buddy, William. Well, that's when the you know what hit the fan. It seemed that the ever-popular William was the source of the misery. No great surprise there. Should've known, right?

"You lousy piece of shit," the traumatized stranger shouted out, and Chuck had to restrain him yet again. "If I ever get my hands on you, I'm going to fucking strangle you."

And, calm as he could be, William looked him right in the eyes and said, "If I was you, I'd be having this conversation with your boyfriend and not with me. I didn't force him to have sex with me. Actually, he was the one who approached me. Practically begged me for it. As a matter of fact, if you were any kind of boyfriend to him at all, you should be thanking me. From the looks and sounds of it, your boyfriend really needed a good fuck."

Then there was the briefest moment of silence in that kitchen. (Well, except for the tinkling of the ice in my glass. Tension makes me thirsty, you see.) And then the other guy just snapped, and it took several men this time to hold him back. I don't think in all my years I'd ever seen another person so full of hatred. Honestly, it was almost scary. Well, it probably would've been scary, but between the drugs and the booze, I wasn't feeling much of anything by that point. Then William, still not the least bit riled, finished fixing himself a drink and walked back out into the living room. A few minutes later, Chuck and his distraught charge were leaving through the front door. And Bruce, me, I was just leaning against the counter, trying very hard to stay awake, or at least upright. Which wasn't too easy, mind you. Nope.

I don't really remember anything after that. But I do remember where I woke up the next morning. I know it had to be really early, because it was just starting to get light outside and the room had a faint blue-gray glow to it. I blinked a few times and forced my eyes open to look around. I say forced, because it felt like my head was being crushed by a thousand-pound weight. Beneath a boulder. Everything looked vaguely familiar, but I couldn't quite place it. It was all sort of déjà vu-ish. So I just rested there, very still, and tried to let my mind go over the details of the night before. And then a new thought popped into my head. Because it suddenly dawned on me that I wasn't wearing any clothes. And, wouldn't you know it, at that very same moment, I felt another person behind me as I heard a rustling noise.

Very slowly, I rolled over. I kept my eyes closed and pretended to still be asleep. Why? Fuck if I knew. It just seemed like a good idea at the time. Remember, I was still new at this (but learning fast). After what seemed like an eternity, I blinked open my peepers, and there they were: those same steel, blue eyes I'd seen just before William kissed me.

"Morning, Secret," he whispered, with a wry grin, probably the same one the Devil gives you just before he tosses you into the lava pit.

"My name's Bruce," I mumbled back.

"Let's stick to Secret," he countered with, drawing ever nearer. I knew I should've hated him. I knew I should've jumped out of that bed, found my clothes, and hightailed it out of there. But, damn it, he just looked so… so… well, he *just looked,* and, like a deer caught in the headlights, I stayed put.

"What time is it, William?" I asked, terrified of the answer.

"It's almost seven, why?" he answered, and my head pounded.

"I have to be at work by eight." I felt like crying. I probably should've asked for the day off, but I needed the money way too much to have done that, smart as it might've been. And I, not in my wildest dreams, ever expected to be where I was right at that very moment.

"Don't worry, you can shower here, and then I'll drive you over to the restaurant. You'll be there in plenty of time, and I guarantee you'll be wide awake and ready to serve your pretty, little ass off." He was still grinning when he said that and then he put his index finger beneath my chin and gently leaned in and gave me the softest, sweetest kiss. *Good morning to me*, I thought. *And what in the world am I getting myself into?*

CHAPTER TWO
HOMO WE GO

Well, that was a lot to take in, wasn't it? But I did have to fill you in with some background tidbits, right? Get all the main characters into play for you, I mean. Okay, maybe now I'll take it a little slower. Huh, what's that you say? You like it fast? Fast and furious? Is that how you like it? Well, *yippy*, 'cause that's how I like to give it, Baby. In other words, you better put your helmet and shin pads on, because here we go...

Needless to say, getting out of bed was tricky. As you may or may not remember, guys who are twenty-one tend to wake up with, how should I put this delicately, a raging hard-on. (Hmm, delicate no, visually appealing, most definitely.) And, even though my head was splitting, I had enough sense not to lead William on, tempting as it seemed.

"Mmm, could you shut your eyes, please?" I pleaded, with as much dignity as I could muster.

"Mmm, no way, Secret. Anyway, I already saw it. How do you think you got that way to begin with? But fear not, Sweetie, I was a complete gentleman. And, uh, by the way, most gay guys these days trim those nasty little pubic hairs. I mean, seriously, I found a spare set of car keys tangled up in there last night."

How, exactly, do you respond to something like that? So I just laid there and looked pitiful until he finally relented and shut his eyes. It was then that I quickly got up, found my clothes, and got dressed. Luckily, boners go down just about as fast as they go up, because I really didn't want to remain naked for very much longer than I already had been.

Modesty, however, may have come easy for me, but not for William. No sooner was I dressed, and there he was, springing out of bed and making his way to the dresser. William, being twenty-two, was just as easily *up* as I was, so guess what I got a gander at? And, no, he couldn't have cared less and merely started rummaging through the top drawer of his dresser. I hadn't a clue what he was looking for and, to tell the truth, I had my eyes on something else. I mean, I'd only ever seen someone else's prick in magazines and in gym class, and then they were soft and non-threatening. *This* sucker was big and hard and pointing right at me, like a divine divining rod.

"Better watch out, it senses fear," he said, with a chuckle, and then tensed something to make it bounce. I gulped and turned three shades of red (they were… wait a minute, we've done that one already. Let's add a fourth one then: fire-engine.)

"I wasn't looking. I was just…"

"Yeah, yeah, right, whatever." He shook his head and walked back over to me. In his hand was a little baggie with some powder in it. Now, I may have been unlearned way back then, but even I knew what he was handing me. "Here," he said.

So there I was, face to face with my first hard-on (that wasn't my own) and my first bag of coke. (Decisions, decisions.) Despite my better judgment, I took the coke, even though *it* was behind curtain number-two and I wanted the box where Carol Merrill was standing. (Twenty-one, friend. Keep reminding yourself of that. It'll make it easier to explain the choices I made.)

"Take it. Trust me, it'll make your day go by a lot faster and easier." And with that, he produced a little, silver spoon, grabbed my free hand, and sat me back down on the bed. Then he reached below his bed and pulled out a little, square mirror. (By the by, his pecker was still standing at attention. Honestly, I didn't know whether to look away or salute the damn thing.) "Okay, I take it, by the look of terror on your face, that this is your first time. (Oh, if he only knew.) So, I'll go first. And if you want to play with it, go ahead," he said, very matter of factly, before glancing down at his manhood and them back up to me.

So, as he gingerly poured the white powder onto the mirror and spread it out with the blunt end of the spoon, I grabbed my first, my very first (oh, I just love this part of the story) penis. Penis, penis,

PENIS! (Shout it like Oprah does; it helps to get the point across.) There it was and there was my hand around it. I, Bruce Miller, was holding onto an honest to goodness, hard as a rock, prick. Hallelujah!

And, as I stroked it, which wasn't easy because my hand was shaking life a leaf, he was snorting the coke from the little, silver spoon. First one nostril and then the other. "Bird can't fly on just one wing, can it?" he said, sniffling, before handing me the spoon, newly filled for yours truly.

I shook my head, not knowing what the hell he was talking about. All I knew was that I had to let go of something that I had waited my whole life to hold on to, only to grab something that I had no desire for whatsoever. In any case, I reluctantly let go of his willy and apprehensively snorted the white stuff. (Bad choice? Please. As if you're so perfect.)

I have one thing to say: yuck-the-fuck-o. It tasted horrible going down and it burned just a bit, too. Then, before I could even get my wits about me, William filled the spoon again and placed it beneath my other nostril. "Toot, toot, Sweetie. Up the hatch now." He sounded like a mother trying to feed her baby. Anyway, I blindly obeyed, shook my head a little, like I'd just taken some bad-tasting medicine, and forced a smile on my tired face. (Okay, I know I've said this already, but drugs are bad. Just say no. Usually. And only do it if the situation calls for it. Which, of course, this one clearly did. Then look up *justification* in the dictionary and find a picture of yours truly.)

"Thanks, William. Much appreciated." Suffice it to say, I wasn't talking about the coke.

"Okay then, let's get me dressed and get you to work," he said, jumping up and back over to the dresser, where he set the baggie down and rustled about for some clothes to wear. Believe it or not, I was kind of relived to see him get dressed, seeing as I didn't know how much more of William naked I could take. Honestly, if Michelangelo really was gay, imagine what he went through staring at the guy who posed for his David day in and day out.

Thankfully, it didn't take William long to get some clothes on, and, before I knew it, we were out of the house and into his little, red Corvette. (No, no song references here, easy as one would've been; he really did have a little, red Corvette.) William looked like he was born for that car of his, too, and when he put his big, black Ray Bans on, man, let me tell you, it was fantasy made flesh. My heart, by then, was racing as fast as the engine. (Oops, did it again; I forgot I was on drugs.) Quite suddenly, my head was reeling, my feet were tapping, my hand was slapping my knee, and I was up, Up, UP and away.

WHOOSH!!!

Well, I hated to admit it, but those couple of bumps really did the trick, and when I looked over at William, he had the biggest shit-eatin' grin on his beautiful face. He was just smiling and nodding and vibrating all over. Least he looked that way to me. Maybe, in reality, it was me that was vibrating and he was sitting still. Whatever. Because the effect was the same. Then he cranked up the radio and we both looked at each other again, and at that exact same moment we both started singing to *Rock Lobster*, something about boys in bikinis and girls in surfboards. (B-52s reference there, Sweetie. Dig it.)

That's when I felt it, too. Do you ever have that feeling of rapture when it just, you know, dawns on you that you're alive and breathing and happy as all fuck? When that great, big slot machine of life tumbles over to triple sevens? Well, that was what I felt like right at that split second. Yes, yes, I know it was the coke and the cool San Francisco air hitting me in the face, but all I was certain of at that moment was that I was happy, and, whatever the cause, I for one wasn't knocking it.

"Secret?" William said, staring at the road ahead, that mesmerizing grin still plastered to his equally mesmerizing face. The sun had fully woken up and, looking in the rearview mirror, I could see the patches of green grass on Twin Peaks as the fog began rolling in over the hills. It was a perfect summer morning in the most beautiful city in America.

"Yes, William," I replied, now staring straight ahead, not wanting to miss a moment of the picturesque scenery. (Plus, looking at William still made me a trifle bit nervous.)

He began to nod. "The way I see it, we have two choices. One, I can keep driving and, in about five minutes, we'll reach Joe Joe's and you'll get out of the car and go into the restaurant, where you'll serve hung over queens and tweeked out clubbers for the next eight hours. Oh, and that shit you snorted will wear off right about the time every one of your tables has been seated and twenty other people are waiting for a chance to fill one of them the split second they become available."

"Or?" I wondered, not really liking the first option.

"Or, two, we can turn around right here and keep driving until we're far, far, far away from Joe Joe's. And far, far, far away from the tweekers, geekers, slackers, hung over, fucked up, drugged out messes of humanity that you call customers, and be somewhere... somewhere (and here he pointed hither to the north)... somewhere where there are no people ordering coffee or asking for change for a five."

"And where, pray tell, would that be?" Forgetting that, not only did I have to be at work in approximately five minutes, and that if I failed to perform that duty, I would, no doubt, be unable to pay for food, gas, rent, or (heaven forbid) a new bottle of Wet.

"Black Sand Beach," he answered, smiling and tapping his fingers on the steering wheel. Blondie was now singing *One Way or Another*. Somewhat prophetic, huh? You betcha!

"You know, I really can't William. You live high up in your ivory tower without fear of starvation or homelessness, but I need Joe Joe's to live. To eat. To sustain my meager existence." I sighed, heavily. "Maybe you should just take me to work." Now, I may have said it, but it was obvious from my tone that I clearly didn't mean it.

"Way too melodramatic, Sis, for this early hour of the morning. I mean, please, you're like twenty-one or something, probably fresh out of college, and Joe Joe's was, like, the first paying thing that came along. Am I right, Secret? Am I?" Of course, he didn't wait for a reply. "Well, just sit there and stop your fretting; Auntie William will take care of everything." (Hey, you up there, are you sitting there screaming at me right now? Are you shouting no, No, NO! Don't do it! No good can come from this. Well, are you? Yeah, smart of you. Bravo, Einstein.)

Well, he was right about one thing; I did take the first thing that came along. And, to tell you the truth, it wasn't all that hard to get that job. There had to be a million jobs just like that or better, in fact. So I sat there for the next couple of minutes, as we drew ever nearer to the aforementioned dining nook, and I tried to convince myself that William was right.

"Fuck it!" I soon relented, throwing my arms up as I motioned William forward, willing my brain not to think of the dire consequences.

Again, I was only twenty-one. William was also right about that. Meaning, common sense and thinking things through were not my forté. And if I'd waited one more minute, I probably would've changed my mind. I do like to eat, you know. But I threw caution to the wind (I threw it, but it came back and whopped me in the face. Yep, the breeze was that strong) and I chose the road less traveled.

"Fuck it!" William shouted back. "Fuck the whole damn thing!"

And we were off. Not surprisingly, the elation I'd been feeling just five short minutes earlier had given way to an awful feeling of doom and apprehension. What, I thought to myself, had I just done?

Naturally, William had the cure. "Oh, I see worry on that adorable face of yours, Secret. I told you I'd take care of it. Here, take this and perk up, Sweetie. Grey clouds are gonna clear up, so put on a happy face." Then he handed me that same little baggie. Well, I was already in it up to my chin, might as well go all the way under. (Yeah, yeah. Enough of you up there. Where were you back then when I needed you?)

I took the spoon and the mirror and took a bump up each nostril. It went down a little smoother this time. (No, a different spoon and mirror than I had used that morning. This one he pulled out of the glove compartment. That should've told me something right there, huh?)

The next few minutes we drove in silence. By then, my mind was racing with all kinds of thoughts. I mean, there I was, zooming to Lord knows where with a man I just barely knew and, at times, couldn't even stand. I was jobless, presumably. I was broke, definitely. And I was now wired for sound. But then we hit the Golden Gate Bridge and I got a shot of the bay and the boats and the hills and the virgin-white fog rolling gently over the lofty, rust-colored bridge, and I just, I don't know, I just snapped out of it. I was free, free from that crappy job and miles away from my rat-nest hovel and driving in a snazzy, red Corvette with Tarzan. And me, Jane, felt just hunky-dory. (Welcome to the jungle, friend. Keep a good grip on the vines. The drop down is a killer.)

***

Shortly thereafter, we arrived at the beach. Well, not exactly the beach, mind you. The beach, as it turned out, was way, way down a dirt and rock path. Going down, in my present *up-lifted* state, should've be a snap, I figured; going back up looked less than promising.

In any case, we were a third of the way down when William stopped short and turned to me, pointing to the vista far below. The sky, by now, had completely cleared of the usual morning fog and was as blue as William's eyes. I took a deep breath and looked up and then to the left and then to the right. The ocean was glistening like a diamond, reflecting under the beautiful California sun. Then I looked down at the beach, which seemed to be littered with quite a few people, actually. We moved along and I kept glancing down as we made our way along the precarious path. That, of course, is when I started to notice something a little unusual. See, all the people appeared to be males. And, getting a little nearer, most of them were, *gulp*, naked.

"Um, William, is this a gay nude beach by any chance?" I was hoping that it was maybe just National Buck-Naked Day that we'd accidentally and quite coincidentally strolled into.

He shrugged. "Yup, is that okay with you?"

"Oh, well, sure. Well, sure, why not?" I croaked out. Thank goodness we were out in the sun, because I was now as white as William's ultra-expensive sheets. *A gay nude beach*. I mean, how was I going to lie there among all those naked gay men? I'd just barely gotten over the shock of seeing one naked gay man, and now I was expected to be surrounded by them. Thankfully, I figured, I could just lie on my stomach. All day. Until everyone else left.

A few minutes later, we'd found a nice spot right in the middle of it all as William threw down the towels that he'd brought from the car. (He must kidnap helpless, out-of-work neophytes regularly, I thought. I mean, he seemed awfully prepared for it all.) Then I helped spread out the blankets and plopped my butt down on one of them.

I looked up as William got undressed: first the shoes and socks, then the shirt, and, finally, the shorts and undies. And then there was naked William again. He was *softer*, no doubt, than he'd been that morning, but no less intoxicating. Especially with the sun right behind him and the waves lapping the shore in the not too distant distance.

"Your turn, Secret," he commanded. "Off with it."

"Er... yeah." I was helpless before him as I slowly started to undress, while he plopped down on the towel right next to mine.

Naked, all too soon, and quite tense from both the coke and the situation before me, I just rested there with my eyes closed and tried desperately to forget about my current circumstances. But then a new thought dawned on me, that old proverbial light bulb turning on above my noggin. "William?" I said, one eye popped open as my head tilted to the side.

"Yeah, Secret?" he rolled over and looked down at me.

I shielded my eyes from the sun, looked over and up at him, and asked, "William, you planned this whole, entire escapade, didn't you?"

He smiled and shrugged. "Yup."

"Thought so."

"Secret, don't look so serious; everything will be fine." And he bent down and gave me a soft, wet kiss on my mouth and then gently squeezed my privates. (Mmm, nice.) "And, if not," he continued, "at least you'll have the best tan on the unemployment line."

The thought made me no less stressed out, needless to say, but I nodded just the same. He smiled even brighter and rolled back onto his towel. Oh well, I thought, at least my hangover had gone away. Things were looking up. (Wait, just wait; *looks* can be deceiving.)

***

We sat out there like that for a few hour, neither one of us saying much to the other. People walked by and stared a lot (usually at you know who), but, for the most part, we had an uneventful morning. In fact, it didn't take too long for me to get accustomed to the fact that almost everyone around us was naked, and, after a brief time, I started to enjoy myself again. I was half-baked from the coke, basking in the sun, and, every so often, gently being stroked by William. In other words, thoughts of Joe Joe's were quickly fading like a forgotten nightmare, like a hazy mist burned off by a brilliant summer sun.

Somewhere in the distance, I could hear Kate Bush singing about running up a hill. William could hear it, too, and started singing along with her. Never one to miss an opportunity to sing along with Kate, I piped in with the chorus. And there we were, two naked, tweeked out, gay dudes singing and having a fine old time. A prettier sight you'll never see. This, I figured, must've been what Lewis and Clark were looking for, had they been coked-out butt-buddies.

"Kate Bush fan?" I asked him as the song ended.

"Isn't every healthy, red-blooded, American queer boy?" he replied.

"I don't know; you tell me." I guessed that I was in for another lesson, and listened intently.

He rolled back over my way. "Well, certainly everyone I've ever met is. Next time you go into someone's home that happens to be gay, go check out their music collection. I guarantee they'll have *Hounds of Love* at the very least, if not everything she's ever done. (And I've done just that for the past decade, and, you know what, he was right. Except for lesbians. Replace Kate Bush with the Indigo Girls, then the rule holds true.)

"Thanks for the tip," I told him.

He giggled. "Bruce, you're kind of new at this whole gay thing, aren't you?" He caught on fast.

"Sort of." I hated to admit it. I mean, Kansas wasn't exactly the place to learn how to be a card-carrying gay boy. I could, however, shuck an ear of corn in no time flat. That was bound to help me make friends and influence people, right?

"How *sort of?*" he asked, eyes now in a squint and an inch away from my own.

"Um, well, I guess about… let's see, um… just under a few months." I looked up at him as I said this. He was grinning down at me and started teasing my left nipple with his index finger.

"Guess that makes you more of a Fag-it that a Fagg-ot," he said.

"And what, exactly, is a Fag-it?" I couldn't help but ask as I propped myself up on my elbows.

"That would be a Fag-In-Training, Secret. Welcome to Graduate School," he proclaimed and gestured down the length of the beach in front of us. (I always was a good student, and school, apparently, was back in session.) "So what exactly am I working with here? What do you know up to this point?" William had suddenly taken on the air of a learned professor, albeit a rather studly, naked one.

"Let's see," I said, tapping my chin. "I know that I like men. (Long pause.) That's it. I like men."

He smiled and nodded. "Well then, at least you have the fundamentals down. That's a good start, Secret. Mind if I give you your first lesson?" Ooh, this should be good, I thought as I looked over at him. And I don't know if it was the drugs (and yes, it probably was) or if it was the sun burning my retinas, but William's eyes and teeth were, well, sort of sparkling. Actually, there was this whole sparkly aura around him just before he started in on his lesson plan.

"William," I said and reached out to hold his hand, "if you're going to continue calling me Secret, and I take it that you are, then I think I should be able to call you something other than William."

"Sounds fair," he replied, looking intrigued at the prospect of a brand new moniker. "And what would that new name be?"

I thought about it for a second, squeezing his hand just a bit, and replied, "How about… Sparkle?"

31

He jumped in place, like a shiver had run down his body. "Oh, I like that a lot. Okay, Secret, Sparkle it is then." And, voila, an era was born. "Well then, now that we have that straightened out, for lack of a better tem, on to our first lesson. Pay attention because there will be a test at the end of this. Lesson One, Secret, is the easiest and most basic of all the things you can learn from me, but it's also the most important. Ready?" he asked, looking over to make sure that I was indeed paying him heed. (Which, of course, I was.) "Right then, Lesson Number One is this: all men are pigs. Straight, gay, bi, curious, and all creatures in between. We all want one thing and we won't stop until we get it. Do you know what that one thing is, Secret?"

"Sex?" I answered, eager to make teacher happy.

"Good boy, Secret. Sex it is. And do you know why all men have sex first and foremost on their brains?"

"Because it feels good?" I thought I had that one for sure.

"Wrong, Secret. Though, yes, it does feel good. But, no, the real reason men, and that is all men, want, need, and have to have S-E-X is because it's programmed into us by Mother Nature herself. See, we're all born with an innate obsession to spread our seed: to propagate the species, as it were." He nodded and continued. "Now then, the difference between straight men and gay men is this: straight men, poor suckers that they are, start spreading their seed at a young age, just like we do. However, at some point, society, and by this I mean parents, the media, and women, start telling them that they have to settle down with one female and spread that nice, gooey, white man-sap in only that one woman. And you know what, Secret? That idiot straight man falls for this trap every time and pays for it the rest of his poor, miserable life. See, Mother Nature never intended for him to share that seed with just that one woman. No, he was supposed to spread it around to any woman, and as many women, that would have it. Much as gay men have been doing all along." (Not me, though. Alas, my white, sticky stuff had only reached my miserable sheets thus far.)

He continued. "Now, gay men, and a few lucky straight men, rarely fall for this trick. Society isn't telling us queers to do anything accept maybe cut hair, wait tables, serve drinks on planes, and choreograph dance recitals. Society, or I should say, straight society, has no clue, Secret. None whatsoever. Gay men, you see, are able to spread that lovely, white peter-glue from one end of the world to the other, just like old Mother Nature intended. And our poor, straight brethren are doomed, year after monotonous year, to spread their tired, old seed all on that same one woman."

"But," I interjected, with a hopeful look on my face, "aren't there gay men that also want to settle down with just one other man and not spread their seed around?" I was hoping for an answer that I knew I would never get. Sparkle, you see, was nothing if not predictable.

"Oh, poor misguided waif. No, society has brainwashed these men just as they have fooled our straight counterparts. If marriage was truly *natural* then fifty percent or more of all marriages wouldn't end in divorce and seventy-five percent or more of all men wouldn't cheat on their wives each year. It's simply not natural for a man to settle down with just one, or even a few, other partners. But because women have a different biological and emotional agenda than men, your average straight man, who is highly inferior to any gay man, is duped into believing that a women's agenda is also his own. Then they grow fat and complacent with their lives. In other words, trapped." He smiled and moved along. "Now we, on the superior side of the coin, have been operating as Mother Nature meant us to, and, as a reward, are able to *maintain* ourselves in a much more desirable fashion. We are artistic, sensitive, intelligent, motivated, caring, compassionate, and better adjusted than the vast majority of men on this planet. Not to mention cuter, hunkier, and just plain old more fabulous. And all this because we aren't constrained to the fallacy of one man, one woman, forever. Gay men have it exceedingly better than any straight man ever will, and this is because we understand our roles as men on this planet better. So pity the straight man, Secret, and revel in your gayness. We may be in the minority, but I for one would never want to be part of that boring, complacent, bourgeois, banal majority. Viva la Fag!" he said, raising his fist in the air.

"Viva la fag!" I repeated, also with my fist in the air, though I was a bit less sure of myself than Sparkle was. Because, truth be told, it was exactly that one-man-forever thing I was looking for. Hoping for. Praying for. Still, far be it from the student to contradict the teacher. In any case, right about then, my stomach started to grumble. The coke, it seemed, was wearing off, and I was quickly realizing that I hadn't eaten anything all day.

"Secret?" said Sparkle.

"Yes, Sparkle?" said I.

"Your stomach is making some funny noises over there and you're starting to look a bit pink. What say we head on out of here and go grab a bite to eat? (Music to my ears.) School is out for today."

So we got dressed, rolled up the towels, and started to head on out. The beach, by that time, was chock full of dudes, too. What struck me as funny, though, was that the majority of the people that were naked were the ones who really shouldn't have been: lots of rolling guts and flabby hind parts. Oh, there were some cuties, to be sure, but they were spread out and mostly sitting amongst themselves. Truth be told, I was looking a lot better than most of the men there. I mean, what had I been so nervous about? This was a piece of cake. And then...

"Bruce! Hey Bruce!" I jumped. Who the hell could've known me down there? I looked all around and back and forth. "Bruce, over here!" I heard whoever it was, but I couldn't see him. And then, lo and behold, I saw who was yelling my name and I froze dead in my tracks. Sparkle stopped as well and gave a, "Well, look who we have here." Yes, it was Chuck and that same guy who was dragged out of Sparkle's apartment the night before. There was also another guy with them. No doubt it was the alleged boyfriend that caused the whole friggin' mess in the first place.

"Sparkle, I beg of you, no scenes please. I've had enough upheaval for one day, thank you very much," I pleaded in a whisper, but Sparkle had the slightest smirk on his face as he put his fingers to his lips and made a tick-a-lock motion, indicating that he wouldn't make a sound. I, of course, had my doubts, but I headed over to where Chuck was lying out, with Sparkle following silently behind me. (No doubt plotting his next evil move.)

Chuck, who I now saw was naked, was waving at me until he saw who I was with. That stopped him cold, and I could've sworn I saw the briefest look of terror on his face as he nudged the guy next to him and whispered something in his ear. That, naturally, caused the guy next to him to bolt up onto his elbows as well. (Kind of a reverse domino effect. And, honestly, it was terrifying to behold.) Now the three of them were blankly staring at us as we approached. All the while, Sparkle was snickering behind me as I made a *please shut up and behave* motion with my hand behind my butt, but Lord only knows what Sparkle interpreted that to mean. Certainly not *please shut up and behave*.

"Chuck, man, it's great to see you again." Of course, what I meant was that it was nice to see him buck-naked and spread out before me like a midday snack. And, ooh, he looked yummy indeed. He was, much to my delight, tighter looking out of his clothes and much hairier than I had imagined. And, yes, he was a *natural* blond, though I certainly tried my darndest not to look. (My darndest, by the by, was rather on the weak side that morning, what with the lack of food and all.)

"Bruce, yes, um, yeah, you too." Poor guy. He really had to struggle not to say something that could set the powder keg off again. And I don't know if it was the coke or what, but I swear I could hear the gears turning in Sparkle's head, just grinding away trying to find exactly the right thing to say. (He didn't disappoint. Shock.)

"Chuck, so nice to see you again. You left in such a hurry last night and I didn't get a chance to say goodbye," Sparkle said, oozing grace. (Well, something was oozing, anyway.) "And, Jeff, no hard feelings, right, old chap?" I wish I could draw you a picture of the hatred on Jeff's face at that very moment, because words cannot do it justice.

Sensing impending fireworks, I grabbed Sparkle's hand and started to yank him away. "Well, we were just leaving. Going to grab a little bite somewhere," I said and pulled hard on Sparkle's hand. This, naturally, caused him to stand even firmer. Surprise, surprise.

"Ah, yes, a little bite. If I recall, that's what young James over their likes. Isn't that right James?" Sparkle had (and still has, except for this coma thing) such a knack for saying just the right thing at the completely wrong time and place. (God bless him. Or, make that, God help us.)

"Why you miserable piece of shit," Jeff spat. "You have some fucking nerve."

"My, my, Jeff, such language. I was just saying…"

"He was just saying goodbye," I interjected and gave another hard yank. Jeez, he was strong as an ox and held his ground, despite my pulling and tugging.

That caused Jeff to jump up and start toward Sparkle. This in turn got Chuck and James up lickety-split. And I, the Switzerland of the beach, jumped in the middle, trying very hard to be the neutral party of the group. (Plus, it got me closer to naked, little Chuckie. See, I might've been fucked up, but my priorities certainly weren't.)

"My goodness, don't they have leash laws on this beach?" Sparkle was in grand form, and, despite myself, I gave a little *tee-hee*. Unfortunately, neither Sparkle's remark nor my guffaw were doing us very much good, and the sight of three naked men struggling in the sand (and one semi-dressed Sparkle) was causing quite a commotion. Several other guys started to approach our little group to see what was happening. (God, I needed a drink, but I was beginning to believe that *He* was no longer listening to my pleas.)

"Bruce, I think you should get your friend out of here ASAP," Chuck leaned in and whispered in my ear. (I know it was tragically inappropriate, but all of this was making me horny as hell.) Still, I agreed wholeheartedly with Chuck that it would be for the best if we could separate this little ménage a mess. So, instead of pulling on Sparkle, I gave him one mighty push. Luckily, I caught him off guard and he went tumbling a good couple of feet away. This was all the distance I needed, and I rushed over, grabbed his arm, and dragged him away.

"Sparkle, fun's fun, but let's get away from this, okay? I mean, please, game, set, and match, good buddy."

"Oh, Secret, such the spoiled sport you are. I was just having a little verbal sparring fun with a few old and dear friends."

"That's what you call fun? And how old and dear, pray tell?" I sensed that a little dish might get Sparkle's mind (and body) away from the festivities. (And yes, you guessed it: I wanted the four-one-one on Chuck. I wasn't exactly having any luck finding out for myself, was I?)

"Now, Bruce, you know I'm not one to gossip." Of course, I didn't know. If you recall, I only knew Sparkle for, like, less than a day by that point. (And just look at all the fun I was having.)

"Spill it, Sparkle. And, by the way, you just called me Bruce." Score one for me.

"Bruce. Secret. Whatever. Do you want the scoop or do you want to quibble?" Of course, I wanted the info on my little, blond stud, but I was learning that flustering Sparkle would probably be a rare occurrence, and I had to take it when I could get it.

"Well, I need to keep my mind off the hunger pains in my stomach, my apparent lack of employment, and this fucking hill of death we're climbing up, so spill it."

"Ooh, okay, take a pill already," he said and literally handed me a pill.

"How did you do that?" I was with Harriett Houdini all of a sudden. It just came out of nowhere. *Poof.*

"Honey, Gay Rule #3," he said, clearly in sync with Kiki's gay rule book, as we trudged up higher and higher with no end in sight.

"Which is?" I asked, huffing and puffing, sweat stinging my eyes.

"Always come prepared," he replied.

"Isn't that the Boy Scout's rule or something?"

"Where do you think they got it from?" Sounded good to me. Anyway, I swallowed the pill. I mean, what the hell, there was no booze in sight and my nerves were shot to hell by that point.

"Okay, so now tell me about those three back there."

"Oh, yes, right, the three little piglets: Chuckles, James, and our high-strung friend, Jeff *where's-my-bottle-of-poppers?* Jessups. I take it from your more than obvious flirtations that really you just want the dirt on Chuckles, though. Hmm, where to begin?"

Luckily, we reached the summit before he started, because I didn't want to miss a thing. "Just the highlights please," I asked, knowing that given an inch, he would take a mile. And speaking of inches...

"Well, let's just say, little Chuckles *isn't* so little," Sparkle said as he got into the now-burning-up car.

"How not so little?" I asked, also getting into the car. Though, thanks to whatever it was I had taken, I barely noticed the searing heat.

"Um, hmm," Sparkle muttered, rummaging around the car. "See this can of Diet Coke?"

I gulped. Certainly it couldn't be that big. "Not that big?" I asked, just a bit frightened.

"Oh, hell no. I just wanted a Diet Coke. Damn, I'm thirsty."

I smacked him hard on his arm. "Fucker, play fair," I yelled and slapped him again.

"Ow, Girlfriend, trim the nails, please," he said, rubbing his arm. "Okay, now, where were we? Oh, yes, we were talking prick size. Um, you know I'm not one to tell such things."

"Tell." I threatened him with another slap.

"Jeez, take it easy. Remember what mine looked like? (Like I could forget that.) Well, add an inch up and half an inch around and I'd say you were about there. You'll find, Secret, that it's the little ones that pack the biggest pouches. And thank the Lord for that."

"And you know this *how?*" I didn't think I really wanted the answer, but I made it that far, so I pressed on. In for a penny, in for a pound, as the Brits say.

"Two years ago I was at a party," he started to explain. "Several beers and a couple of hours into it, Chuckles walks up to me, grabs me

37

by the hips, stands on his tippy-toes, looks up at me and says, "I live next door." Now, as you might have guessed about me, I'm not one to miss an opportunity, and, within two minutes, I was next door. I think you can fill the rest in yourself, Secret, but, suffice it to say, it was a memorable evening. We've been passing acquaintances ever since. He's been at every party I've thrown in the last two years. So has his friend, Jeff, for that matter."

"Well, I doubt Jeff will be at your next one," I couldn't help but add.

"No, doubtful, but let me tell you something, Secret, that Jeff is no Miss Snow White herself. She was cruising everything that had a pulse last night, and I've caught her more than once on the dance floor locked in a vise-grip with someone other than James. Who, by the way, is Dud City in the sack, but you didn't hear that from me."

"No, of course not," I replied, feeling no pain by that point. Whatever he had given me was making me mellower than a James Taylor album.

"By the way, just where are we going? This isn't the way we came up," I made note.

"It's a surprise. So just sit back and relax and we'll be there in a few." (Yippy, more surprises. Well, what was one more?) As commanded, I sat back and enjoyed the view. It always seems so funny to me that you can leave the hustle and bustle of San Francisco, and fifteen minutes outside the city is nothing but rolling green hills (or brown, depending on the season) and stretches of land with either small herds of cattle or acres of vineyard on them.

As promised, in about five minutes, we pulled up to an adorable wooden house in the middle of nowhere, and Sparkle, with his arms thrown up, proclaimed, "We're there."

"And where is there?" I asked, with about as much curiosity as my current state of mind would allow.

"Casa d'Astan!" He pointed grandly to the home before us.

"Huh?" I wasn't formulating sentences too well either by that point.

"Well, this is my parent's summer cottage, but they aren't due up for another week or so. See, they always come up the same time every year. Anyway, there's bound to be some cans of something in the house that we can make due with to tide us over until we can get back into the city."

So we got out of the car and walked up the little stone path to the house. There were lemon and avocado trees all around the periphery and patches of wildflowers here and there. In truth, you couldn't have asked for a more serene setting. It was hard to imagine Sparkle, and the apparent hullabaloo that was his life, in such surroundings. But he was telling the truth, because he produced a set of keys and we were in the house in two shakes of a lamb's tail.

The inside of the cottage was just as rustic as the outside, very Martha Stewart meets Betsy Ross all over. There was lots of dark, antique wood furnishings and beautiful, old quilts and tapestries strewn about. The walls were painted in muted pastels and the paintings were all of scenes from times long past. Homey, quaint, and cozy. Everything Sparkle was not. Picture Sadam wintering in Martha's Vineyard, and you wouldn't be far off the mark.

"Strange," I chirped, "this strikes me as very *un*-Sparkle like. You must be nothing like your parents."

"Fuck, no," he was quick to respond. "My parents and I are nothing alike, but it's no wonder, really. I mean, as a child, I was raised by nannies and butlers and maids and cooks, while they were always off to Europe or up here. I was never allowed to join them. No big loss there, seeing as they're massive bores. In any case, I had much more fun and learned way more from the people they left in charge of me and my brother than I ever could have had with them. Honestly, we barely ever see each other now, thank goodness. I mean, they don't exactly approve of my lifestyle. But you know what I say, Secret? Fuck 'em. I was able to take control of my trust fund when I turned twenty-one and have had very little need or desire to associate with them ever since." Now I was beginning to see how Sparkle got to be Sparkle. I could also sense that he wasn't exactly as happy about his family situation as he was letting on to be. Not if that frown on his face meant anything.

I got a quick tour of the house as we hurried to the kitchen, where we found a note that Sparkle snatched up and started to read out loud. "Mother and Father, I have stocked the refrigerator and cupboards with the provisions you have asked for. I am looking forward to our little visit and will see you on Wednesday evening. Yours lovingly, Lance." He paused and then looked back over at me. "Well, well, well," he said, appearing a bit crestfallen, "it would seem that Mummy and Daddy are arriving sooner than usual, and my dear brother, Lance, will be joining them. How lovely for them." Sparkle again paused for a moment to collect himself. I couldn't begin to imagine what was going through his head, because, except for the fact that my family had no clue that I was gay, we were a fairly tight-knit group. If it was me, and my family was in town and had no intention of calling and letting me know that they were there, I would be devastated. Still, I had a strong suspicion that Sparkle did not devastate so easily. He was like a storm shelter that way, buried deep into the earth, with lots of provisions, mostly of the prescription kind.

"Well, fuck 'em," I tossed in, trying to cut through the tension. Besides, it seemed to be the answer of the day.

"Exactly, Secret. Fuck 'em. And, anyway, my dear brother was kind enough to provide us with what I'm sure will be a fine lunch. Let's just see what we have here," he said as he walked over to the refrigerator.

He opened the door, and, as he had predicted, it was full of meats, cheeses, fruits, and juices. The cabinets were full of equally fabulous things: crackers, spreads, cereals, breads, canned items, and, most importantly, wines. My stomach was doing back flips, as, by that time, I was ravenous.

"It would appear that my brother has outdone himself," Sparkle commented, with obvious traces of derision in his voice. I sensed that there was no love lost between the two of them. "So, what'll it be, Secret, turkey on white or ham and cheese on rye?"

"Yes, please," I answered, hungrier than Karen Carpenter on a liquid die, before adding, "Sparkle, can I ask you a question?" he shrugged as he went about preparing our lunch. "Now, you can tell me to fuck off if this is too personal or anything, but I get the distinct impression that you care just a little bit more than you're letting on that your family didn't let you know that they were in town this week."

"That wasn't a question, Secret; that was a statement. And, yes, fuck off."

"Well, fine then; we won't talk about it. I just thought you might like to get it off your chest or something. But if you don't want to talk about it, we won't talk about…"

"Okay then, let's stop talking about it," Sparkle interrupted. Obviously, I'd hit on a touchy subject.

"What would you like to talk about then?" I asked him.

"Whatever. Just not that, okay?" He looked at me, and I could tell that he meant business. Besides, he had a massive kitchen knife in his hand, which he waved around, menacingly. I could just see the headlines: *gay virgin hacked to death in Marin cottage*. Not the way I wanted to go. Especially the virgin part.

"Fine then… um… let's see… what to talk about?…"

"Secret, what was your major in college?" Sparkle stopped cutting the meat. I think he was starting to get a bit angry with me by that point.

"Um, English Lit. Why?"

"And you can't think of anything to talk about except why I don't get along with my parents?" He started preparing our lunches again and was shaking his head.

"Dickhead," I said, under my breath.

"What was that?"

"Huh? Nothing. Hey, Sparkle, did you ever notice that there are girls named April, May, and June, but never July?" He stopped putting the lettuce on the sandwich for a second to contemplate that. "And, Sparkle, did you ever notice that there are girls named October and December, but never November? Why do you suppose that is?" Again, he stopped for a second before putting on the tomatoes. "And then there are girls named Summer and Autumn, but not Spring, and only rarely Winter."

Then he put the knife down, propped his hands on the counter top, looked me deep in the eyes and said, "You win, Secret, I'll tell you why I don't get along with my parents if you'll stop with the Jerry Seinfeld routine. Deal?"

I merely nodded in the affirmative and told him to finish with the sandwiches first. (Score one in the plus column for yours truly, by the way.)

***

Five minutes later, with plates in hand, we made it into the living room. Sparkle ran back to the kitchen for napkins, silverware, and, thank goodness, a full bottle of red wine. I began eating half the sandwich and drinking a full glass of wine before even two words were said.

"Ready," I announced as I poured my second glass of wine.

"Sure?" he asked, still on his first glass and only two bites into his sandwich. "I can wait for piggy to finish his meal."

"Nope, you may proceed." I motioned for him to start with a grand flourish of my hand and a bowing of my head. It's amazing how

41

doing gay things like that comes naturally. How many straight men talk like that I wonder? I mean, did you ever hear a conversation between two gay men and realize that only gay men could ever have that exact same conversation? Case in point: I was with Kiki the other day at Home Depot (or as we like to call it, Homo Depot) and we were arguing about which color to paint his bathroom. Kiki wanted robin's egg blue and I was arguing for a mix of powder blue with a touch of vermilion. Now, you tell me, could you ever, in your wildest dreams, hear two straight guys having that same conversation? They would just say *blue* and leave it at that. What a drab life they must lead. But I digress. Where were we? Oh, yes…

He nodded and began. "I already told you, Secret, that my parents were almost never around and that they left me in the care of the house staff. Well, honestly, that really wasn't so horrible. I mean, it was the only life I ever knew. Lance, my brother, and I were only a year apart and, even though I was older, we were about the same size and liked pretty much the same things growing up. When school was in and my parents weren't home, the house staff did all the same things any parent would do, raising both of us to be fairly normal boys. And that's pretty much how it went until we got too old for looking after, when Lance and I took divergent paths."

Sparkle stopped to catch his breath, finished his first glass of wine, took a couple of bites of his sandwich, poured us both some more, and continued. "By the time I was sixteen and Lance was fifteen, our interests were suddenly nothing alike. Lance was playing J.V. football, basketball, and running track. I, on the other hand, was into more ethereal pursuits such as drama and reading. My one and only athletic ability lay in swimming. Not team swimming, mind you, but swimming in our pool at home. Lance could never beat me at that, you see. As he bulked up and I lithed down, I would out-swim him in distance and in speed, time and time again. He hated me for that, Secret, really hated me. I mean, he couldn't care less that I wasn't into any of the activities that he was into, but the fact that I was better than him at even just one sports-related thing really ate him up inside.

"So, in order to get out of racing my brother and inevitably making him angry with me, I stopped going home after school and started going to the library instead. After a few weeks of this, I noticed another boy reading there almost every day, too. He looked a bit older than me, was a few inches taller, blond hair and blue eyes. Not what I would call a real looker, but cute enough. And I was only sixteen and really didn't have the experience with cruising that I do today. But still, when he'd look up from his book and see me staring at him, one of us would nod or smile or something, and I knew, just knew, that this was more than mere politeness."

"Bourgeoning gaydar," I tossed in, knowing it quite well.

Sparkle nodded, refilled our glasses, and finished his sandwich. Mine was long gone by then, and I'd already gone to the kitchen, fixed another one, and was back in time for the juicy parts. "Then, one afternoon, instead of reading in the library, I decided to read on the lawn by the playground. It was a beautiful spring day, really warm, so I took off my shirt, lied down on my back, and read my book. Sometime later, I had the strangest feeling that there was somebody else out there with me. So I put the book down and propped myself up on my elbows, and who should be standing there but my library buddy. Naturally, my heart started racing, but I remained cool and introduced myself. He did the same. Bradley was his name, and he had a book in his hand and said that he had the same idea as I had, to come outside and enjoy the weather. My guess, he was really coming to look for me. Still, whatever the reason, I was glad for his daring-do. I mean, I would probably never have been so brave."

Sparkle sighed and closed his eyes for a second, obviously visualizing the scene in his head before continuing. If the gulp that followed meant anything, I was beginning to think that this story would not have much of a happy ending. "I asked him to sit down, to read with me. He politely accepted and also yanked off his t-shirt. That's when I knew that he was probably older than me, because he had about a dozen fine blond hairs on his tight, little chest. At sixteen, you see, I was quite hairless. Today it's an affectation, but back then it was just sweet youth.

"Anyway, Bradley got on his back, opened his book, and started reading. He was just inches away from me, and, for about ten minutes, neither one of us said a word. Suffice it to say, in all that time, I didn't read a single word; I just kept turning the pages of my book every few minutes in order to appear like I was reading. I mean, I was terrified. Excited, yes, but terrified. Big time. Then he put his book down and turned sideways onto one arm and said that it was just too nice outside to read, and, besides, it was a crappy book. I agreed, put my book down, as well, and rolled over to face him, eye to eye, with butterflies whipping around inside my tummy. Then he asked me why I was all of a sudden always in the library after school, and I told him the truth. He told me that he was there because his mother didn't get home until about five and she didn't want him to be alone in the house. He chose to hang out in the library and read. He said he really didn't mind, and I, for one, was glad for his circumstances."

Sparkle again stopped to refill our glasses, but I'd barely been drinking by that point as I was intently paying attention to his story. This kind of stuff didn't happen in Kansas when I was a kid. Of course, not many gay men get to sip wine in a remote cottage with a slice of heaven like Sparkle, either, so maybe my luck was changing.

In any case, he continued soon enough. "Then the conversation turned interesting. See, Bradley was looking at my torso and asked me if I had gotten my awesome body while swimming. I said that I guessed that was how I got it. Of course, I'd never really given it a thought before then, but it did make sense. Then, Secret, he did something that took me totally by surprise: he reached over and gently ran his hand over my stomach and chest, saying that he figured it was the swimming, too, seeing how hard my stomach was and how solid my chest was. I didn't know about that, but I did know that both my stomach and chest were moving up and down really fast all of a sudden. Noticing my perplexity, he quickly took his hand away. Still, not wanting to miss my chance and, seeing that fair was fair, I reached over and ran my hand across *his* chest. I asked him when he started growing his chest hairs, but of course that was just a pretense. Then he told me that they started growing in the year before, when he was sixteen, and they were coming in pretty regularly now. I noticed that, while he was talking, his chest was also rising and falling pretty rapidly. Meaning, two teenage dudes, same boat. In any case, I let my hand linger a little while longer before removing it. Guess I've always been a bit brazen."

He paused and chuckled. Brazen, of course, was a gross understatement. "Well, after that, we were both sort of at a loss for words. That's when Bradley said that he needed to get going, that it was nice meeting me, and that he'd see me around. Then he turned to go...."

"Oh, God, no!" I screamed. "He didn't just leave, did he? Don't tell me nothing else happened!"

"Jeez, Secret, like, duh, of course something happened or else this would be a pretty useless story, don't you think?" He sighed and slapped my arm. "So, anyway, he turned to go, but before he even took two steps away, I called back to him and asked if instead of going to the library after school the next day, why not come home with me and hang out, and that the butler would drive him home later on. He turned to look at me, paused a moment, and then nodded his head, his smile big and bright and wide, those butterflies of mine making their triumphant return. Then he waved a farewell and walked away. My heart was racing and my head was spinning, as you can imagine, but damn if I didn't just make my very first date."

Sparkle sighed and caught his breath before picking up where he'd left off. Despite the joyfulness of the story, I could tell there was a pain there, something worming its way up. "Needless to say, I was a wreck that night and the whole next day, but I made it through, and the next afternoon I met up with Bradley at the library before we headed to my house. I told him that my parents were in Spain for the next two nights and that my brother was at football practice, and that the servants pretty much stayed on the first floor of the house. I was hoping that he was getting the hint that we'd be pretty much alone and that he could ravage me at will. Not that my suaveness was at a peak at the age of sixteen, but still.

"In any case, when we finally made it home, he was in awe of my house. Well, honestly, it was actually more of a mansion, but to me it was just *our house*. Anyway, Bradley was all wide eyes and gaping mouth from one end of the place to the other. He told me that his whole home could fit into just our basement. And that's when I knew I had the upper hand.

"I made sure to show him the backyard last," he said, continuing ever onward, his face taking on a bittersweet quality to it, a poignancy I'd yet to see. "That's where we kept the pool and the hot tub. And that's when Bradley really went nuts. He'd been to homes with pools before, but never a hot tub. *Bingo*, I thought to myself. Then I told him that we should get in. Well, I could sense the instantaneous fear at that thought. I mean, there he was, poor boy, alone with a young harlot trying desperately hard to seduce him. Needless to say, he looked ready to run. I wasn't about to let happen, of course, so I told him that I got in the thing all the time with my other friends, a bold-faced lie, by the way, and that it was no big deal. The logic of that seemed to sink in, because he brightened up and said that he'd love to go in, seeing as he'd never been in a hot tub before.

"Well, I started shucking off my clothes before he had a chance to change his mind, and I was naked and in the hot tub before he could even take his shoes off. That also gave me a distinct advantage, Secret.

See, now I could look down at him as he got undressed. Which he then proceeded to do. He already had his shirt off and was taking off his shoes, while I got comfortable in the tub. Then he unbuckled his belt, looked up to see if I was watching, which of course I was, and then quickly took off his pants. Then he stopped and stood there in his white Jockeys and looked up at me again and asked if the water was warm yet. Now, I don't know if you've ever seen a seventeen-year old boy in white skivvies before, but I could've sworn I was staring at an angel. An honest to goodness angel. I gulped as I told him that the water was perfect, willing him to hurry the fuck on up with it.

Sparkle took a swig of wine before the story continued. "Then he did it. He took off his underwear and started to climb up the stairs of the hot tub. In just one minute, I was about to be naked with another boy, and I was, needless to say, absolutely petrified. He reached the top of the hot tub and just stood there. Never having been in one before, he wanted to get the lay of the land before he hopped in. That was just fine with me, because I was getting the lay of the land as well. And, needless to say, his land looked very layable indeed. Up close and in the lights of the tub, Bradley looked kind of sexy, truth be told."

"Wait," I rasped. "Fill me up." I held out my glass, hand suddenly trembling.

Sparkle kept right on going after topping us both off. "Anyway, then he turned around so he could climb down into the tub, offering me a view of his stellar butt. It was also covered in a fine spray of blond hairs and looked hard as a rock. I had the strangest desire to just reach up and grab it and... and... and, well, I had no idea what I would do with it once I grabbed it; I just knew that I needed to grab it. And then he was in the tub and was turned around facing me. We just sat there like that for a while, getting used to the water and the newness of it. For him, the newness of the hot tub, for me, the newness of a naked boy with me in the hot tub. He said that it was *neat* and I said that I was glad he enjoyed it. Then nothing. Neither one of us could think of a single thing to say. That lasted for what seemed like an eternity, until Bradley finally said that he had better get on home before his mother started worrying. As he stood to get out, something inside of me snapped, Secret, and I screamed, 'Wait!', and I suddenly jumped up and grabbed his dick."

"You didn't!" I shrieked, hopping up and down on the couch.

Sparkle nodded and grinned. "Yup. And something like that could've gone in one of two ways: he could've been really pissed at me

46

for doing that and beaten the shit out of me or he could do what he did and just stood there getting a boner. He didn't look at me as all this was happening and I wasn't looking at him either. Well, at least I wasn't looking up at his face, but I was looking at him. Then I let go and he climbed out of the tub. I was frozen in place after that. What had I just done? Was he going to run home and tell his mother? Was he going to blab it to the entire student body tomorrow? Was I about to be the only *out* sixteen-year old boy in my high school?"

"Were you?" I asked, nearly in a pant.

"Thankfully, no, I wasn't. He got dressed fast enough, but as he got ready to go back inside the house, he looked back over at me. Then he paused at the patio door, took a deep breath, and said that he'd like to come back over tomorrow if it was all right with me. *If it was all right with me?* Was he joking? Of course it was all right with me, and I promptly told him so. And then the butler drove him home."

I grinned and giggled. "The butler drove him home, huh? Talk about icing on the cake."

Sparkle grinned, too. "I suppose he was just as taken in as you clearly are, Secret. And thankfully so. In any case, the next day was Friday, and Bradley had one-upped me when we met at the end of our classes. He told me that his mother said that it would be fine if he spent the night at my house. This time, he was looking me straight in the eyes. I gulped, nodded a yes, and squeaked out a *that would be great.* Then he lit up with a smile, patted me on the shoulder, and we walked out of the school together."

"Hand in hand?" I couldn't help but ask, ever the hopeless romantic that I am.

"No, dumbass, not hand in hand," came the reply. "He might not have wanted to beat me up, but that didn't mean the rest of the school wouldn't if they saw us like that. Anyway, to continue, when we got home, I lent him a pair of swimming trunks and he dove into the pool as soon as he had them on. Honestly, he looked like a kid with a new toy or something. I jumped in and sprayed him with a nifty cannonball. This, of course, led to the standard teenager splash fight. And that, cue the doom and gloom music, is when Lance walked up."

"Uh oh," said I, hearing said doom and gloom music in my head, cranked up to max.

"Yup. Oh oh," Sparkle agreed. "See, never having seen me with another boy at our house before, he was kind of surprised to see us there in the state we were in. In any case, I introduced the two of them, but Lance was standoffish and, I could've sworn, jealous. After all, he was used to having me at his beck and call, and now, here I was with some stranger in our pool. He left us alone after that, but I felt uncomfortable and asked Bradley if he wanted to go up to my room and listen to some music instead. Bradley, thankfully, said that that sounded like a good idea, and so we got out, toweled off, and headed into the house. I told the cook that we would come back down for dinner later and then take it up to my room."

"The cook?" I couldn't help but ask.

Sparkle shrugged. "The cook, yes. Anyway, she said that she would just bring it up to us, and then Bradley and I hightailed it up to my bedroom. For once, I was truly glad that my parents had beaucoup bucks, and not just because they were out of town and I was mostly alone with Bradley, but mainly because I had a lot of cool things to show off to him."

"Besides a chauffeur and a cook," I interrupted.

"And a limo and a mansion, Secret. Yes. In any case, he jumped from one thing to the other like he'd never seen such things before. From the television to the telephone to my games, ultimately flipping through my albums. And that's when I knew that I'd found Mister Perfect. See, he knew every one of the records I had in my collection and was really jealous that I had both Pat Benatar albums and Blondie's *Plastic Letters* and even Andy Gibb's *Shadow Dancing*. He chose one of my Berlin LPs before we hopped on the bed together and sang along with Terri Nunn to *Sex (I'm A...)*."

"Love that song!" I shouted.

"Fab-u-lous," he agreed. "Anyway, by the end of the album, we were exhausted from laughing and singing, and, just in the nick of time, the cook came up with our dinners. I forgot that I was nervous until we were forced to take a break and eat. I mean, so long as we were rowdy and loud, I felt relaxed, but as soon as silence overtook my room, *POW*, I was a wreck again. This was made even worse by the fact that we were sitting so close and our arms and legs kept touching as we ate. I never realized before then just how small a single bed was. Then, when we were done eating, I flicked on the television and we watched Entertainment Tonight and made fun of Mary Hart's hair." He sighed and shot me a crooked grin. "Love, Secret, was in the air."

As was my hand, asking for another round. "Please."

He poured and the story continued. "By the time eight o'clock rolled around, we'd pretty much exhausted all the possibilities for anything entertaining on television, so I jumped up and popped a tape in the VCR, then went over and turned off my bedroom lights. As I turned to get back in bed, Bradley was taking off his pants and shirt. He said that he was making himself comfortable. As if I cared why he was taking off his clothes in my bed, right? I mean, he could've been on fire, just so long as he was getting undressed. I, of course, being the good host that I was, followed suit and also took off my clothes, jumping into my bed with nothing on but my Fruit of the Looms and a smile."

"Hot" I managed.

"And about to go scorching," he amended. "So there we were. Alone, undressed, and in bed. Now what? All of this was new to me. I'd managed to catch *Parting Glances* on HBO, but even that couldn't have prepared me for this. Thank God the movie I'd selected for us was funny, and, after a bit, both of us got decidedly more comfortable. Each time we would start laughing, we would bump arms or legs. Well, somewhere in the middle of the movie, we managed to be completely side by side and touching each other, and guess what?"

"What?! What?!" I shouted, almost spilling my drink. Almost.

Sparkle giggled and shot me a grin. "Yours truly had a hard-on. I looked down to see if it was noticeable or anything and, well, you've seen me in that state before; of course, it was noticeable, but even more noticeable was Bradley's. And that's when I also realized that Bradley wasn't watching the movie anymore. Not knowing what else to do, I grabbed his now straining basket. Secret, this may surprise you, but I've never been more terrified in my whole entire life. Still, there was no turning back at that point, and I had no idea how to go forward. I was probably just lucky that Bradley was seventeen and more mature than I was, because he took complete control of the situation. Thank God, because we would probably still be in that bed fumbling with each other's undies if it was left up to me. In any case, he rather deftly had us out of our underwear in about two seconds flat, and, before I knew what hit me, we were making out. Honestly, there have been many, many men since that night, but that's about the only one that I can remember like it was yesterday. I've never felt so utterly alone with just one guy before. The bed and the room faded into nothingness and it was just me and Bradley, naked and hard.

"Yeah, been there done that," I interjected.

"Quite. Anyway, the rest of it went rather quickly and easily. Not knowing what else to do but beat each other off, that's all we did.

And with two horny teenagers, that didn't take very long at all. I remember that moment, too, because we both shot straight over our heads and hit the wall. Even to this day, I don't think that I've surpassed such distance. We both laughed about it and then laid there for what seemed like forever just hugging and making out until we both fell asleep. Honestly, I couldn't have asked for a better first time. That is, until the next morning."

I simpered. "I don't think I want to hear."

He shrugged. "You asked for it, Dear One. And here it comes. In Spades. So, Bradley and I repeated our evening step for step when we woke up and then showered and prepared to go down for breakfast. But, before we could make it there, we ran into my brother. Lance had a look on his face that I'd never seen before, which scared me half to death. He said that he'd heard weird noises the night before when he got up to go to the bathroom and again that morning when he went to shower. That's when he figured out that it was Bradley and me having sex. He looked disgusted as he was telling us this, and, try as I might to deny it, Lance just kept calling us faggots and queers. Then he said that if I didn't get Bradley out of the house immediately, he was going to get my father's gun and shoot us both."

"No," I managed, hand over my mouth.

"Sadly, yes. And it wasn't a hard decision to make. In other words, Bradley and I were running down the stairs and out of the house in minutes, and shaking pretty badly as we started to walk back to his house. It took about an hour to get there, with neither of us saying much the entire time. What started out to be the most fabulous experience of my whole young life, Secret, was quickly becoming a nightmare. And all the while I kept telling myself that everything would be okay and that Lance would be a good brother and never mention the events again."

"But you were wrong."

He nodded, frowning as he did so. "I was wrong. I didn't make it home until it was getting near dark, figuring it was best if I let Lance simmer down a little before I talked to him. But as soon as I walked in the door, I knew that that would never happen. See, my brother and both my parents were sitting in the living room waiting for me. And, as angry as Lance looked that morning, my parents looked decidedly more so that evening. Secret, I can't even begin to tell you how horrible it all was. Between the yelling and the crying, all I kept thinking of was how I would never get a chance to be with Bradley again. I was right, of course, because my parents, never ones for being reasonable, had things under control. Their control. They had me out of my school and enrolled in a military academy by the next day, and had the butler drive me up there immediately. There were no teary goodbyes or kisses for me. I was just up and out of the house." Sparkle shook his head and clenched his fists. "The poor butler. He had no idea what was going on, and I for one wasn't about to tell him. He just dropped me off at the headmaster's house and was gone."

"This story sucks, dude," I told him, eyes wet, head tilted down.

"Uh huh. Sucks. And life for our family was never the same after that. I went home for holidays and for summers until I went off to college, but my parents and brother were only civil and nothing more. There were only two things, Secret, that I was quite lucky about regarding that whole nasty mess. Firstly, it was an all boy's school they sent me to and, needless to say, there were a lot of horny teenage boys there. Bradley, it turns out, was the first in a long line of seventeen-year-olds that wanted to have sex with me. And, secondly, my grandparents had left me my trust fund, my parents having no control over it. When I turned twenty-one, I collected the loot and was out from under their reign forever. To this day, we've never discussed my sexuality, and my brother and I have barely said two words to each other. They let me come up here when I want to, but I think it's more like a consolation prize. Lance gets the love and I get the use of the house in the country. Not a bad deal, I would say. So there, Secret. There is your story. Happy now?"

"No," I said, with a pit in my stomach and a lump in my throat. "Not happy. Depressed. Here, pour us some more wine. I don't think I can handle this sober (as if we were even close to that anymore), especially since I haven't come out to my own parents yet."

"Then please, Secret, don't let my little story stop you from doing so. You need to tell your parents who you really are. I certainly regret how my parents found out that I was gay, but I never for a minute regret them knowing. You'll never be able to be yourself around them if they don't know the real Bruce." Sparkle had a point and was quite touching in making it. (Either that or that was some really great wine we were downing. I assumed, all things considered, that it was probably the latter.)

And then Sparkle did something completely surprising. He got up from his side of the sofa and sat down next to me and put his arms around me and gave me a nice, warm hug. Then he said, in a really quiet voice just loud enough for me to hear, "Thanks." I guessed that he meant *thanks* for letting him get that off his chest, or maybe thanks for me being his friend. I sensed he had very few true ones. Whatever it was, I hugged him back. There's nothing quite like a nice, warm hug between friends, after all. And that's how we were sitting when the front door popped open.

As the door swung in, letting in sheets of light, I had to shield my eyes with my hand to get a better look at our intruder. It only took about five seconds for them to adjust, but it was unmistakable who was standing in the doorway, looking mighty pissed.

"Lance," Sparkle grunted, pulling away from me all at once, "how nice to see you again. It's been way too long." Sparkle came off about as sincere as a used car salesman.

"Faggot," his brother barked. "I seem to have a knack for finding you in these situations. Now get your faggot ass out of this house and take your faggot boyfriend out of here with you."

"Or what?" Sparkle was now on his feet, and, thank goodness, was a good two inches taller than Lance and in a hell of a lot better shape. I mean, I don't mind a little rock-em, sock-em action every now and again, but only if I know for certain that there's little chance of me getting my ass completely kicked. I figured we had a keen advantage here, so I too stood up to face the prick.

"Or next time I see you I'm gonna take my gun and shoot your fucking queer ass off the face of this planet. Now get out of here and stop causing this family so much shame and grief." The entire time, Lance was waving his arms and pacing back and forth. Ignorant straight people are so utterly silly that way. Making a big deal out of nothing. If anything, they should be grateful for the lack of sexual competition. As if they could compete against us anyhow.

Now Sparkle, to his credit, was taking all of this remarkably well. He simply stood there for another minute and shook his head. I, on the other hand, was not so calm. I'd finally come out to myself and most of my world, and here was this moron screaming at me and calling me a faggot. Who did he think he was, Anita Bryant?

I was just about to let him have it, too, when Sparkle, sensing my impending rush of venom, grabbed my hand and started to herd me out of the room. "Lance," Sparkle said, in an even tone, "as always, it's been a rare pleasure seeing you again. Please tell Mother and Father that I send my love and that I will see you all again during the holidays." Sparkle was walking us out of the living room and toward the front door as he was saying all of this. I for one was surprised at his total calm demeanor. But, just as we got within about a foot of the door, Sparkle let go of my hand and jumped toward Lance, pinning him against the door and knocking the air out of his lungs at the same time.

"Listen, you little piece of shit," Sparkle said, still in complete control. "This is not *my boyfriend*. This is my *friend*, Bruce, not that it's any of your damn business. And I will bring whomever I want to this house, whenever I want. This, like the rest of our family's wealth, was our grandparent's, not our parent's and certainly not yours. It belongs to all of us equally. So get over your ignorant self and get a fucking life. Besides, I don't see a wedding band on your finger. Is there something you'd like to share with us, Little Brother?" Sparkle let go of his shaken sibling, who quickly backed into the house. We departed slowly and awkwardly. Needless to say, I was good and ready to leave by that point.

"Sparkle?" I said as we got into the car.

"Yes, Secret?" Sparkle was looking at me as his hands rested on the steering wheel. Clearly, that little melee had taken its toll on him.

"You okay?"

"Getting there, Secret. Now let's get the hell out of here; I need a drink in a nice, wholesome gay bar."

"Well, amen to that, my friend. And do you want to know something, Sparkle?" I asked. "I think I figured out what Gay Rule #4 is."

"Yeah, Secret, and just what might that be?"

"That straight people and gay people *are* different. *We're* better. Hey, that would make a great slogan: *We're here. We're queer. We're better.* Pretty nifty, don't you think?"

"Needs some tweaking, Sweetie, but we'll work on it."

"Looking forward to it, Sparkle," I replied, patting his back. "Looking forward to it."

CHAPTER THREE
FROM FAGS TO RICHES

So I bet you're wondering from the nifty little title above what I did exactly to go from my near state of destitution to the aforementioned *riches*. Okay, riches might have been a slight overstatement. Let's just say that I was no longer broke. See, Sparkle did indeed take care of me, just as he promised he would. How, you are no doubt asking, did he manage to do that? Well, before you make any judgments, let me just say on my own behalf that this is going to sound much worse than it actually was. Okay, so here goes: I became Sparkle's, um… Sparkle's… well, his houseboy, if you must know. (For a while, we toyed with calling me Glint to his Sparkle, but that, thankfully, didn't pan out. Besides, I had a feeling that Secret would be my name for quite some time to come.)

In any case, it was just temporary until something better came along, and I wasn't about to look a gift horse in the mouth. And, hell, it paid much more than I could ever have earned at Joe Joe's. Besides, as you're soon to find out, it was just a stepping-stone to the next better thing that did indeed come along.

Basically, I cleaned his apartment, paid his bills (which were considerable), kept his date book (even more considerable), and ran his errands. All of this, believe it or not, kept me fairly busy, but it also afforded me a lot of down time. Probably the best part about it, looking back, was that I never had to go to work before ten o'clock, the hour at which Sparkle usually woke up. I also got to meet a ton of truly interesting, if not outright bizarre, people, because Sparkle, it turned out, had a lot more going on than met the eye.

My very first excursion into the wilderness that was (and still hopefully is) Sparkle's life was the very first time I went to brunch with him and some of his friends. Brunch, if you're new to the madcap world of queer, is to the gay man what church is to a Catholic: something you do every Sunday whether you want to or not. And, I was soon to find out, Sparkle never, ever missed brunch. He was like the mailman of brunch: come rain, or sleet, or even jail (followed by bail, long story... wait), Sparkle was at a brunch or throwing a brunch. This also was one of my duties: to put brunches together. (You should be able to include that on a résumé, by the way: *throws a fabulous brunch.* It's not easy, mind you.)

Now that first brunch, it was a doozie. We went to Jellies, rhymes with nellies, which is just what that restaurant was full of that day. I'd never been around so many queens before in a single afternoon. Joe Joe's was much butcher and more rugged; Jellies was pure zaniness compared to that place. And Jellies had something Joe Joe's didn't have: a full bar. Honestly, whoever had the idea to put a bar and a restaurant together, well, that guy should get a Nobel Prize or something. Because, I'm here to say, brunch without booze is like sex without coming. Why bother?

If you've never been to San Francisco, there's something you should know: space is at a premium here. Offices are cramped, apartments are tiny (with bedrooms that are closets), and restaurants have their tables so packed together that by the time you're done eating you've just had your first date with a guy you didn't even arrive with. Jellies was just such a place. As a matter of fact, if you didn't have a twenty-seven-inch waist or less, you couldn't work there. This, compounded by the situation we had, which was that there were six of us, made for quite an interesting and enlightening afternoon.

***

Sparkle and I arrived second to last, and were greeted uproariously by (now get this) Jim, Tim, and Slim. The three of them were roommates as well as frequent fuck-buddies, and each one was more outlandish than the next. They were also, not surprisingly, completely adorable. In any case, I sat down next to Slim, who had on hot pink nail polish and a t-shirt that had obviously been meant for a twelve-year-old girl, plus, on top of his head, big old Jackie-O sunglasses. He was glamour and glitz rolled up into a hard, little fairy body. I would've eaten him up alive right there and then if I wasn't so sure that he would've given me cavities.

"Double Bloody Mary," I implored the waitress.

Jim and Tim, though equally adorable, were working a different angle than Slim. They both had on army boots with the whites of their socks just barely showing. There legs were neatly trimmed with just a hint of hair on them and they both had on shorts that were shorter than any Daisy Dukes I'd ever seen. Meaning, when they stood up to great us, I saw nothing but bulge. For shirts, they both went with a classic white tee with rolled up sleeves. And both had striking blue eyes and raven-black hair.

"Waitress, is that drink coming?" I croaked out, because if it didn't, I soon would be.

Suffice it to say, this was more like it: not a muscle clone in sight. The décor was also upbeat and not the least bit trendy. *Kitschy*, I would call it. None of the tables or chairs matched and neither did the plates, cups, or silverware. The walls were covered with old movie posters and faded pictures. And, best of all, when the drinks did show up, they were in huge hurricane glasses. This, I must say, was how a Bloody Mary was meant to be served.

And then our last brunch guest arrived.

Number six was decidedly more butch. Her name was Millie, and she had on army boots that she wore over her baggy fatigues. She was wearing a loose white tee that said: *Nobody Knows that my Girlfriend Fists Me*. I couldn't even begin to imagine (or didn't dare try) how that one worked. *Blech*. And she had Lesbian Haircut #3. You know the one: feathered on top and short all around, with a rat's tail in the back. I swear, there must be just one lesbian hairdresser that travels around the globe giving Lesbian Haircut #3, because you can go to any town in any country in the world and see this haircut on at least one dyke.

Introductions and air-kisses were given all around, with Millie sitting down to my left. Apparently, this little group knew each other well and was already comfortable with each other, because the conversation turned raunchy almost immediately.

"So, Tim, how was your date with Randall last night?" Sparkle asked.

"Well, you'll notice he's not with us this morning," Jim answered for Tim.

"Amen for that," Tim added, nodding his head. "You just never know about some people."

"Ooh, do tell. I've only heard secondhand accounts, and none of them were encouraging." Sparkle scooted up his chair as he said this, even though the six of us couldn't have gotten any closer if we were sardines in a can.

"Well, everything started off nice. He drove over from his house in Berkeley…"

"Oh no," Sparkle interrupted.

"What?" I inquired, with the five of them answering in unison, "He's geographically challenged".

"Oh." (Whatever.)

"Anyway, he does own. So points for that. And he did show up with a beautiful bouquet of wild flowers. So again, pointage for that. Actually, he was racking up the points all night long: dinner at Chez Moi, he paid, drinks at The Stud, he paid, and then back to my place, and…

"You paid." This time it was Millie who interrupted.

"Boy howdy, did I ever. Everything started off nice and sweet. I fixed us some drinks before we sat down on the couch to do the whole chitchat thing. And chitchat quickly turned to lip-smack and, before I knew it, we were back in my bedroom and were naked as the day we were born. Sort of."

"Sort of?" I asked.

"Well, Randall had some added features that I'm pretty sure he wasn't born with. The tattoos were okay. I mean, that's kind of sexy and everything, but he had both his nipples pierced with these two huge barbells."

"Gross!" we all said together. (Remember, this was the mid-nineties; piercing was still fairly nouveau at the time. Not like today, where every Tom, Dick, and Mary has their dick, balls, butt, lip, nose, eyebrow, and bellybutton pierced. Back then, we were still squeamish about such things.)

"Gross is right. I mean, I had no idea what to do with them. Do you play with them or hang your shirt up on them or what? But, okay, I figured, let's roll with it. He was just expressing himself or something, right? Plus, he looked and felt really hot, once I dimmed the lights and took my glasses off. Anyway, things were going well, lots of kissy-kissy and some sucky-sucky and licky-licky, but then he gave me this little punch on my chest. Okay, I can deal with that, I thought. No biggie. And then he did it again, but harder. I mean, look at me, y'all, I'm what, one hundred and forty pounds and just barely five

57

seven. I'm meant for the gentle cycle, and he was rough and tumbling me."

We all giggled and took healthy swigs of our drinks before he continued. "So, anyway, I decided to move my chest away from his fists and I swung my butt around for some sixty-nining instead. Big mistake. No sooner was my nice little rump in his face when he started slapping it, and hard, too."

"So that's what I heard last night," Slim interjected, squeezing my knee. (Hmm. Things were starting to get interesting. Below the table, I mean.)

"Tu-huh. Sorry about that," Tim replied. "Then I did the sensible thing and I removed my butt from his face and said, 'Look, Honey, you're no Chad Douglas, so would you please stop slapping my ass?' (Chad who? I got that one later on when Sparkle showed me a video. Yikes!) Well, that stopped him, anyway, and he apologized and went back to some nice gentle rubbing and kissing."

"But...?" Sparkle asked.

"Butt is right. Pretty soon I felt a finger creeping towards my love-hole (snickers all around). Now, I don't mind telling you all that every now and again I like getting my butt plugged, and one little finger wasn't going to stop the festivities, but one finger quickly led to two fingers, and when he started in on finger number three, well, let me tell you, cut, print, that was a wrap."

"You asked him to stop?" asked I, taking mental notes should the same situation present itself to me in the hopefully near future. (Yes, *that* story is coming up, too. Don't get your panties in a wad.)

"I asked him to leave," Tim answered, emphatically. "Lord knows what else he had up his sleeve, and I for one was not going to find out. Needless to say, he wasn't at all thrilled at the prospect, but quietly got up, got dressed, and got the hell on out. *Phew!*"

Now, a little side note on this whole story to show you just how strange and wonderful gay life is. See, Tim has stayed in the periphery of our lives for the past eight years, popping up at a party or a brunch or a chance run-in in the streets or a bar, and let me tell you, the vanilla Tim you just met has blossomed into a man of many colors. (Hanky colors that is.)

In fact, soon after that brunch, we ran into Tim at The Eagle for their beer bust, and he was wearing jeans and a leather vest. Nothing strange there; it was The Eagle, after all. But September rolled around and we ran into him again at the Folsom Street Fair (The biggest leather street fair you've ever seen. You should make it a point to check it out.) and he was utterly transformed. His clean-shaven face now sported a full mustache and thick side-burns. Again, he had on a vest, but this time he was shirtless and we could see that his left nipple was pierced and his right arm had a brand new tattoo. And, to top it all off, he was wearing tight, tight chaps and nothing but a codpiece underneath. We actually walked right past him before he called our names out and we turned around. It took us a few seconds to figure out that it was actually him.

A few years later, we heard that he'd made several fisting videos, both giving and receiving, and in 1998 he was voted *Mister San Francisco Leather Boy*. So you see, friend, gay life is ever-evolving. I certainly am not the same man I was all those years ago, or even three years ago, for that matter. How many straight men get the chance to change personas, careers, fashions, lovers, etc. like your average gay man does? Not many I'd imagine.

Anyway, back to the brunch...

Our meals were served and we were all on our second round of drinks when the conversation again turned to sex. Sparkle had noticed Millie's t-shirt and had commented that he never realized that lesbians fisted each other.

"Sure. I mean, it makes sense," Millie said, very matter of factly, "what else do we have to stick up there, right? Plus, look at my fist. Girls have much smaller hands than guys do and they fit rather nicely in pretty girl pussies."

"Gee, thanks Millie," Slim said, looking rather green around the gills, "that was certainly, um, a visual."

"Please, Mary, it's no worse than any conversation I've had to listen to from you queens over the years. Bruce, watch this," she said, looking at me with a grin and a glint in her eye. "What is the strangest thing that any of you have ever had up your asses?"

"Ooh, I like that one," said Tim, rubbing his hands together as he licked his lips. "Okay, me first, me first. Let's see. I was dating this guy, Hobart, about a year ago, and Hobart had this thing about dildo fucking. I don't know if it was, well..."

"He had a small one, right?" Sparkle the Sage guessed.

"Well, yes, he did, actually. Maybe that was it. Anyway, he really got off on stuffing this enormous array of dildos up my ass. Every time I went over to his house, he had a new one, and no two looked alike. It got to be that I would get really excited each time I made my way over to his flat just to see what he was going to stick up my butt. Then one night he came over to my apartment and things were getting kind of hot and heavy, and he asked me if I had any *toys* for him to play with. 'Well, actually, no I don't,' I told him. Man, you should've seen the look on his face. It was this mix of surprise and sadness. I actually felt sorry for him."

"So what did you do," Jim asked, "or do I want to know?"

"Mmm, um, no, not really. See, having nothing in my room that would satisfy Hobart's fetish, I went to the bathroom…"

"The bathroom you and I share?" Jim interrupted.

"Yup. And since I use spray-on and you use roll-on…"

"You let him fuck you with my deodorant?" Now Jim looked peeved.

"Uh-huh. And I replaced it, so stop your freaking."

"And how was it?" Jim asked, calming down as his curiosity got the better of him.

"Well, they could have called it *Arrid Extra-Wet* after we got through with it; and, not that I'd do it again, probably, but I've had worse things up there." He smiled and looked at each of us in turn. "Okay, so who's next?" he inquired, finishing his drink and ordering another one. I noticed that the drinks were going faster than the meals, by the way.

"I'll go." This time it was Sparkle's turn, which should've be interesting, I thought, and, needless to say, was not disappointed.

"Do you all know Benny Turner?" he asked, taking a healthy swig of his drink.

"Hey, isn't that the guy you're always calling Batboy Benny? Why is that anyway?" Jim asked.

"Um, because, like, he was a batboy when we met, duh," Sparkle responded, in his usual endearing way.

"Oh, wasn't he kind of old to be a batboy?" This time it was Tim asking the obvious. (Slim, by the way, was working his way up my leg with his dexterous fingers. By that time, I was on my third Bloody Mary and was becoming one rather *horny* Mary. Not surprisingly, I was getting very little eating done. But, to be fair, no one likes a cold omelet.)

"Actually, yes, he was too old to be a batboy, but he'd entered this stupid contest that *The Examiner* was running, one that they obviously forgot to put an age limit on. They probably thought that no one over the age of ten was going to enter the contest. They, of course, were wrong, because Benny entered one hundred and fifty times. Seems it was his dream when he was a little boy. So for one full season, *almost*, he was Batboy Benny. The fans loved it, and Benny got way more than his fifteen minutes of fame."

"Fine. Got it. So what was the strange thing shoved up your ass?" Jim asked, rolling his hands to indicate that my friend should continue to the juicy parts.

"Hold your horses (Slim was holding mine by that time), I'm getting to that." Sparkle was not one to be rushed, in case you hadn't figured that out yet. "Anyway, one night, Benny and I were driving around looking for something to do and we were coming up with nothing. You know how sometimes this city can be so small and you've, like, done everything five times and there's just nothing left to do? (Everyone nodded except me.) Well, that was the kind of night we were having, until Benny had an idea." He took a big gulp of his drink, as did the rest of us, and continued. "See, Benny knew of a way sneak into the ballpark, and, it just so happened, the Giants were at an away game that night."

"And how exactly does one sneak into the park?" Millie asked. (I think she spotted Slim's wandering fingers, and so we switched to playing handsies beneath the table.)

"Well, the night cleaning crew sometimes leaves one of the side entrances open so they can have easier access to the park and their vans," Sparkle explained.

"And why, pray tell, do they need that?" I think Millie liked pestering him, and it was working.

"Because, and that had better be the last interruption or I'm stopping here (Millie saluted an okay), because they went out to their vans to get stoned, which they couldn't do in the park, because they didn't want to get caught. Anyway, back to the story." He ordered another drink first, and we all followed suit. We let the waitress take the food; by then it was kind of pointless. "So there we were, creeping around in the dark outside the park looking for the entrance, and having little luck. Probably the night crew had gone home or they weren't working at all, because there were no lights on whatsoever. Well, that made us both incredibly horny for some reason and, before I knew it, we were pressed hard up against the wall with our pants down around our ankles surrounded by nothing but pitch blackness. Benny started going down you know where and I braced myself on the wall.

That's when I felt the doorknob. Of course, I waited to tell this to Benny for a few minutes."

"Why'd you wait?" I asked, stupidly, and sat there as everyone at the table looked at me like I was the dumbest thing since Milli Vanilli (maybe not that dumb, maybe more like Right Said Fred). They kept looking and I kept staring, and then, "D'oh. I get it. You were getting head. Sorry, please continue. Very funny. Go ahead."

And he did, "Anyway, I opened the door for us and we were inside in a flash. We followed the dark corridor down to the visiting team changing room and turned on the lights. All in all, not a bad set up. Kind of like a really large hotel bathroom. It had that ultra clean look and you got the feeling that no one was going to stay there for very long. Still, they couldn't quite get rid of the pungent odor of sweaty men. That, combined with the excitement of the break in, made for two horny boys. Meaning, before we knew it, we were both naked. Benny had my back on a long bench and my legs up in the air before I could even say *play ball*. That's when he spotted the jar of Vaseline sitting next to the baseball bat…"

We all screamed at one time, "Oh my God, you didn't!"

"Didn't what?" Sparkle asked, surprised at our outburst, and then, "Oh… OH!… like, gross… what kind of freak to do think I am? Have you *seen* the end of a baseball bat? Get real, people."

"Well what then?" Jim asked, with all of us nodding, waiting for the answer.

"As I was saying, and you people are sick by the way, he spotted the jar of Vaseline sitting next to the baseball bat, which was leaning on a big, black dildo…"

"Whoa, wait a minute," Millie shouted, standing up, "what in the world was a big, black dildo doing in the locker room?" (Good point, I thought.)

"Um, oh, well, you see… okay he fucked me with the baseball bat. There, are you happy now? Batboy Benny fucked me with a baseball bat!" (It figured.)

"William Astan," Jim procalimed, shaking his head back and forth, "you never cease to amaze me. So who's next?" he asked, but looked like he knew that the game was over and that there was no way anyone was going to top that one, short of a Buick up someone's behind.

"Wait," Sparkle interrupted, "the story isn't over yet."

"What, was there a second baseball bat lying around?" Tim joked. (We hoped.)

"No, smart-ass, there wasn't a second baseball bat lying around. One was plenty." Sparkle smirked, and I could tell that he thoroughly enjoyed shocking the hell out of us. I, for one, am still shocked to this day, but, c'est la vie. "See, unfortunately for Benny, though it's true there was no one in the park that night, there were surveillance cameras situated throughout the locker room. The evening's events were taped for posterity's sake and poor, ignorant Benny was quietly relieved of his duties as batboy."

"God, he must hate you," I surmised.

"Actually, the last thing he said to me was, 'If I ever catch you alone, I'm going to take that baseball bat and smash you over the head with it until you're a bleeding pile of flesh. Even your own mother won't be able to recognize you.' I may be paraphrasing, but you get the idea. *Now* who's next?"

"How about Bruce," Slim shouted, quickly cooling any feelings I may have had for him up to that point.

"Um, well," Sparkle knowingly interjected, "how about Jim?"

"No, how about Bruce?" Slim was adamant.

"It's okay; I'll tell them," I said, dreading my straightforwardness. Damn Bloody Marys; I should've just made something up, but... "Well, you see, I've never been with, um, anyone before, and have only used the port-side for withdrawals, not deposits. Not yet. Sorry, so who's next?" I hoped that would be it and that Jim or Millie would go next, but, of course, that was too juicy a tidbit to let slip by.

"Wait a minute. Let me get this straight, if you'll pardon the expression. You've never made it with a guy? Never?" Slim looked shocked. Actually, everyone looked kind of blown away, except, of course, for Sparkle. He was taking long swigs from his drink and was looking around the room, anywhere but at me.

"No. Not yet, but I hope to soon, and, besides, twenty-one is not too old to be a virgin, right?" I was hoping for a *right,* but I was not to get one. No one answered, in fact. They all just stared at me in disbelief. Like I'd farted at a funeral or something. It was that awful, really.

Then Sparkle jumped in for the rescue. He looked at me and said, "Hey, don't we have somewhere to be at three o'clock?"

"Oh my goodness, is it almost three already? Yes, we do have to get going." Saved by the bell.

That woke everyone out of their shock, and they all agreed that it was getting late and that they had other places to be as well. So we paid the bill and said our goodbyes. All the while, Slim was giving me the strangest looks. I don't know if he was repulsed or mystified by my admission, but he did give me a nice kiss as we walked out the door. All in all, it was a perfect way to end brunch.

***

"Thanks, Sparkle," I told him as we made our way down the block

"You're welcome, Secret. No sweat."

"Sparkle…?"

He sighed. "Yes, Secret, I really did get fucked by that baseball bat."

"I thought as much."

We started walking toward The Castro. I had no idea why, but it looked like Sparkle was headed to somewhere in particular. "Where are we walking to?" I asked.

"Secret, Honey, who do you work for?" Not exactly an answer, but I knew where he was going with it.

"Why, you, Sparkle, of course."

Here it came. "Then please just enjoy the walk and no more questions."

"Another surprise?" I asked, timidly.

"That would be a question, Secret, but yes." (Uh-oh.)

When we arrived at where we were going, Secret said, "Ta-dah!" I looked around, but all I saw was the Subway sandwich shop. Seeing my perplexity, Sparkle turned me around until I was facing the door right in front of me. The sign above read: The Gauntlet.

"What's The Gauntlet, Sparkle? Or do I want to know?" I knew I didn't, but what the hell; sometimes I just like hearing myself talk. In any case, Sparkle was pushing me up the steps and into the shop.

At first I thought we were in your plain old run of the mill jewelry shop. There were a few cases in the shop that contained what looked like earrings and studs and the like, but on closer examination, the jewelry looked less like it was for your ears and more like it was for certain other body parts. I gave a long, hard gulp before I turned to look at my employer. He had his face right up to the glass of one of the cases and was looking intently at the merchandise.

"Um, Sparkle, what *exactly* are you planning on doing here?" All the while I was praying that it was just window shopping, but I knew deep down that Sparkle had other plans for us. After all, he never stopped at just the window.

"Now, Secret, Darling, I've been giving this some serious thought for a week now, and that conversation we had over brunch just, you know, made me realize that I really want a nipple ring. And don't worry, you don't have to get one if you don't want one." I listened as he said it, but for some reason I had a giant pit in my stomach. All the while I could hear music in the background like the kind you hear in a movie just before someone gets killed. Namely the cute, little virgin boy.

"Good, because I'm not getting one. Period," I insisted, my hand slapping down on the glass countertop.

"Fine. I am. Now help me pick out a ring."

Not having a clue as to what a good nipple ring should look like (I had never even seen one before that moment), I just picked out the most colorful one that was in the case. It was a green hoop, but, instead of going full circle, it had yellow metal balls on each end. I thought it was cute and said so. Sparkle had other thoughts on the matter. Cute, after all, was not what he was going for. Eventually, he ended up picking out a sterling metal bar with silver balls on each end. The clerk showed us some pictures of what it would look like once it was in, and, Lord only knows why, I actually thought it looked kind of hot; it was almost appealing looking in a sick and twisted sort of way. Still, it was pretty gross once you realized that there was going to be a hole in your nipple.

"C'mon, Secret, come back with me while they do it," he said, dragging me back to a curtained cubicle. It was clean and sterile enough, sort of like a miniature dentist's office without the spit-sink. Still, I could think of a half dozen other places I'd rather have been: prison, Iraq, Cleveland, etc.

Pretty soon, a short, extremely tattooed, shaved-headed, multi-ear-pierced man walked in and introduced himself as *Tree*. Tree was very matter of fact about what he was going to do and how he was going to do it. He said that the actual piercing was over in a split second and that the pain was very bearable and, to some, even

65

enjoyable. This I personally found very hard to swallow, but, looking at Tree, I sensed he fell into the latter category, the one's that found it enjoyable. He also said that in many cases the nipple ring added to the sensitivity of the nipple with the overall effect of a more pleasurable experience when someone played with it. Not worth the effort, I thought, but Sparkle had a smile on his face as Tree explained this.

Okay then, if you're squeamish, you should probably skip this part and read ahead about a page.

(Hey up there, good for you! Anyway, it's not *your* nipple getting pierced, right?)

First, Tree had Sparkle take off his shirt and lie down. Then he put surgical gloves on and proceeded to wipe the nipple with some disinfectant before he marked each side of it with a pen. The whole time he was doing this, I was getting more and more nervous. Sparkle, as per usual, was cool as a cucumber. He didn't even look down to see what was going on. Though, of course, I, *gulp*, had ringside seats.

Tree then took the metal nipple bar, which he had been sterilizing in an oven up until that point, and placed it next to a metal stick sitting on a table by the short bed that my friend was lying on. It appeared really sharp at the end and it turned my stomach just to look at it. (Last chance to skip ahead up there.) Then he told Sparkle to breathe normally, which he did. (I, needless to say, was fairly close to hyperventilating.) He then grabbed the nipple and lifted it up a bit. Sparkle grinned at that, sick fuck that he is, and, before I knew it, Tree had *shoved* the metal stick right through the nipple and out the other end. *OW! OW! OW!* I was thinking as I sucked in my breath and shut my eyes really fast. When I opened them back up, the stick was just sitting there on Sparkles' chest, skewering his nipple. (If I was feeling any lingering effects of the Bloody Marys up until then, I wasn't any more.) Tree then took the nipple bar, which had one ball on one end and nothing on the other end, and threaded it on one end of the stick before yanking the stick all the way through the nipple, thereby pulling the bar through as well. He then put the remaining silver ball on the other end of the bar and, voila, it was all over. (Though clearly not forgotten. Ever. As much as I've tried.)

Sparkle, for his part, barely moved a muscle the whole time and never so much as let out a gasp or a shriek. I, however, was in shock. I couldn't even believe that I just witnessed someone get a stick rammed through their nipple.

Then Sparkle asked, "So, how's it look?" Honestly, I had to admit, it looked sexier than hell on him. It sort of detracted from his nelliness. Too bad you had to go through the actual piercing to get the end result.

"It looks great," I professed as Sparkle got up slowly and stood in front of the mirror to get a gander at it. I could tell immediately that he loved it, seeing as he simply glowed as he stood there, grinning from ear to ear. I, too, was staring at it and, once I got over the experience of witnessing the *operation*, I also had a smile on my face. It did look great, and I said so, yet again. Sparkle gave me a peck on the cheek and said the words I was dreading to hear, but was expecting just the same: "Great, now it's your turn."

"No fucking way am I going through that," I said, shaking my head back and forth.

"C'mon, you just said it looked great, and it only took a minute and it didn't hurt at all. And it'll be this great experience that we can share together. We'll be Nipple Sisters!" He was exceedingly convincing (or I'm an even bigger idiot than I thought).

I just stood there for a minute and stared at his face and then his nipple. Then back at his face and then back at his nipple. And then over at Tree, who was waiting to see if he could inflict his pain on yet another victim. (Tell me something, do you have to have a degree to perform this rite?) Then back at Sparkle again and then… and then… "Okay, fine; I'll do it," I said, feeling like I'd just lost complete control over my life. And, yes, if you're counting up there, for, like, the millionth time since I'd met him. Meaning, I was soon to have a hole in my nipple to match the one in my head.

"Yippy," Sparkle squealed (so much for looking butch). "He'll take the green one with the yellow balls." (Can you say *sucker*. He knew it all along.)

And before I could think of an excuse to get out of it, I, too, was lying on the short metal bed with my shirt off and two black dots painted on my poor, little nipple. Then one, two, three, I, too, had a sharp metal stick sitting comfortably on my chest and through my nipple. And, finally, I, too, had a shiny, metal nipple ring through my nipple.

"You lied, Sparkle," I said, teeth grinding together.

"Lied, Secret?" he asked and pointed innocently to his chest.

"That hurt like a big, old mother fucker."

"Oh, that. Yes, I guess you're right. But if I told you that beforehand, you wouldn't have gone through with it, now would you?" The asshole had me there. "Stand up and take a look," he commanded. I stood up very, very slowly, not wanting to move my chest even a millimeter. Then I was standing in front of the mirror and looking at the new addition to my body. Again, I hated to admit it, but it did look rather sexy just hanging there. Plus, with the metal pushing through it, my nipple was now twice as big as it was before. (Bonus!) "See, that wasn't so bad, Secret." I just stood there and stared blankly back at him. Actually, it was more traumatic than bad, but I was getting over it quickly and, pretty soon, the adrenaline rush was making me somewhat euphoric.

Tree then gave us a quick lesson in nipple care: how to clean it, what not to do with it, and what to expect in the healing process. I barely listened to him; I was too dazed from what I'd just done. Luckily, it was all written down and Sparkle was paying attention. And when it was finally time to leave, and we had to put our shirts back on, that's when I started to panic. I just knew that putting that shirt on over my nipple would be painful as hell. Thankfully, it wasn't, but the next few weeks should prove interesting, I thought. Then, just before we were about to leave, I looked at Sparkle and said, "Nipple Sisters, huh?" He smiled at me and took my hand, squeezed it once and led me out of the shop, newly sobered and newly pierced.

***

Sparkle and I started back to his house, but not before we headed into the Double Rainbow to get us some comfort food. Nothing like a good scoop of double chocolate anything to ease the pain, of which, strangely, there wasn't any. There was a dull throbbing coming from my chest, but it was all, thus far, very tolerable.

Walking through The Castro, ice cream in hand, I felt like the world should've been oohing and aahing at our accomplishment. It was like we had undergone some magic ritual and no one was there to bear witness. At first, I was a little disappointed at the lack of adulation from the masses, but then I realized that I hadn't been alone back at The Gauntlet. In fact, Sparkle and I had shared something special. And then, all of a sudden, I felt really glad for what I'd just done. As stupid as it was, it was also a very adult decision and something my mother would have a cow about if she ever got a gander at it. And that, of course, made me doubly happy. Double Rainbow happy, in fact.

"To the Nipple Sisters!" I proclaimed and lifted my ice cream cone up to the clear, blue sky.

"To the Nipple Sisters: Secret and Sparkle!" My friend followed suit and raised his cone as we headed up Castro Street looking for a cab to take us home.

It didn't take long to catch one, either. Cabbies know that we gays are good tippers, and they flock to The Castro. Disposable income is certainly one of the perks of being queer, you see. At least for Sparkle it was, not for me (not yet). And before we knew it, we were back at his less than humble abode and firmly ensconced on his sofa.

Being newly pierced had taken a lot out of us. (Well, the petering out of the adrenaline and the wearing off of the booze was more likely the culprit, but still.) So we just sat there, didn't say anything, and grinned for a solid ten minutes. That's when Sparkle noticed the flashing red light on his answering machine, letting him know that he had a message.

He popped up, hit the play button, and plopped back down on the couch. And wouldn't you know it, it was my new friend Slim. And guess who he was calling for? "Hi, William. (Sparkle's new moniker hadn't yet reached the masses). This is Slim. Thanks for the lovely afternoon. Oh… and, um… by the way, if you happen to know how I can get in touch with your friend, Bruce, I'd love to give him a call sometime. Major yummage there. Anyway, give me a call. Ciao." And then click and silence.

Looking over at Sparkle, my face must have said it all.

"Go give him a call, Secret," he said, motioning over to the phone.

"You think I should?" (Duh.)

"Of course you should. There's nothing like an easy fuck. And we wouldn't want to break Gay Rule #5, now would we?"

"And that would be…?" (Get a pen, here comes another one.)

"Never look a gift ho in the mouth… or maybe that's never come in is eye. In any event, you shouldn't pass on a sure thing" (Good point(s).)

"He is awfully cute. But, just out of curiosity, what exactly does he do for a living?" I asked, knowing that I would call, but still wanting to know what I was getting myself into.

"He owns a bookstore, Classics, it's called. They specialize in hard to find books and rare additions. They also host book readings. Apparently, he does very well for himself, according to Tim. (Finally, potential!) I was at the phone quicker than Tammy Faye Baker could say, "Pass me the eye shadow."

"Hello, Slim? This is Bruce. William relayed your message," I said into the receiver. My heart was racing and I had trouble breathing, so, luckily, the conversation ended up being on the short side.

"Well?" Sparkle asked, after I'd hung up.

"I'm meeting him at eight at that little oyster bar in The Castro," I answered, a little panicky and excited at the same time. My first gay date (and he wore nail polish and a midriff shirt). Oy. If my mother could only see me now. (Then again, maybe not.)

"Well, it's five now. Why not take a nap here, borrow some clothes, and leave from my place. It's a lot closer than from yours, and, besides, you look way better in my stuff." He had a point. Of course, considering what he spent, his clothes *should* look damn well better. The cost of one of his outfits equaled about half of my wardrobe, and all he ever wore were jeans and t-shirts.

Sadly, however, I couldn't sleep because of the dull ache in my nipple, so Sparkle and I just sat on the couch and watched some television. When seven o'clock rolled around, I asked him if I could take a shower. He said sure, and, just as I was about to get in, I remembered the nipple ring. Naturally, I couldn't recall Tree's directions for cleaning it. Plus, I really didn't want to touch it. I mean, sure, it looked cool and all, but the thought of putting my fingers anywhere near it kind of freaked me the fuck out. Would it hurt like hell moving the ring around to clean it? Would it be gross to move a piece of metal through a part of my body that, just that very morning, was in one piece?

Sparkle showed me the instructions for cleaning it, but I really didn't want to do it. Truthfully, I was more scared about cleaning it than getting the damn thing in the first place. I guess I didn't want to relive that brief yet intense pain again. And that's when Sparkle had an idea.

"Okay, I'm sensing some apprehension here. Why don't I get in with you and you can clean mine first and then I'll clean yours?" As illogical as that sounded, I did feel a sense of relief. It was easier to let someone else inflict pain on me than it was to inflict pain on myself. (Why? I have no fucking idea. Just go with me on that one.) Anyway, by that point, I was getting used to being naked around him, and the thought of showering with him didn't phase me as much as it may have a week earlier.

"Nipple Sisters!" Sparkle shouted, edging me closer to being naked and in the shower.

"Nipple Sisters," I mumbled, fearing the pounding of the water on my newly adorned protuberance.

I entered the shower with my back to the water and my arms crossed safely over my chest. Sparkle gingerly entered and stood behind me. Despite his bravado, I could tell that he was feeling just as nervous at the prospect of cleaning a hole in his nipple. Then, millimeter by millimeter, I slowly worked my head under the water and let it run over my body, while Sparkle watched apprehensively, knowing that his turn was next.

"Nothing out of the ordinary," I said, with a heavy sigh, proudly emerging from under the stream and nodding to him. Still, he looked at me warily as we scooted around each other in order to change places. Then he wet his body just as I had, again with no direct splashing on his chest. Funny how I should've been excited at the prospect of showering with a naked (and very hot) man, but I was more concerned with getting the ring and my nipple cleaned than copping a feel. In any case, both of us shampooed, soaped up, and rinsed off, careful not touch either our own or each other's chests. And then, *groan*, it was time.

Sparkle reached outside of the shower and came back in with the bottle of Hibiclens: the antibacterial cleanser that Tree had given us. I think it's what doctor's use to scrub up with. In any case, the directions said to put a small bit in your hand and then dilute it to fifty-fifty with the shower water. He handed me the blue bottle, and I did as the directions said to do. Then I looked at him and asked if he was ready. He nodded, bracing himself up against the shower wall. Personally, I think I was more nervous about touching the thing than he was about me cleaning his nipple, but I carried on with my duties, nonetheless.

I gently cupped my hand over his chest and let the bubbly, blue Hibiclens flow over the prescribed area. Sparkle nodded to indicate that I should continue, so I took my index finger and rubbed the cleanser around his nipple and over the ends of the metal. Then, using the Hibiclens like a lubricant, I grabbed one end of the bar and, with the tiniest tug, I slid the metal in and out. At first, it gave some resistance. (Tree told us that it would do that for a while; it was just the scab forming.) Sparkle said that it felt funny, but that it really didn't hurt. That is until I torqued it a tad. Then he let out a wincing yelp and quickly shoved my hand away.

"Okay, all done. Let's get out now," I said, making a move to turn off the water.

"Oh hell to the no. We still have one more nipple to go," he said, switching places with me. Heck, I was fine with the state it was already in. I mean, I had years to clean it. What was one more day?

Sparkle followed the same procedure I did and very gently began to clean the ring and the nipple. True, it didn't hurt so much as just plain felt weird, but I was anxious to get it over with and told him to hurry, which he did, because I don't think he was enjoying cleaning my nipple any more than I was enjoying having it cleaned. Then, missions accomplished, we got out of the shower and slowly and carefully toweled off.

Luckily, the production of nipple ring cleaning took my mind completely off the reason we were cleaning it in the first place, namely my date with Slim. Really, I barely had time to think about that before I was quickly dressed and out the door. Needless to say, I wore a loose, untucked t-shirt. Sparkle called a cab for me, and within minutes I was at the restaurant and facing my super-sexy date.

"So, do anything exciting after brunch today?" Slim asked, not knowing how truly exciting my afternoon had been.

"Um, I'll tell you later. Let's order first; I'm starving." I tried to steer the conversation away from my nipple, because I had no idea how he would take the news and I wanted to get him alone and at home before bringing it up. I figured he was less likely to run away screaming if I had him behind a bedroom door. (I sure as hell hoped so, anyway.)

We ordered a dozen oysters on the half shell to start with and clams marinara to split for dinner. Kind of ironic that we were ordering a known aphrodisiac. I mean, I, for one, needed no help maintaining an erection. Honestly, if I'd stood up at that very moment, my napkin would've remained hovering over my lap. Naturally, before the waiter could place our order, I ordered us a bottle of white wine. Between my nipple and my date, I had no idea what I was more nervous about, so I figured the wine would help to settle my nerves.

"So, Slim," I said, starting the conversation. "Sparkle tells me you own a bookstore."

"Who?" he asked.

"Oh yeah, I forgot." And so I explained the whole Secret/Sparkle thing. No surprise that he liked our ingenuity. After all, not many people are born already called *Slim*, but in his case, it was befitting. (And yummily so.)

"The whole bookstore thing started right out of college," he began. "I'd just graduated with a degree in English Literature and had no idea what to do with it (shhh... I know, ironic), and so I went to work at Classics. The owner at the time, Mister Graybare, who we all called *Gay Bear*, was really cool, a total gay, hippie throw-back with long, gray hair and tie-dyed clothes. The store had a stream of steady regulars and he had to do very little in order to turn a profit. Luckily for me, his only employee had just quit after working there for seven years and he hired me on the spot."

He shot me a wicked grin, the tenting in my jeans suddenly going full tilt, and then he continued. "It didn't take me very long to get in the swing of things at Classics. I opened the store up in the mornings at ten and closed up at seven. In between, I straightened up, rang up the orders, made recommendations, and placed special orders. See, it's the special orders that really set Classics apart from the rest. Gay Bear had developed quite an incredible network of rare book collectors through the years and could find just about any title and any edition a customer could ask for. But the best part about the job was that I could read throughout the day. It was, as the saying goes, like having my cake and eating it too."

By the way, somewhere in the middle of this story, Slim reached over to hold my hand and was playing footsies with me under the table. So, between the pounding coming from my nipple and the pounding of my crotch against my jeans, it was a wonder I could pay the least bit of attention to what he was saying. But I did, which was lucky for me. (Just you wait and see.)

The story moved along. "Anyway, things were going just great until I started to get a little bored. I suppose it was the routineness of the work or something, and so one day I asked Gay Bear if he would show me how to do the accounting books. He was delighted that I took the interest in his work and gladly took me on as his apprentice."

Slim stopped his tale there and just stared at me as I drank my wine. I, of course, stared back, waiting for him to continue. He didn't. "Yes?" I asked, setting my drink down. "Is there something on my face? What? Why'd you stop?"

"Nope. You just looked so cute sitting there. (Sweet-talking will get you everywhere... ooh, ooh... hey, Gay Rule #6! Gay Rule #6!) Needless to say, I melted at that one. And then he leaned in (as did I) and he gave me the softest, sweetest kiss. I know I use the word *yummy* a lot, but yummy it was. Also, he looked me in the eyes the whole time he was doing it, never closing them even for a second. That is, like, the sexiest thing ever. Then he slowly eased away and finished with the story.

"Um, yeah, where was I?" He scratched his head and squinted his eyes. "Oh, yeah. Right. So, never having any finance or accounting classes in college, much of what he was teaching me was falling on deaf ears. So at night I took classes in bookkeeping and small business management. It was great, really, and within six months I was doing all the finances and running the shop. Pretty soon, Gay Bear was leaving the store for hours and then days at a time. He trusted me completely and I had no problem wearing all the hats. Actually, I preferred it, because it gave me little time to get bored. Then one day, Gay Bear came in and said that he had bought a little cabin in the woods and was retiring. But before I could panic, he told me that he was going to sell me the store and that I could pay him in monthly installments for it. That was six years ago; I made the last installment two years ago. After he left, I jumped on the coffeehouse bandwagon and put a little café in the front of the store. Business doubled and, voila, here I am: gay businessman extraordinaire." He smiled and tossed his hands up in the air.

"Wow," I said, totally impressed, "that's really a great story. Bravo for you." He got flustered and gave me the cutest *aw, shucks* look. (I'm sorry. One more time. Yummy.)

"So, Secret, if you don't mind me calling you that (I didn't), what's your story?"

"Well, I just graduated from college with a degree in English Literature and I have no idea what I can do with it," I said, crossing my heart (and avoiding my nipple). "Honest injun."

"Get out!" he shouted and slapped my hand.

"Already am!" I shouted back and slapped his hand in return.

"Well, and you can turn me down and it won't upset me, but I'm about to open up a Classics II and I could use some help. Interested?" (Seriously, what do you think?)

"Yes, very. When can I start?" I know I sounded a tad too anxious, but, please, this sounded so perfect, so ideal.

74

"How about Monday?"

"You mean tomorrow Monday?" I asked, unsure how Sparkle would take the news about losing his attaché.

"Yes, is that a problem?"

"Oh, no, no problem at all. I'll be there at ten o'clock when you open the door." My heart was racing. I mean, I was beyond excited at the prospect of working in a bookstore. And for Slim, no less!

"Great. This will work out for the both of us. I was dreading having to interview for the position, and you foot the bill perfectly," he said and gave my hand a squeeze.

After that, dinner went by fast. In between slamming down the oysters and slamming down the wine, we made polite conversation. But mostly, we just rubbed each other under the table with our legs and smiled back and forth a lot. Then the plates were filled with empty shells and the bottle was empty and it was time to pay the check. Uh-oh, now what? I mean, do I invite him over and then go to work for him the next day? Damn, what to do, what to do?

Slim picked up the bill and told me he'd work it out of me tomorrow. Fine by me, I thought. And then he asked if I needed a ride home. Also fine by me. In other words, I was just gonna let this one play itself out, because thinking about it too much wasn't going to help anything. (By the way, drinking and driving is wrong. Really. But cut me some slack, okay. There were extenuating circumstances here. Remember: twenty-one-year-old *virgin*. So no lectures up there.)

When we got to my building, he asked if he could come up to see my apartment. "You're the boss," I said, with a leer. He liked the way that sounded and readily agreed. Twenty minutes later, he found parking and we were in my eensy-bitty-teeny-weeny loft.

"Cozy," he said.

"That's one word for it," I said, nodding my head. (*Hovel* was more like it.)

I gave him the tour, which took about ten seconds, and we quickly got into swapping some serious spit. Then he started to pull my shirt my head. *Ouch*, for one, as he also managed to snag the ring, and, *no way*, for two, as I had no intention of letting him witness my latest addition without some warning first. In other words, I grabbed his hand away from my shirt and led him over to the bed where I laid on top of him and continued with the bumping and grinding of crotches, *without* any contact to my chest. That made him happy for, well, a minute or two and then he went right on back to my shirt.

75

"Um… wait a sec. Let me get the lights." Maybe if he couldn't see it he would never know it was there.

"No, don't," he replied and pulled me back down. "I want to see you." (Damn romantic.)

"That's sweet Slim, but the glare from the light is just murder on my contact lenses, and I'd rather not pop them out just yet." I was grasping at straws, never having worn contacts a day in my life, but things were moving too fast to come up with anything better (or, God forbid, to tell the truth).

It worked, though. *Phew.* "Okay, Secret, douse the lights." I did and then took my shirt and pants off before climbing back into my bed. Hearing this, Slim did the same. *Mega-gulp.* Now I had to have sex and keep him away from my nipple. Not an easy situation to be in. I mean, the sex part alone was terrifying enough, right?

We went back to kissing and, man, was it ever nice. He was so soft and tender and slow about it all. Plus, my luck was holding out, as he concentrated on my other nipple and completely avoided the mutilated one. Then he reached down between my legs and stroked my crotch outside of the underwear. My moaning must have said it all, because he sprang up and slid my briefs off. Still holding them in his hand, he lay back on top of me and went back to his glorious kissing. When he was done with my lips, he made his way down my neck and sucked and licked me until I was covered in goosebumps. His deft tongue then made a beeline for my exposed nipple (the whole one, as he was covering my other one with my underwear and his hand) and he tickled and plucked at it until I thought I'd explode. Then he moved down to suck my harder-than-granite prick. This move, sadly, was made in conjunction with his raising his other hand away from my chest, thereby lifting my underwear away as well. Unfortunately, my underwear had somehow gotten snagged on my nipple ring. And, as you can imagine, the loudest bellow of pain and terror you've ever heard immediately sprang forth from my mouth. Honestly, the walls rattled. Heck, even the neighbors' walls rattled.

"Oh my God. What? What's wrong?!" he shouted, terrified that he was killing me or something. Or maybe I'd just had a bad bout of Tourette's.

I quickly shot out of bed, raced to the bathroom mirror, and flicked on the light to make sure that my poor nipple was still in one piece. Thankfully, it was. Not even a scratch. I breathed a heavy sigh of relief, but now I had to explain what had happened. Poor Slim, who was hovering nearby trying to see what I was staring at, looked white as a sheet in his reflection in the mirror. That's when I crossed my arms (gently) and turned to face him.

"Um, I'm, like, so sorry. I'm fine, really. It was just... um... you just, well, sort of, accidentally yanked on *this*," I explained, poorly, exposing my chest for him to see. This caused a quick gasp from him. Then he looked up at me, back at my nipple, and then started laughing uncontrollably. Of course, I began laughing right along with him, without having the slightest idea why.

When my giggles subsided, I asked him, "And this is funny why?"

And he answered, "Because I can't believe you went to so much trouble to hide that from me." And then he started laughing all over again.

"Well, you made it sound so gross over brunch today." I offered up the excuse that made the most sense.

"True, it is sort of gross, but not gross enough to not have sex with you," he countered.

"Oh... oops." I guess that honesty is the best policy, sometimes. (No, that's not even almost a Gay Rule, so don't go writing it down. Mostly, it just gets you into a lot of trouble.)

"Come here," he said and reached out for me. Then he hugged me nice and soft so as not to do any more damage to myself *or* his hearing.

We ended up making love the entire night. In truth, once the terror subsided, it was incredible. Was it worth waiting that long for it? Probably. I don't think I was really ready for it before then. Not mentally, anyway. I guess everybody's different when it comes to making contact for the first time. Some people are prepared for it as soon as they reach puberty, and for some, like myself, it just takes a bit longer. I certainly enjoyed the hell out of it, though, let me tell you. And, once I started, man oh man, watch out, because there was no stopping me then.

As for Slim, we both agreed that it wouldn't be in our best interests to continue with a relationship, seeing as he was about to be my boss in just a few short hours. (Of course, that didn't stop us from fooling around every now and then after we closed up shop.)

Thankfully, I still have fond memories of that night. Slim was a great teacher to me, both at work and in the sack. Probably the most important thing I learned was how joyous it can be to be held softly as you're drifting off to sleep. That's what he did for me as I lay there, barely able to move after so much exertion. He just held me close and nuzzled my neck with his cheek. But just before I totally drifted off, he shook me a little and whispered in my ear, "Don't you want to take your contacts out before you go to sleep?"

I grinned and answered, "They'll be okay, thanks. And good night, Slim." (Yummy.)

CHAPTER FOUR
MARY, MARY QUITE CONTRARY

Well then, I suppose by now you're wondering how our old comatose friend is doing. As for that, honestly, I really don't know. It's been, like, four hours since I got to the hospital, with Sparkle just lying there in his white gown, basically not moving a muscle. (If he knew he was wearing white before Labor Day, he'd be mortified.) The doctor told me that we would just have to wait and see. The bullet, apparently, went through his chest and out the back, just barely missing his lungs and heart. But he did lose a lot of blood before the paramedics could get to him. (The five-story walk up is great if you want a nice view, but it's a bitch if you've been shot.)

The scary part was just a little while ago, when the police came and started to ask me questions. The doozie, as you can well imagine by now, was, "Did he have any enemies, anyone that would've wanted to kill him?" Surely, an honest answer would've taken hours, and they would've ended up questioning half the population of San Francisco. And, really, I didn't want to put all those people through that. (Plus, it would've given way too many people the satisfaction of knowing that someone finally did try to kill Sparkle.) So I fibbed a bit and said that no one wanted to shoot him any more than your average person (if your average person was Hitler, Mussolini, or Jesse Helms). I'm sure they'd find out for themselves in the short run, anyhow.

After all, if you were paying attention up there, there were several death threats already. Batboy Benny ring a bell? Or Lance, his brother? Or that angry Jeff dude, both from the party and the beach? I mean, come on, how was I going to answer the police when these were just the tip of the iceberg?

Then, just when I thought they were about to leave, they asked me yet another tough one: did I know that Sparkle had been arrested several years earlier for assault with a deadly weapon and that the person he'd assaulted had threatened to kill him? They also wanted to know if I knew where I could find that person.

Oh yeah, I knew all right. (And you better sit down for this.)

"Yes sir, sir, I know who threatened Mister Astan," I stammered.

"And do you know where we can find this person," the cop asked me, poised to write down my answer.

"You're looking at him, officer." (Told you to sit down. Betcha weren't expecting that one, huh?)

"And, Mister Miller, where exactly where you last night?" the cop asked, menacingly.

"Oh… er… um, well you see… oh, come on now, you don't really think it was me? I'm his best friend. Why would I want to shoot him? And if I did, would I be here right now, worried sick about him?"

"Sir, he was arrested for attacking you, and you were heard threatening his life at the time of the arrest. It was documented and a half dozen people were witness to it." (You know, if policemen didn't look so macho in their tight, little polyester uniforms, I would find it really difficult to like them.)

"Well, yes, if you want to be technical about it, he did attack me and I did threaten him, but there were extenuating circumstances. Besides, that was years ago. I would never hurt him, let alone try to kill him. Never." I was shaking a little by then. I was telling the truth, though. I mean, I love Sparkle with all my heart and, even though I could see why someone would have shot him, it wasn't me. Honest!

"Sir, if you say you didn't shoot Mister Astan, then where were you at approximately eleven last night?" the cop persisted.

"Oh, yes, that. Well, I was out at the time, and several people can vouch for me," I replied, knowing that this wasn't what they were after.

"And where was *out* exactly?" he asked.

A hot flush of red rose up the side of my neck. "Blow Buddies," I whispered.

"Excuse me? Where?" he asked again, cupping his ear.

"Blow Buddies. From ten until around midnight last night I was at Blow Buddies, and there are at least a dozen people who saw me there (or at least saw parts of me)."

"I see," said the officer, also now a little red in the face. "I'll check into that, but until then, please don't leave the city without notifying the police."

"No, sir, officer; I won't," I promised, crossing my heart. (It's hard to turn off the nelly sometimes.)

And then the police left and I was alone again with my thoughts. It's funny, I hadn't thought about that afternoon for a long time. Who knew it would come back to bite me in the ass? I suppose you're just waiting for me to tell you all about it, huh? Well, it is sort of a funny story in retrospect, but at the time it was all pretty miserable.

***

The whole mess had started three weeks prior to the actual confrontation. I was, by then, running Classics II for Slim. Business in both stores had been great, and once I got the hang of the bookkeeping, Slim pretty much left me on my own. On occasion, we'd meet to discuss how things were going in both locations (and every now and again we would slip into the back room and *play*), but, for the most part, I was pretty autonomous and happy as a clam. As a matter of fact, I was a might too busy at times and had decided to hire a full-time assistant. During those first two years, Slim and I had shared a girl named Sharon who would go between the two stores and help out wherever needed, but even that wasn't enough on some days.

So it was decided that Sharon would work full-time for Slim and I would get my very own *Boy Friday*. And, since Slim let me do the hiring, I made sure that my assistant would be gay by placing help-wanted ads only in the gay rags. I know that seems extremely heterophobic, but if I was going to spend eight hours a day with someone, they sure as hell better be gay. I mean, it wasn't that I thought I couldn't get along with a straight person as much as I didn't think a straight person could get along with me. Mostly, though, since Sparkle spent quite a lot of time at the store, I also made sure that there wouldn't be any *run-ins*. (Oh boy, was I wrong on that one.)

In a week, I interviewed about a couple of dozen men and a few women for the position. None of them were even almost as qualified, though, as my last interviewee, Mack. Just like I'd been, he was fresh out of college with a degree in English Literature, but he knew what he wanted to do with his studies. See, at night, he was taking courses towards his Masters Degree and was hoping to find a day job where he could study a bit and also have some flexible time off to take exams. If that wasn't enough, his ultimate dream was to teach Queer Studies in college. Now *that* I was totally floored by. I mean, I had no idea that such a career even existed (and back then, it just barely did). Needless to say, I hired him on the spot.

And let me just add this as a side note: Mack was P-I-P-I-N-G hot. Like, Sssssizzlin', friend. Blond hair, blue eyes, and an almost white goatee on top of a lean, tight, gym-toned body. And I mean this with all sincerity; I hired him for his ideals and his dreams. A man like Mack, I figured, could change the future for the next generation of gay men and women. I say this because it does have some significance to this recounting.

Immediately, I was thrilled with my decision to hire him, too. Not only was he bright, but he also had a gift for schmooze. Heck, he talked up almost every customer that came in; and when you're as good looking as Mack is, people just like talking to you. (Sad but true.) The first week he was at Classics II, I watched him from the sidelines and I was amazed. A customer would come up to the register and, within seconds, Mack was in full conversation with them. And not just about books, but about the entire range of small talk: the weather, news, TV, science, children, and on and on. It was incredible to watch. And what was even more spectacular than his ability to make seemingly uninteresting and bookish people open up was the way he got them to buy even more books than they'd come in for. *Cha-ching!*

A person would come in to buy children's classics and they'd leave with child psychology books or computer books. I was glad that Slim had decided to include current books in Classics II, because Mack was selling the shit of everything. That first week alone, business was up fifteen percent. And when Mack needed to study, I was only too glad to let him sit in the back and pour over his work. It was wonderful to see such a dedicated young man. Every so often, I'd take a break and go back and sit with him, and he would tell me what he was studying. If I hadn't loved my job so much, I'd have been jealous of him. I mean, I'd been so ready to graduate from college that I never really considered signing on for another three or four more years of it.

Now, what really got Mack psyched was when the topic of gay literature came up. And, naturally, he wanted to know why we didn't carry any gay classics. Funny that two stores that were run by gay guys didn't carry any gay books. But, since Slim's expertise by that time was in classic editions and rare books, that's pretty much what both stores sold, stuff dating much farther back than most of the gay books did. When he opened up the second store, he had a larger space to work with, so he decided to put in some additional sections of books, ones that would appeal to a more brainier and refined clientele. He never even thought of a gay section. Mack, however, had other ideas and was eager to share them with me.

I guess with my upbringing and background, I never really had access to gay literature. Actually, until I moved to San Francisco, I didn't even know that there was such a thing. (The only gay reading I did was in between the covers of the Playgirl's I stole, and I doubt the male models' stats could be considered *literature*.) Still, I never so much as went into a gay bookstore since I moved here. I mean, I worked in a bookstore all day; why would I go into another one in my free time? (I wonder if straight gynecologists avoid pussy at home. But, don't you worry, I don't think about that conundrum all that often. Too much of a visual. *Yuck*.)

In any case, in between reading his books and selling the store's books, Mack would tell me about the authors that had paved the way for the gay writers of the nineties: Randy Shilts, Gertrude Stein, Edmund White, Andrew Holleran, Robert Ferro, James Baldwin, Oscar Wilde, Rita Mae Brown, and Paul Monette, just to name a few. These were openly gay people who made money (albeit limited amounts) writing queer books. And listening to Mack, I could see why the customers were so taken with him. He had such a charm about him, speaking with such authority and zeal about whatever topic he was engaged in, that you gladly got sucked into the conversation. By the end of that first week, he'd convinced us to start carrying gay classics in Classics II, with him in charge of stocking the books. In truth, I can't even begin to tell you how exciting the prospect was for me.

Now, coinciding with Mack's first week at the store was Sparkle's vacation to Cancun. He desperately wanted me to go with him, but I could never take that much time away from work. I also didn't like for him to spend large amounts of money on me, which he would've needed to do if I went along. Dinner and drinks here and there were okay, but plane tickets and hotel accommodations were another matter entirely. Sparkle had enough control over my life already without being my sugar daddy, after all. So I politely declined and Sparkle went solo.

Needless to say, that week with Mack had been a busy one, what with training him and keeping up with my work at the same time, and I was glad for the hiatus with my best friend. (Also, I think you can guess by now, too much of Sparkle was not necessarily a good thing.) And, Sparkle being, well, Sparkle, he didn't so much as call me during his entire vacation. (Perhaps vacation isn't the right word here, since it implies taking a break from work. Sparkle was, for all intents and purposes, merely plying his trade along different routes.) Still, by the end of that busy week, I was glad for his return to my life.

That happened, grandly, at the beginning of Mack's second week at work. I'd been covering the register for him while he studied in my office, when Sparkle, festooned with gift bags, pranced into the store wearing loose, white gabardine slacks and a cream-colored, silk chemise tied into a knot below his chest. He was so dark from the sun that when he walked into the shop I could've sworn it was that actor from the Sprite commercials. You know the one: the *un*-cola-nut guy with the rolling letters. The same guy who played the zombie in the James Bond movie. I have no idea what his name is, but I'm sure you'd recognize him. Anyway, that's who Sparkle reminded me of as he ceremoniously laid down my gifts on the countertop. Every person in the store turned to watch the event, which, of course, only fed fuel to the fire. I could've charged admission, in fact, for the show we were all about to behold.

First came the emotive hugs and kisses, followed by the opening up of one tacky gift after the next. Honestly, he must've wiped the airport out clean before he got on the plane back home, I was guessing. There was a veritable cornucopia of mini bottles, Cancun t-shirts, snow-globes, pens with scenic beaches on them, and little stuffed animals in native clothes. In other words, crap on top of crap.

"Aren't these for the man who already has everything?" I asked, without a trace of sarcasm.

"And you don't?" he answered, also with a straight (whatever) face.

"That would be *you*, Darling." I grimaced.

"Oh, yes, I suppose you're right. I guess that these would be for me then." And he took all the gifts and dumped them back into the bag they came in and then he set the bag on the floor and sat down on a stool and asked, "So, what's up?"

"Um, you're kidding, right?" I asked and gave him a *you've got to be kidding* look.

"Um, about what?" he answered and gave me a *I have no idea what your talking about* stare.

I sighed in return. "You've been gone a whole week and there's nothing in that bag for me? That is, nothing I would want to keep?"

"In the bag, no. Check your back pocket." Now he was smiling and motioning to my butt.

I reached into my jeans and pulled out a gorgeous silver I.D. bracelet with *Secret* etched across the flat metal in the center. Well, that explained all the carrying on. It's no wonder I didn't feel him tuck it into my pocket. I went to hug him for the beautiful gift, but he blocked my advance and said, "read the inscription."

I did. It read: *Nipple Sisters 4ever!* That's when he got an even bigger hugging and kissing reception than I did. Honestly, it was the best present I'd ever gotten, if not, well, the most twisted. Then he lifted his arm and jangled an identical bracelet in front of my eyes. His was etched with *Sparkle* across it and had the same inscription. Heck, you can say what you want about him, but, at times, he could be the sweetest man in the world. (True, those times were few and far between. And usually only reserved for when he was asleep. But still.)

"I love it!" I shouted and slapped his chest.

"I knew you would," he said, knowingly, and slapped my chest in return. We had that whole Jerry and Elaine thing down pat. (He was Elaine, naturally.)

"So, now that we have that all out of the way, really, what's up?" he asked again, and I got all excited.

"Miss Thing," I answered with glee, "guess who's got a brand spankin' new assistant?"

"Let me guess. That would be you, right?" he deadpanned.

"Yup." I beamed.

"And do you really get to spank him?"

"No, that was just a figure of speech."

"Pity." Then he put his elbow on his knee and rested his chin on his palm. Jet lag, apparently, was creeping up on him. Or a recently swallowed pill. Take your pick.

"No, not a pity. Wait until you meet him. He's fabulous and has one of the most amazing personalities you've ever met." I was hoping to rouse him with my excitement for Mack, but he just sat there, head in hand, and stared at me. "Okay, Miss World Weary Traveler, he's fabulous *and* dazzling to look at." Now *that* got his attention. He was up off the stool in the blink of an eye and asking me where my fabulous new assistant was hiding himself. "You're nothing if not predictable, Sparkle," I told him and led him to the back room to meet Mack.

When we got to my office, I opened the door, motioned to Mack, and said, "Sparkle, this is my new assistant, M..."

"Why, Miss Mary Mack, I do declare," Sparkle interrupted, all southernly-like. Really, I should've known that those two beautiful creatures knew each other already. There must be some club or something that they all belong to. (Meanwhile, the only things I belong to are Costco and Blue Cross. *So* not fair.)

"I take it you two know each other then?" (Duh.)

"Oh my, yes, indeed we do," Sparkle quipped. "We go way, way back. What's it been? Three, four months already? We met at Jason's birthday party, right?"

"Um, sure. Right." Then silence. I guess we'd interrupted Mack's studying, because he was strangely quiet and not his usual friendly self. I apologized for disturbing him, and then Sparkle and I made our way back to the café at the front of the store, so we could have a cup of coffee and chat about Cancun.

"Secret," Sparkle said and immediately grabbed my arm as we sat down with our coffees, "I can't believe that Miss Mary Mack is, like, working for you. Have you any idea how long I've been after that piece?"

"Um, four months?" I guessed.

"Try ten. We *met* four months ago, but I've been trying to finagle my way into his world way before then. Every time I saw him, I tried to catch his eye, but he was always into his books and never seemed to look around at anybody. I even thought he might be straight until I met him at Jason's party. Now I run into him all over the place. It's, like, fate that our paths keep crossing. Fate! And now, now, my dear Secret, here he is, right under our noses and ripe for the picking."

"Bad analogy, Sparkle."

"Granted, but you get my point. And you know what they say, Secret: William Astan always gets his man."

"Er, I thought that was the Mounties?"

"Where do you think they got it from?" I saw that one coming, but what the hell; knowing Sparkle, it could damn well be true.

"Okay, I get it. You like Mack. Now onto Cancun. How was it?" Truly, I wanted to know. I'd never been anywhere besides Kansas and San Francisco, and I lived vicariously through those that did get to travel. Sparkle was like my window unto the world. (Unfortunately, the glass was horribly stained pink and just a tad bit cracked.)

"Oh, Honey, it was so fucking hot and humid. I'll take those cold San Francisco summer days anytime. First, the plane landed in this rinky-dink little airport…"

"And you headed straight for the airport bar…" I interrupted.

"And I went straight for the bar," he continued. "Child, don't think you know little old Sparkle like the back of your hand, because you don't. (Uh huh, right.) Anyway, I just wanted to get into the spirit of Mexico (He pronounced it Me-hee-co.) So I finished my drink, got my Louis Vuitton's, and strolled outside. All I can say is, now I know what a roasted chicken must feel like, because as soon as I stepped outside, I was hit by this incredible blast of hot air. Right away, I understood where my first mistake had been."

Curiously, I asked, "And that was?"

"Never date your travel agent," he answered.

And I countered with, "No, never date your travel agent and then break up with him while he's booking you a vacation in the middle of August."

"Whatever, Secret. Don't be smug; it's unbecoming. Anyway, being the trooper that I am (he shot me a *don't you dare* leer before I could interject something else), I wiped the sweat from my brow and hailed myself a cab. Thank God for that drink I had is all I have to say about that one. It's like they have no lines on the roads down there. The cabs swerve this way, they swerve that way. Honestly, you take your life into your hands just by getting into the damn things. (Melodrama, thy name is Sparkle.) Anyway, I can say this about the cabs, though: they sure get you where you're going and fast. One minute I was at the airport and the next I'm at my hotel. And that was another experience altogether."

"Not exactly four stars?" I asked.

"Two, at best," he replied. "Apparently, there had been a hurricane the summer before and the area of the island that I was staying on was particularly badly hit. Half of the hotel was still under reconstruction. Guess which half I was staying in? I'm sure my ex-boyfriend/ex-travel agent had something to do with that as well. Fucker. Still, I told myself that I wasn't going to let it get to me. I

87

mean, really, how much time would I be spending in my room anyway, right?" He looked at me with a sad face.

"Let me guess," I guessed, "it rained a lot while you were down there?"

"Very perceptive of you, Watson. Yes, it rained five of the seven days. I don't think maid service had ever filled a mini bar that many times before. Instead of asking me if I wanted fresh towels each morning, I was offered an assortment of gin and vodka and scotch. God bless you, Margarita," he said and made the sign of the cross over his chest.

"Was that the name of your housekeeper?" (Ask a silly question…)

"No, Sweetie, I had a blender in my room." (…and get a bitter answer.)

"And the tan?" I dared to ask.

"Store-bought, I'm afraid. Looks real, doesn't it?" I nodded a yes, though he did look a bit on the orange side. Still, who was I to kick a man while he was down?

"And the men?" (I was hoping that I wasn't going to be three for three.)

"To my surprise, there were two gay bars in the town of Cancun, but none on the tourist island across the bridge. That should've been my first tip off. Apparently, the money that was being made on the island resort wasn't trickling down to the town where the natives lived." He sighed and shook his head from side to side. "Now, the first bar was a video disco, and the music was coming from videos that had been taped years earlier from *Superstation TBS's Friday Night Videos*. I never thought I would have to dance to Prince's *Purple Rain* ever again, Secret, but I was sadly mistaken." And now he bowed his head in defeat. (I guess I was three for three, after all. Some days you just can't win.)

"The next bar," he continued, "was mostly a neighborhood bar. Let me ask you, have you ever seen a very short and rather rotund Mexican man do an impersonation of Madonna singing *Like a Virgin?* (I nodded a no.) Well, let me tell you, if she were dead, she'd be turning over in her grave. God rest her soul." We both made the sign of the cross this time. (I'm not really religious or anything, but it was Madonna we were talking about.)

"So, no men, then?" I guessed.

"Well, I didn't say *that*, did I?"

I should've known better. "Then you did at least have sex down there?"

"Almost. See, after about a half an hour of supremely bad drag and watered down drinks, I decided that I'd had enough and I left. The bar had been on the edge of some kind of town square, and at night it was mostly dark and somewhat cruisy. Well, when in Rome..."

"Cruise for a Mexican?" I hazarded a guess.

"Exactly. The problem, though, was that it really was awfully dark. I could see people sitting here and there, but I couldn't make out what they looked like, and I was certain that not all of them had been there looking for what I was looking for. So I decided to play it safe and I took a seat to let the action pass me by. That, as it turned out, was a much better plan. Lots of men walked by, and it was quite obvious that they were looking for some white ass for a change of pace. Being the equal opportunity whore that I am, I had no qualms with that whatsoever. The only problem was that the vast majority of men walking by were either old, fat, short, or a hideous combination of the three."

"Not a happy trio," I made note.

"No," he agreed, with a frown. "Then, just as I was about to give up and go back to the hotel, I spotted what looked like a good prospect. He, too, was sitting alone on a bench about thirty feet away. From that distance and in the dark, I could only tell that he at least wasn't short or fat. What I could also tell was that every time I looked up, he was looking back at me. And, so, I had a dilemma." He stopped to take a sip of his coffee.

"Which was?" I asked, impatiently. Sparkle, you see, has a way of telling a story and stopping right at the juicy parts. I know it's for effect, but it still drives me crazy.

"Gay Rule #7," he answered and gave me a look like it should've been obvious. See, even after several years, I hadn't mastered all the rules and I feared I never would. (I think he made most of them up as he went along, anyhow, but they did seem to come in handy.)

"And Gay Rule #7 is?"

"My dear Secret, Gay Rule #7 is one of the most important rules of them all, and it's *the* most important rule whilst cruising. Simply stated: *distance* is a girl's best friend. Case in point: I can't even begin to tell you how many times I've stared from afar at what I thought was a cute, young thing only to find upon closer inspection that what I was cruising was indeed a lesbian. I mean, they all have these thin, little boy bodies and short haircuts and tattooed arms, so it's a natural mistake. Still, it gives me the creeps every time it happens. And then, of course, there are the related but no less depressing *neck-downers.*"

"Neck-downers?" That was a new one on me.

"Neck-downers are those unfortunate souls that have stupendous bodies, but are less lucky in the looks department. From a distance, they look really yummy, but up close, run away, Girlfriend, run away. Anyway, while sitting on that bench, I was thinking about Gay Rule #7. I mean, he looked fine from thirty feet away, but what if I made an effort to go over only to discover that he was some malformed hunchback or something far worse. Would it be worth the risk? See, that was my dilemma."

"But you went over anyway?" Because, yes, I did, in fact, know him that well.

"Didn't have to; he came over to me. At first, I thought he was getting up to leave. He walked away from me and around the square, but about five minutes later, he was sitting ten feet away from me and to my left. I was thrilled, because I thought I lost my only chance for some nookie. And then I casually glanced over, and there he was, staring back at me and nodding."

"Cruising, apparently, has the same rules from country to country," I guessed.

He nodded. "Thankfully so. Still, I could just barely make out what he looked like. He was definitely a Chicano and had very dark hair and what appeared to be a thin mustache. That and he had on loose white pants and a loose white shirt and sandals. I could also see that he was thin and my height. So, finally, I thought, here was a decent prospect. After a couple of looks away and then back at him, only to find him still staring at me intently, I made my move and asked, 'Where did you disappear to?' He slid over to the bench next to mine and answered in a wonderfully thick accent, 'The bathroom.' Thankfully, Secret, up close, he looked much better than I had anticipated. He had beautiful brown skin and deep dark eyes and was cute and young and, from the looks he was giving me, quite eager to get it on."

"Which made two of you," I couldn't help but add, stating the obvious.

"Duh," came the also obvious reply. "Anyway, I made the next move, hopping over to the bench he was sitting on and plopping down next to him. He smiled up at me as I did this and introduced himself as Hector. Said with his accent, it was music to my ears. He was chatty and friendly and his English was great. Living in a resort apparently helped greatly with his pronunciation and diction."

Sparkle got up and put two chairs facing each other. Then he jumped from one to other as he recounted the rather short conversation.

"'Do you come here often?' Old line, but it seemed appropriate, said I."

"'No, not often. Just sometimes,' he answered and gave me a mischievous grin."

"'And since you're sitting here with me, I take it you like Anglos?' He answered my question by taking my hand and placing it on his crotch. There was a noticeably hard lump underneath the thin cotton fabric and he let out a barely audible groan when I squeezed his growing prick. 'I'll take that as a yes.' To which I promptly added, 'Would you like to come back to my hotel with me, Hector?' He nodded and we were up and off the bench in about a half a second.

"We hailed a cab and headed back to my hotel after that. And the ride back, Secret, was not without its highpoints. See, Hector's thin cotton pants had no zipper, just a flap in front, and, it turned out, he wasn't wearing any underwear. A few minutes into our ride, I looked over at him, and he was smiling back at me and motioning with his eyes for me to look down. I did, of course, and was greeted with a semi-hard, short, thick, brown dick. I was in foreskin heaven, but resisted the urge to reach over and grab it. Lord only knew what the cabby would've done if he had caught us. And, since I, too, was not with underwear, I returned the favor and gave Hector a gander at my own manhood. He obviously liked what he saw, because his was now standing at full attention.

"When I realized that we were getting near my hotel, I put my prick away, with Hector followed suit. Not that it mattered, really, as you could still plainly see it beneath his pants. Fortunately, it appeared to have settled down by the time we got out of the cab. I mean, I didn't want any scenes in the hotel." He sighed, loudly. "But, alas, that was not to be."

"Uh oh," I interrupted.

"Understatement, Secret," he told me. "Anyway, Hector and I made our way through the lobby, and were walking toward the stairs when we heard a voice telling us to stop. We turned around to see the front desk person running at us and shouting, 'No, Senor.' He kept shouting this until he got just in front of us. Then he nervously informed me that they didn't allow prostitutes in the hotel. Now then, whatever word goes beyond mortified, *that's* what I was at right at that very moment.

"I looked over at Hector and he was looking down at his feet. I took that as a sign that I had made a truly grievous error in judgment. Then the hotel guy pointed a finger at Hector and told him to get out. Without saying a word or even looking at me, Hector did just that. Honestly, I felt horrible for the both of us. Then the hotel guy put the icing on the cake. He apologized for the scene, but he said that the hotel had very strict rules about such things. He also told me that Hector was no more than sixteen or seventeen years old and that I was very lucky not to have been caught by the police. I agreed with that, thanked the man, and turned quickly to go back to my room. Needless to say, I was not a very happy Sparkle. Horny, yes, happy, no. And in two languages, no less."

"So," I ventured, "was there anything about your trip that you are happy about?"

"I'm happy I'm back. I'm happy to be able to shower under a nozzle that isn't five and a half feet from the ground. And, mostly, I'm happy that Miss Mary Mack is working right here at Classics II. That's it," he answered, emphatically.

"And you're happy to see me, of course."

"Oh, sure, of course. (So much for the nice, sweet guy I missed so much.) Anyway, my beloved Secret, I must dash and shuck this nasty South of the Border aura off of me. I'll call you later. Ta!" And then he rushed out, bags in hand, ass swaying like a palm tree on a windy day.

Honestly, I was glad he was back, all things considered. Sadly, not everyone else felt the same. See, ten minutes later, Mack came out to the front of the store and asked, "Is he gone yet?"

It wasn't what he asked so much as how he asked it that made me nervous. I sensed impending doom. Gingerly, I inquired, "Why? What's wrong with Sparkle?" (You'd have thought I'd know better than to ask a silly question like that one.)

"That guy is the phoniest, most vile, slickest piece of vermin I've ever met. And, oh... oh... when he calls me Miss Mary Mack, I just want to slap the shit out of him. I swear, if he calls me that one more time, I'll... I'll... I'll strangle the son of a bitch." Mack was fuming. It was sort of scary, really, as I'd never seen him anything but pleasant before. Of course, I had seen Sparkle cause this reaction before, so I wasn't all that surprised. "Is he really a friend of yours?" he asked me.

"Best." I cowered as I said it.

"You're joking, right?" I shook my head that I wasn't, and he relaxed a bit and gave me a grin. "Well, there must be something good about him then if that's the case. How's about, when you know that he's coming down here, you let me know and I'll retreat to the back office to study?" We shook on it. I knew that it was just forestalling the inevitable, but why do something today that you can put off until tomorrow? (*That* you can quote me on.)

That night, Sparkle came over and looked considerably more relaxed. Actually, he looked somewhere between drunk and stoned. "Girlfriend," I asked, "have you had one, or six, too many?"

"No, I haven't had a drink all day," he answered, calmly.

"Why? What's wrong?" See, that concerned me.

"Nothing's wrong. But there was one itty-bitty thing that Mexico had to offer that did make the trip somewhat tolerable." He reached down as he was talking and came back up, slowly, with a little tote bag that had four medicine bottles in it. "These." I reached into the bag and looked closely at one of the bottles.

"Xanax?" I asked. "What's Xanax for again?"

"I think it's for stress. I'm sure not feeling any, so it must be working." He definitely looked relaxed as he plopped down on my couch. "FYI, you can buy prescription drugs over the counter in Mexico. You know, I have this whole new respect for the Mexican people now. Oh, and look what else I got." He shoved the tote bag back at me.

I stared down. "Valium, Percoset, and Vicodin. Oh goodie, it's a Judy Garland Christmas come early." (Oh well, if it's good for the Mexican economy, then it's okay by me.)

"By the way," he continued, onto a new but frightfully worse topic, "did M.M.M. have anything to say about me?"

"Oh... well, no, not really (think, Secret, think). He did mention though that he has a boyfriend already. (Hey, that could work.)

"Boyfriend, schmoyfriend. This is San Francisco. If anything, that makes it even more of a sure bet." (Nope, didn't work.)

"You know, he's really busy studying for his Masters and everything; I doubt he has much time for any *extra-curricular* activities,"

I added and then prayed. And then crossed my fingers behind my back. And my toes within my sneakers.

"You know something, Secret? If I didn't know any better, I'd swear that you liked him and were trying to keep him for yourself. Well, Sweetie, I saw him first. So hands off." He was wagging his finger at me now. I suppose, with all the drugs in his system, that was about the most rage he could muster, which meant that I planned on keeping him medicated as much as possible if this little *problem* was going to continue. (Thank goodness there were enough drugs in that tote bag of his for the both of us.)

***

Immediately, I came up with a plan to keep Mack and Sparkle as far away from each other as I possibly could. I told Sparkle to call me before he came over, at least for a little while, because we would be doing inventory for the next two weeks and I would be too busy to entertain him for most of that time. Since Sparkle requires constant entertaining, my request was agreed upon quite readily. Granted, it was only a Band-Aid on a gaping wound, but I figured that during those two weeks I could either try to convince Mack to like Sparkle or convince Sparkle not to like Mack (or at least not lust after him so obviously). Easy as pie, right? Then again, have you ever tried to bake a pie? Shit takes forever and never turns out near as good as the stuff you buy down at the bakery. Plus, it costs about three times as much as just buying it pre-made. In other words, well, that was enough words already. You figure it out.

In any case, just before Sparkle would show up, Mack would disappear to the back somewhere and I would convince Sparkle that he was either busy doing inventory or studying. For the most part, my plan was working. The two of them were well-separated and there was peace in the valley. Only once in those first few days was there a run in. Sparkle and I had been out front drinking our lattes when I excused myself to go to the bathroom. Upon my return, there was no Sparkle in site. Fearing the worst, I headed for my office.

Sure enough, he was back there flirting with Mack. Now, for his part, Mack was obviously playing nice for my benefit. He laughed at Sparkle's jokes and kept up his share of the conversation, but even with the smiles and the jocularity, I could tell that, behind it all, Mack was seething with hatred. After a few minutes of this, I convinced Sparkle to let Mack get back to his studying. He agreed and, as he turned to leave, he said, "Ciao, Miss Mary Mack." Then he walked back to the café. Just as he left the office, I turned to look at Mack, whose fists were clenched, lips pursed, eyes tightly shut. He was, apparently, totally ready to explode.

"Count to ten, Hon," I whispered to him.

Instead, he mouthed back, *I hate him.* So much for getting Mack to like Sparkle. Maybe I'd have better luck with the reverse strategy.

When I got back to the café, Sparkle was sitting there and was all smiles. "What?" I asked, curious about the look of happiness that spread across his face.

"Oh, nothing," he said and paused for effect. "But I'm making headway on the Mack front."

"And you know this how?" I couldn't help but ask.

"A girl just knows. Anyway, I could see it in his eyes."

Strange, all I saw was disgust. So I tried a different approach. "Let me ask you something, Sparkle. Could it be that the only reason you like Mack so much is because you can't have him?"

"Who says I can't have him?! I will have him! Have you ever known me not to have a man that I wanted?"

Oops, wrong approach. "No, it's just…" I tried.

"It's just that you want him and you don't want me to have him. That's it. Well, Miss Thing, he's mine, so back off." He was way serious this time, so I backed off. There was no use, I finally realized, in trying to get these guys to change their minds. In other words, I'd just have to think up a different strategy.

"Fine, fine. Mack is yours. Take him. Anyway, on to a different topic," I said, hopefully defusing the situation. "Did I tell you that we're going to start carrying classic gay books around here?"

His smile returned. "Hey, that's a good idea. This place needs some queering up. That straight stench kind of hangs in the air around here. Have you noticed it?" he asked.

"Um, I believe that's the old books," I replied.

"Well, they both have that same tired smell to them then." He was right about that. The women reeked of dead flowers and the men all smelled like they'd just come from the office or a bar. Honestly, I couldn't wait for the gay influx. (Maybe, I hoped, I could even get a date out of it.)

***

95

The next few days had been especially hectic for me. Besides my normal duties at the store, I was busy helping Mack pick out the gay books and then ordering them. It was fun, though, because I was getting a crash course in gay literature. I also had the added bonus of being too busy to play with Sparkle, so there were no more confrontations at the store. Two birds, one stone. Then again, one is all it takes to do some heavy damage.

By Friday, we'd ordered all the books and had set up some new bookcases in what was to be our gay section. And, really, I couldn't have been more proud. I mean, I was actually doing my small part for gay culture. I felt so... so... Quentin Crisp-ish (but with much less eye shadow).

When it was finally time to close up shop, Mack and I were both exhausted, but also exhilarated. To celebrate our achievement, I suggested that we grab a bite to eat at a nearby Italian restaurant. He was all for it, and so we headed on out. When we got to the restaurant, it was dark and crowded and it smelled wonderful. We were quickly seated and given a hard baguette to nibble on. That's when I reached over the table, shook Mack's hand, and congratulated him on a job well done, and he, in turn, shot me a smile and thanked me for the opportunity to help out.

Just then we were greeted *not* by our happy waiter, but by a very unhappy Sparkle. I instantly knew what he was thinking, and pulled him to the back by the bathrooms so that we could have our conversation in private (or at least not smack-dab in the middle of the restaurant and in front of Mack).

"Before you start screaming at me and accusing me of whatever it is you're about to accuse me of, let me just say that Mack and I are here just as friends and nothing more. Nothing. I swear," I protested, but I could tell that it was falling on deaf ears.

"Please, Secret, I saw you two playing handsies. You're obviously here on a date, even after I told you to lay off of him. I cannot believe that after all I've done for you, you slap me in the face by coming here with him. You're one lousy mother-fucker!"

"All you've done for me?" I shouted. "All you ever do for me is get me into trouble or embarrass me. If anything, I'm always the one doing things for you. If it wasn't for me, you wouldn't even have any real friends. And besides, Mack can't stand you!"

At that point, the restaurant manager came over and politely asked us to either stop shouting or to please leave. Neither, of course, was about to happen. If anything, the battle escalated and the manager, seeing that we weren't quieting down or leaving, walked away. That should've been our clue to stop, but we were too hot under the collars to pay attention.

Sparkle let the next volley go. "You're nothing but a jealous little twerp. I can't believe I've let you hang around me this long. If I really wanted Mack, I would've had him already. You, on the other hand, are way out of your league. It must really kill you to watch me have any man I want while you have to scrounge around for anything you can get." (Ouch.)

That's when Mack came over to try and intercede. "Boys, boys, please stop with the yelling. Remember that you're best friends, okay? Is this really worth your friendship?"

Sparkle turned to him and, with a sneer, said, "Um, excuse me, Miss Mary Mack, but this is an AB conversation, please C yourself out of it." (Uh-oh, that did it.)

"Why, you snide asshole," Mack shouted, "you're so full of yourself that you can't even see that you're fighting over a man that absolutely despises you and you're doing it with your best friend. You have to be the biggest jerk on the entire face of the planet. As a matter of fact, I can't stand to even be in the same room as you." Mack turned to look at me and frowned. "Bruce, I'm sorry, but I'm leaving and I quit. I never want to see this reprehensible excuse for a human being ever again."

Mack turned and walked back to get his jacket, while I ran after him to try and convince him that we could work it out. (Not that I thought we could, mind you, but I had to give it a shot.) Sparkle followed close behind, and, a split-second later, we were all back at the table. I tried my darndest to try and talk some sense into Mack, but he had his mind made up and was intent on leaving. I, of course, was frantic. I not only needed Mack to help me with the new section, but also I wanted to continue working with him. It was hopeless, though, as he was quickly out the door before I could think of good reason for him to stay. And, to make matters worse, as I turned to say something mean and nasty to Sparkle, he beat me to the punch by calling me a wanna-be before throwing his I.D. bracelet down to the floor.

Well, that did it. I exploded and proceeded to call Sparkle every bad name I could think of. This, sadly, ended with my final words of the event: "William Astan, I hope the next time I see you you're cold and dead and in a morgue somewhere, and you better watch out, because it may be me that put you there." At the same time I was saying this, Sparkle reached over, grabbed the baguette, and smacked me over the head with it. Also at that same moment, the police came in and heard and saw the entire thing. Hence, assault with a deadly weapon for Sparkle and a threat against his life by yours truly. (Talk about your bad timing.)

By that point, the two of us were really ready to kill each other and were about to lunge when the police interceded and separated us. I went immediately limp and let the policeman bring me to a corner of the restaurant. Sparkle, suffice it to say, was not so helpful. He put up quite a fight before several policemen had him under control. To make matters worse, as if they weren't God-awful already, the restaurant manager had come over and was pointing a finger at Sparkle and was telling the police that he had started the whole thing. Of course, this was true, but I immediately felt sorry for him as they dragged him out of the restaurant and into the street. Seconds later, I could hear them reading him his rights as they handcuffed him and threw him into the back of their car.

I, however, was substantially luckier. After I told the police what had happened (or at least the abridged version), they released me and gave me a warning. They also said that I should be careful not to threaten any more lives. Needless to say, I haven't. Then I asked them where they were taking Sparkle and how could I get him out of this mess. They were shocked by my request, of course. For that matter, so was I, but that's what being best friends is all about. (Peaks and valleys, Sweeties. Peaks and valleys.) Besides, I couldn't picture Sparkle lasting more than a few hours in prison without becoming someone's bitch.

The police released me, and I made hasty apology to the restaurant manager. I also left the waiter a huge tip, even though we never ordered any food; I figured he deserved something for the trouble we caused. I probably shouldn't have bothered, though, as I was pretty sure that I would never be eating at that restaurant ever again (not that they would have let me, anyway). Luckily for me, there was a phone booth just outside, because I knew immediately who I needed to call.

"Hello, Kiki, this is Bruce. I sort of need a favor," I began, guiltily.

Kiki and I had remained good friends over the years, but since he didn't particularly get along with Sparkle, or vice-versa, I didn't get to spend a lot of time with him much anymore. Still, we did see each other periodically, and he knew all about Sparkle's shenanigans over the years, so he wasn't at all surprised at the story I told him. Still, it wasn't Kiki that I needed, you see, so much as Larry, mainly because he was pretty much the only *adult* I knew and certainly the only professional I had for a friend. I seriously doubted that any of our other friends had an attorney or even personally knew one. (Bail bondsman, maybe. But that was only a quick fix.) Meaning, Larry was our only hope. At least I prayed as much.

Kiki put me on hold and went to get him. As I stood there in the cold and ruminated on the events of the past hour, I started to cry. I mean, I had lost two friends in a matter of seconds and was relying on a third to help me out of the sad state of affairs I was in. What, I thought, had happened? Certainly, I tried my best to make it work out, but my good intentions just weren't good enough in this case. I swore that if I could put things back to normal, I would only tell the truth from then on out. (Stop your snickering up there. Dire situations call for desperate measures. Besides, you and I both know that that wasn't really ever going to happen, right?)

The next voice on the phone was Larry's telling me to calm down. As soon as we got off the phone, he said that he would call his lawyer and the three of them would meet me at the police station. He also told me not to worry and that everything would be okay. I felt at least a little better upon hearing this. I mean, at least I'd made one good decision that day.

I hung up the phone, hailed a cab, and was at the police station in no time flat. This was not necessarily a good thing, however, because I then had to wait for Kiki and Larry. Needless to say, police stations are downright creepy, and the ones in San Francisco are no exception. Between the drug dealers, prostitutes, and homeless derelicts, I was beginning to feel dirty just by being there. (Especially with the baguette crumbs still tenaciously hanging around in my hair.)

As for the station itself, the least they could do was hire a good interior designer, I thought. I mean, come on, was all that overhead fluorescent lighting really necessary? It gave everyone that washed out look. And they hadn't bought a new stick of furniture in something like ten years. It was pitiful, really, but the prospect of redecorating (at least in my head) gave me something else to think about besides Sparkle behind bars. (Sounds like a made for TV movie: *Sparkle Behind Bars,* with Richard Chamberlain as Sparkle and co-starring Tom Cruise as his faithful sidekick, Secret. What? It could happen.)

I was still thinking about whether or not to go with hardwood floors and chintz rugs when Kiki and Larry came swooping in with what must have been Larry's lawyer in tow. Introductions were made before I hastily told the lawyer, Mister Horowitz, what had happened. He told me that since I wasn't going to press charges and he doubted that the restaurant would either that he should be able to get Sparkle out sometime that evening and that we should all just sit tight. (Had there been a bar there, *tight* is exactly what I would've been. Alas, there wasn't one, but in my redecorating fantasy there certainly would be.)

Larry went with Mister Horowitz to post Sparkle's bail, while Kiki tried his best to cheer me up. I mean, I was feeling pretty lousy at that point. Plus, I was uncertain how Sparkle would react to seeing us all there. After all, we hadn't exactly parted on good terms. To top it all off, I remembered that Mack had quit and I would have no one to help me in the store the next morning. So I decided to call Slim and tell him what had happened. Maybe he could send Sharon over, I figured.

I reached Slim quick enough; he told me that he'd already heard the whole story. Mack had called him to apologize for quitting and then explained why. Since Slim was old friends with Sparkle, he completely understood. He also offered to switch Sharon over to Classics II and offered Mack a job at Classics. Sparkle never went over there, and Mack happily took the job. Score one measly point for yours truly. I was so relieved that I started to cry all over again. Thank God Kiki was with me because I was fast becoming a total wreck. Naturally, I thanked Slim up and down, and, by the time I hung up, Larry and Mister Horowitz were already on their way back.

"Well?" I asked the lawyer, anxiously, with tears streaming down my face.

"He'll be out in an hour. They just need to process the paperwork. Plus, the clerk owes me a favor. (Mister Horowitz winked at me as he said this. *Hmm.* A gay, Jewish lawyer. I really needed to hang out with Kiki more often if this was the company he was keeping.) No one is pressing charges, but he'll still have to go before a judge for disturbing the peace and resisting arrest. Oh, and don't worry about your friend; they let me go back to see him, and an hour before they arrested him, they raided an illegal gay dance party. He's back there with a dozen of the cutest drugged-out boys you've ever seen. He actually told me to take my time."

"Sounds like Sparkle," I said, with a sigh of relief. "Thank you so much for your help. I can't even begin to express my gratitude for all you've done."

"Well, perhaps I can find a way for you to do just that," he said, with a wink, and handed me his business card. Maybe the night wasn't going to be a total loss after all, I thought, and shot him a smile while tucking the card into my wallet.

"You guys don't have to wait with me anymore," I said, with a relieved sigh. "I'm sure you'd all rather be anyplace else but here, and I doubt Sparkle will want a huge reception when he gets out." I was hoping they'd agree, and, knowing Kiki's feelings toward Sparkle, they did. I thanked the three of them repeatedly and walked them outside. Then I gave Kiki an extra long hug, telling him how lucky I was to have friends like them. He said that I was right about that and he would call me in the morning to see how I was doing. He also said, rather cryptically, that Sparkle and I would get our chance to make it up to him, and soon. Not wanting any more surprises, I let it go and went back inside the station.

Twenty minutes later, Sparkle came walking toward me. My heart was pounding a mile a minute and I was nervous as all hell. Would we still be friends? Would the feud still be in full-force? My questions were answered as soon as he got within a few feet of me, because he reached out his arms and beckoned me toward him. I gladly hugged him while he apologized over and over again. Both of us were crying up a storm and swore we'd never fight again, especially over a man. (A good pair of jeans, though, were fair game.) We stood there like that for about ten minutes and cried and laughed until we had no more tears left.

Then I reached into my pocket and pulled out the discarded bracelet. Sparkle reverently took it and put it back on his wrist. That put a smile on both of our faces as, arm in arm, we made our way out of the police station. It was only then that my breathing finally returned to normal.

"Horrible lighting," my friend said to me on our way out. (Told you so.)

"Oh my God, yes. Some indirect lighting would be so much better." I couldn't help but laugh. "So how was prison?" I asked as we walked down the street in search of the nearest bar.

"Not bad, actually. I had company." We rushed into the pub on the corner.

"I heard. Any cuties?" I ordered a double gin martini, putting my arm over his shoulder.

"All of them. Yumminess from one end of the cell to the other," he answered and ordered the same.

"Any dates?" I tacked on as I gulped down my drink.

"Just one; tomorrow night. Of course, it depends on whether or not he gets out of jail by then. If not, I promised to visit him there. I've never made out in the *big house* before, by the way. Definitely sexy, but I'll pass on the repeat performance." He downed his drink even faster than I and ordered a second.

"I think I may have a date as well," I informed him, producing the business card.

"The lawyer? No way; I saw him first. He's mine!" said he, but before I could respond, he added, "Nah... just joking. He's all yours, dude."

I gave him a hard punch on the arm and finished *his* second martini. "Sparkle, my friend, life with you is never dull," I said, with a happy sigh. "It's a pain in the ass, but it's never dull."

"Amen to that, Brother. Amen to that." And then we ordered another round.

It was then we noticed that we were in a straight bar. See, just like I told you: dire times, desperate measures.

CHAPTER FIVE
WHAT A DRAG

What's the weirdest dream you've ever had? Was it that classic one where you're back in school after not being there for years and there's a test that very day? Or maybe the one where you're running really, really fast and all of a sudden you're off the ground and you're flying through the air? You know, they say that flying in your dreams is a sign of good luck to come. Personally, I'm terrified of heights, and those flying dreams are a real pain in the ass. It's like, hey, I'm flying, cool, but, *whoa*, I'm way too high for my own good. (I think a good therapist could really do me some good, don't you?) Or is it that one where you're back living at home with your parents and your mom and dad are being their usual interfering pain in the asses and you're, like, screaming and totally going off on them? With that one, I always wake up in a good mood, but with just a slight twinge of guilt. (I know, I really do have issues. See back to the therapist question.)

Well, let me tell you something, those dreams are nothing compared to this recurring one that I've had ever since Sparkle and I became friends. Maybe you can interpret it, because I can't make head nor tail of what it could mean. In any case, it appears now to be entirely prophetic.

See, it starts out normal enough, with Sparkle and I sitting around his living room listening to music. I'm pretty sure that it's Heart that's singing in the background, but it sounds like Pat Benatar. And the funny thing is, I know that that can't be, but I don't know why. (Personally, I wish it were the other way around. I think Nancy Wilson could sing the shit out of *Love is a Battlefield*. But, then again, Pat could

103

probably do *Barracuda* some justice.) Anyway, during this dream, Sparkle and I are sitting around doing nothing in particular, and every time I turn to look at him, he has one less layer of clothes on. First he loses his shirt, then his pants, and then his undies, all while I remain fully clothed. Now, before you think the obvious, that I secretly desire Sparkle or some such foolishness, let me just say that there's no sexual tension in this dream; it seems perfectly natural that Sparkle is becoming nude. (Of course, that is perfectly natural for him in real life, but no judgments, please.)

Well, after a short time, Sparkle is naked and the two of us are carrying on a normal conversation like nothing is out of the ordinary. That's when things turn freaky. Next, whenever I turn to look at him, he slowly becomes… well… sort of, well… *a woman*. His short, dark hair becomes long, luxurious, and very blonde. His nice hard pecs turn to big, bouncy boobs and all of his body hair just all of a sudden disappears. Thankfully, he retains his penis, which alternates from erect to flaccid. You know, I think that part of my dream is just a reflection of my utter lack of sex. I mean, I seriously doubt that I'm attracted to he-shes. (Or as Sparkle affectionately refers to them: chicks with dicks or pussy on a stick.) And I'm certainly not obsessed with Sparkle's dick, pretty as it is and all.

In any case, the dick thing is not an integral part of the dream (really). And, pretty soon, it's out of sight and hidden by a billowing gown. Then, always at this point, I get up off the couch and I stand directly in front of a mirror. Well, lo and behold, I'm also in a dress and my hair is long and flowing and whorishly red. What scares me is that the dream-me isn't the least bit upset about the transformation. If anything, I'm happy to be so outwardly feminine. As that old song goes: *I enjoy being a girl.*

The dream always ends the same way, and that's with Sparkle and I as full-grown women. It's not that I feel like a woman in the dream or anything, but I certainly look like one. And, of course, Sparkle makes a glorious woman: all tall and lean, with achingly high cheekbones. Sadly, even in my dreams, I get the short end of the stick, as I look more comical than alluring. My makeup never looks quite right, my hair is always just a bit askew, and my dress hangs weird. Sparkle ends up looking like *Elle* and I end up looking like *Hell.*

Sparkle gets a big kick out of this dream. Me, I just find it kind of weird. I mean, honestly, I've never had the least bit of desire to be a woman. And I certainly have never wanted to be with a woman. The thought is just so, well, *icky*. I constantly meet gay men who came out after years of dating women, and most have had sex with a girl at least once in their lives. I thank God that I don't have that awful memory etched forever in my head. Seriously, the only bush I've ever seen up close was in my mother's garden, and I plan on keeping it that way. Please don't think of me as being overly misogynistic; I'm simply more than happy being a man. (Granted, a somewhat affected man, but a man just the same.)

And while the dream never feels threatening to my masculinity and it doesn't make me wake up with night-sweats or anything, I am kind of curious as to why I keep having it. I often wonder if it has some hidden meaning. That is to say, I *used* to wonder. My questioning, you see, stopped shortly on the morning after we rescued Sparkle from jail.

That night, after we finished our drinks and were significantly more relaxed, we both got into cabs and headed our separate ways. I had to go to work in the morning, after all, and I was still upset about the whole Mack thing, but Sharon was more than qualified to help me run the store and I liked her an awful lot, so, as I often say, glass half-full. Plus, Sharon being my first official bisexual friend, I always felt so worldly around her. Or at least less Kansas.

On a side note (yet another one), something I swear I cannot grasp is the notion of bisexuality. I mean, I have a hard enough time dealing with men, sexually speaking, without also having women in the picture. Of course, they say that bisexuals are extremely well adjusted, again sexually speaking. And, certainly, I can see where it would be convenient to have no preference between the sexes. I mean, can't get sex from one, go onto the other. But still, there seems something wrong with the whole notion of it. Call it a lack of sticktoitiveness or something. Regardless, Sharon was a real pill, and I was, if not happy, then at least relieved that I had an assistant whose company I enjoyed. Heck, even Sparkle liked her, and that's saying something. (Well, everything, really, given the whole Mack debacle.)

She was already at the shop when I got there the next morning and obviously knew most of how and why she all of a sudden was working alongside me and not Slim. In any case, I don't think she cared either way. She adored working with all the old books and had a true yearning to read every last one of them, whether in my store or the other one. In truth, I've never ever seen a more dedicated and driven reader before. Every few days, I'd catch her reading a different tome and always on a different subject. When I asked her why she was so voracious in her reading habits, she had a purely original response. And a very Shirley MacLaine one at that.

See, she said that she's a strong believer in reincarnation, dreaming of her past selves every so often. Sort of like she's at once herself and a total stranger all rolled into one. She told me that she has this gut feeling that in one of her past lives she was illiterate and that it was her complete undoing. And so, in this life, she not only cherishes books, but also it's like a compulsion for her to always be reading one. She says that she has overweight friends who say that they were malnourished in one of their past lives and never let themselves get hungry in this one. In my case, I must never have had sex in a past life, because I find myself looking for it around every corner in this one. Or maybe I had too much sex in a past life and I'm being punished in this one by never getting any. (It's actually a blessing to be able to blame my past incarnation for my lack of sex instead of blaming myself. It's good for my ego at any rate.)

Well, anyhow, Sharon was all smiles and good cheer when I arrived at work the next morning, thereby brightening my spirits considerably. At least I didn't have to come up with any more schemes to keep Sparkle and my assistant apart. (I don't think scheming is my forté, huh?) Also, she was just as excited as I was about the new gay section. Hallelujah for that, because it was quite an undertaking getting it off the ground.

After my first cup of coffee, I felt back to my old, cheerful self. I was obliged to let Sharon in on the whole story of Mack and his departure, and she thanked me for my honesty. I also told her that I was glad she was working with me fulltime. She blushed a little, then thanked me again. All in all, things were turning out better than expected. I honestly felt that. Really, I thought that my life was now back on track and as normal as it was ever going to get. (Yes, we're about to take a turn for the bizarre. What a shock. Ready? Here goes.)

We were both sitting there, letting the caffeine surge through our veins, when who should walk in but Sparkle. Nothing strange about him being at Classics II. I mean, he was there all the time, for that matter. What was odd was that it was before ten o'clock and, for the life of me, I could only remember a handful of times when I'd seen him at such an early hour. Conscious, I mean.

"And what do we owe this vision to? Catching the proverbial worm, are we?" I asked, in utter amazement. Barring earthquake, flood, or other natural disaster, I couldn't imagine what could get him out and about at such an ungodly time of day.

"What, can't a man just enjoy the rewards of an early morning jog?"

Now *that* wasn't the answer I expected. "You jogged over here? Are you feeling all right?" I knew that Sparkle exercised. I mean, you don't look like him without a little sweating, but I never actually saw him work out and he never really talked about doing it. I think he wanted me to believe that it all came naturally for him. But since it didn't come naturally (or any other way) for me, I figured that he must pump the iron or some such thing when I was at work and he was left to his own devices.

"Yes," he answered, incredulously, "I jogged over here. Why is that so special?"

"It's not special," I responded. "I've just never seen you do it and I've never seen you out at this hour before without being forced into it. Not unless I spend the night at your house, and, even then, you're not nearly this alive. What gives? Sale at Macy's you just have to get to? Cruisy bathroom opening up in the park?"

He shook his head and grimaced at me. "Well, if you must know, it was my prison internment."

"But you weren't in prison; you were in a small county jail's holding cell. And, for that matter, you were only there for a few hours, during which time you met a man and made a date. How traumatic of an experience could that have been to cause you to be up, out, and jogging at this hour of the day?" I couldn't wait for his answer.

"A few hours in a cell feels like years, Secret. You cannot possibly imagine what it's like to lose your freedom. So, here I am, enjoying my freedom. From now on, I'm going to grab life by the balls and take off running. (A painful expression, if ever I'd heard one.) Instead of *no I can't, no I won't, no I don't want to*, it's going to be *yes I can, yes I will, yes I want to!* Hello world, here I am! (He was quoting Barbra Streisand, so I knew he was serious.) So, damn it, pour me a great big cup of coffee 'cause my head is saying *go, go, go* and my body is saying *back to bed, back to bed, back to bed.*" And then he promptly slumped into the spare chair at our table and plopped his head down on it.

"Now that's the Sparkle I know and love," said I, getting up to get him his much needed coffee.

"Bless you," he moaned, soon adding, "Good morning to you, too, Stryker." He was talking to Sharon, and, no, he wasn't referring to that gay icon, Jeff, of the large endowments Jeff. He called her Stryker because it was a combination of straight and dyke. (Befitting if not original, I thought, for a bisexual woman.) Sharon also enjoyed the name and referred to Sparkle, on occasion, as Cheat. Which is a combination of cheap and slut. (Also befitting.)

"Here ya go, Sweetie. A nice, big cup of joe for the newly freed."

Sparkle eagerly grabbed the cup and took a swig. "To Freedom," he toasted, and we joined in, all our mugs held up high.

But our freedom was short-lived, for just as soon as our cups hit the table, the three of us were joined by a fourth.

"Well, well, well, just the two men I was looking for. And, Sharon, always a delight to see you." It was Kiki. And just as soon as I spotted him coming through the door, I remembered what he'd said the night before. It had something to do with returning the favor. (Fuck.)

"And to what do we owe this pleasant visit? Aren't there hairs to be clipped and necks to be shaved?" It was Sparkle, who was clearly no fan of Kiki.

That, of course went both ways. "On my way to work now. You remember work don't you? Oh, no, I suppose not." Yup, Kiki was no fan of Sparkle, either. Still, underneath it all, I suspected that they enjoyed the shared cattiness. "But before I open up shop," he continued, "I wanted to poke my head in and ask something of our friend, Bruce, here. Luckily, *you* are here as well. I trust you survived your little ordeal last night?"

"Yes, thank you and your husband for coming down and bailing me out. It was much appreciated." Sparkle raised his mug in a toast, but I could tell it was forced conviviality. Sparkle simply hated to be indebted to anyone, especially someone he didn't particularly care for. Which was pretty much everyone outside of his little circle and Cher.

"What are friends for?" Kiki responded.

"Indeed." Sparkle knew something was up, but he was playing the game out.

"Well, that brings me to my little request. In case you were unaware, Larry and I belong to a gay softball league..."

"My goodness," Sparkle interrupted, "I had no idea you all were athletic. I thought you were looking bigger these days. I figured it was just too much red meat in your diet. Now I know better. Softball?

My goodness gracious." I was grinning despite myself. Honestly, this was the first I'd ever heard about any gay softball league. I couldn't imagine those two suited up and on a playing field, not unless there was a bar just off of first base.

"Yes," Kiki continued, "well, anyway, we joined last year in an effort to be less… stationary. Larry played some in college, so he suggested the league. Granted, I was a wee bit hesitant at first…"

"Not wanting to ruin your shearing hand and all." Sparkle was on a roll and rapidly gaining bitch points. I could tell that Kiki was remaining civil just long enough to get his request on the table.

"So to speak, yes. But, once I got involved, it was really quite fun. It didn't take too long for the two of us to play with a modicum of talent, and now we are, if you'll pardon the expression, in the swing of things." (Groan from Sparkle.)

"Well, good for you," piped in Sharon. (Yes, softball + dyke = heaven. Bisexuals included.)

"And the reason for this unexpected and simply delightful visit?" Sparkle asked, with as much sarcasm as he could muster at such an early hour.

"That would be," Kiki continued, looking at us nervously, "to help the team out with some fundraising. There's a northwestern, gay softball tournament in Seattle in two months, and we need to raise the money to get us all there. Unfortunately, since most of the players are doctors, lawyers, and other assorted professionals, there are only a few of us that can spare the extra hours needed to raise the money."

"And since I'm practically awash in spare time," inferred Sparkle, "and our dear friend, Secret, here has his evenings free (meaning I never have any dates, which really sucks), you figured we were available to come to your aide."

"For the most part, yes. However, I think you'll both enjoy the particular fundraising project we have in mind; it promises to be quite the event." Kiki put on a cheerful expression, but I had a feeling it was all for show.

"Now, let's see," Sparkle began guessing, "could it be, um, an all-nude carwash? That could be fun, except, well, cold water does make one's genitals shrink just a bit. And it would have to be during the day, when Secret wouldn't be able to participate, so I guess it's a nix on that. Perhaps keep that as a contingency plan, 'kay? How about, let's see, oh I know, you'd like us to go door-to-door peddling assorted candies. Hey now, I think that could be fun, especially in The Castro.

One is bound to meet a nice array of eligible bachelors with that plan. Of course, the ones that would actually buy the candies might be, well, a little on the chunky side, no offense Kiki; so maybe that wouldn't be as enjoyable in practice as it appears to be on paper. Hmm... what else? Wait, I think I have it! (Kiki was arms akimbo and tapping his foot by then. He really must've needed our help to be taking Sparkle's abuse for so long.) It's a Jell-O wrestling fundraiser? I'm right, aren't I, Kiki? I can tell by your delighted expression that I'm right. (Kiki was sneering, actually.) Well, as good an idea as that is, I have to tell you that Jell-O isn't exactly my medium of choice. Pudding maybe, mud definitely, but not Jell-O. You know, it's made out of horse hooves and pig snouts, and I'm a strict vegetarian. (He ate meat almost everyday of his life.) So, sorry, I think we'll have to pass on that plan, too. Well, I guess I'm fresh out of ideas, so please, Dearie, what, pray tell, do you have in mind for us?"

Kiki stopped tapping his foot, dropped his arms to his side, paused a second to gain some confidence, and said with conviction, "A drag show emceed by one or both of you. You'd be the stars!"

The three of sat there staring at him, mouths agape. Personally, I was waiting for him to say it was all a joke. *Gotcha*! But nothing, he just stood there staring back at us and waited for one of us to speak up. I did the honors. "No fucking way in the world am I going to get up on stage in a dress and make a complete jackass out of myself just so that you can go play in some softball tournament in Seattle. No way, no how, not a chance. I think I like the door-to-door thing better. At least that way there's something in it for me: sex, candy, or, if there's a God in heaven, both. Sorry, Kiki, thanks for busting Sparkle out of the slammer, but nuh uh." I folded my arms in an *I'm serious about this* way and hoped that Kiki would understand.

But before he could make any objections to, what I thought was my final decision on the topic, Sparkle spoke up and said, "We'll do it. Just name the place and time and we'll be there with bells on, or possibly boas... or both, depending on our outfits."

"You will?!" the three of us shouted at him in amazement.

"Delighted to repay the favor to our dear friend here. Now off to work with you; we have a show to plan." I was completely shocked, or I certainly would've argued. Kiki, realizing that he'd gotten what he'd came for, quickly thanked us and hurried (if memory serves, I think he ran) out the door and yelled back that he'd fill us in on the details later.

I stared at my friend in stunned dismay. "What in the world has come over you? Did they knock you around your head in that jail last night? Do you realize what you just agreed to do? Plus, and this is a great big plus, as far as I know, neither one of us has ever done drag before. And, except for a brief role in my summer camp's version of *The Sound of Music*, when I was eight, I've never been on a stage before. Hello, Earth to Sparkle, what the fuck were you thinking?"

Sparkle sat there for a moment to collect his thoughts before he answered. Then, as calmly as he could, he said, "Okay, I realize that we have no experience as drag queens, that neither of us has any stage experience, and that I don't even particularly like your friend, Kiki, but I woke up this morning and made a solemn oath to myself that I would take on more adventures in my life before I was too old to enjoy them. I think we should look on this as a blessing. God put me in jail so I could help others." And then he rested his hands on the table and sat back in his chair, cool as a cucumber and looking rather Buddha-esque.

I was not so relaxed. "What?! Are you insane? God didn't put you in jail; the police did. And the schmucks that you'll be helping are a bunch of Mary's that are too lazy to raise money that they probably already have but are too cheap to spend, just so they can fly up to Seattle and toss a ball around. And knowing Kiki as I do, throw it badly. Now is not the time for you to all of a sudden become Saint Sparkle just because you spent a few hours behind bars." This time I meant business. There was no way I was going to go through with it. No fucking way.

"Are you going to tell him that we're not going to help?" Sparkle asked.

"No, you got us into this mess and you're going to get us out," I answered.

"Nope. I said it and I meant it. If you don't want to help out your friends, then that's your problem, but you're gonna be the one to tell them, not me." Damn, I couldn't believe that after all this time Sparkle was the good guy and I was the bad one. Fucker.

"Fine!" I harrumphed and went off to help a customer who had walked in a few minutes earlier.

"Fine!" Sparkle shouted back to me and got up from his chair and walked out of the shop.

"Well," added Sharon, who had remained silent throughout, "working here should be interesting." And then she cleared and cleaned the table. Needless to say, none of us had any idea just how interesting it was going to get.

**

The next morning, I arrived at work in a truly foul mood. I didn't have the heart (nerve) to call Kiki and Larry the night before to tell them that Sparkle had jumped the gun and that, though we really would love to help out, we just couldn't, what with all the many and various things going on in our lives. It sounded like a crock of shit, even to me, but it was the best I could come up with at the spur of the moment. The truth may have worked, but, as you've seen, it wasn't my usual modus operandi.

As it turned out, time had run out either way because, for a second day in a row, Kiki came barreling into the store with more surprises in hand. This time he was noticeably more excited, and I knew right away that I was in trouble.

"Well, Secret," he began, "the team had a practice game last night and Larry and I told them how Seattle was a fete accompli, as we now have our star performers lined up and..."

"But I..." I tried to interrupt.

No good, he continued on through. "... that, between Sparkle's good looks and large circle of friends and your, well your, um, *energy* and all (gee, that made me feel great), the night would most certainly be an enormous success. So, just a quick FYI before I get going to work, the show is three weeks from this Sunday at The Stud and starts at nine sharp. I'll touch bases with you sometime before then, but basically do whatever you want up there. (He was starting to move toward the door now and was talking a mile a minute.) There will be four other performers, all from the team. You'll have bios and stuff beforehand, so you'll be able to prepare some appropriate shtick in between acts. (Now he was at the door.) Call me if you need anything."

"But we..." I tried, really I did, but he was way too fast for me.

"Ta for now, Sweetie, and thanks for everything. Tell Sparkle thanks as well." And he was out the door and running down the sidewalk before I could say or do anything more.

I moaned to myself. "But we can't do it. Sorry, but we're just too busy." It was a lost cause; Kiki was well out of earshot by then.

"Too late, Bruce," said Sharon, draping an arm around my shoulder. "It looks like you're going on, after all. Hey, if it makes you feel any better, at least Sparkle will be right up there with you."

"Big whoop," I grumbled.

And then who should walk in but Miss Freedom Lover herself. "Hey, was that Kiki I saw running down the sidewalk?" he asked.

"Yes, you lousy fuck fucker." Sadly, calling him names didn't make me feel any better.

"So I take it you told him that we weren't going to do it and he was running away in a mad rage?" he guessed, as way wrong as he could be.

"You know," I began, "I think I liked it better when you slept in late and my life had a semblance of normalcy. One night in jail, and suddenly I'm a performance artist. Damn."

"Drag queen, Honey, and I take it that means you didn't tell him and we're about to be starlets." He was positively beaming at the revelation. I was just pissed and walked away.

"Exactly," Sharon told him, "but I think Bruce is less than enthusiastic at the prospect."

"Just you wait, Stryker, our friend is going to be a huge star," I overheard him say, but if I managed to get through it all without having a nervous breakdown, then I would consider the night a resounding success.

In any case, it was three weeks away. Maybe it would be cancelled. Maybe the whole tournament would be postponed until the following year. Maybe Seattle would sink into the ocean. Maybe...

"Hi, Bruce. Hi, William." It was Mister Horowitz entering the store with a wave and an adorable smile. (Classics II was becoming Grand Central Station all of a sudden.) "Kiki said that if I couldn't find you at home that you'd probably be here. Guess he was right." He was talking to Sparkle, but he was giving me that *come hither* look. (I returned it with a *come yon* leer.) He sat down with Sparkle, while I rushed to get him a coffee and a scone, on the house, naturally.

"Well, my friend," he said, patting Sparkle on the back, "your court case has been set for two weeks from today. I have a friend (wink, wink) that got it pushed way early for you. We'll be in and out of there right quick. Unless you go off on a rampage before then (no, no foreshadowing; he behaved himself for a change), then you should be off with a slap on the wrist and some hours of community service."

"Can we push for a slap on the ass and call it a day?" Sparkle deadpanned.

"Sorry, no can do. Just no more shenanigans until then, okay?" No small request for Sparkle, but he nodded his ascent and gave a solute for good measure.

"But that's only one of the reasons I came down here to see you both this fine morning," he said with a grin. "The other is to thank you guys for volunteering to help us out with the fundraiser. The whole team is looking forward to it."

"You're on the team?" I asked as I scooted a chair in between his and Sparkle's.

"Pitcher, three years and counting."

"Well, Mister Horowitz, what a Renaissance man you are," I gushed.

"Allen, call me Allen, please. And, no, not really; I force myself to play so I can get at least a little exercise and social time for myself. Otherwise, I'd be stuck in court or preparing for a case all day, and you know what they say?"

"Never mix beer and liquor?" guessed Sparkle.

"No, all work and no play, yada, yada, yada," responded Allen.

"Oh, yeah. Those yadas can be a bitch." I was trying to be cute. It worked, it seemed, and Allen shot me a coy grin and nudged my leg beneath the table. I had visions of a half-Jewish, half-Catholic wedding passing before my eyes. (My mother would be so proud. That is, once she found out that I'm gay, I mean.)

"Are you also going to be in the show, Allen?" Sharon asked, interrupting my reverie.

"Well, despite my better judgment, yes, yes I am. I figure you only go around once, so might as well do it all."

"I couldn't agree more," I agreed, Sparkle and Sharon both throwing me a *get real* look. "As a matter of fact, I was just sitting here telling my friends how much I was looking forward to the performance."

"You were?" Sparkle, as usual, wasn't playing along.

"Come on, you know I'm just thrilled at the idea of helping out the team. Tell Allen how happy I am to do this little favor for them," I said and grabbed his arm, tightly, and kicked him a bit under the table. (Violence always brings the idea home to Sparkle, you see.)

"Oh, yes, that's right. Our Secret here is just a regular old Florence Nightingale, always eager to help out our men in uniform."

"Yes, well, weren't you just saying that you had an errand to run?" I told Sparkle more than asked him. See, I was pushing for some one-on-one time with my new lawyer friend.

"No, I don't think..." I kicked him again and nodded with my head for him to scat. "Oh, yes, that's right; I was just headed to Walgreen's for some Preparation H. I'm simply busting out down there. Thanks for reminding me, old chap." And he got up to go. Sharon also got the hint and went back to the register.

"Well, I hope your friend will be all right," Allen said, with a concerned look.

"Oh, he'll be fine. Something's always falling out or popping back into Sparkle."

"No, I mean, you kicked him awfully hard."

I blushed. "Oh, you noticed, well..."

"No need to explain. I'm flattered. Look, I've cleared my caseload a bit for the next month in order to get some rehearsal time in before the big event. If you have a free night this week, would you like to do dinner or something?" he asked and rested his hand on mine. The *or something* sounded promising. Meaning, I nodded a hearty yes.

"Great, how about tomorrow night then? I'll come by before you close up shop and we can head on out from here. Sound good?"

"Sure," I beamed, "that would be great."

"Terrific. Then I'll see you tomorrow night," he said, getting up from the table. "Gotta go now, criminals to try, innocent men to defend, and all that. See you then." And he was out the door with a wave and a smile. Maybe this whole show thing would be fun, after all, I was beginning to think. (Uh uh, I'm not going to tell you just yet. You'll just have to wait and see.)

***

The next day, I let Sharon go home a half an hour early, so that when Allen came to get me, I'd have him all to myself. I was giddy as a schoolgirl as the hour approached. I mean, the novelty of going out with my first lawyer and my first Jew was driving me crazy with anticipation. I felt so, so... *cosmopolitan.*

It didn't hurt that Allen was dreamy. Throw in a pair of horn-rimmed glasses and a big, bumpy nose to boot, and that would be Allen. I had butterflies in my stomach just thinking about him. Not to mention a boner the size of Cleveland. (Well, Detroit, at any rate. Okay, okay, Palm Springs, but still.)

The proverbial icing on the cake was when he strolled into the shop, right on time, with a beautiful bouquet of roses. Usually, when it comes to picking me up or meeting me somewhere, most of my gay friends are twenty or more minutes late, which is something I can never quite figure out, since all they have to do is throw on a pair of jeans and a t-shirt. Must be the hair gel that holds them up. That and the necessary cruising they do along the way.

Allen walked over to the register, where I was closing out the day's receipts, and handed me the flowers. I thanked him and told him how lovely they were and quickly shot him a glowing smile. Suffice it to say, inside, I was a nervous wreck. No one had ever given me flowers before, let alone an adorable man with a steady income, and I became speechless and awkward. In any case, I took the flowers, found a vase, filled the vase with water, and arranged the flowers just right (being gay has so many advantages), and barely looked up at Allen or said more than two words to him. Then I quickly walked over to the door, mumbled some passing comments to him, locked up, pulled the shades down, and started arranging the chairs for the morning. A couple of minutes into this, I felt a hand on my shoulder and I turned around slowly to face him. He, oh joy of joys, was looking straight into my eyes and was smiling.

"Stop," he whispered.

"But I just..."

"Come here." He grabbed my hips, pulled me near him, and gently kissed me on the lips. I was picturing the witch at the end of the Wizard of Oz. *I'm melting, meeeelting...* "Can we go now?" he asked as he slightly pulled away.

"Uh uh. Not yet," I told him.

"How come?" he whispered into my ear, swirling his tongue around for good measure. Needless to say, I was getting some massive lumpage in my pants by that point. (Chattanooga!)

"Because." And this time I grabbed him by *his* hips, wrapped my arms around him, and kissed him hard. He tasted just as good as he looked, and I felt some heavy lumpage in return from his side of things.

"Yum." We both said, simultaneously, as we pulled away.

"Shall we," I said, motioning to the door.

"Not yet. Is the door locked?" He had a truly wicked grin on his handsome face, which sent my heart to fluttering.

"Um, yes, what did you have in mind, Mister Lawyer Man?" I asked as seductively as I could muster, his piercing green eyes burning right on through me.

"Take your shirt off, Bruce." He said it without any rise or fall in his voice.

It was more of a statement than a command, and I only hesitated for the briefest moment before I obeyed, slowly undoing the buttons on my shirt (I knew how to give a show when it was called for) before setting it down a nearby table. "Better?" I asked, returning his leer with one of my own.

"Much. Shoes next." He grabbed a seat about fifteen feet away and sat down to watch me untie my shoelaces, kick of my sneakers, and roll off my socks. I looked up when I was done and raised my hands in a shrug to indicate that I was ready for the next request. "Take your belt of, Bruce." And the belt was on the table with my shirt. He never took his eyes off of me nor mine off of him. "Bruce?"

"Yes, Allen?"

"Are you wearing any underwear beneath your pants?" This time his voice was just slightly off beat, more raspy and quick, and growing thicker by the second.

"No, Allen, I'm not."

"My, my, going commando? Was that for my benefit, Bruce?" I nodded a yes, though I certainly wasn't planning on this little scene. Sometimes Sparkle does give good advice, you see; this seemed to be one of those times. "Good. Walk over here," he said, motioning with his finger at the same time. "Stop," he added, when I was no more than a couple of feet away. "The pants, Bruce, take them off." He was still looking me right in the eyes, and, without looking away, I removed my pants. And then there I was, in the middle of the store, naked and hard as a rock.

"Nice, Bruce. Did you have a good day today?" he asked and stood up. I nodded that I had, and he continued. "I had a good day as well. Mostly, I sat in my office picturing you just like this, naked and waiting for me to do this." And then he walked up to me and put his hands on my chest and ran his fingers up and down my torso. As soon as he felt my goosebumps, he let out a barely audible moan.

I reached down to grab his right hand, pulled it lower, and wrapped it around my prick. Then it was my turn to moan. He liked that, and, within a heartbeat, we were kissing like crazy. His lips moved in perfect synchronization with mine, and when he let go of my dick to embrace me, I sank into his arms. I couldn't remember a time when I felt so absolutely turned on by another man, and I had the feeling that it was reciprocal. That feeling, of course, being his turgid tool in my grip.

Several minutes later, we were both naked and rolling about on the floor. Not being the kind to kiss and tell (well, not more than I already have, sorry) let me just say that the next hour was, how shall I put it, *memorable*. Sometimes I wish we hadn't done it right there and then, because for years I measured all my other sexual experiences against that evening. Very few of them even compare. Well, at least it's one more thing to blame for my utter lack of any meaningful relationships. God forbid it should ever be solely my fault. To be fair, on my own behalf, I have managed to maintain a great deal of long lasting friendships. Allen, alas, was not to be one of them, as you shall soon see. But for now, let's just bask in the glory of that evening... *aaah*... okay, enough of that.

When we were finished, we cleaned up, got dressed, and went out to dinner. I was ravenous by then, as was Allen, but we managed to learn a lot about each other in between wolfing down our dinners and gulping down our cocktails. He seemed, by all accounts, to be a remarkable man, putting himself through law school, graduating near the top of his class, and then giving free legal advice to several gay organizations, all while working fulltime for a law firm. I was completely smitten with him by the end of the evening and was thrilled when he invited me back to his place to spend the night.

When we got back to his apartment, we had a fabulous repeat performance of our earlier antics and drifted off to sleep in a comfortable embrace. In the morning, he drove me home, waited for me to change, and then drove me to the shop and dropped me off. I was smiling from ear to ear as I walked in. It had, spine-tinglingly enough, been a perfect first date.

"You got yourself some last night, didn't you?" That was how Sharon greeted me.

"Jeez, how in the world could you know that?" I asked and went to fix myself some coffee.

"Oh, just call it female intuition. Let's see, exhibit A, you're smiling way too much for this hour of the morning. Normally, you're in your own little foggy world until that first cup of java kicks in, and, even then, you're not usually perky until at least eleven. Exhibit B, I noticed that you were dropped off this morning in a nice, shiny Cadillac. Not your normal mode of transportation. And then there's exhibit C."

"Which is?" I was almost afraid to ask.

She walked over behind the counter, bent down, and came back up with one of the rags that we used to wipe the tables down with. "Exhibit C," she proudly waved over her head. "These have that decidedly Clorox-like aroma that can only mean one thing."

"Other than Clorox, you mean." I played along. I mean, I'd been found out, so why bother denying it?

"Exactly. At first I thought it was probably just little old you releasing some steam. But then," and she bent down again and came back up with a second rag, "I figured you alone wouldn't need two towels. Sorry, but even Sparkle isn't that virile. So let me guess, it was that cute lawyer guy, right?"

"Uh huh." I nodded and grinned. "And it was fab-u-lous."

"I can see that," she said and waved the towels one last time before putting them back. "Good to know we can use this place for other things than reading. Maybe we should start selling lube and condoms." I thought about that for a second, but I doubted that Slim would go for it. Instead, I decided to keep some spares around after that, though. Just in case.

Sparkle jogged in a few minutes later, walked straight up to me, looked me deep in the eyes, turned me once around for good measure, and then proclaimed, "Miss Thing, you got yourself some man-pussy last night."

"What? How in the world did you know that? I know it's not an every day occurrence (or any day), but I seriously doubt they were broadcasting it on the news this morning."

"No, Honey, get real. I called up this morning to see if you were in yet, and Sharon told me." I looked over at Sharon, but she was making herself look busy in order to avoid my *what a big mouth you have* stare. "Anyway, spill it, Sis. Is it true what they say about Jewish men?"

"And what do they say about Jewish men?" I asked, without a clue as to what they said.

"You know, big noses, big…"

"Oh, who says that?"

From behind the register came, "People who aren't Jewish, I would imagine." I'd hoped we wouldn't wear off on Sharon, but I was quickly learning that it should've been the other way around.

"Well," I spoke up, "let me lay your immature inquisitiveness to rest." They both stopped to listen to what I had to say on the subject. Pitiful, actually, how low people can sink. "None of your damn business." (Okay, I'll tell you, though. It was huge! That must be what they mean when they say *God's chosen people.*)

"Fine," Sparkle relented and went back to fixing himself some coffee, "be that way. Next Friday, I'll just have to hang out in front of the temple and find out for myself. Anyway, I did come here with a purpose, other than to be read."

"I love that your life has purpose all of a sudden, Sparkle. Mine is so much more vibrant now that I can start my day with a cup of coffee and some words of wisdom from yours truly," I said, with a flourish, and bowed to her highness.

"Asshole. I'll just leave if you insist on treating me this way."

No way would he ever leave before blabbing whatever it was he came down there to tell me, but I acquiesced just the same. "So sorry, my love, what is it that you came all the way down here to share with me?" I asked and sat down across from him. I sipped my coffee and batted my eyelashes for good measure.

"Well, it's only the name of our fabulous new duo." He looked up from his coffee, a beautiful grin spreading across his already too stunning face. Truly, I needed some less attractive friends. It was like being with George Hamilton. Perfect hair, perfect tan, perfect teeth. Of course, Sparkle is significantly less macho than George, but you get the picture.

"And what, pray tell, would that be?" I leaned in and set my coffee down. I mean, it's not every day that you're given a drag name, and I was, despite myself, rather agog with excitement. (Nifty little word, *agog*. One rarely gets to use it. *Aplomb,* too. Great word, but almost never seen. Shame really.)

As if a spotlight had suddenly hit him in the face, Sparkle stood up, raised his right hand out in an oratory gesture, and bellowed, "Ladies and Gentleman... please welcome to the stage... with a thunderous round of applause... the ladies... Miss Trinidad aaaaand Tobago!"

Sharon and I jumped up and applauded and cheered.

"I love it!" I shouted.

"Me too!" Sparkle rejoiced.

"Me three!" joined Sharon, and it was unanimous. In the traditional of Abbott and Costello, Kukla and Fran (I never liked Ollie), and Sodom and Gomorrah, a great team was born. I felt like Marilyn with her first prescription bottle: like I was floating on air.

"To stardom!"

***

Stardom, however, did not come without a price: *Hell,* thy name is stiletto. See, for three solid weeks, I breathed, ate, walked, and talked drag, and I did it from atop an ungodly high pair of red high-heels. I have no idea what Eartha Kitt was singing about, but you can keep your cha-cha heels far away from me, thank you kindly. How women spend their entire day perched on these torture devices I have no idea. Better yet, why? Honestly, everything below my thighs was in severe pain, but, thankfully, by the night of that fateful show, I was walking like a pro. Granted, it was more like a pro football player, but I did have a certain charm, something akin to poise, about my stride. Truth be told, I was actually proud of myself.

Of course, Sparkle took to it like a duck to water. He was working the runway within a week. (Just between you and me, I seriously doubt that that was Sparkle's first time in heels, but I humored his initial awkwardness.) It was Sharon, though, who was truly our savior. She instantly became our *Drag Master,* as she liked to call herself. We both figured that, since Sparkle was becoming our regular first customer of the day (though he never paid for anything), he might as well help us out with the morning rush. This he did every morning for three weeks, always in heels. Sharon gave us our first lessons, and, within a couple of days, we were up and running. (Hobbling, to be precise.) The customers didn't know what to make of it, but this is San Francisco, after all, so live and let live they probably figured.

I, never being the overtly showman-like type, kept my heels on behind the counter, but shucked them when I worked the floor. (At least for the first week; then you couldn't get me out of the damn things.) Sparkle couldn't care less either way. Actually, I think he rather liked it. They made his calves look amazing, as many of the female and a few of the male customers expressed. Sharon even took to wearing her heels so that we could all be about the same height. And when there was a lull, she would start belting out some show tune, and the three of us would make up a routine. It was great practice, but even greater fun.

Allen was not having such a good time of it, however. The two of us saw each other periodically over those few weeks and we began to feel comfortable around each other fairly quickly. It was, well, *nice*. At least for the most part. There were, however, some bad times, some unfortunate bumps in the road. Allen, almost immediately, regretted volunteering for the show, you see. He couldn't work the heels and walk and talk at the same time. At first, he'd practice with us after work, but once we started getting good at it and he was still rocky, he quit and only practiced in private. He wouldn't even tell me his drag name or anything about his routine, saying that he wanted it to be a surprise. Heck, whatever floated his boat, I figured, and let it be. Besides, we had our own numbers to worry about.

In any case, overall, we had a nice time together. He was good company. And it'd been forever since I had any adult friends or had an intellectual conversation. Sparkle was more of a chit-chatter and gossiper, certainly not a world class conversationalist, mind you. And the sex, well, that was spot-on. As quiet and reserved as Allen was when he was dressed, he was the complete opposite when naked. We sucked and fucked the hell out of each other for three glorious weeks, let me tell you.

That all being said, Allen worked long hours and we only got to see each other a few times a week, at most. So, in my spare time, I practiced being Tobago, or Toby, as Sparkle called me. I called him Trinny. (Trinny the tranny. It has a certain ring to it, yes?)

"Hey, Trinny, coffee at table six and hustle it," I would shout at him from behind the cash register.

"Eat shit, Toby," he would shout back, with a snicker and sneer.

Well, after about a week of the heels training, Sharon started bringing wigs in for us to try on. Why she seemed to have an endless supply of wigs I had no idea and was afraid to ask. But she had every color and style, and the three of us had a blast wearing them around the store. Pretty soon, we had a whole new bunch of regulars in the mornings and all where there to see what the three crazy people would have on next. Sparkle looked best in the Roaring Twenties pageboy, Sharon in the seventies Cher, and yours truly in the Kate Pierson/Cindy Wilson beehive. Every time I had it on, I had this strange desire to shake my ass and make strange noises. (Dance this mess around, 'round, 'round.)

Drag was fast becoming our lives, in fact. So much so that I feared that once this whole thing was over, we would need some twelve-step program to get us back into sneakers. Anyway, no sooner had we mastered the pumps and the wigs, and Sharon had a whole array of smart party frocks and long glamorous dresses for us to wear as we sold books and served coffee. (Strange, but tips were up fifty percent.) Sparkle, naturally, wore no underwear beneath his gowns, insisting on no panty-line, but I was modest in my BVDs. And Sharon, she had the best time of all, and started wearing the shortest of the short skirts, along with a jet black Cleopatra wig and six inch black stilettos. Lesbians were arriving in droves. (Actually, I think a group of dykes is called a gaggle, but I'll have to check on that and get back to you.)

Then the pièce de résistance, and for that we needed Kiki. It was obvious what we were lacking once we had the heels, the clothes, and the wigs: makeup. No surprise, Kiki was an expert painter of faces, and, once he saw the condition of our wigs, *they* were jacked up to heaven. Hell, my modest beehive became an insurmountable termite's nest.

He started slow and did Sharon's makeover first. When she came out of the office newly coifed and shellacked with makeup, I almost didn't recognize her. *Va-va-va-voom*. She went from nerdy geek to slutty chic, and obviously loved the transformation.

Next came Sparkle. Honestly, words can't describe the outcome, but I'll do my best. Nearly an hour after they went into my office, Kiki emerged and triumphantly announced with aplomb (hey, I worked that one in after all), "Ladies and gentleman... may I introduce you to the lady... Miss... Trinidad." Everyone in the shop came back to see the spectacle.

At first, all we were privy to was a single foot, encased in a stunning, two-inch-heel, white leather pump. Sparkle must've bought them himself, because I know that Sharon couldn't possibly have afforded shoes like that with what I paid her. The foot was then replaced by a whole leg, and that's when we got a glimpse of the dress. Honestly, I'd never seen so many white sequins before. Bob Mackie, eat your heart out. Next, he lifted the dress to show us his shapely leg and stylish pantyhose. Several whistles and cheers went up from behind me. That caused a white gloved arm to pop out from behind the door, which was quickly followed by an entire Trinidad, mouth wide in a smile, eyes twinkling like the midnight sky.

There was complete silence as she stood there. See, as handsome as Sparkle was as a man, he was equally as striking as a woman. I was transfixed as I stared at him, as was, apparently, everyone else in the shop. Then, one by one, all the people watching started to applaud, until there was a din of hands clapping and voices shouting. And Sparkle, as calm as he could be, crossed his legs at the knee, gently lifted his gown slightly off the ground, and, with absolute ladylike grace, curtsied. Then he motioned with his hands to Kiki, who also curtsied. I had a whole new respect for Kiki after that moment, because, seriously, he'd created a masterpiece. I couldn't even begin to imagine what I would turn out looking like.

Alas, there was no hidden beauty lurking behind the façade of poor Bruce. Try as he might, Kiki just couldn't work his magic on me. Luckily, my wig was so large and overpowering that it completely took attention away from my face. For some reason, whatever Kiki tried, I would always end up looking like myself with makeup on. Nothing more, nothing less. And, honestly, I think Kiki felt worse about his failure than I did. "Well," I tried to tell him, "two out of three ain't bad. At least Sharon and Sparkle look fabulous."

But it wasn't just the makeup that didn't work. My gown was lumpy and bunched in the most unappealing places, my fake breasts looked just that, and nothing I was wearing seemed to go together. And the more Kiki primped and prodded, the worse it got, until, finally, I had to tell him to just give it up. Crestfallen, he emerged from my office and blandly announced, "Ta-da… Tobago." I felt much like a rabbit being pulled out of a hat. Ass-first.

There was, sadly, no gradual unveiling for Toby. I just lumbered out and watched as, one by one, all the smiles on the faces of the spectators turned to frowns. They were expecting gorgeous and they got grotesque. Only Sharon and Sparkle remained smiling, and, strangely, that was enough.

"Honey," announced Sparkle, "I do declare, you've been reborn."

"Yes," I agreed, "but it turned out a stillbirth." Nervous laughter came from the crowd.

"No, no, you look positively radiant," he insisted.

"If you like that Carl Malden meets Imogene Coco look, then, yes, I'm sure I look stunning." Again, more laughter, followed by a couple of claps. "I mean, please," I began the routine, "look at me; my ass looks flatter than a pancake, my tits are all over the place… hey, get back there," I screamed down at one of them and pushed it back in place, "and my face, oh man, I wanted demure, I wanted wholesome, I said to Kiki, I said, 'Kiki, give me… Doris Day.' But Kiki, he must've heard Tammy Faye. Yikes, the last time I saw this much makeup on one face… well, I don't think there ever has been this much makeup on any one face. I'm sure glad they test this crap on bunnies and kittens, 'cause this, I think, would be a lethal overdose if it were the least bit unsafe. Ladies and gentleman, at this very moment, not one pore on my face is actually breathing," I announced and moved my hands around my face as if to offer it up for their inspection.

Laughter and applause broke out in the shop, followed by an overpowering surge of adrenaline suddenly rushing through me. That's when it dawned on me: *pretty* isn't what makes you a star; charisma makes you a star. And, judging from the reaction I was getting, I think I was well on my way. Sharon and Sparkle were patting me on my back and smiling from ear to ear. Even Kiki, who was truly devastated by his failure, was all smiles. And I, well I felt like Bette, Barbra, and Liza all rolled into one. I felt like, well, a diva!

Sparkle leaned in and whispered, "I think we found our respective fortés."

"Yep," I whispered back, "beauty and the borscht. I feel like Mel Brooks on estrogen."

Well, the show was over and the customers went back to their shopping, and Sharon went back to the register, and Sparkle and I went back to my office to catch our breaths. I was feeling so, well, *alive*. And as soon as the two of us were behind closed doors, we clasped hands and began jumping up and down and silently screamed, so as not to let the customers know that that wasn't the first time we'd been fabulous as a team. (By the way, jumping up and down in spiked heels is a very bad idea. Word from the wise.)

Then, in mid-jump, I saw it. I'd caught our reflection in the mirror and immediately stopped jumping and grabbed Sparkle and pulled us right up to that mirror and pointed.

"That's it, Sparkle, that's it!" I screamed, and this time not nearly so silently.

"What's it? Have you decided that you're going to do this fulltime? You know, *snip-snip*, look, Ma, you have a daughter. 'Cause I'm here to say, Precious, you would not make a pretty woman. Even as a drag queen, you're on the bottom of the totem pole. Maybe even the part that's buried in the ground. Uh, *woof.*"

"Okay, okay, I get it. I wasn't born to have the face that launched a thousand ships. Enough." I stopped him from continuing.

"Honey," he continued anyway, "you couldn't launch a raft in a flood with that kisser. No offense."

"Fucker!"

"Sweet talker!"

"Okay," I ended it, "anyway, that's not what I meant. What I meant," and I grabbed Sparkle's face and pointed at it in the mirror and then looked into it myself, "what I meant is, that's my dream."

"*The* dream?" he asked, now stunned.

"*The* dream," I confirmed. "This is exactly what the two of us look like when I see us in that dream of mine. Now I get it. Now I totally get it. It makes complete sense now. I don't want to be a woman. I don't, *yuck*, want to be with a woman. I want to be… I'm going to be… a…"

"A drag queen," Sparkle said, interrupting my epiphany.

"A star!" I corrected.

"Whatever, Mary. But I will say this for ya, you got guts going out there looking like that." And the two of us left my office and went back to finish the afternoon rush. I felt a change coming on, friend. A mighty big change.

***

Over the next few days, Sparkle and I practiced being Trinny and Toby as our audience grew and grew. Word had apparently gotten out about the two wacky drag queens at the bookstore, and we became standing-room-only. Kiki came by before he went to work each day to make our faces and Sharon brought us new outfits and wigs. And though they dug their claws into each other as often as possible, secretly, I think Sparkle and Kiki were starting to appreciate each other. Their digs got less and less caustic and more, well, sort of chummy.

I for one was glad for it, too. It was hard having my friends on separate teams, and if it took a fake ass and falsies to bring us all together, then so be it. Which brings up something I'm sure you've been waiting patiently for: another gay rule. So here goes, Gay Rule #8: your friends are your family. It's a short one, and it carries a lot of baggage, but the quicker you find it out, the better off you'll be. And, even though I'm not sure if I picked this family or if it picked me, I knew for certain that I was glad to be a part of it, sick and twisted as they all were, because, at the end of the day, they were all mine.

Of course, as we got closer to the big event, we also got closer to the trial. Sparkle didn't say as much, but I knew he was nervous about it. Still, I had faith in my Allen. As it turned out, though, we had very little to worry about. The whole thing lasted about ten minutes. With no one pressing charges and it being Sparkle's first offense, the judge told him to behave himself in the future, fined him five hundred dollars, and gave him sixty hours of community service. Sparkle whispered into Allen's ear to ask the judge if the drag show could be considered community service. That, of course, was a big no.

Allen, anyway, already had something lined up for Sparkle, and it wasn't what I had imagined. Sparkle, in fact, was even more against it, until Allen told him the alternatives. See, for the next six weeks, Sparkle was to be, and this is only funny in retrospect, a big brother to a troubled gay teen. The alternatives? Feeding the homeless, picking up garbage on the side of the road, meals on wheels, and a whole array of depressing and/or messy alternatives. Sparkle balked, but in the end agreed to Allen's choice.

Honestly, I hoped that this kid was emotionally stable enough, because I couldn't imagine what good Sparkle could do for him short of teaching him how to accessorize or mix a good martini. Granted, these are two very important abilities, but not ones a troubled teen desperately needs.

Luckily, and I use the term quite loosely here, Sparkle's ward would not need mentoring for another two weeks, as he was still in a youth detention ward upstate. So, at least for the next week, Sparkle could concentrate on our act. Allen whispered to me that he thought that a little responsibility might be good for Sparkle. I had my doubts, as it never seemed to help in the past, but I nodded my head in agreement anyway. It seemed a hell of a lot better than standing on the side of the road in an orange jumpsuit picking up trash. (Sparkle is a spring, not an autumn, and orange just washes him out.)

After the trial, or whatever it was that we'd just experienced, Allen dropped us off at the store and went back to his office. Sharon was waiting for us with two cold gin and tonics and two brand new wigs. Just what the doctor ordered! Once safely ensconced in someone else's hair, we felt one hundred percent better. So we cranked up the tape deck and lip-synched our way through two Tori Amos songs, one

Kate Bush, and a few Barbra Streisand's for good measure. With each song, the crowd got more lively and dense, and by closing time we were chock-full and had completely forgotten about the day's bad start.

Kiki came by once he finished for the day, and the three of us closed Classics II with a rousing rendition of The B-52's *Wig*. Kiki did the Fred Schneider parts and Sparkle and I did Kate and Cindy. Each time he screamed, "What's that on your head?", we would throw a wig into the audience. By the end of the song, everyone was wearing one. It was a glorious sight to behold. Wigs, as it turns out, are the great equalizer. (Who knew?) Someday, we intend on taking a big truck-full of wigs to the U.N. in New York, where we plan on convincing all those dignitaries to put one on. We're sure that world peace will be realized shortly thereafter. (Hey, they laughed at Washington, Jefferson, and Franklin a couple of hundred years ago, and they all wore wigs, didn't they?)

***

And then, before we realized it, the three weeks had gone by and we were at The Stud getting ready for our premiere. I had the strangest feeling of absolute joy and excitement mixed with abject terror. Sparkle, though I had no idea how, was as calm as he could be.

"Sweetie," I stormed over to him as he sat before the tiniest of tiniest makeup mirrors, and asked, "how in the world are you so relaxed?"

"Secret?" he said.

"Yes, Sparkle," I responded.

"How long have you known me?"

"Jeez, it seems like eons, but I guess it's somewhere around three years now. Why?" (I know, I know. By now, you'd think I'd have known better. But in my own defense, I was wearing a *blonde* wig.)

"Secret?" he said again.

"Yes, Sparkle," I answered again.

"What are these?" he asked and pointed down at the table to a lump of pills that I had somehow overlooked.

"Oh, damn it all to hell, why did you let me get all flustered when you had those the whole fucking time?" I demanded and grabbed one of each.

"For pure entertainment value, Secret. Besides, we have a full forty-five minutes to go until the show, which gives you plenty of time

128

to get relaxed. Hey, how many of those things did you take?" he asked, counting what was left of the pills he'd set down. "Forget relaxed, catatonic is more like it. You better tell me now what it should say on your gravestone."

"Mom and dad, I'm gay. How's that?" I replied and pushed him out of the way so that I could get my turn at the mirror. Kiki and Larry were dressing at home, and so Sparkle and I were on our own until Sharon could make it to put on the finishing touches.

"Well, that's one way to avoid the issue," Sparkle commented and started in on his makeup using a hand-held mirror.

"Really, are there more ways to do it. Because, if there are, could you please write them down?" I guess I was mostly joking, even though I knew I had to tell them sometime. Lately, it had been really nagging at me. Of course, *lately* I was dressing up as a woman, so maybe my judgment was just a tad impaired. I mean, between the too tight shoes and the two-pound wigs, I probably wasn't getting enough oxygen to my brain in order to make a sound decision anyway.

Just then, Sharon arrived with Allen, Kiki, Larry, and a terrified looking stranger in tow. All four men looked liked they would rather be anyplace but there, and I figured that the unknown gentleman was the last of our drag troupe. They were already in their outfits for the night, so all Kiki had to do was start in on their makeup, while Sharon finished off Sparkle and myself. Ten minutes later, we were six overly dressed, overly buxom, overly everything wo-men.

With only a few minutes to go until our curtain call, Kiki handed us some note cards and wished us luck. Of course, we had practiced our songs, but neglected our introductions. Oh well, the drugs had kicked in by then and I no longer cared. Sparkle said we'd just wing it, which was fine by me. Besides, what could go wrong? (Stop snickering up there.)

Before we could even look at the cards or wish each other luck or escape for our lives, we heard music coming from the other side of the door, which was Kiki's cue to go out and introduce us. Kiki, who for the remainder of the evening was (are you ready for this?) Miss Eta Bug, looked at us apprehensively and lurched forward through the stage door.

Immediately, we heard a loud cheer go up from behind said door. And when I say loud, I mean nearly deafening. Loud enough to slice right through all those lovely pills I'd taken. Even Sparkle, who, without pharmaceutical intervention, was naturally unperplexable, looked panicky and made a quick grab for my hand. We both squeezed for dear life.

And then we heard it…

"Ladies and gentlemen and all forms in between… please welcome to the stage… the lovely, the glamorous, your hosts for this evening… Miss Trinidad aaaand Tobago." If my heart hadn't stopped it had at least skipped a few beats. Kiki rushed back to us and handed us each a microphone and promptly collapsed at Larry's feet. Drama with a capital D.

Sparkle went out first, and his hand in mine was replaced by Allen's. In all the excitement, I had fairly ignored my paramour. It didn't help that my hot lawyer-man was now a towering mess of drag. Secretly, I was glad that I wasn't the only one who didn't make a pretty woman. Allen was, let's see how to put it… *arf, arf, arf*. Plus, he was sweating profusely beneath his makeup and wig as I gave him an air kiss and wished him well. He did the same before we both peered out the door.

From my viewpoint in the wings, all I could see was the stage and Sparkle. And though I couldn't see the audience, I could most certainly hear them. The din was ear splitting. The crowd was screaming and banging their feet on the floor and their hands on the bar and walls. Sparkle, remarkably, was retaining his composure. Actually, he appeared to be reveling in the ovation. That, thank goodness, had a calming effect on me. I knew that he would be there for me (the drugs helped, though) and so I stood and waited in anticipation for my introduction.

That took awhile, as the crowd was slow in quieting down. Sparkle, for his part, was giving them a show. A little leg here, a little shoulder there, and a hair flip every few seconds, and the audience would be whipped up all over again. I had to admit it, he looked amazing. You know the outfit that Marilyn had on when she was singing happy birthday to JFK? Well, that was close to it, only tighter and sluttier. And, as always, no underwear. Sparkle may have been happy dressed as a woman, but he wanted no mistakes that he was all man underneath. I'm sure the people up front were getting quite a deluxe view. (See, when they say ring-side seats, I doubt they mean cock ring.)

After several minutes, Sparkle finally made the *okay, quite down now* motion with his hands, and the audience reluctantly obeyed. Then it was show time.

"My, my, my, aren't you a stellar crowd?" he began, and the audience went back to their hootin' and hollerin'. "Well, ladies and gentlemen, as you well know, we're here tonight to help send our boys off to Seattle. And I for one am always willing to do my part in helping out anything that involves playing with large, hard sticks and round, tight balls." Sparkle licked his lips and grabbed his crotch for effect. Naturally, it worked, as the shouts and clapping erupted forth again. "Of course, as you all know, Trinidad never works alone, so let's hear it for my partner in crime and your co-host for the evening... the lovely... the talented... the ripped up to her britches... Miss Tobago... (Not yet.)... Miss Tobago... (Still not yet.)... (Pause.)... Toby, get your fat ass out here!" (That was it.)

"Yeah, yeah, yeah, I hear you," I rasped into the microphone and then slowly made my way on stage. Again, my ears were greeted to an uproarious shout. It was like nothing I'd ever heard before and I was instantly covered in goosepimples from head to throbbing toe. It was like an orgasm without the sticky, gooey mess. Naturally, I loved it, and my fear quickly gave way to elation. Then I put my hands over my eyes like a visor and scanned the crowd.

I'd been to The Stud on numerous occasions, but had never seen it anywhere near as packed as it was that night. Virtually all of our regular customers were there, as was just about every person I'd ever seen Sparkle talk to before. He'd obviously been a very busy beaver (pun intended) over the prior several weeks. But now it was my turn to shine.

"Excuse me, excuse me," I announced into the microphone. "Could everyone please settle down for a moment? Thank you." I waited for absolute silence and crossed my arms over my ample-bosom and tapped my foot so they'd know that I was serious. "Now... that's better. You, you over there," I was pointing over at the adorable bartender closest to the stage. "Double gin and tonics, and keep them coming. And speaking of coming... (I made a lascivious gesture to the bartender, who promptly turned red and fixed us our drinks.) Sparkle and I waited patiently for them to be delivered.

"Oh, yes, yes... much better, Toby," said Sparkle, downing his entire drink in one fell swoop. The audience loved it. And, never one to be upstaged (granted, it was my first time on stage, so I needed to set a precedent), I also downed my entire drink and then reached into the audience and downed someone else's. (Yuck, bourbon.)

131

"Ah," I ahed and wiped my mouth with my sequined sleeve. "Yes, lovely. Now, where were we? Oh yes, Bartender..."

"No, Toby," Sparkle interrupted, "we've done that already. Tell them about the show. Remember the show?"

"Trinny, my love, of course I remember *la show*. I was just going to thank the bartender. Now, let's see." I began running my hands around my dress like I was looking for some pockets. "Oh, pooh, I haven't any money on me to tip... to tip... what's your name, Sweetie?"

"Chester," yelled out the barkeep.

"Ah, Chester. Yes. How quaint. Well, Chester, it appears I have no money stashed away in my lovely gown to tip you with." I kept searching around my dress until my hand landed on my crotch. "Oh my. Say, Chester, I believe I've found something to tip you with after all."

"Leave the poor boy be, Toby. Besides, that's clearly not even close to the twenty percent gratuity he so richly deserves."

"Wicked bitch!" I hissed at my partner as I shot her a sly wink. "Well, anyway, Mister Chester, I'll leave you my number in case you should want to retrieve your tip at a later time." I shifted my crotch around, again for the enjoyment of my audience. Mostly. "Well, enough of that," I said and flattened out my gown and poofed up my hair. "Now, on to the business at hand... (pause)... um, er, why was it we're here again, Trinny?" I scratched my head and tilted my wig out of sorts.

"The softball league in...," he tried to tell me.

"Oh, yeah, right. What's that about anyhow? A bunch of old sissies sweating, spitting, and running around looking silly is not my idea of fun."

"Toby, Honey, I've been to Blow Buddies with you; what's the difference?"

"Trinny, Darling, you've got a point. So let's raise some beaucoup cash for this bunch and get them the hell out of here. Whatta ya say to that, you fabulous people out there?" I shouted at them, giving them all an air hug. They apparently were thrilled and let us know it.

"Good to hear it," shouted Sparkle. "Now, on to our first entertaintress. Let's see here," he said and looked down at the notes that Kiki had given us. "Oh, yes, our first performer and personal stylist to your co-hosts is none other than the delicious... the scrumptious... the one and only... Miss... Eta Bug. Let's hear it for her ladies and gentleman!"

Kiki came running out, gave me a quick squeeze, and promptly yanked the microphone out of my hand. That was our clue to exit the stage. By that point, I was only too happy to stay, but it looked like Kiki wanted his shot at stardom, so Sparkle and I reluctantly went backstage. Sharon was there to greet us with a hug and another drink. (With all the free booze we were getting, it's a wonder we didn't turn professional.)

"You were both fabulous!" she whisper-screamed at us so as not to be heard out front. Though, judging from the sound of the music, I didn't think she had anything to worry about. Then we had about two and a half minutes to relax before Kiki was through with his act. He had performed it for us about a week earlier and, truth be told, it was unreal.

Dressed in complete Bjork garb and looking as close to Icelandic as he could possibly get, he lip-synched to the Sugarcubes' *Sick for Toys*. With a little imagination, I think you can imagine the prop potential there. Yes, dildos, butt-plugs, and nipple clamps were soon flying all over the stage. And coming from the pixy-like Eta, it truly was a sight to behold. At one point, he was faux-humping a ten-inch black dildo while belting out the lyrics. Though I guess it's not really lip-synching if you're actually singing. Personally, I find it a lot easier to sing rather than to mouth the words. The music is usually loud enough so that nobody knows any better, unless they come up to tip me, and then I take it down a notch so as not to scare them away.

With barely enough time to catch our breaths, Kiki finished his routine to an enormous ovation. The look on his face said it all. I couldn't remember a time that I'd seen him look so ecstatic. Well, except for the time that Paul Lynde came into his shop for a haircut. (Kiki saved the hairs.) The look on Larry's face was even more charming, though. He looked like the proud papa at his daughter's first ballet recital.

With a quick hug and air kiss for Kiki, we all switched places again, and Sparkle and I were back in the spotlight. (Damn it, okay, I'll say it... where we belonged!) The audience welcomed us back with the same zeal as before, my adrenaline shooting off the chart.

"Wasn't she fabulous folks?" I asked the crowd and applauded at them so they'd get the hint. "Let's hear it for her ladies and gentleman... Miss Eta Bug!" And they did let her have it, until she came back out and gave them all a deep bow. I smacked her on the ass and shooed her offstage; there was, after all, only enough room on there for two divas. (Honestly, the thing was swatch-sized.)

"I say, I say, Trinny, wasn't she fabulous?" I sounded tipsier than I actually was, which was fairly close to outright drunk due to the pills and the booze combined. (I swear, those warning labels on the side of the bottles, the ones we read and then drive heavy equipment on the very next moment, well, they're pretty much right on target. When it says *No Alcohol*, that doesn't mean that it doesn't contain alcohol; it means don't drink alcohol while taking the medication. Got it?)

"Um, who was fabulous?" answered Sparkle, looking indifferent and bewildered.

"Why, Trinny, Eta, of course!"

"Eta? Who the f… oh, Eta… yes, fabulous," he was looking down at his nails as he said it.

"Trinny, Honey, what in the world is wrong with you? Hello… Earth to Trinny." I walked over and gave a knock on his overly-sprayed quaff. My hand bounced off the wig, leaving no impression that it had touched down even for an instant.

"Oh, Toby, I'm afraid that something is terribly, terribly wrong with me," he replied and kicked his heel up, looking just a little like a young Miss Shirley Temple. (Okay, you have to use your imagination a bit for that one, but, if you squinted and looked out of the corner of your eye, you might've seen it.)

I walked over to him again and put my shimmering arm around his neck and asked, "Trinny, what is it? You can tell me. I promise not to breathe a word of it to anyone." I made the tick-a-lock motion in front of my lips (and I threw away the key) and then I crossed my heart and hoped to dye… my hair back to its original color, whatever that might be.

"But…," he whispered and pointed to the audience, who by then was leaning in close to be able to hear her horrible secret. (That, or they were looking up Sparkle's dress. Probably a little bit of both.)

"Oh, they won't tell. Will you ladies and gentleman? (Shouts of *no* rang throughout the place.) See, Trinny? Now, tell Auntie Toby what's making you so blue, other than that tight-ass dress. Honestly, how do you breathe in that thing, anyhow?"

"Well… you see… uh," he whispered and, with his chin down, looked up at the audience, all sheepishly-like. That got them all cheering him on, of course, and he waited until they were at a fevered pitch, and in a deep baritone and as loud as he could, he blurted out, "I'm pregnant!"

"You're what?" I shouted and backed away from him.

"Pregnant," he repeated and feigned holding back the tears.

"Honey, pregnant? Honestly, I quite doubt it." I tried to explain to him how highly unlikely that was, but he was adamant.

"I'm showing all the signs. One, I feel bloated," he started with.

"Trinny, you've had at least six drinks tonight. I would say that's more gin-logged than bloated."

"Then, two," he tried, "I haven't had my *monthly friend* in, like, forever."

I gave him a doubtful expression and struck down number two with, "Sugar, unless you're thinking about that nasty yeast infection you keep getting, I seriously doubt that your *monthly friend* is the same one your mother used to get. More than likely, the penicillin is finely working."

"Okay, then how do you explain the water retention and swollen ankles?" he offered, still holding on to his contention.

"Trinny, hand me one of your ultra-glam heels, please," I asked of him, and he reluctantly offered me one. "Honey, these are a size ten, and you're clearly a twelve," I said and showed the audience the sticker on the underside. "It's a wonder only your ankles are swollen."

"Well, they only came in a ten, and look at them; they were made for this dress. I had to get them!" He stamped his other heel and grabbed the one in my hand back and slipped it on his stocking feet, looking completely annoyed at me by that time. "And the water retention, Miss Smarty-pants?"

"Easy," I told the audience and reached into my wig, pulled out a pin, and proceeded to pop the water balloon boobs in Sparkle's dress. Water poured out all over him, and the audience went mad with laughter. Sparkle, feigning rage, stormed off the stage and left me alone to introduce the next act.

"Ladies and gentleman," I began, "she's awfully pretty, but she's one french fry short of a Happy Meal sometimes. Anyway, moving on, let's bring to the stage that fabulous bella donna... you know her... you love her... Miss... Anita Cab." Cue for Larry to enter and for me to depart.

Larry, bless his heart, really went out on a limb for his routine, and in vintage Stevie Nicks attire, did his hell-best *Edge of Seventeen*.

With his diaphanous, multi-scarved dress and glorious long, curly blonde wig and bandana, he stormed onto the stage and pranced and lip-synched his heart out. Granted, he rarely had his lips going in synch with the song, but for pure effort and effect, he got a roaring reception from the audience. Kiki was crying in the wings, actually. I put my arm around him as he stood there blubbering, feigning back my own tears.

Turning to Sparkle, who was now changing out of his wet gown and into his new outfit, I gave him a wink and a thumbs up and then blew him a kiss. He returned the compliment by mooning me as he got into his dominatrix garb. With a short black wig, smudged black eyeliner, tight, black, rubber dress and six-inch spiked heels, he looked like he could inflict some major damage. The whole effect was topped off with an impressive bullwhip, which Sparkle had been practicing with for the last three weeks, much to the chagrin of his downstairs' neighbors.

Finishing up just in time, he came over and hugged Kiki from his free side, and the three of us stood there and watched Larry take his bows. Amazingly, he had a line of at least a dozen men waiting to offer him their tips. Could being a doctor be that rewarding? (I mean that spiritually, not monetarily, of course.)

I ran out on stage and dragged Larry off. He didn't go peacefully, but I reminded him and the audience that we had much more to go and that my big number was still coming up. (See, I knew my priorities.) Eventually, I pushed the zaftig faux-Stevie off and grunted into the microphone, "I think she *Anitas* a diet, ladies and gentleman, more than a cab." I downed my drink and winked at them. "Now, let's welcome back to the stage, the one and thank God only... Miss... Trinidad!" I shouted, and the audience drowned me out. The lights dimmed and I ran off the stage so as not to be in the way of Sparkle's cracking bullwhip, which let out a tremendous *pop* as it lashed out across the empty stage. When the lights came back up, the audience was greeted to the vision of Sparkle looking like he'd just stepped off the cover of *Heavy Metal* magazine. Appropriately, he was doing a knock out performance of Chrissie Hynde singing *Bad Boys Get Spanked*. The audience went into a frenzy as Sparkle cracked his whip over their heads. (Dangerous, but well worth the effect.)

I was riveted by the performance, and it wasn't until he was more than halfway through it that I noticed Allen standing beside me, also in a black dress and high heels and furiously looking out to the stage. I asked him what was wrong, but he just kept staring straight ahead and wouldn't say a thing. And that's how Sparkle saw us as he finished his routine and made his way off, followed by what would've been a standing ovation had the audience not been already standing.

Approaching us, he immediately sensed danger. "What's wrong?" he asked us both as he hesitantly drew near.

"You know what's wrong, you sick fuck!" Allen screamed at the very top of his lungs, nearly scaring the group of us half to death.

"No," Sparkle attempted, "I don't. Please be so kind as to fill me in." Sparkle always has this way of remaining perfectly calm in the presence of those who are not, which usually results in the other person getting even angrier. It worked like that then as well.

"That was *my song* you just did," he shouted. (Uh-the fuck-oh.)

"But, Allen," I tried, only to have Allen put his hand up to warn me to stay out of it. In his heels, Allen towered over me by a good six inches, so I reluctantly obeyed.

"I can't believe after everything I've done for you that you would have the audacity to completely steal my routine. Of course, I shouldn't be surprised; you never did strike me as the type who could come up with an original thought on his own. It's no wonder that even your best friend threatened to kill you." And here, all red in the face and trembling with rage, Allen pushed Sparkle's back up against the wall and screamed out this threat before he stormed off and out the back door of The Stud and out of my life forever: "If I wasn't a minister of the court and I didn't have the utmost respect for the law, I swear that I would kill you with my own hands right now!" (Yep, add him to the growing list of suspects, which still has a lot of growing to do, sad but true.) Needless to say, the group of us was left there, completely stunned by the outbreak.

Realizing that a full to two minutes had gone by and there was nobody on stage, Kiki ran out with the microphone, announced the next entertainer, and then ran backstage so as not to miss any more excitement. The poor stranger in our midst, who hadn't uttered so much as even a few words to us all evening, and for all intents and purposes seemed the most timid of men and least likely candidate for a drag queen, shot us all a look of terror, as he hadn't quite counted on going on stage just yet. Still, he rallied his courage and dashed out there just as his music started.

Honey, if it isn't true that the meek shall inherit the earth, it's at least partially true that they shall, for a brief moment in time, rule a tiny little drag stage south of Market Street. Our heretofore previously unknown friend, whose drag name was simply *Bitch*, came storming onto that stage to the music of Shannon's *Give Me Tonight* and proceeded to high kick, butt-wiggle, and split his way into Stud history. We all forgot the past few minutes and were at once stunned and awed by the Bitch's mastery of female impersonation. Larry, shouting over the din of the crowd and the music, informed us that Jack (that was his name) was the only male cheerleader for his college football team, as well as a Karaoke enthusiast. Well, let me tell you, one plus one equals *Yow!* because he was simply amazing out there.

Kiki leaned in to tell me how sorry he was for Allen's behavior and assured us that at least he and Larry knew it wasn't our fault. He also told me that Allen had frequent *fits* like that out on the softball field as well. (Thanks for warning me sooner, right?) I told him that he shouldn't worry about it and that the experience as a whole had been truly enlightening. Sparkle, hearing our friendly banter, leaned in and group-hugged us to let us know that there were no hard feelings on his part either. Larry joined our little love-fest, and we all stood there, shimmering away, and waited for Jack to finish. A happier group of drag queens there never was before or since.

Finishing up his number, Jack was given what was yet to be the evening's most sincere applause, with the four of us shouting and clapping the loudest. In tears and in shock, he bowed graciously and fairly stumbled backstage and into our waiting arms. Years and years later, as it turns out, only Jack continued (for any appreciable length of time) to remain a drag queen, and the name *Bitch* is now synonymous with numerous other drag queen titles that Jack has earned. Anybody that was there that night was witness to the birth of a legend. Of course, the evening wasn't over yet. Not by a long shot.

Needless to say, Sparkle and I still had our grand finale ahead of us. And, no, I never did go on solo that night; I was more than happy being a part of a duo. (At least, if we failed, I could always blame Sparkle.) And with the audience still reeling from the Bitch's routine, we made our way back onto the stage.

"Well," shouted Sparkle, "how do you like them apples?"

"I know, I know," I shouted back at him. "Last time you tried doing a split like that we found a ring, a prosthetic finger, and a spare set of car keys."

"Tramp!"

"Slut!"

"Okay then, ladies and gentlemen, enough about us, did you all enjoy yourselves this evening? (more hooting and hollering) Well, that's just dandy. I think we raised more than enough money to send those fine fellows up to Washington. And, more importantly, Trinny and I had lots of free booze! But you know what we need now? (shouts of *what?* from the audience) Some fine man-loving, that's what."

The crowd couldn't have agreed more, with quite a few of them offering up their assistance. (I always knew that love was blind, but I had no idea that it was deaf and dumb, too.) Sparkle, however, was shaking his head back and forth and was standing there with his arms crossed in front of him. "No, I don't think so," he stated as the cheering died down.

"Excuse me? Did one of the Bitch's high-kicks land on your head or something? Did you just say that you didn't want any man-loving? Ladies and gentlemen... *Hell* has just frozen over."

"You heard me; I'm just sick and tired of all those men out there using me for one night of pure, unadulterated passion and then never calling me again. I give and I give and I give..."

"Honey, if you gave anymore," I interrupted, "you'd be the crowned Pope of whores."

"Exactly my point. Enough is enough," he said as our music cued in.

"It's raining," he mouthed.

"It's pouring," I returned.

"My love life is boring me to tears." And we finished the evening with those two legendary divas, Barbra and Donna. The crowd, in full agreement with Sparkle's sentiment, sang along with us, and, just before the end, we were joined by our three cohorts. Round after round of applause was followed by bows and many thanks from all of us, and then, all too quickly, it was over and done with. Trinidad, Tobago, Eta, Anita, and Bitch once again turned back into Sparkle, Secret, Kiki, Larry, and Jack. But to this day, all five of us carry at least a little bit of our alter-egos wherever we go. Because you know what they say: once a diva, always a diva.

And amen to that.

CHAPTER SIX
AN ADDITION TO THE FAMILY

Well, that was exciting, huh? I bet you've never witnessed the birth of a legend before. Am I right? Too bad it wasn't yours truly. I mean, I'm sure I could've been a star. I had what it takes, after all: the looks, the talent... the, uh... the... oh, okay, maybe I didn't exactly have those things, but I did have one thing... *moxie*! Oh well, I guess sometimes looks and talent do count for something. Of course, even though we didn't become the grand divas that we expected we'd become, our lives did indeed change as a result of those few weeks.

I never did see Allen again. Fuck it, though. I say goodbye to bad rubbish. (I say goodbye, but I'm thinking, *come back rich lawyer-man, come back.*) But guess who I did start dating almost immediately after that glorious night? (Tick-tock... are you thinking?) It was Chester, the bartender!

Yup, right after the show, as the six of us were heading out of the bar, Chester came running up behind us and asked if we minded a tag-a-long to our little troupe. "Hell no," I answered for everyone. I mean, it's not every day that a tragic drag queen gets hit on by an adorable bartender. (You know, who am I kidding? I bet that happens all the time.) And, lucky for me, Sharon went right home and volunteered to open up the shop in the morning, so I could sleep in a little. Bless her heart.

And we weren't out of surprises just yet, either. Lo and behold, there outside The Stud, waiting for us with open doors, was a jet-black stretch limousine that Larry had hired for us as a *thank you for risking your reputations* present. Of course, I had none to uphold and Sparkle's reputation couldn't have gotten any lower on the rating scale, short of digging up Harvey Milk and shooting him all over again. (Sorry for the un-P.C. and downright gross analogy.)

"Well, Chester, it looks like there's room for you, after all," I said as we piled on in. I, for one, was way glad that we'd gotten out of our drag clothes before leaving the club. And thank goodness the inside of the limo was on the dim side, because I was certain that I still had traces of mascara around my eyes. And the glitter was murder to get off. That, however, as it turned out, was what our quirky friend, Chester, was after. You've heard of drama queens and opera queens, well, Chester was a new breed of queen: the drag queen queen. See, he loved drag queens. Well, lust really, but same difference.

And, apparently, my drag charms must have had their effect, because Chester was all over me like white on rice. (Oh yeah, there are rice queens, too.) Honestly, I didn't know whether to be delighted or insulted. After all, I'd never been chased after for the woman inside of me before. Then again, I'd never been chased after period, so live and let live, I figured, and I let Chester fawn.

"Where to folks?" came a voice from a well-hidden overhead sound system that we heard just after we all piled into the limo.

"Well, I don't know about you all," offered Sparkle, "but I could use a little bit-o-butch right about now. How about The Eagle?" The rest of us whole-heartedly agreed with the sentiment. Drag was great, but in small doses only. Underneath it all, we were still men. Mostly.

"Yippy, The Eagle," squealed Kiki. (Okay, maybe some of us were more men underneath than others.)

Sparkle gently rapped on the dividing window until our driver lowered it. "To The Eagle, my good man," he ordered, which caused the chauffeur to turn his head around in order to look back at our little posse.

"Yes, sir," the driver said, "with pleasure." Wow, the pleasure was definitely all ours, because staring back at us from beneath his blue cap was the blondest man I'd ever laid eyes on. And the only thing that was more striking than his nearly white locks were his dazzling blue eyes. In other words, Sparkle fairly sprang into action.

Leaning his arms on the open window, he poked his head into the driver's cabin (or whatever you call it) and asked, "And what would your name be, Mister Driver Man?"

"That would be Sven (I kid you not)," he said, then grinned and nearly blinded us with his pearly whites. I couldn't say for sure, but I think I heard Sparkle's pants tighten up right along with Sven's smile. Even Chester, who had been paying an inordinate amount of attention to yours truly, stopped to gawk at the vision that was now driving us around.

"Nice to meet you, Sven," Sparkle gushed and then introduced himself and, begrudgingly, the rest of us lowly folk.

I leaned into Larry and asked if he knew if our driver was gay or not. But before I could get an answer, Sven piped in with, "Um, you're whispering right beneath a microphone, and, sorry, it's on. And the answer, sir, is a resounding yes; this is a gay limousine service."

"Should've figured by the name on the door," I said. After all, it was the Pink Triangle Limo Service. So, like, duh.

San Francisco being the tiny city that it is, we were at The Eagle in just about five minutes. The parking gods must've been watching over us, too, because the limo fit in a space just out front. Eagerly, the six of us exited our carriage and headed for the entrance to the bar before we realized that Sven was still sitting inside.

"Dude," Sparkle said as he walked back over to the limo and tapped on the driver's side window, "aren't you coming in with us?"

"I'm not sure it's really appropriate, sir, as I'm just you're driver for the evening"

"If you're lucky," smirked Sparkle.

"Besides," continued Sven, "I'm not exactly dressed for The Eagle." He pointed to his outfit. See, like all The Eagle's worldwide, this one was primarily a denim/leather bar. And, no, Sven was in neither.

"Wait!" I shouted, "look above the door!"

"Well, well, there appears to be a uniform contest tonight," Sparkle said and pointed to the banner over the door. "First place is one hundred dollars and a door prize." He turned and grinned at our driver. "I think you're more than dressed appropriately, Sven. Now get your butt out of that limo and let's get inside the bar before my liver throws a hissy-fit."

"I do aim to please, sir," he said, with a grin, and promptly exited the limo. That's when we found out that not only was Sven gorgeous but also a good six foot-two and built like a brick shit-house.

"Um, Sven," Sparkle asked, "do you have anyone else in that suit or as that all you?"

Sven laughed as our happy sextet grew to a ravishing septet, the group of us entering the bar en masse. Needless to say, we immediately drew some attention to ourselves. I think, for the first time since I'd met Sparkle, that nearly none of the eyes were on him. And our dear new friend seemed oblivious to the hysteria that he was causing. Sparkle, however, was noticeably pissed off. Guiltily, I must admit, I felt just a twinge of delight at the switch. I, after all, had been going unnoticed for years. The pump, you see, was suddenly on the other foot.

The seven of us got our drinks of choice and headed on out to the patio. Indeed, Sven fit right in. There was every kind of outfit to be had out there that night. There was the ubiquitous motorcycle cop, the ever-present sailor man, every branch of the military, actually, and several combinations of leather, rubber, vinyl, Velcro, metal, and various other assorted materials to be found. No other chauffeurs were present, so Sven stood out like the sore Viking thumb that he was. If there had been anyone attired in feathers in the competition that night, they'd surely have been ruffled.

To be quite frank, though, I found the scene to be utterly ridiculous. I mean, really, can anybody truly look sexy in a pair of jodhpurs? I think not. Still, I was up for a good contest, and had only a few minutes to wait. We'd barely sat ourselves on one of the benches when an announcement came over the loud speakers that the competition would be starting in five minutes. (Of course, in a gay bar, that usually meant fifteen.)

"You have to enter this, Sven," I said to him. "You can't possibly lose."

"Well...," he tried to get out of it, but the six of us were all at once pushing, prodding, and cajoling him, until he simply couldn't refuse. Besides, first place was a hundred big ones and a shiny, new, three-pound butt-plug. See, truly, taste and elegance never go out of fashion. That's my motto. (Actually, my motto is: I'll take the thirty bucks and you can keep the latex corkage.)

Minutes later, the festivities were underway. One by one, tragically overweight, over-dressed, and decidedly under-sexy men paraded across the stage in one ridiculous outfit after the next. The smattering of applause was polite if not pitiful and we had little doubt that our Sven would be the victor. Sadly, that's when the real competition approached the stairs to the platform. Kiki noticed him first and nudged me to get my attention. "Yikers," I said, under my

143

breath, as our little group turned their heads in unison to behold the walking behemoth.

There was complete silence as he climbed the stairs and walked to center stage. I have no idea how tall he was or how much he weighed, but standing there before us, I can tell you that he was larger than large. Honestly, I'd never witnessed so much bulk on one single man before in my entire life. It was frightening. (Well, maybe a little arousing, but just a little.) The uniform was equally as impressive, too. Actually, it was silly as hell, but, on him, it was impressive. Yep, he truly made the most stunning Boy Scout you've ever seen.

Where he found the outfit, I have no idea. My guess is that he made it himself. I got a closer look at him just after the show and I seriously doubt that the Boy Scouts give out fisting badges. But who knows, maybe they do. Times have indeed changed, after all. Anyway, he filled the damn thing out fabulously. His bulging, veiny, tree-trunk legs fairly ripped at the seams of his tiny, tan trousers. And his chest could barely be contained in his equally tight, tan top. (Hey, maybe I should write for the J. Peterman catalogue.) Topping it all off was a spiffy neckerchief, odd-shaped chapeaux, and a whole collection of merit badges that seemed to have very little to do with building fires, mending sprained ankles, or surviving the wilderness. Unless you consider his badge for Most Improved Sling Bottom surviving the wilderness.

In any case, regardless of how silly he looked, the crowd loved him. They hooted and hollered and called out all sorts of interesting activities that they would like for him to do in order to earn more merit badges. In other words, our rag-tag little group had little hope for our poor driver, who, amazingly enough, had a curious grin on his stunningly Nordic face.

"If you want to back out of this," Sparkle suggested, "we would all understand. Wouldn't we?" he asked, looking at all of us in turn. We nodded in agreement that indeed we would. I mean, who would want to follow that act? Shockingly enough, though, Sven shook his head and made his way to the stairs and waited for the crowd to simmer down a bit. That took a while, with the Scout Daddy standing there the whole time, relishing the adulation. After what seemed like an eternity, however, he made his way off, and Sven took center stage.

Oohs and *ahs* could be heard throughout the patio, but there was no screaming, no cheering, no shouts of lurid profanities. Admittedly, I felt guilty for coaxing our poor driver up there. Then, very slowly, Sven took off his shirt to reveal his glorious chest and tummy. The shouting picked up to a low grumble. Shouts of *More!* went up, but Sven stood his ground and waited for the crowd to urge him on with more gusto. When he felt they were truly wanting more, he, again very slowly, removed his snazzy slacks, leaving him standing there in his shiny black shoes, black socks, and black jock strap. Now The Eagle was starting to buzz with some excitement. The previous contestant may have looked great fully clothed, but our contender was fast becoming fully naked, and he was looking considerably better with each passing second to the horny bunch of revelers that stood before him.

Scout Daddy, sensing he was about to lose his title (or the butt-plug), reacted swiftly and bounded back onto the stage. (Loped was more like it, but you could tell it took quite a lot of inertia to move his heavy legs.) Rapidly, he removed his shirt to reveal the ripped and bulging pecs and abs hidden beneath. Sven just stood there and grinned. I sensed he had something up the proverbial sleeve. Shouts for Sven were outnumbering his competitor two to one, and, so, within seconds, both men were standing before us in nothing but shoes, socks, and jocks. (Kudos for their creativity in finding one black jock and one tan jock to match their respective outfits.)

When the chanting grew to a roar and it was unclear who the victor was, Sven calmly turned his back to the audience, bent down, and removed his undies. With his hands in front of him, he stood there with his glorious rear in our faces while he waited. When shouts of *Turn around!* filled the patio, he slowly put his hands behind his back and gradually turned to face his audience. Clearly, it wasn't something up his sleeve that Sven had waiting to surprise us all with.

Like Thor with his mighty hammer, Sven stood there with a dick big enough and hard enough to crack the clouds open. The crowd, needless to say, went wild, until you couldn't hear anything but the din of cheering. Then, as it subsided a bit, he turned to the other man on stage with him and gave him the *your turn* gesture. Red in the face, Scout Daddy picked up his crumpled outfit and stormed (loped again) off the stage. With renewed vigor, the crowd went wild. Never had a hundred bucks and a butt-plug been so richly deserved.

And that, friend, leads us to Gay Rule #9. Which, however much we hate to admit it, and it isn't always necessarily true (keep telling yourselves), is: size *does* matter. It certainly did that night, anyway. And by the hungry look in Sparkle's eyes as Sven approached us with his reward, it mattered an awful lot. I mean, we didn't know whether or not to hug him or back up for fear of getting ram-rodded. What we decided on instead was that it was probably best to get him back to the limo and dressed before the revelers turned ugly (er) and started to pounce. It was getting awfully late, anyway, and we'd certainly had our fair share of excitement for one evening.

***

Well, of course, the excitement wasn't exactly over. At least not for Sparkle, myself, nor our newfound friends. Still, I'm sure you've been over stimulated enough without having to hear the recounting of all the juicy details of our night of pleasure. (Separately, not together, as interesting as that may sound.) Suffice it to say, from what Sparkle told me the next day, both of us had our hands (as well as other body parts) full that evening. I think you can use your own imagination for the rest of it, but I will draw you one picture to start off with. See, it wasn't Chester and Bruce that had sex so much as Chester and *Toby*. Get the picture? (Kind of freaky, right? But well worth it!)

More eventful than Sparkle getting fucked by Attila the Hunk or Toby getting some drag booty, however, was the addition to our little group the following week. As ordered by the court, Sparkle was sentenced to sixty hours of community service, and, through Allen, agreed to be a (cough) mentor to a needy gay teen. So, on a chilly, bright Sunday morning, the two of us drove his Corvette to a shelter for runaway teens located smack-dab in the middle of the seediest part of the Tenderloin district. We agreed (he forced me) that I should stay and watch the car while he went in to got his *little brother*. And, trust me, if you've never sat in a spiffy, red Corvette in the center of a slum before, you have no idea what you're missing. Meaning, I was grateful that the two of them were back in just a few minutes. Needless to say, if there was a choice between Sparkle's hubcaps and my life, I think you can guess which one I'd choose.

Coming out of the shelter, Sparkle was walking slowly on his new ward's right. Neither one said a word to the other, and I could tell that they were both extremely uncomfortable with the situation at hand. The walk across the street afforded me a good once over of the boy, though, and I can tell you that what I saw was more than a bit disconcerting.

However old the boy actually was, he looked much older. Certainly much older than most of the teenagers I'd grown up with. In fact, he looked like the teenagers you see on TV, the ones that are twenty-seven in real life, but are playing high-schoolers. He was lean, but in an unhealthy way, and not at all like your normal gangly teen. His clothes were baggy and looked like hand-me-downs from hand-me-downs. I guessed that, because I didn't think that anybody still wore acid-washed jeans and certainly no one his age could even remember the group Styx or would care to wear one of their t-shirts. As they got closer to the car, I could see, too, that he was, or at least had the potential to be, a real looker. With dark hair and piercing blue eyes, he easily could've been Sparkle's real life little brother. Odd, but true.

As he approached the car, and I motioned for him to jump in the tiny area behind me that could barely be considered a back seat, I smiled at him and said, "Domo arigato, Mister Roboto, domo." He gave me this strange look that all at once said a.) I have no idea what the fuck you're talking about and b.) maybe you should avoid conversation with me if you know what's good for you. Clearly, however, I didn't know what was good for me. "Um, your shirt," I said and pointed, "was from the Mister Roboto tour." Again he gave me that look.

Luckily, Sparkle saved me by interrupting what was certainly a lagging conversation. "Secret, this is Peter. Peter, this is Secret. Peter please excuse my friend, he's mildly retarded at times." I smiled and nodded, and Peter gave a barely discernable nod in return. If first impressions were a sign of anything, we were both in a mess of trouble.

"So, Peter," I tried again, "what would you like to do today?"

He paused for a second before answering. "I could use a drink".

"Oh, sure, we could stop and get a soda. Or perhaps you'd like a smoothie or something like that," I responded.

"No, a drink. You know, scotch, gin, vodka. A drink. I need a drink. Get it?"

I got it. "How old are you, Peter?" I asked, nervously.

"Sixteen. What's the difference?" he answered, smugly.

"Well, where I come from, sixteen-year-olds don't drink." God, I sounded like my mom, which rightly scared the hell out of me.

"And where are you from?" he asked, with a slight sneer on his face.

"Kansas."

"Well, Mister, where I come from, you drink. You drink, you get drunk, you get high, you get laid. You get whatever you can. Do they do that in Kansas?"

I shook my head. "Not that I ever saw, no."

"Thought not. So how 'bout it, Sporto? What say we go to the nearest queer bar and you guys buy me a gin and tonic." (Common ground, but not exactly what I'd been hoping for.) When I was sixteen, I was still reading Superman comic books and eating Twizzlers. Now *that* was fun for me. I certainly wasn't getting laid, and high was something you got on a Ferris wheel.

Again, Sparkle came to my rescue. "No queer bars, *Sporto*, and no drinks, drugs, or drama. Got it." Sparkle put his foot down and I for one was shocked. Drinks, drugs, and drama were Sparkle's idea of fun pretty much every waking hour. Now he was laying down the law, and it wasn't the side that he was normally on. I wondered if my mom and dad said one thing and did the exact opposite as well. Funny, I never thought of my parents as anything but what they were. Maybe I was wrong about them the whole time. Spooky, huh?

"We're going to get something to eat and then we can play the rest of the day by ear, okay?" Sparkle told us more than asked. I nodded an okay, while Peter just sat in the back and stared out at the passing scenery. I wished I could be back at the shop with Sharon instead of there in that car with them, but I knew Sparkle couldn't handle the outing by himself, least not without a drink, drugs, or drama. (Irony. Woohoo.)

The three of us decided on pizza and drove to The Castro. Peter became noticeably agitated when he realized where we were going.

"Problem with the pizza idea, Peter?" Sparkle asked, while he parked the car.

"Um, no, it's just... well... it's... (there was now a look of pain on his face)... see that person over there?" he asked, pointing far down the sidewalk.

"The dyke in the chaps, the drag queen leaning on the ATM, or the shirtless guy that should've known better?" I asked, squinting in the sun and trying to see who was upsetting him. (P.S., yes, The Castro is that tragic at times.)

"No, on the ground," he responded, with a total look of despair on his face. This time, when Sparkle and I looked up the street, we knew who he was talking about, because sitting on the sidewalk with a cup placed directly in front of him was a boy around Peter's age. He looked dazed as he sat there. I'd seen the same kid sitting there several times over the past couple of months and dropped a couple of quarters in his cup not two weeks prior.

"Should we seek Mexican in The Mission, Peter?" Sparkle asked as he sat back in his seat. Peter nodded a yes and balled himself up in the rear of the car. I also got back in and the three of us drove away.

"Friend of yours, Peter?" Sparkle yelled back. The top was down and it was the only way he could be heard above the wind.

"Used to be," we barely heard him answer.

"Not any more?" I asked, turning around to face him.

All of a sudden, Peter looked his age. He was small and scared and not nearly the adult he let on to be. "Not any more," he repeated and shook his head to confirm it. He continued, haltingly, with, "Not since the shelter. His name's Gus. Least that's what he calls himself. See that look on his face? (He was looking down at the back of my seat and you could tell he was playing something over in his head.) That's heroin."

Nervously, I asked, "And you used to do it with him?"

That snapped him out of it, "No, Sporto, only the stupid ones do that shit, or the ones that really have something they want to forget. Not me; I stuck with the speed, the pot, and the booze. (Jiminy, I felt so much better at hearing that. At least he didn't shoot up, right? Jeez.)

"But then you got yourself into the shelter, right? To get off the street?" I ventured.

"Not exactly. That was the State that decided that. I'd been busted a couple of times already and they said that either I clean up my act and go to the shelter or I go to some juvenile detention camp up in the north."

"So you chose the shelter?" Sparkle asked, pulling into a spot not far from where we were headed. "Judging from your friend up there, I'd say you made the right decision." Peter nodded that he thought so too and hopped out of the car. Sparkle and I quickly followed, and we were, thankfully, finally off to lunch.

"Are you glad you're in the shelter now, if you don't mind me asking?" I asked, before we reached the restaurant.

"Yup. Well, sort of. I mean, I miss my friends and I sort of miss the drugs sometimes, but I'd rather have the shower, the bed, and the food. I don't so much like being told what to do and where to go, though." Now he was sounding like a teenager. A fucked-up one, but still.

"And the State," asked Sparkle as he held the door open for the two of us, "they told you to go with the two of us, am I right?"

"Now you're getting it," Peter said, with a sly smirk.

"And I take it you're not exactly thrilled about it, right?" Sparkle also asked, bending down a little to look Peter in the eyes.

"No, not exactly," he answered, staring right back at him, defiantly.

"Well, kid, the State is making *me* be here as well, so order up, chow down, and make the fucking merry best of it, because you and me got us fifty eight and a half more hours of this happiness to go. Got it?" he said as calmly as he could, still looking straight at a now not so cocky Peter.

"Got it," came the reply, along with a nod, "if you're paying for it."

"Oh, I'm paying for it, all right. I'm paying out the fucking ass for it." I don't think Peter caught the innuendo. Instead, he eagerly ordered a super burrito. Sparkle and I ordered regular ones, as we were watching our figures. (In order to make sure other people watched them as well.) We ate mostly in silence due to the fact that Peter barely so much as took a breath between bites. I couldn't imagine what they were feeding him at the shelter, but I took it that the food was not what was keeping him there.

I, for one, was glad for the lack of conversation. See, this kid scared the shit out of me whenever he opened his mouth to speak. For one thing, I wasn't used to being around teenagers any more. And for another, I certainly wasn't used to being around semi-homeless wards of the State. Sparkle was basket case enough for me to handle without Junior Sparkle thrown into the picture. Thankfully, once we finished eating, we all agreed that perhaps lunch would be enough for one day; there would be plenty of time for bonding in the weeks ahead. And so we drove Peter back to the shelter, with Sparkle dropping me off at the shop a short while later. Gladly, I went back to work, knowing that I'd done my good deed for the day. Next time, I would let Sparkle go mono a mono with the kid. (Though homo a homo was more like it.)

***

Next time was three days later, in fact. I was closing up for the evening when Sparkle came in looking completely worn out. He lumbered in, took a seat, and put his head on the table.

"Let me guess," I guessed, "been doing the big brother thing again, right?"

"Uh huh," he mumbled, without lifting his head off the table.

"Wanna talk about it?" I tried as I locked the door and pulled down the shades.

"Nuh uh."

"Wanna drink?"

"Uh huh"

"How 'bout a Big Girlie Drink Drunk Night?" Now his head was off the table.

For those of you who don't know what a Big Girlie Drink Drunk Night is (And why would you? We made it up.), let me tell you, it's fun as hell for a few hours and you're guaranteed a nasty hangover in the morning. So why do we do it? Because it makes you appreciate the plain, old gin and tonics all that much more. Plus, you get to be a big girlie drunk. Makes sense to me. Anyway, Big Girlie Drink Drunk Nights help you to forget your troubles. At least for a few hours.

What you do is, you go from one bar to the next and you order a different girlie drink at each one. Girlie drinks (and again, no misogyny intended here) are drinks with cordials in them. You know, like Amaretto Sours, Melon Balls (with Midori), White Russians (Khalua and vodka together, yippy!), anything blue, or anything with Schnapps, etc., etc.

Then we occasionally make it interesting by alternating between full drinks and shots. Girlie shots only, though, in keeping with the spirit of things. Our favorites are Sex on the Beach, Slippery Nipples, B-52's, and, again, anything blue or anything with Schnapps in it. If you think you're man enough to play this game, let me give you a piece of advice: stay away from the Jaegermeister. And Goldschlager is a no-no except when it's in an Oatmeal Cookie. (The shot, not the actual cookie.) Now you see why the hangover is a necessary evil of this game. Anyway, if you try it and you like it, let me know. If you try it, puke, make a jackass of yourself, or destroy your liver, blame yourself. I mean, if you made it this far, I think you're an idiot if you follow our example on anything.

In any case, Sparkle quickly helped me close up, and we were firmly ensconced on a ledge at Moby Dick's within twenty minutes.

With frosty, green Grasshoppers in hand, we sat and talked about Sparkle's outing with Peter.

"It was horrible, Secret," he began. "I thought I had it bad growing up, but this kid has the sob story to end all sob stories. What he needs is a team of shrinks to help him, not one lousy big brother. Honestly, the poor guy is barely hanging on by a thread. That shelter is his last chance, with juvenile detention camp constantly looming over his head. It's amazing that he made it this far. Given the same circumstances, I'd probably be dead by now."

Okay, drink one down. Those damn Grasshoppers are just way too yummy. So off we went, and, within seconds, were at the video bar, The Midnight Sun. Why this bar is a perennial favorite is truly one of nature's great mysteries. I always leave with a stiff neck from looking up at the monitors. Anyway, they made a mean Brandy Alexander, so I wasn't complaining. Any more than usual.

Sparkle went on with the story. "So here's this fifteen year old kid. He's happy and well-adjusted. He's on all these junior varsity teams, he's on the honor roll, and he's in love. And, get this, the guy loves him back. At fifteen! So what does he go and do? He tells his parents the whole story, thinking that the meanest thing that they could do to him was to ground him or something. And I thought my life was the worst case scenario; like I said, this kid's got me beat, hands down."

Sorry, it was a decent enough drink and the glasses were awfully small, so, of course, we were off again. This time we landed our girlie asses at Daddy's. Not exactly cordial-central, but they did have the necessary ingredients, and we happily ordered and then drank our Bocce Balls. Which, by the way, are Amaretto and orange juice. Mmm, mmm, good.

The story went on, barely slowed by the booze consumption. "So they, like, totally freak. They start screaming at him and calling him faggot and queer and an abomination before the eyes of God. And they aren't even religious or anything. Typical, so fucking typical. In the face of ignorance, preach the Bible. And, by then, Peter is totally hysterical and in shock. His parents had never so much as raised their voices to him before and now they're treating him like he's a pariah. But, wait, here comes the best part. See, when they were through shouting, and Peter thought the nastiest had come, they tell him that they don't want him living under their roof with them anymore. They say that it will ruin their standing in the community. I mean, what the fuck is that supposed to mean? His mother's a housewife and his father's an accountant. I seriously doubt that either one was about to seek public office or anything. Anyway, what else could Peter do? He packed his duffel and left.

"Then it was out of the frying pan and into the fire. Thinking he could convince his boyfriend that they should run away together, he hightails it over to the guy's house. When he tells him what happened, *boom*, relationship over. Apparently, the other dude's parents were practicing Catholics and he wasn't about to take any chances. Sorry, teen lover, but bye-bye."

We did try to drink a little slower, but you know how it is. So out of Daddy's and into The Phoenix we did go. The Phoenix, at that time so long ago, was The Castro's version of a disco. I use the term lightly, by the way. Basically, they played horrible music and had a dance floor. The bar, the clientele, and the drinks were all awful. Funny how The Castro is this big gay Mecca and it's made up of a bunch of tragic bars and over-priced clothing stores. Gay ghetto indeed. (Though, of course, I wouldn't want to live nearby to anyplace else. After all, it's my gay ghetto.) Anyway, we ordered a shot of peach Schnapps in anticipation of getting the hell out of there fast.

Half of it downed, Sparkle continued with Peter's plight. Sadly, the girlie drinks had barely squelched his anger and sorrow. "So there he was: no family, no boyfriend, and, he figured, no school, as he knew that word would get out somehow about his condition at home. So what does he do? He hitches rides to San Francisco, the one place he knew, or at least heard, that it was okay to be gay. But what he quickly learns is that it's okay to be gay only if you have a job, if you have a home, if you have an education, and, mostly, if you have money.

"Having none of the above, he finds himself with other homeless teens in the same situation. Not exactly the best role models for an impressionable teenager, but at least he felt relatively safe with them. Of course, life on the street has its drawbacks. Aside from the fact that he rarely has a roof over his head or three square meals a day, he has to make ends meet by begging, stealing, and selling drugs. Somehow, he miraculously avoids tricking. He wanted to maintain some bit of his integrity, he told me. Amazing."

The story needed one more drink, so we ran out of The Phoenix and right on over to The Pendulum, where men went to meet other men of color. The Pendulum was livelier than the other bars we'd visited and significantly cruisier. Our final drink of the evening was a blue Hawaiian. Thank goodness gay bars carry the necessary ingredients for these girlie drinks, and, feeling quite tropical, Sparkle finished the tale. Just in time, too, because I was feeling quite tipsy by then.

"Anyway, for the past year, that's how he's lived. He tried calling home on several occasions and begged his parents to let him come back, but they hung up on him. Times get rough, he increases his drug trade. That, of course, increases his drug use. Which, in turn, makes him sloppy. In other words, he got caught. Twice. Each time he makes it back to the streets, however. This last time, he ends up at the shelter with a promise that if he gets caught again it's off to a juvenile detention camp. And that's a big no-no in his book. Then, to top it all off, the State decides that it's in his own best interest that he has a gay big brother. Namely moi."

"So much for wise thinking," I interjected.

"Exactly," he responded. "And fuck you very kindly."

"So what do you really think of our new young friend?" I asked.

Sparkle sighed and finished his drink with a hard gulp. "Well, hard to say, really. I mean, I was glad that he opened up to me and all. See, apparently, there are no young gay counselors at the shelter. And I did end the day with a huge respect for the kid's willpower and determination, but, still, I just don't know; I'm not exactly a role model, you know. I just hope that I can do some good for him, because I've never met anyone who could use a break more than Peter could. Anyway, the sixty hours should go by fast and then..."

"And then *what*?" I wondered, aloud. I mean, how do you leave a kid in that kind of situation?

"...then we have to wait and see what happens, I suppose. But I'll tell you one thing, the whole time I was with him today, I kept thinking, there but for the grace of God go I. I mean, really, if my parents weren't super wealthy, that probably would've been me out there. And that's some scary shit, Secret."

"Boo yeah. You on the streets wrecking havoc on the masses? Yikes," I readily agreed.

"Yikes is right. Anyway, let's just pray that Peter stays on the straight and narrow, for lack of a better expression, because I'm not visiting him in that youth prison. No sir. The shelter is depressing enough," Sparkle said, grabbing my hand. "Now let's get out of here; I officially declare Big Girlie Drink Drunk Night over and done with."

"Amen," I responded, staggering out of the bar and into the chilly San Francisco night air.

***

Over the next few weeks, Sparkle spent an increasing amount of time with Peter. It was refreshing to see him take responsibility for something or someone other than himself. And Peter, for his part, was opening up and calming down. I think it helped that the shelter enrolled him in school and set some much needed boundaries in his life. On the weekends, we took him on outings: museums, galleries, plays, Macy's. You know, *wholesome* gay activities. During the week, Peter would come by the shop after school, I'd help him with his homework, and he'd help out around the store to earn some much-needed spending money. All in all, though it was a work in progress, things were going quite nicely for our newly formed family.

On the personal front, Chester and I dated casually, but the whole *put the dress on and let me fuck you* thing got kinda old, kinda fast. Psychologically, I had no idea what was going on in the poor bloke's head, and I didn't really want to find out. Still, beggars couldn't be choosers, and he was awfully cute, so, well, cut me some slack, please. As for Sparkle, he had his hands full with Peter, and Sven had strange work hours, so they, too, dated here and there, but nothing serious. Of course, there were certain advantages to having a stretch limo at your beck and call. (Though what exactly is a beck?) Sharon, in the meanwhile, was raking it in all of a sudden. Lesbians were coming in droves (ooh, that sounds pretty) to the shop, now that the gay section was open. Meaning, Sharon had her dance card filled for weeks on end.

One night, several weeks after Peter entered our lives, and with only five hours remaining in Sparkle's community service, Sparkle, Sharon, and I all decided to go on our first triple date. I took Chester, Sparkle took Sven, and Hester, a practicing witch, accompanied Sharon. (Yes, San Francisco is truly unique in its abilities to draw all kinds to its shores.) We decided on Italian somewhere in North Beach. I forget exactly where we ate, but like all the Italian restaurants in that neighborhood, it was yummy, a bit pricey, and mega-straight. (On a side note, most of the waiters really are Italian and drop-dead-gorgeous, so you can see why we opted for it.)

Anyway, it was nice having the gang together somewhere outside the shop for a change. Plus, the evening started off with something out of the ordinary, besides being driven to the restaurant in Sven's limo. See, as the six of us sat down to our table, Hester asked us all to hold hands and to close our eyes. We obeyed. (I mean, never fuck with a witch, right? Remember the *Wizard of Oz*?) I had no idea what she was doing, but I could hear soft murmuring and chanting coming from her side of the table. Must've been the witch's version of Grace, I figured. In any case, when she told us to open our eyes again, the entire restaurant was staring our way. We feigned nonchalance and started perusing the menu.

"We don't have to do that again in between courses, do we?" Sparkle whispered to Hester, much to Sharon's chagrin.

"No, once ought to do it. The table is now cleansed of all bad spirits that might've been lingering," she replied. And I was certain she was serious.

"Oh, great, nothing worse than bad spirits ruining a perfectly good meal," he joked, but it went right over Hester's head. It didn't, however, go over Sharon's. She made a face at Sparkle that indicated that he better settle down.

"Oh, I know, but they're gone now, so we can eat in harmony." Hester was spooking me out big time, but Sharon looked happy, so I let it pass.

"So, Hester, um, like, how long have you been a witch?" This time it was Chester that picked up the ball, giving me a little leg squeeze under the table as he asked her the question.

"Oh, let me see," she said, sitting there thinking about it. "See, that's a tough one... it must be... oh... six... no, make that seven... no, six... yes, definitely, *six* lifetimes." (*Ding, ding, ding*. Hello, Sharon, are you listening to this? Where the hell did you find this chick? At the poison apple booth at the farmer's market?)

"Wow, long time," Sven spoke up, adding to the underscore of low-key jocularity, all at Hester's expense. Still, it went, *whoosh*, right over her head.

"Yeah, well the seventh time didn't really count," she tried to explain. Sharon, sensing defeat, merely bowed her head.

"No?" asked Sparkle, with a concerned furl in his brow. "How come?"

"Oh, because that was the time that they accused me of being a witch and I really wasn't one. Pretty ironic, huh?"

"Wow, yeah," Chester whole-heartedly agreed and then again nudged me under the table.

"Yeah, ironic," I added, with a nudge back. On my other side, sadly, Sharon was brutally kicking me under the table.

Luckily for her, though, the waiter came over at that point and took our orders. Seriously, I wasn't sure if she was upset about dating this woman or bringing this woman on a date with us. Probably the latter, if history proved anything. But, honestly, you'd think she would've known better on both accounts. In any case, we did stop picking on Hester eventually, but that had more to do with the food arriving than any real concern for our witch friend's feelings. Whichever the case, the food was wonderful, the wine was superb, and the conversation, as per usual, was raunchy and inappropriate. In other words, I was having a marvelous time.

Sometime, midway through our meal, Sparkle excused himself to go to the little boy's room. A few minutes later, Hester stopped eating and had this weird look on her face. One by one, the rest of us noticed this and stopped eating, all of us staring at her instead.

"Um, is there something wrong, Hester? Are you in need of a Heimlich or something?" I asked, with some real concern.

"Um, I'm getting this strange feeling that something is wrong with your friend Sparkle. You better go check on him." It was the way she said it that made me jump up. I didn't really believe she knew anything, but I believed that she believed it, and that was good enough for me.

"No, wait," she commanded me, "Sven better go in with you."

Sven stood up, hesitantly, and we both made our way to the john. We walked in just in time, too. Sparkle was jacked up against the wall with a strange and fairly large man's hand wrapped tight around his throat by then.

"Is there something wrong here, gentlemen?" Sven calmly asked.

"Mind your own fucking business," the stranger replied, without turning around to look at us.

"Um, the man at the end of your arm *is* my business. I'm his chauffeur." That got him to turn around, of course, but his hand was still firmly placed over the neck of an ever whitening and gagging Sparkle.

"What the fu... (he started, and then looked up at the much larger Sven)... who the fuck are you? No wait, I don't give a flying fuck who you are. This faggot here was staring at my dick while I was pissing."

"Be that as it may," continued Sven, "I'm going to have to ask you to remove your hand from around his neck."

"Or else what?" Straight men are so stupid sometimes.

"Or else this…" Sven walked further into the bathroom and, with one hand, gripped the stranger between his neck and shoulder. This had a dual effect. Firstly, he released his grip on Sparkle, who then fell to the ground gasping for air. Secondly, the stranger sank to his knees in what seemed to be a tremendous amount of pain. This was followed by a long string of obscenities.

"Now, I do apologize for my friend's behavior, but I must ask you to remove yourself from this restroom immediately." Sven was firm and remained cool and collected the entire time. The guy, realizing he had little choice, stood up, looked at Sparkle, told him that if he ever saw him again without his bodyguard he would finish what he started, and then he left. (And, yup, there's yet another suspect. Gee, and some people just rack up frequent flyer points. How boring.)

"Well, well, well. Was it worth it?" I couldn't help but ask.

Sparkle, rubbing his neck and wiping the tears from his eyes, answered, rather characteristically, "Guy had a big fucking dick."

Sven and I had to laugh at that. Then Sparkle looked up at us and a big grin replaced the grimace that had been there. "Thanks," he said, massaging his throat, "lucky for me you guys had to pee."

Sven and I stared at each other, remembering the real reason we'd come back to the bathroom. We told Sparkle the story as we made our way back to the table. Our three remaining dinner companions were staring up at us anxiously when we arrived.

"Well?" Sharon asked.

"Hester was right; Sparkle was in need of saving," I volunteered. Sharon beamed with pride as Hester turned red in the face. The three of us then thanked her up and down, while she graciously accepted our gratitude. (Only in San Francisco, friend. Only in San Francisco. And, for that, I'm grateful.)

By the time we finished dinner, dessert, and some much needed wine, we'd put the whole bathroom scene out of our heads and were treating Hester like she was one of our own. Sharon was noticeably happier, and I, in turn, was happy for her. It appeared that a witch in the family might be a good thing. Sparkle certainly seemed glad to have her there. Then, uh oh, it happened again.

"Shit, what now?' Chester asked, looking at Hester. "What could be wrong this time? We're all here at the table."

"It's not one of you. It's someone connected to you," she looked shaken as she said it. "We better pay the bill now; I sense a need to rush out of here." We called the waiter over and started chipping in for our shares of the meal.

"Well, who is it then?" I asked, with some real urgency. Now I believed her and I wanted to know who was in trouble.

"That I can't tell, but wait, let me try something before the bad news gets to us," she said and reached into her purse before pulling out a handful of items. Quickly and precisely, she grabbed a dessert plate, piled on some twigs and some gemstones, poured on some oily liquid, and commenced to chanting again. This time, when the other restaurant patrons stared, we didn't care; we knew that whatever Hester was doing, it was for our own good. When she was done with her mantra, she lit the oily mess, clapped her hands, and shook her bracelets. Chills ran up and down my spine. I prayed that her spell would work. Then I realized how silly that sounded and prayed twice as hard.

"There," she whispered. "Whoever is in trouble will now be protected from harm, though one of you will have to do a selfless deed in return. I hope you don't mind, but I had to work something fast, and it was the first spell to pop into my head. Your friend is safe for the time being, but one of you has twenty-four hours to fulfill the bargain.

"Any idea when we'll find out who's in tr…" I started, but, at that very same moment, Sparkle's cell phone started ringing. He paused before he answered it in order to collect himself. I could tell that he was shaken by the whole experience. I, for one, was not looking forward to hearing who was on the other end of the line, either.

Sparkle didn't say more than a couple of words, but he nodded a lot and murmured a few *uh huhs* before he clasped the phone shut. I could tell immediately that the news was bad. Plus, the first thing he said when he got off the phone was that the news was bad.

"Who is it?" I fairly screeched. "Is it your mother? Your father? Your brother? Who, who is it?" I was suddenly semi-frantic.

"It's Peter," he replied, his face suddenly pale, which was saying quite a lot, considering how much he paid to stay perennially dark. "That was the head of the shelter, Dan, calling to tell me that they caught Peter smoking pot. He barricaded himself inside one of the rooms, because he doesn't want to get shipped to the camp," he told us, nodding his head in disbelief the whole time, my stomach sinking with each miserable word.

"Fuck," I groaned. "Are they gonna do that?"

"The head honcho seems to think so. He said that I should come down and try to talk him out of the room before they have to call the police."

"Let's go," commanded Sharon, and the five of us fairly raced out of the restaurant and over to the limo. Sven gave the old girl all it was worth and we made it to the shelter in about ten minutes flat. Sparkle and I were dropped off, while the rest of our group got driven home. There was nothing they could do but wish us both luck, anyway. Of course, I was wishing the same thing right about then. I mean, Peter didn't belong in a detention camp. That would've been two giant steps backward.

We both raced up the stairs to the shelter and were greeted by Dan. He shook our hands, recapped what had happened, and led us to the door of the room where Peter was holed up. Sparkle took charge as soon as we got there.

"Peter," he spoke loudly but with control, "this is Sparkle. (Times like that I wished we called him by his given name.) You have to come out of there and talk to us."

There was a silent pause, and then from behind the door came, "No! I'm not coming out of here and I'm not going to that juvi prison, so fuck off."

I looked at Dan with pleading eyes. He whispered to us that rules were rules and that Peter had broken the biggest one of all: absolutely no drugs in the shelter. Still, I tried reasoning with him. "But Peter's been coming along so great over the last month. His grades are good, his behavior has improved remarkably, and, as far as we know, this is the only time he's fallen back to his old ways. Can't you make one exception?" I was nearly in tears, and Sparkle looked twice as bad as I felt.

"Look," Dan began, "I know all those things. And it kills me to do this, but you have to understand my position here. For every Peter out there, there are a dozen other kids who want and need to be in this shelter. Funds are limited, space is limited, and there just aren't enough places like this for all the needy teens throughout the city. Many kids that come through here are just like Peter, and many make headway only to fall back to their old ways. But many also come here and manage to succeed and then leave here and lead normal, productive lives. Those are the kids we need to have room for here. Peter understood the rules and he knowingly broke them. I'm sorry, but we can only afford to keep the ones here that at least try to make a go of it. I agree that sending him up north isn't the best solution, but it's what has to happen."

Sparkle's answer to that was, "Okay, I understand where you're coming from, but let's at least sit down and talk with Peter and try to found out why he did what he did. It just doesn't sound like him. I mean, before you make any final decisions, can't we at least give him the benefit of the doubt and hear his side of things?" I'd never heard Sparkle speak so from the heart before. In fact, mine was breaking as he pleaded with Dan.

"I'm not going to promise anything, and I seriously doubt that whatever he has to say will change what simply must happen, but I agree that we should at least hear him out," Dan said, and I could hear in his voice that he really didn't want to send Peter away either. His hands were probably well tied by the Department of Social Services when it came to matters like this.

"Peter," Sparkle faced the door and tried again, "you have to come out right now. You're only making it worse the longer you stay in there. Please come out and talk to us, and maybe we can work this all out."

A minute past and there was silence from behind the door. Then we heard movement from inside the room and we knew that Peter was unblocking the exit in order to make his way out. Suddenly, we heard the lock click open before Peter poked his head out and looked at us. His face was red and tears were streaming down his cheeks as he walked outside and stood in front of us. Honestly, I didn't know whether or not to punch him or hug him. After all, he'd done a really stupid thing, and, deep down, I felt betrayed. I mean, Sparkle and I had invested a lot of ourselves toward Peter's welfare, and this was not a good way to repay us.

"Why don't we all go into my office and talk?" Dan suggested, and we followed behind him to do just that. Sparkle tried to put his arm around Peter, but he was pushed away. I could see the hurt in my friend's eyes when that happened. I mean, both of them had come so far in such a short amount of time; it was such a shame that this had to happen after all that.

"Now, Peter," Dan began as we all took seats in his office, "perhaps you can explain why we caught you doing drugs in the shelter when you know we have strict rules against such behavior."

Nothing. Not a peep out of him. Peter just sat there with his arms folded in front of his chest and didn't say a word.

"Peter," Sparkle tried, "if you want us to help you, you're going to have to tell us why you did that. I thought you were beyond such things. At least, I hoped so."

"Fuck that," Peter mumbled. "Like you care."

That, of course, stung both Sparkle and me. "Peter, if we didn't care we wouldn't be here right now, would we?" Sparkle countered with.

"Please, Mary (we taught him that), we both know you're running down the clock on the time you have left with me." He wouldn't so much as look at us as he said it.

"What the… now listen hear…" I was pissed at the thought of that and I tried to explain that what he was saying was utter nonsense, but Sparkle raised his hand for me to stop.

"Wait, Peter, can you step outside for just a minute and let Secret and I have a word with Dan?" That caused Peter to look up at us, finally, and he looked mighty pissed. I couldn't remember if I'd ever treated my parents that way and I certainly hoped that I hadn't. Really, Peter had no reason to be mad at us considering he brought this misery upon himself.

Peter begrudgingly left us after we made him promise to wait outside for just a few minutes. We were a bit concerned that he would run away if we left him on his own, but I think, deep down, he knew we were on his side and that we might be his last chance. Actually, it really did seem like Sparkle was his only hope, because I hadn't a clue how to get him out of this.

"Well, I think I know what's happening here," Sparkle said. "He knows that I have only a few hours left of my community service and he thinks I'm going to leave him. Damn, I can't believe I didn't see that coming."

"It still doesn't excuse what he did," Dan argued, "but I can see what motivated the bad decision. He was afraid to lose another family. But, guys, listen, there's nothing I can do about this. The State made these rules, and I have to enforce them."

I looked over at Sparkle. His head was down and he looked like he was thinking hard about something. Dan and I sat there and watched him, waiting to hear what he had to say. Then, slowly, he lifted his chin and looked toward me before he reached over and grabbed my hand and gave me a slight grin. What he was thinking, I had no idea, but I anxiously waited to hear what he had brewing in that twisted, gin-soaked brain of his.

"Secret?" he whispered to me.

"Yes, Sparkle?" I whispered back.

"Remember Hester's spell?" he asked me. I had remembered and it suddenly dawned on me what he had in mind. Meaning, my smile quickly echoed his.

Sparkle looked over at Dan and asked, "Um, the rule, as I see it, says that if you do drugs in the shelter, you can no longer stay in the shelter, right?"

"Pretty much, yes," Dan answered, bewildered at where Sparkle was going with this.

"The rule doesn't state, however," Sparkle continued, "that the only alternative is that he goes to the juvenile detention camp, does it?"

"No, but that's what the court usually decides. It's the only place he can go. He has to be supervised by somebody," Dan answered, but toward the end, it started to dawn on him, too, what Sparkle was getting at.

"Dan, what are the odds that the court would let Peter come stay with me until he's legally an adult?" Even after I heard him ask it, I was still uncertain that I didn't imagine hearing him say those exact words. I knew that Hester's spell had come full circle, but I never dreamed that it would be Sparkle that would do the selfless deed. Presumably, his first ever, no doubt.

Dan sat there looking at us for a minute and then a grin appeared on his face. Must've been contagious, because we were all sporting one by then. "Good question," Dan replied, with a hearty laugh. "Honestly, I have no idea, but I think they would rather see Peter in a home with someone who cares about him than in a juvenile camp for two years, surrounded by people who don't."

"But you'd put in a good word for us, right?" I asked.

"You bet. It's obvious to me that this is what would be in Peter's best interests. Luckily for you, this is San Francisco; judges here are a lot less prejudiced by that kind of arrangement. In fact, I think they'd overlook this little error of judgment if you got Peter some drug counseling. Plus, I also think they'd agree to your plan, seeing that he's sixteen and has little hope without some adult supervision and caring."

"So you're saying we can try it our for now?" Sparkle asked, with a trace of hope in his voice.

"I'm saying that you can bring Peter home with you for the time being and that I will file the appropriate papers with the court to get the ball rolling on some kind of foster care arrangement. The rest is up to the State and Peter. During the time that he's with you, he has to show signs of improvement and adjustment or they're gonna come and take him away from you and place him in that camp, no doubt about it."

"Deal," said Sparkle, beaming now, and stood up to shake Dan's hand and hug me. It was, truth be told, either the craziest idea that Sparkle had ever had or the out-and-out smartest. Probably a little of both, but it was certainly the bravest. Now all we had to do was tell Peter.

With straight faces (heinous term), we asked Peter to come back into the room. He looked nervous as he sat down between us, his usual bravado clearly vanished. He obviously knew he was teetering on the brink and that whatever we said was ultimately going to decide his fate.

"Peter," Sparkle gravely said, "I'm going to have to ask you to go to your room and pack your bags."

Peter's jaw dropped and it appeared that he was trying desperately hard to hold back the tears. I felt for him, but he deserved this for putting us all through this hassle. Rather than argue, however, he stood up and made his way to the door. Try as I might, a tear ran down my cheek, just the same. It was followed by one down Sparkle's, too.

"Peter," Sparkle said, calling after him, with a slight tremor in his voice, "after you pack your stuff, you're coming home with me. Dan's going to try and keep you out of that camp if you can behave yourself under my supervision."

Peter stopped in his tracks and turned toward us. His face was dripping wet from crying, and, as he looked back and forth between Sparkle and me, he said, "If you're gonna be watching me, who the hell's going to be watching you?"

Sparkle let out a laugh and then opened his arms. Peter went running into them, followed by both of them hugging each other and crying. I think we all knew the answer to his question, by the way. Obviously, I was going to be the proud papa of two spoiled brats whether I wanted to be or not. Lord help the three of us.

We all made our way out of the office and over to Peter's room to help him pack. He only had a handful of belongings, which he quickly stuffed inside a duffel. He was grinning from ear to ear as he packed, and within a couple of minutes we were ready to leave. Dan said he would keep us up to date on the proceedings and that we should expect to hear from him within a week. He then warned Peter that he better keep his nose clean, because there wouldn't be any more chances for him after this one. Peter whole-heartedly agreed to those terms and fairly rushed us out the door and away from the shelter, where Sven was waiting for us as we exited the building, the doors already opened, the engine revving.

"I thought you might need a ride home," he said and ushered us into the limo. Peter, though in a daze from the events that had just occurred, was awed at the idea of leaving the shelter in a limo. I couldn't say that I blamed him, really. It was, after all, a fairy tale ending to a fairy's tale. Sparkle sat in front with Sven and gave him a big, juicy kiss for being so sweet.

After a few minutes of driving in silence (We were all collecting ourselves. It had been quite an evening, after all.), I looked over to Peter, who appeared about as happy as anybody possibly could, and I asked him, "Peter, just out of curiosity, was it all worth it?"

"You mean, if I had to do it all over again, would I tell my parents that I'm gay?" He paused to think about it for a second. "Yeah, Secret, I sure would. I'd rather live in that shelter or even on the streets than live a lie under their roof. I might have waited until I was eighteen, but still, I don't regret telling them."

Funny, I'd been living the lie a lot longer than that and it took a smart-ass sixteen-year-old to show me the light. He had everything to lose by his decision and still did the right thing in the end. What was I waiting for? If I lost my family by telling them the truth, I still had another one to fall back on. Meaning, I now knew what I had to do.

"Sparkle?" I said into the microphone.

"Yes, Secret?" His voice boomed over us.

"We're going to Kansas!" I pronounced, with glee.

"Jeez, I gotta go home and pee first," he responded.

"Fucker, not at this moment, but soon, and you're both going with me. If I'm gonna get tossed out on my ass, I'm gonna need some help getting back up."

"Deal," Sparkle said into the microphone.

"Deal," Peter said and put his hand in mine.

"Deal," I said to no one in particular, suddenly feeling like a million bucks. I tried not to think of the worst thing that could happen, though the worst thing that could happen did, in fact, happen to the two men sitting there with me. Still, I knew that I had to do what I had to do, and I was glad that the people I loved were going to be with me when I did it. (Okay, I was scared shitless. I mean, the ones I loved were complete fuck-ups, but at least they were my fuck-ups.) Now I just had to call my parents and tell them that we were all coming home. I thought about that for a long minute and then promptly shuddered. Maybe, I figured, I could just write them a nice letter instead.

CHAPTER SEVEN
COME OUT, COME OUT WHEREVER YOU ARE

Okay, I know what you're thinking. Maybe you underestimated our comatose friend, right? Well, so is not the case. Granted, in a moment of weakness (we had been drinking beforehand), Sparkle came through in a grand way, but it was simply a lapse into normal human behavior. (Since it was brought about by Hester's spell, let's say *para*normal behavior.) Honestly, once Peter was settled in, which took, like, a day, Sparkle was back to his old, bitchy self. And I for one was glad. I mean, goody-two-shoes is fine if you're Martin Luther King, Jr., or Gandhi, or Jesus, or someone like that, but, please, not for dudes like us. And, by the way, look what happened to the lot of them: shot, starved, and crucified. No, for a best friend, I'll take demented, perverse, and selfish any time. (Again, I'm so sorry for these gross analogies; they seem appropriate in my head, but then I hear myself saying them and, man, horrible, horrible, horrible.) In any case, I was glad for what Sparkle had done for Peter. If anyone deserved a second chance, it was our young friend.

And, just so you know, the first thing Sparkle had to do, per Dan's advice, was to rid the apartment of any alcohol or drugs, prescription or otherwise. We agreed, after all, that there should be no temptations in the apartment for Peter. Plus, Social Services would be snooping around regularly. See, Sparkle hadn't counted on that when he offered up his home. Of the two good deeds, the second, the purging, had to have been the hardest to endure. Anyway, at least with Peter there, Sparkle had a maid, cook, and errand boy all rolled up into one. And Peter, for his part, was only too glad to oblige. At least at first. But without life's little helpers, i.e. most everything that comes in a bottle, Sparkle was lost. Just imagine going from Xanax and Vicodin to Tylenol and aspirin, and I think you'll get the picture.

Still, remarkable as it may sound, Sparkle did his utmost to make Peter feel safe and secure. He was up every morning to see Peter off to school (yes, Peter made them breakfast, but he could've gotten that anywhere), he was home every day at four to welcome him back from school (okay, Oprah was also on at four, but he could've watched that anywhere), and he drove him over to my house whenever the two of them got bored. Okay, yes, as you might've guessed, the drugs and the booze were stashed at my place, but I think what I'm trying to get across here is that Sparkle was making sure that Peter knew there were people around him who cared, sober and bored though those people were.

Peter, for his part, went through quite a few changes as well. For one, he had his own room for the first time in over a year. And he had a blast redecorating it, too, with a little help from his fairy godfathers. Why gay men have this innate ability for interior design I have no idea. My guess, we're simply fabulous at everything that requires a bit of imagination. In any case, when we were through, Peter's room could've been in any issue of Architectural Digest or Better Homes and Gardens. (Well, maybe Better Homos and Gardens, but still.) And, to top that, I'd set up a spare bed in my modest quarters so that Sparkle could have a break every now and again. (I mean, so he could get laid, of course.) Actually, I enjoyed the company. Living alone, after all, can get pretty dreary when you're not getting any.

Secondly, he got a new wardrobe full of clothes. Now I got a chance to see why having a kid is so much fun. After all, it's a blast to dress them. All the things my mom wouldn't dare let me wear were quickly becoming a part of Peter's collection: sleeveless shirts, baggy denims, anything shiny, anything retro, and anything tight. They all looked fabulous on our lithe, little friend. Truth be told, we were spoiling Peter something rotten, but after the year he had to endure, he certainly deserved the extravagance. Besides, Gay Rule #10 is the most fun rule of them all: any excuse to shop is a good one. (Occasionally, we replace *shop* with *drink*, but I think you might've guessed that already. Oh, just so you don't worry about us, Sparkle and I got rid of most of our internal organs years ago. We pretty much have one enormous liver each now. I mean, please, who really needs an esophagus or a pancreas anyway, right?)

But those were just the obvious changes in Peter's life. The stuff on the inside took a little longer to catch up with the stuff on the outside, you see. Psychologically speaking, Peter was a wreck. (And Sparkle's boat had slowly been sinking for most of his adult life.) The few times Sparkle wasn't home when Peter got back from school, Peter had a cow. He literally flew off the handle. Also, he would suddenly erupt into small fits of rage without any provocation whatsoever. Through Dan, we enrolled him in an intensive psychological program, but results were slow in coming. What we soon discovered was that his mental scars were obviously running a hell of a lot deeper than we previously thought.

Quickly, we found that keeping Peter busy was the best medicine, because it seemed to keep his mind off what was troubling him, and, for better or for worse, his spirits were always elevated when he had lots of responsibilities. That was the easy part for Sparkle and I. See, around the house Peter did *everything*. If Social Services had ever gotten wind of what Sparkle had him doing, they would've surely removed Peter from his home and then arrested Sparkle for slave labor. And around the bookstore, Peter was waiter, stock boy, and cashier all at once. Honestly, he must've been drinking the coffee behind my back, because I'd never seen anybody with that much natural energy before. (More than likely, I'd forgotten, through lack of brain cells, what it was like to be a sixteen-year-old boy.)

I don't want to paint too a bleak picture of it, though. For the most part, Peter was fast reverting back to what, we assumed, was his old, normal self. He was bright and cheerful around us, most of the time, and, with the customers at the shop, he was extra friendly. (Especially with the gay ones.) He was, much to our dismay, a born flirt, in fact. If Sparkle wasn't worried sick about him the majority of the time, I think deep down he would've been most proud of that one attribute. Actually, when he lectured him about the consequences of flirting, I didn't know if he was actually upset with Peter because he was only sixteen and shouldn't have been making googly eyes with the older male customers or because Peter got to them first, thereby beating Sparkle to the punch.

Still, our lives were melding smoothly together and we were all relatively happy. We were no more or no less like your average dysfunctional family. It was then and only then, when all was back on track, that I decided that it was time to go home. My real home, that is, in Kansas. I cleared it with Dan and the Social Services people first, because I thought it would do Peter some good to get out of the city for a while. They agreed, so long as he didn't miss any school. That was fine with me, as I thought a weekend at home with the two of them and my parents would be plenty enough time to do what I needed to do and then get the hell on out of there.

Also, I doubt I had the balls to do it without them pushing me along. What I'd come to realize, with their help, was that the longer I took to come out to my parents, the harder it would be to ever tell them the truth. Living the lie, you see, had become the norm for me, and, the more I lied, the more I felt guilty for waiting so long to tell them, but not guilty enough to actually bite the bullet (oops, bad phrasing there, all things considered) and tell them the truth. It was one of those double-edged swords, for sure. Still, with this whole Peter thing brewing in my head, I knew I had to do it. *How*, I had no idea, but *when* was going to be the very next weekend. Peter and Sparkle, in fact, were thrilled at the prospect of going to the land of Dorothy and Toto. I had my doubts, however, and was praying for a twister to come swoop me away to Oz.

I arranged for the three of us to fly out of San Francisco right after Peter's school ended on Friday. (I arranged. Sparkle paid. Not bad.) Much to Peter's delight, we picked him up outside of school in Sven's limo. He approached us as if being picked up in a stretch limo after school was an everyday event for him. Then, after he got in, he squealed in delight and kicked his feet about a hundred times on the plush carpeting.

"That was, like, so cool," he shouted. "I'm starting to dig this limo trick you guys keep pulling."

"My pleasure, Master Peter," boomed Sven's voice, directly overhead.

"Hey, Chauffeur Man," Sparkle shouted back, "less drivel more drive, okay? And you," he said, turning to Peter, "my little man, I wouldn't get too used to this if I were you. And make sure to thank your Uncle Sven when he drops us off." He smirked and looked up at me. Sven's eyes were looking back at us through the rearview mirror and I could tell that he had a big grin on his face as well. And, damn, even his crow's feet were sexy. Personally, I was starting to dig the whole limo thing, too. Sure beat the hell out cabbing, any day.

Not wanting to be upstaged, Peter countered Sparkle's fun by yelling up to Sven, "Uncle Sven?" To which Sven replied, "Yes, Master Peter." And he answered with, "Uncle Sven, will you tuck me in to bed when we get back? I've been an awfully good little boy lately." Which caused the two of us to smack Peter on his arm. (Not too hard. We don't believe in corporal punishment, except between consenting adults.)

"Stop flirting with the help," Sparkle reprimanded Peter. "Besides, that's my job. Go pick on someone your own age."

"I'm trying. Believe me," he uttered, scaring us both to death. Emotionally, for him, it probably wasn't such a good idea. Emotionally, for us, it *definitely* wasn't a good idea. I don't think either one of us was ready to start meeting beaus just yet, and, all at once, I started feeling very overprotective of our young charge. We both left Peter's comment alone, however. After all, we were still young enough to know that telling him not to do something was tantamount to giving him the go ahead to do it anyway. He would just have to learn from our mistakes, and, between Sparkle and myself, that shouldn't have taken too long, all things considered.

In any case, it simply amazed me how utterly different this parenting stuff was than what I was expecting. Every day with Peter made me have this totally knew appreciation for my own mom and dad. I prayed that they would still appreciate me in return after this weekend. After all, my little troupe was zero for two with the whole coming out thing, and I knew that bad luck runs in threes.

A short drive later, Sven dropped us off at the airport, hugged and kissed us, and drove off. That turned more than a few heads on the sidewalk outside, let me tell you. "What?" Peter announced to no one in particular. "Haven't you ever kissed your chauffeur goodbye before? Jeez."

"Shut up and walk, boy," Sparkle mumbled, ushering us inside. "Nice one," I whispered into Peter's ear. Sparkle turned to glare and mouthed a *dickwit* at me. Naturally, I mouthed a *bitch* back at him. (Ah, friendship.)

"Look Thing One and Thing Two," said Peter, breaking it up. "You're both a couple of lunatics, okay?" And before we could scold him for being a smart-ass, he added, "And that's what I love best about you both." Granted, he was being sarcastic, but it nearly melted my heart to hear him say it. And though Sparkle wasn't showing it, I knew it choked him up as well.

Within minutes of our arrival at the terminal, they started boarding the plane. Sparkle turned to me and asked, "Ready?"

Was I? I suppose as ready as I was ever going to be. But what kept going through my head was that this really shouldn't be as difficult as I was making it out to be. It was so stupid that anyone had to worry about this kind of thing. I mean, I was gay, I'd always been gay, and always would be gay. Why should it make any difference at all to anybody? Clearly, it had no effect on anyone but me. So why was it such a big deal? And, yet, it was. Literally, I was terrified to tell the people I loved the most in this world something about myself that was so fundamental and yet had absolutely nothing to do with them whatsoever. That's fucked up, right?

As soon as the plane was in the air and level, I snapped my hand up and ordered a gin and tonic. The flight attendant handed me my can and my mini-bottle and gave me the ubiquitous nod and smile. (You know what? I like the term *stewardess* so much better. Sorry.) Sparkle tapped me on the shoulder and added to my joy with a pretty little blue pill held out in the palm of his hand.

"Bless you," I whispered, downing it and the drink in one quick gulp before turning to the flight attendant, whose name badge I noticed said Bethany, and asked, "Miss, can I tell you something?"

"Certainly, sir, what would you like to tell me?" A little forced, but I was rolling with it.

"I'm gay." I proclaimed. She gave me a strange grin and a head tilt and then looked over to Sparkle for some direction.

"He's practicing," my friend explained. Not knowing what to say or do, she simply nodded, continued to smile, and gave me a bag of peanuts. My reward? For being brave or being gay or both? In either case, I ate them with pride. Sparkle patted me on the back, while Peter just sat there and shook his head back and forth. Minutes later, the other flight attendant, Mark, came over and introduced himself. (Thanks Bethany!)

And then, before I knew it, our plane was landing. Little blue pill or no little blue pill, I was nervous as all get out. God, I wished I'd done this years earlier. We departed the airport, rounded up a rental car, and proceeded with the twenty-minute drive to my parent's house. I told them not to meet me at the airport, as five people in their car, plus our luggage, would've been too much. The real reason was that the five of us trapped in a car for that amount of time could only have led to disaster. Needless to say, I was in no condition to drive, so Sparkle took the wheel while I gave directions.

I hadn't been home since I moved to San Francisco several years earlier. I couldn't afford it and neither could my parents, but we did talk on the phone every week, and I still felt as close to them as ever. Thankfully, seeing the flat, arid countryside reminded me of my youth, and my nerves started to settle a bit as we drove down the highway with my Aldo Nova tape cranked up to full blast. (Life *is* just a fantasy.)

And then we were home. We sat in the driveway for a few minutes while I caught my breath, but I was only delaying the inevitable. Sparkle and Peter, for their parts, were upbeat and excited and were trying desperately hard to keep me in good spirits. But, honestly, I don't want you to get the wrong idea; I love my parents deeply. It was just the thought of hurting them was making me a total mess.

As we sat there waiting, the door to the house flung open and my mother emerged. "What are you waiting for, a personal invitation?" she shouted out as us.

"Coming, Ma," I shouted back.

"Secret?" Sparkle said to me just before we exited.

"Yes, Sparkle?"

"No matter what happens, I love you."

"I know, Sparkle, and thanks, but if you embarrass, mortify, or otherwise destroy my world this weekend, I'm going to kill you," I said, threatening him with a smile and a pat on the shoulder.

"No promises, Secret," he responded. Meaning, I prayed to God for a miracle.

The three of us got out of the car with our duffels and walked up to my mother. She was beside herself with happiness and ran up to throw her arms around me. She smelled like home, like everything that was happy in my life. It was, suffice it to say, good to see her.

"Your father should be in from the office soon and dinner will be ready in fifteen minutes." She beamed as she walked us into the house, with Sparkle immediately taking stock of the home I was brought up in. I could hear the gears shifting in his head as he scanned the living room to find signs of why I was who I was. I was sure he would use my past for dish at some future date. Peter, too, was looking around, but his expression was significantly different than Sparkle's. It had to be the first home he'd been in since he was thrown out of his own, and it was apparent that he was going through something, if not painful, then at least uncomfortable.

My mom was oblivious, of course, as I introduced her to my companions and she hugged and kissed them both. Inside my head, I was chuckling. I mean, the thought that my mother just kissed three gay men was strangely humorous to me. Then she dragged the three of us around the house for the grand tour. Sparkle snatched up every picture of me as a child as we progressed through each room. Few comments were made, but I knew he had a bitchy thought for each one that he was keeping tucked away somewhere in his devious little brain, destined to emerge at the most inopportune moment far in the future.

By the time we were through and had made it back to the living room, my father was walking through the door and dinner was ready. My dad and I gave each other a big, manly hug before introductions were made all the way around. Five minutes later, we were sitting down to eat. It all seemed so surreal. I mean, I never for a second imagined my parents eating dinner with Sparkle, but there, in fact, we were.

Smalltalk was made throughout the lovely dinner that my mother had prepared. You know, the usual: who moved where, who married who, who got divorced, who they ran into recently. The standard stuff. I couldn't even begin to imagine how I would work the gay thing into the conversation. But, I figured, what the hell, I had all day Saturday to do it; why spoil a great meal? And then I relaxed a bit knowing that the pressure was off, however temporarily. That's when, unfortunately, the conversation turned to a more personal level.

"So, Bruce," my mother began, "are you seeing anybody special in San Francisco?"

Oh, God, why? Why me? "Um, not really. There's this, er, *person* I met at a show recently, but nothing serious," I semi-truthed it.

"Oh, what kind of show was it?" she asked, oblivious to my internal turmoil.

"It was a benefit for our men in uniform," Sparkle answered for me.

"Oh, that's nice. So, tell me, why is it nothing serious?" *Damn*, I thought, *I should just tell her now. Tell her now, Bruce; tell her now.*

Except, it wasn't the right time, and so I answered with, "Well, you know how it is. I work just about every day and night at the shop and there aren't enough hours in the week for a relationship as well. Don't worry, though, Ma, it's okay. I'm young and there's plenty of time for that. Besides, I love the work and Spar... er, William visits me almost every day." (Lift up foot, place foot in mouth.)

Then my father picked up the ball. "Why does William have the time to visit you every day? Maybe you need an assistant, William; I mean, I'd also love to have my days free." Can you imagine the training process to be Sparkle's assistant? Poor dad, if he only knew what he was asking.

I answered before Peter or Sparkle could further deepen the hole I was digging for myself. "No, Dad, William came into some money and he doesn't work, exactly." I should've known better than to phrase it that way, though, because my father was a stickler for the standard fifty-hour workweek, and he immediately became irked at the thought that a strong, healthy, young man didn't work for a living.

"Huh?" my father began, wiping his mouth and setting his fork down to show that he meant business. "You mean you do nothing all day but sit in a bookstore? When I was your age, I had two jobs and a family to support. Even if I had all the money in the world, I would still work. Keeps the brain juices flowing."

The hole was getting deeper and my mouth was now full of feet as I said, "Well, Pop, William doesn't exactly do *nothing* all day; he takes care of Peter." I knew I should've just dropped it even as the words were coming out of my mouth. I mean, how was I going to explain that arrangement?

"Um, if you don't mind me asking," my mother asked, without waiting to see if Sparkle minded, "how does someone so obviously young as yourself come to have the responsibility of taking care of someone Peter's age?"

Now no one was eating and all eyes were on Sparkle, who, in return, was staring back at me in the hope, I can only figure, that I could somehow telepathically send him the answer to *that* tricky question. Peter, however, beat us both to the punch. And, as much as I would've preferred answering the question myself, I knew Peter's motivation. He, after all, owed a lot to Sparkle and just wanted to stick up for him.

"William takes care of me because my parents won't and because the State was going to put me away," he offered up.

Both of my parents' jaws dropped and simultaneously they asked, "What do you mean your parents won't take care of you." I knew that there was no turning back now, and braced myself for the answer and the subsequent reaction.

Peter paused for a second before he answered. Coming out to anybody, even total strangers, is never an easy thing to do. In fact, it feels so strange to have to say the words *I'm gay* to somebody. I mean, really, you never hear someone saying *I'm black* or *I'm straight*. These are just things that should go without saying, but Peter wasn't going to turn back now; he owed it to my friend.

"About a year ago," he began, slowly, "I told my parents that I was gay, and they, in turn, threw me out of the house. (My parents blanched.) I lived on the streets for a year, and they refused to even talk to me on the phone. Now William takes good care of me."

No one said a word. The three of us sat there and waited for a reaction from my parents, while my parents waited for, well, I have no idea what they were waiting for, but they were noticeably upset by what Peter had just said. My mother was the first to say something, however.

"Peter, I'm so sorry," she said and started to cry. My father walked over and put his arms around her. She continued, but she was obviously very upset. "I… I just can't believe any parent could do such a horrible thing. I'm just so, so sorry."

She stopped, and my father added, "William, I apologize for my comment just now. It's a wonderful thing you're doing for Peter here."

"No problem, Mister Miller; I'm only too glad to help out," Sparkle assured him. Still, the whole group of us looked tense, and all for completely different reasons. Mine was that the whole gay thing was now on the table and I thought that in seconds I would be coming out to my parents.

But, before I could say anything, my mother wiped the tears from her eyes and said, "Peter, I can't begin to imagine why your parents did what they did, and I certainly haven't a clue as to how you managed to survive, at your age, without a home, but I truly believe that all things happen for a reason. It was a very brave thing telling your parents what you told them. You did the right thing. Unfortunately, your parents didn't, but it looks like you have people who care for you now, which is all that matters. If you need anything, anything at all, you can count on Mister Miller and me to help you out. And Bruce, I can't tell you how proud I am of you right now for being a part of Peter's life. It makes me feel, and I'm sure your father as well, that we did something right to have such a caring and responsible son such as yourself."

That was it. That should've been my moment. I had the opening. It was the perfect time to tell them, but hearing them call Peter brave for telling his parents that he was gay when he was only fifteen and then hearing them tell me how proud they were of me, well,

I just felt like the worst little shit in the world. Peter was the brave one, but I was nothing but a coward and a liar. And so, as much as I wanted to tell them the truth, I just couldn't. It would look like I waited all those years to tell them because I didn't trust their love for me. And so, feeling quite awful and foolish, I merely sat there in silence.

My father went back to his seat and we all finished our meals, but the rest of the evening was strained. We all passed on dessert, agreeing that it had been a long day for everyone. Before we retired to bed, however, my mother tried to perk us all up by saying that she was going to take us all out shopping the next day and then out to a big dinner at my aunt and uncle's home. The shopping sounded reasonable, but I knew that a day at my aunt and uncle's meant no time to do what I'd come there to do. Plus, I knew that Sparkle and Peter would be bored to tears. My mother looked at me with such joy at the thought, though, that I knew that I had to put on a happy face and tell her that it sounded like a great idea. Both my parents perked up when I said it, and I was, at least, happy for that. Of course, Sparkle, I could tell, was ruing this trip more and more with each passing moment.

And so, with one night down and a full day of family fun ahead, we went off to bed. I kissed my mom and dad goodnight and assured them that I couldn't wait to see the rest of the family the next day. I could tell that both of them were thrilled to hear me say that. Family, you see, meant the world to them, and now, in their eyes, our family had increased by two.

Truly, I loved my parents so much at that moment, and my heart was breaking knowing that I was deceiving them. So, tomorrow, tomorrow definitely, I promised myself, and went off to my old bedroom.

Peter went to the guest bedroom after we hugged him goodnight, and my parents had fixed up a spare cot in my room for Sparkle, who was waiting for me when I got there with an impish grin on his face. I'd seen that look many times before and, uh oh, I knew he was cooking something up.

"Before you even begin, let me just say this: NO!" (Just be quiet up there; even I knew I was going to do whatever he had in mind for me, but I at least had to put up the obligatory objection first.)

"No what?" he asked, all innocently-like.

"No to whatever mischief you're about to foist on me. Need I remind you that a.) we are in my parent's home in the middle of Kansas and b.) whatever it is you're about to get me into is probably illegal in this state, c.) it will certainly get us into trouble and d.) we have to set a good example for Peter." (Hey, I almost convinced myself.) Then Sparkle whipped out a book that I immediately recognized as the latest Damron Guide. (If you're out of the loop, that's the book that tells you where everything queer is in the known universe, Kansas included.)

"Oh no, no fucking way. There can't possibly be somewhere around *here* in *there*." I felt pretty sure about that, but Sparkle already had the page bookmarked and was waving it in front of my face to prove me wrong.

"Look here," he beamed, "right here on page two hundred. There's a gay bar not twenty-five miles from here. We have the rental car and can sneak out without anybody being the wiser. Besides, I know you can really use a drink right about now and I noticed that your parents have no liquor in the house." Damn him. That's why he was carefully scoping out the place. He wasn't looking for dirt on me; he was looking for a way to get me to go to a bar.

"Sparkle, you're amazing. You totally planned this before we even got on the plane, didn't you?"

"Secret, how long have you known me?"

"Oh, forget it; I've played that game before. Fine, I do need a drink and I know you're going to convince me to go anyway, so let's save us both the time and let's just get going." He had me. He always did. But, to tell you the truth, the thought of going to a gay bar in Kansas had been a dream of mine my whole life. This, I figured, might've been my only chance, and I, for one, wasn't about to pass it up.

"That's the spirit," he said and slapped me on the back. "Let's wait until everyone is asleep first and then tiptoe out of here. I promise, one drink and we'll be back before anyone suspects anything."

"Sparkle, my love, in all the years I've known you, there has never been just *one* drink, but I'm willing to go, just the same. So sit there and shut up and we'll go in a half an hour."

"Deal!"

He won, as usual. Like, duh.

***

As it is with many small towns, Sonny's was located in a nondescript strip mall and showed no outward signs that it was a gay bar. It was small and cramped, but it was, at least, full, what with it being a Friday night and all. Sparkle and I bee-lined it to the bar and ordered us some gin and tonics. Doubles. Strong with a capital S. In all honesty, much as I hated to admit it, I was glad we were there, because I felt like I was coming full circle at long last.

So, with drinks in hand, Sparkle and I scoped out the scenery. Strangely, it could've easily been any bar in San Francisco. The same music was blaring, the same videos were playing, and the crowd was neither overly attractive nor overly tragic. Gay America, I was finding out, was pretty much the same all over. And, just like back home, it only took something like three minutes for the flies to start swarming around Sparkle. I'd learned what to do in those situations a long time ago and walked to the other side of the bar to mark my own measly territory.

Minutes later, the music faded out and was replaced by a Broadway overture that I didn't quite recognize. Still, I'd been to enough bars in my lifetime to know that a drag show was about to begin. Sure enough, seconds later, a glamorous drag queen appeared on a tiny stage that I hadn't noticed until that moment. She was tall and lean, and the glittery dress couldn't hide the fact that she'd regularly been using her gym membership. And, as soon as she started her shtick, I had this funny feeling that I'd met her somewhere before.

Her name was Gloria Hole, and you could tell by the crowd's reaction that she was a town favorite. All eyes were facing the stage and the cheers started as soon as she opened her overly-lipsticked mouth.

"My, my, my," she started, "what an attractive crowd we have out there tonight. Wait," she said, and pulled out a thick pair of glasses before putting them on. "Oh... sorry, my mistake." Then she ripped the glasses off and threw them off stage. "Well, that's better," she continued. "Now, if someone would be so kind as to pass me a drink, I think I might be able to make it through this evening." A large glass of something alcoholic was passed through the crowd and landed in my hand. Naturally, I took a gulp before handing it to Gloria.

"Hey, handsome, no sharesies. Remember, no booze, no Gloria; so get your own." She looked down when she said it and stared right into my eyes. Then she paused for a second to see if she knew me. Strangely, I sensed some recognition.

"Sorry," I shouted back at her, "but I can see you without the glasses and *I* needed something."

A mixture of boos and shouts went up, and Gloria put her hands on her cushioned hips and said, "Sugar, come here." I inched up a little. "Closer," she commanded. Again I moved a couple of inches. "Sweetie, I won't bite," she cooed.

I yelled up at her, "It's okay, I've had my shots."

Ooh, now I was in it up to my ears. "Darlin', come here to your Auntie Gloria and I'll get you a drink of your very own."

"Hey, you don't have to tell me twice," I announced and bounded onto the stage.

"Well, well. You're either an alcoholic or a drag queen, Sweetie," she surmised.

"What's the difference?" I deadpanned.

"Oh, Honey, you're a drag queen alright. The bitter scale goes from one to ten, and you're definitely an eleven." I was glad for the distinction.

"Gloria, I've got eleven for you right here," I said to her and grabbed my crotch. *Now* the crowd was on my side.

"Bartender," she breathlessly spoke into the microphone, "get this man a drink and a big bottle of lube for yours truly. I think I might've found Mister Right This Second." Several of the men in the audience were vying for my attention at that point as well. Even Sparkle stopped what he was doing to catch my act.

"What's your name, Honey?" she asked, once I got my drink.

"On stage, it's Tobago. In bed, you can call me *Sir*."

"Oh, yes, Sir. So, Tobago, where's Trinidad?" she asked. I pointed to the area where Sparkle was standing. I could tell, by the look on his face, that he was none too thrilled that he'd been drag queen outed, but he was the one who hauled my ass down there and that's the price he paid. Tough fake-titties. Besides, it didn't look like any of his suitors were backing off, and I, for one, was having a blast.

"Well, it seems like you're here with your own troupe, Sweetie. Care to perform a number?" she asked, and I was seriously tempted, until Sparkle shouted out, "We're on sabbatical."

"Too bad," Gloria pouted, "we could use a couple of good drag queens up on this stage."

"Honey, I'd settle for *one* good drag queen," I quipped.

"Now, now, no hitting below the belt, which, by the way, is going to come down over your pretty, little ass if you don't behave," she threatened.

"Promises, promises," I dared back.

"Ladies and gentlemen," she announced into the microphone, "there's going to be a ten minute intermission while I go and teach this randy bitch a thing or two about Midwestern manners." Then, before I knew what hit me, and much to the crowd's delight, she grabbed my hand and pulled me off stage into a small office. Then she sat down and pointed to a seat next to her and motioned for me to sit down, too.

"Gloria, I was only kidding out there. I'm sorry if I upset you," I offered, suddenly a little worried.

"Sugar, you were great. That's not why I dragged you back here," she said and took off her wig.

"Um, why then?" She had my curiosity aroused and, as she continued to de-drag, she was having the same affect on certain other parts of me.

"Bruce, it's me Sonny," she, now closer to he, said. Again, he looked familiar, but I couldn't quite place him.

"Sonny? Sonny, hmm, let me see… no… no bells. Give me another clue." It was killing me that he knew who I was and I still hadn't recognized him. Then he unzipped his dress and shimmied out of it. Standing there in his panties, it was his chest that was the final tip off. "Holy shit," I shouted and jumped up. "Sonny Leary! I'd recognize those pecs anywhere. You used to drive me crazy in the boy's locker room. What the fuck are you doing here? Better yet, since when are you gay and a drag queen? Last time I saw you, you were practically engaged to Samantha Peskow. (Sonny, you see, was my boyhood crush. He was captain of every team and had the girls swarming all over him. Samantha kept them all at bay.)

"Funny story, that one," he said and sat back down. "See this dress?" He pointed to the beautiful beaded number now hanging on the door. "It's Samantha's. Least it was. She's a big, old bull dyke now and couldn't begin to fit into it anymore. Lucky for me, I got all her hand-me-downs."

"Did you both know about each other in high school?" I asked, now in near shock.

"Oh yeah. We were each other's beards. We've been friends since we were three or four and we never kept anything from each other. When I was twelve, I told her that I thought that I liked boys. In return, she told me that she thought that she liked girls. Right then and there, we came up with the arrangement. Even at that age, we knew we'd need each other somewhere down the line. And, hey, it worked out great, except for the fact that neither one of us ever got the chance to be with someone of our own gender. And, boy, did that ever suck."

"Jeez, I know just how you felt," I sympathized. "Damn, I had the biggest, fucking crush on you back then."

"I know," he said, "you were pretty obvious about it. Every time my shirt came off, there you were with your eyes practically glued to me. I wish I could've let you known back then that I felt the same way, but, well, you know."

"Man, I wish you had as well. I used to beat off thinking about you every night. It kills me to think that I could've been doing it with you all that time." I couldn't believe that he was telling me those things. Seriously, I would've given my left nut to have known it way back then.

"Well, Bruce, there's no time like the present," he said and brushed his hand over his panties.

"What? Here in the office? Won't you get in trouble?" I was hard as a rock and really didn't care if he got in trouble or not; I was just nervous about finally getting to live out a childhood fantasy of mine.

"Bruce, silly boy, I own this dump. Actually, I do quite well for myself. See how crowded it is out there? (I nodded a yes.) It's always like this, seven days a week. This is the only place for them to come to within a fifty-mile radius. Now, if you're done asking questions, why don't you take those pants off and join me here on this comfy, little chair?"

As I said, he didn't have to tell me twice. Meaning, I was out of my jeans and on top of his lap in no time flat. My mind was buzzing and my entire body was tingling as I touched his chest for the first time and pressed my lips to his at long, long last. It was all so unreal, so mind-blowing, so perfect. All those years later and there I was, nearly naked and making out with Sonny. Wow, I should've come back to Kansas a hell of a lot sooner.

The whole event was over in about five minutes, but it was well worth it. (By the way, moisturizing cream makes for a great lube.) Funny how things have a way of working themselves out in the long run. I would never, in my wildest imagination, have believed that one day I would get off with Sonny Leary. And in a gay bar and with him in drag no less. But there I was, cleaning his you know what off my hands and grinning from ear to ear.

I gave him my number and he gave me his, and we promised that if either one of us was traveling anywhere near the other again that we'd give the other a call. Honestly, though, I didn't much care either way. It couldn't have gotten any better than those brief moments in that office at that time and place. And so, all cleaned up and completely satiated, I made my way back to the bar, while Gloria got redressed and back up on stage. Quickly, because it was a small bar, after all, I regrouped with Sparkle.

"Girlfriend," he said, wiping his fingers over my apparently lipstick-smeared mouth, "this color is all wrong for you. You know, I never would've figured you for drag trash. By the way, is she hiding much in her tucker?"

"Very funny. I'll have you know, we're old friends from high school and we were just doing some catching up." I tried to hide the obvious.

"Honey, unless you were doing some laundry back there, I'd say that funky smell on you came from something other than *catching up*. Anyway, I take it from the look on your face that you had a nice time and are ready to go. I, being the great friend that I am, will capitulate."

"Slim pickings, I take it." I could always read right through Sparkle's bullshit.

"The slimmest. You'll be glad to know that you missed nothing by waiting to come out until after college. These Kansas boys are a total bore. Plus, they actually measure the amount of booze they put into the drinks. How primitive." (He said it, not me.)

"Well, tomorrow is going to be a long day, and I think I've experienced enough gay culture for the evening. Let's go home and try to catch a few hours of sleep before our shopping extravaganza," I suggested.

"Agreed," he agreed and steered us out into the clean, crisp night air. "So, how ya doing?" he asked as we drove through the quiet streets back to my home. In truth, I missed the noise and commotion of the city.

"Okay, I guess. I just want to get it over with. That whole Peter thing was a bit much to take. Honestly, I should've seen it coming, but my brain has been a bit scattered of late," I told him. "And how are you?"

"I'm okay. Your parents are a trip, by the way. It's like being with the Cunninghams. I mean, I feel like The Fonz and you're Ritchie. I had no idea that there are actually families like yours. It explains so much about you, too. Anyway, stop worrying about Peter and me and do what you came here to do. I have plenty of pills to keep me stabilized throughout the ordeal and enough for you to recover with." (Always the trooper.)

"Thanks, Sparkle. I'm sure I'll be taking you up on the offer. By the way, you might want to slip my mom some beforehand; it might make it easier on the both of us." I was semi-serious.

"Ooh, how very Grace Slick. When she's not looking, I'll slip one in her coffee. What fun that would be." (Sorry if you don't get that one. Sixties trivia is so eighties, don't ya think? Anyway, it's funny, so laugh.)

Minutes later, we were pulling into the driveway and sneaking back into my house. I felt seventeen all over again. So many feelings and emotions were running through me as we tiptoed back to my room and climbed into our beds. In any case, I fell asleep dreaming about Sonny, but this time we were back in high school and he was begging *me* for sex. All in all, it'd been a good homecoming. (Emphasis on the coming.) Now it was time to batten down the hatches and prepare for darker waters.

***

The next morning, we woke up, showered, and lumbered downstairs. Peter and my parents were already chowing down on a sumptuous breakfast.

"Thanks for waiting," I grumbled and sat down.

"The early bird catches the worm," Peter replied, in between bites.

"Really, I hadn't heard that. Thanks for the advice. Next time they're serving worms, I'll be sure to set my alarm. Now pass the toast." I was grumpy without my first cup of coffee. (Okay, maybe my third, but then I was all sunshine and roses.)

"What do you say?" my mother admonished.

"*Please*," I added, feeling like I hadn't been away for all those years.

"That's better," she said, with a motherly look, before patting Peter on his head. I think he was having a great time of it. Certainly no one cooked like that for him or mothered him like that around Sparkle's apartment. Naturally, he was eating it up. Literally. Heck, there was enough food at breakfast to feed certain third world countries, and Peter was making his way through it all. I wondered if I ate like that when I was his age. Probably, because I remember that my mom always used to cook that way when I was growing up. It's a wonder, I suppose, that I'm not big as a house.

"I have some fabulous news," my mom soon uttered, once she made sure that we all had everything we needed. (Short of a shovel, I'd say we did.)

With trepidation, I asked, "What would that be, Ma?"

"Your cousins, Tess and Albert, are going to be at your Aunt Rose and Uncle Jesse's today. They're driving in all the way from Iowa to be with the family and to see you. Isn't that wonderful?" She was busting with joy. My father, however, looked less enthused. See, he always hated my mother's side of the family, and, truth ne told, I could see why; they were a bunch of flakes.

Aunt Rose and Uncle Jesse were the only two hippies in the state of Kansas back in the sixties, and their kids were raised rather permissively, in my fathers' eyes. What that means is that they were brats when we were all growing up together. Plus, they were older than me by at least ten years and always made me feel like the baby. Meaning, they teased me incessantly. I'd hoped never to see them again, but, alas, life has a funny way of bringing people back together again. Just look at what happened with Sonny and me.

I hadn't seen either one of my cousins since I left for college, but my mother gave me regular updates on their lives. (As if I cared.) I felt a certain righteousness, even at a young age, when Tess had a baby out of wedlock at the tender age of nineteen and Albert dropped out of high school to pursue a field in music. Three years later, he was driving trucks cross-country. I guess my parents knew what they were doing in terms of child-rearing, and I was always glad that they were my parents instead of my aunt and uncle. Also, Dad felt the same way about them as I did, letting us know it whenever the subject was brought up.

"Oh, goodie," I proclaimed, with mock enthusiasm. My father grinned, ever so slightly.

"Be nice," my mom said, waving a finger at me. "We haven't had the whole family together in ages."

For that, I was grateful. Still, it was good to see my mother so happy, and I did love my aunt and uncle. They were so un-Kansas when I was a kid. And anything that goes against the grain when you're a child is far superior to the norm. Still, it was always kind of scary and kind of exciting going over to their house. That weekend was no exception.

Shopping with my mother was an experience, too. I thought she went to extremes over breakfast; shopping with her went beyond that. Way beyond. Truly, I think she sometimes regretted being just a mom, even though I was finding out that being just a mom was a fulltime career. I mean, I couldn't imagine what it would be like if Peter was any younger than he was. The responsibility was enormous enough, and I was only seeing it secondarily to Sparkle.

In any case, I think that what she would've liked to have done with her life was to go into a career in fashion. Which is not to say that she had any fashion sense in the least. It was just that she just adored dressing other people. Picking out a single outfit could easily take two hours with my mother. Heck, as a child, I would frequently be sweating by the time we were though. To leave with a shopping bag of just a few shirts and some slacks, I had to try on somewhere around sixty different combinations of clothes. To this day, I get hives just stepping into a J.C. Penny's or a Mervyns. Once, I could've sworn I heard the salesperson that was helping us break into tears while we were in the changing room.

Now she had three boys to clothe and only a few hours to do it in. Funny, they could invent a whole new Olympic sport around my mother: marathon dressing. Ironically, as much as I hated the whole experience, Sparkle and Peter were in heaven.

Surprisingly, over and over again, I was finding that I took my parents for granted. What would it have been like not to have a mother who cared for me so much that she would agonize over every outfit I wore? Well, that's what my friends' childhoods were like. Again, I had it all wrong. Is this what it was like becoming an adult? Finding out that your parents were right all along? God, I'd hoped not.

The problem was, even though my mother's heart was in the right place, her tastes in fashion was somewhere nestled between New Jersey and Hell. The only reason you never objected to the final decision was that you were so glad that the ordeal was finally over with that you would gladly have worn Bermuda shorts and a cashmere sweater just to get the heck out of the mall and away from any more articles of clothing.

Luckily for us, shopping stores in Kansas had caught up to the rest of the country by that time and our choices were considerably more acceptable than when I was a kid. Plus, my mother must've watched enough television and read enough magazines over the last decade since my childhood to finally know what was generally in style.

In other words, the outfits we ended up with weren't all that bad, all things considered. At least I wasn't in a pair of Wranglers and an Izod shirt. And Peter, needless to say, made out like a bandit. By the end of the day, he was calling my mom, Mom. I didn't mind one bit, either, and my mother, well, she couldn't have been any happier if she'd won the lottery. Even Sparkle, who was obviously never one for family life, started calling her Mom towards the end of our shopping spree. I think it was more out of respect for her tenacity than her prowess, though.

So, arm in arm, we left the mall and made are way back home to get ready for the family get-together. Sadly, if there was no way to tell my mom that I was a flaming queer while shopping, I saw less of a chance over dinner. I mean, how do you tell your parents that you're gay surrounded by your family? (Okay, I see how silly that sounds. Of course, that would've been the perfect setting. Talk about killing two birds. But, honestly, I wanted it to be just her and me. She could tell Dad, because I didn't think I had it in me to handle them both simultaneously.)

After we got home, the three of us showered and changed into our new clothes and paraded past my parents like models on the runway. My mother couldn't have been any more proud. My father, though, just sat there and shook his head. Poor guy. He never did fit in quite right with the family, but he did love us dearly, loons though we all were. Fashion show over, we headed to the car and on to my aunt and uncle's house thirty miles away. (My parents actually had a Bobby Vinton tape in the car. I hid it beneath my seat. One crisis at a time, friend. One crisis at a time.)

We arrived, piled out of the family sedan, and, in a neat little row, headed on up the walkway to the house. Sparkle double-upped on the pills to be on the safe side, while Dad and I joked about the other side of the family. Only Peter and Mom looked tickled to be there, and had been feeding off each other's family hysteria all day. In truth, it was fairly nauseating. Even without the coming out thing hanging over my head, the reunion would've been the last place I would've ever chosen to be.

My relatives were waiting for us at the door, and there was five minutes worth of hugging, kissing, and introductions, followed by more hugging and kissing before we finally made it into the house. Everyone looked the same as the last time I'd seen them. My aunt and uncle were a little pudgier and grayer, but they were still just as laid back looking as ever. My parents wouldn't be caught dead in a pair of jeans and a t-shirt in front of company, even if it was family.

My cousins, though certainly more adult in appearance, still basically looked the same. Tess had aged more than Albert had, though. I suppose that was what you got for being a parent at such an early age. Albert, surprisingly, looked like he did when he was a gangly teenager. He still had the ratty ponytail, ripped jeans, and a cigarette dangling from his lips. There were, of course, the telltale age lines appearing, but the road, apparently, was good to him. In any case, it was creepy seeing them all again. How this family grew up together was and still is beyond me. Hell, we couldn't have been more different if we tried. (And we did try.)

The only surprise to the gathering was my cousin, Sam, Tess' fifteen-year-old son. He, at least, looked like one of my side of the family. Which is to say, normal. I hadn't seen him since he was really little, and, thankfully, he'd grown up nicely. His father, whoever he might've been, must've carried some good, strong genes in him, because Sam shone out in the meager looking group that was his family. Right away, I could tell that Peter was glad to be there, and I knew that I'd better watch out. Sparkle also caught on and firmly placed himself in between the two of them. Peter, you see, was just bold enough to do something, even surrounded by all of us. Or especially because he was surrounded by all of us. See, that's just the way he rolled.

In any case, we sat around catching up with each other before dinner. Weirdly, it was like I'd never left. Same old complaints and trivial problems that have plagued both families since I was a child. And, trust me, I couldn't have cared less as I sat there and listened to it all. And I certainly wouldn't want to thrust it all on you now. Suffice it to say, families are better off together only at weddings and funerals. Everything in between is B-O-R-I-N-G. Heck, I had more interesting things happen to me in one week at the bookstore than these people had happen to them all year. The only person that looked the least bit interested was Peter, especially when they were talking about Sam. Honestly, I was seriously contemplating telling them all that I was gay just to break up the monotony.

Unfortunately, I never got the chance, because dinner proved way more interesting than expected. Oh, sure, it started out normal enough. *Please pass this, please pass that.* Drinks were poured and re-poured. (The one weakness my family allowed was alcohol consumption, thank God, but never in their own home.) Then polite conversation was made. Really, it was your typical sit-down, family-style dinner. No voices were raised and no real issues were addressed. Then, as was her way, my mother just had to start asking questions.

"So, Tess, tell me how things are going with you," she politely asked. I knew the two of them didn't speak regularly. Actually, Tess didn't seem to speak much, period. I think adulthood had worn her down. Funny, because, as a teenager, she was spunky as all get out. Well, at least that's how I remembered her.

"Fine, I suppose," she answered, without so much as lifting her head to look at my mother.

"Well, that's... nice." Obviously, my mom didn't know where to take Tess' almost non-reply, and so she decided on a different approach, moving in from the side. "And, Sam, anything new with you?"

Now that caught Tess' attention. As soon as my mother asked the question, she looked over at her son and gave him a *if you know any better, you'll keep your mouth shut* look. I'd seen that same look from my own mother when I was growing up when an adult asked me a point-blank question about a subject that my mother had warned me not to talk about. Like when my Uncle Jeremy was in rehab, and our neighbors asked about him. (Yes, I told them the truth. See, I only got proficient at lying as I got older and saw the point to it.) As for Tess and Sam, I was wondering what the two of them were hiding. And, as they say, the apple doesn't fall too far from the tree, because my mother, I could tell, was dying to find out as well.

Sam mumbled a, "nothing," and half-heartedly returned his attention to eating. His mother kept staring at him, though, just in case. Needless to say, everyone was now facing poor Sam, to catch him should he slip up.

"Oh, come on now, a handsome boy such as yourself must get himself into all kinds of mischief. There must be something going on with your life." My mother was nothing if not relentless.

Again he stopped eating and looked up at Tess for direction. Now we were all certain that something was up. And that's when I noticed that Aunt Rose was fidgeting beneath the table. Meaning, whatever was up, she was in on it. Uncle Jesse, who simply ate and ignored the conversation entirely, was obviously out of the loop. Typical. Still, my mother persisted with her line of questioning when she got no response from Sam.

"Now, I refuse to believe that your lives are so uneventful that you can't think of one single thing to tell your Aunt Karen. After all, we've barely seen hide nor hair of each other in years." She was adamant by that point. I think she was legitimately hurt by their lack of up-frontness. In any case, we were about to find out why.

Tess tried to back herself and her son out of the conversation. "No, really, Aunt Karen, our lives just keep rolling along. You know, there aren't a lot of twists and turns in Iowa. Besides, we haven't heard much about Bruce's exciting new life in San Francisco." Uh-oh, I'd been praying that the conversation wouldn't turn to me, because I'd had just enough booze to do you know what. "Bruce," she continued, "tell us all about the big city. Are you dating anybody special out there?"

Damn, that was it. Sparkle and Peter looked at me expectantly. My mother, flustered by the change in the conversation, also turned to me. I guess she figured that anything from me had to be better than what she was getting from the other end of the table. Even my father, never one to care either way, looked up to see what I had to say.

So that was my chance. I took a deep breath, looked at my family, and a few short seconds later I heard it said loudly and proudly, "I'm gay!"

Only it didn't come from me. My mouth was just getting ready to say it, honestly, it was, but someone beat me to the punch. I blinked, then looked around the table for the culprit. Suddenly, it was obvious by the way Tess was looking at Sam that it'd come from him. Damn, I couldn't believe my gaydar didn't pick up on that. I guess it has a certain threshold and doesn't detect fifteen-year-olds too well. Peter, I think, had it figured it out from the get go.

I didn't know whether or not to be relieved or pissed that the kid had blown my chance. Everything else was a blur beyond that, anyhow. Tess immediately blew up at Sam, who, for his part, had a strangely peaceful and relaxed look on his face. Having never come out to my family, I could only surmise that he was just so happy to get it off his chest that the consequences seemed of little importance to him.

"Damn it, Sam," Tess stood up and shouted at him, "I asked you not to bring that up tonight, didn't I?"

"Doctor Samuelson told me that there was nothing to be ashamed of and that I should be honest about it," he tried to explain to us all.

"Who's Doctor Samuelson?" Uncle Jesse asked, finally getting into the conversation.

"It's the boy's psychiatrist," Aunt Rose told her husband.

"How come you know that and it's news to me?"

Uh-oh, I was right. Aunt Rose was in on it and my uncle was way out of the loop. Poor Uncle Jesse looked downright hurt, while the rest of us just looked extremely uncomfortable. Peter kept his eyes on Sam, however, and Sam, for his part, could only look down at his food. I was beginning to feel better about not spilling the beans myself. Family reunions, it was fast turning out, are not the appropriate place to air ones laundry, dirty or otherwise.

"Tess had to tell someone, and she made me promise not to tell anyone else." Aunt Rose knew she was in trouble, and now Tess was in trouble as well. Albert, her brother, never said a word. I figured he was carrying a shit load of baggage himself and was glad that the ceiling wasn't crashing down on him, too.

"Well, damn it, it's nice to know that my family has such a high opinion of me," grumbled my uncle, quickly adding, "Well, Sam, good for you. You're right; you have nothing to be ashamed of." Then with a frown he stood up from the table. "Now, if you'll excuse me, I think I've been insulted enough for one evening." And then he left us, but not before walking over and giving Sam a kiss on his forehead. (Yippy for Uncle Jesse!) Sam, by then, had turned beet red.

"Fine, Pop, leave. You're not the one who has to deal with this; I do," Tess shouted after her father.

Uncle Jesse turned back around and said to her, "It's Sam's life, Honey; just be there for him and love him the same way you always have, and let the good Lord do the rest. I'm sure he'll be fine and I seriously doubt he needs to be seeing a shrink. Jesus, you all are seriously screwed up." Wow, I had a lump in my throat as big as an orange. I knew that my uncle was a cool guy, but he was full of surprises that night. The rest of the family, not too surprisingly, wasn't holding up nearly as well.

Tess sat there dejectedly with her arms folded in front of her and didn't look at anybody. Aunt Rose, feeling sorry for not telling her husband the truth the whole time, ran from the room in tears, while Albert lit up a cigarette and muttered something that sounded disparaging, which I couldn't quite hear over his mother's wailing. Anyway, that was our cue to leave. *Phew.*

Dad went and got our jackets and tried to usher us all out quietly. Mom went and hugged her sister-in-law first and thanked her for the lovely meal. I went and kissed Uncle Jesse, who was now in the living room, and thanked him. He didn't exactly know what for, but he gave me a hug and a kiss and told me not to be a stranger. Peter, well Peter was nearly in tears as he walked over to Sam and told him to call him anytime he needed someone to talk to. Sparkle gave him his card so he'd have their number. I was so proud of my boys right then and there that I could've just busted.

My mother told Cousin Tess to get her head out of her ass and then she told Albert to get a haircut. (I kid you not. She used those exact words.) And then we were out of there, letting out a collective sigh as we left. Honestly, I doubt any of us were expecting such an eventful evening. And, man, it sure was nice to see my dad put his arm around Peter as we walked to the car. You know, just when you think you have your family all figured out, you find that you barely know them at all. But still, even after all that, I just didn't think my mom and pop had it in them to deal with two coming out announcements in one night.

No, it's not that I didn't trust the outcome anymore. I knew they'd handle it better than Tess or Aunt Rose or Sparkle's family or, for that matter, Peter's. It's just, well, I wanted it to be my mom and me, together and without an audience. I figured that I owed her that much. Then I'd tell my father afterward. After all, he was certainly a much cooler dude than I ever expected.

***

I barely slept through the night with all the thoughts racing through my head. See, the whole trip back to Kansas had really opened my eyes to my family. More than likely, I'd played the whole coming out scene in my head so many times and in so many ways that I'd simply convinced myself that they were less tolerant and loving than they actually were, clearly forgetting just how amazing they could be.

At around six in the morning, not being able to lie in bed anymore, I got up and went downstairs to the kitchen to fix myself a bowl of cereal. My mom had beaten me to the punch and was sitting there already slurping down some non-fat, healthy, oaty stuff.

"Got anything with sugar or color to it?" I asked.

"Of course. I prepared for just such an emergency," she replied and reached up to one of the cupboards and pulled down a new box of *Fruit Loops*. I knew that she would throw it away after I left, seeing as she only ate cereals that were good for you. Me, I preferred taste to quality.

"Thanks," I said, pouring myself a big bowl before sitting down next to her. Then I looked at her and said, "Mom, do me a favor and watch out for Sam. It doesn't look like Tess is handling the situation all that well."

"Don't you worry about Sam. If I know my brother, he's already taking caring of the situation. He may have been a lenient disciplinarian to those kids when they were growing up, but he would never tolerate any kind of bigotry in his house or in his family. No matter what you think of him, Bruce, he's a good man."

"I know, Ma. I know." I went back to eating my cereal, with the two of us sitting there in silence for a few minutes.

"Bruce?" She suddenly stopped eating and looked over at me.

"Yeah, Ma?"

"I have a feeling that there's something else on your mind besides your cousin Sam." (Damn, she was good.)

"You're right, Ma, there is." I sat there looking at her for a moment. She had so much love and warmth in her eyes, so much tenderness. Honestly, there's no look like the look that your mother gives you. No one can give you as much unconditional love as your mother, after all. And, at that moment, it was just what I needed.

"Mom... um... well, I'm gay, too." I don't think I've ever felt such a rush of adrenaline before as I had at that moment. I also felt this tidal wave of relief wash over me as she looked deep into my eyes and then reached out to hug me.

Then she said something completely unexpected, whispering in my ear, "Bruce, we already knew."

I pulled away from her and said, "You know? What do you mean you know? Who told you?"

She grinned and let out a motherly giggle. "Son, just because we're from Kansas doesn't mean we're blind. I mean, really, you never dated in high school or college, or at least you never brought any girls home with you to meet us, and, whenever we talk on the phone, you only mention your male friends and that girl Sharon. Generally, you tend to veer clear away from the subject of dating whenever we bring it up, and, the clincher, you live in San Francisco."

She had me there, but I never thought for a minute that she might know. Man, I was a real idiot. All that fuss for nothing.

"But why didn't you tell me that you guys knew?" I asked, also giggling myself now, more out relief than because I thought it was funny.

"Well, Bruce, your father and I figured that you would tell us when you were ready to. I guess it took you a little longer than we expected, but better late than never."

"And it doesn't bother you?" I was probably pushing my luck, but I needed to know.

"I'll be honest with you, when it first dawned on us that you might be gay, we were upset. It's just not what we wanted for you. We thought you'd live a miserable and lonely life, which, of course, broke our hearts. But, over time, we got used to the idea, and you always seem very happy and well-adjusted, so, now, it doesn't bother us. That's all any parent wants for their child, you know, for them to be happy." She smiled and stroked my cheek. "Are you happy, Bruce?"

"Yeah, Ma, I really am." And I really meant it, too. Especially at that very moment.

"That's good, Bruce. Your happiness is all that's important to your father and me."

"I'm sorry I can't give you grandkids, Ma," I added. That always weighed heavily on me, you see.

"Oh, we're fine with that now that we see that you have your own family. It's not the one I imagined you with, but it looks like it works for you." Again she giggled. "That William is a gas, by the way."

"I know, Ma. I know. And, Ma?"

"Yes, Bruce?"

"I love you very much."

"I love you too, Son, but can you do me just one favor?"

"Sure, Ma, anything you want."

She nodded and walked over to one of the cabinets. "Can you just *try* this cereal? It won't kill you to eat healthy you know."

"Fine, Ma," I replied, wiping the tear from my cheek. "I'd be happy too."

This one time, anyway.

CHAPTER EIGHT
TIT FOR TAT

Tits are cool. Now, seeing as that's just about the straightest (and strangest) thing you're ever gonna hear me say, I promise I won't repeat it or dwell on it all that much. But they do play a relatively major part in the story I'm about to tell you, and I wanted to get it out in the open so as not to confuse or upset you later on. Okay? Are you ready to move on? You're looking a little green around the gills up there.

Fine, I'll continue then...

First, let me say that, back in the present, Sparkle hasn't gotten much better. Granted, he hasn't gotten any worse, either, thankfully, but a little cooperation on his part would be nice. It's been three full days now since he was brought to the hospital and, basically, he's just been lying there in that awful coma. The doctors told me yesterday that his brain functions were normal and his heart rate and other vitals were looking better all the time, and that it's just up to him to snap out of it. They also warned me that the longer he stayed asleep, the worse off he would be when he did finally come back to us.

But it's what the police told me that truly had me concerned. (I mean, really, Sparkle barely uses the remaining brain cells he has. What's a few more down the drain in the grand scheme of things?) See, apparently, Sparkle has a gun registered under his name, and the bullet that shot through him matched to the type of gun he owns. That, oddly enough, can mean two things. One, it's merely a coincidence and whoever shot Sparkle used the same kind of gun; or two, he was shot with his very own gun. I told the police that there's no way in hell that Sparkle tried to commit suicide, seeing as he loves himself way too much to do that, but they pointed out that there was no forced entry into the apartment and that his gun was still in the house with only his fingerprints on it. I knew that meant that the police would barely keep up the search for whoever did shoot Sparkle, but I also knew better than to think that Sparkle tried to take his own life. Besides, right now the most important thing is that he comes out of the coma, not who put him there in the first place.

In order to accomplish that goal, the snapping out of it, as they put it, the doctors encouraged me to talk to Sparkle and rub his arms and legs in the hope that he could possibly hear and or feel me and decide that he was better off out in the real world and not wherever the hell he was. I didn't know if it would do any good, but I decided to give it a try. That's why I'm here in his room right now telling you this little tale. After all, it's one of his favorites. It's also got the requisite amounts of sex, drugs, booze, and woe. Oh, and there's a smidge of good-deediness as well. After all, I like to tell a well-balanced story, in case you hadn't guessed that already.

So, in order to tell you what happened, I'm gonna have to jump a few years from where we left off. I guess, if I'm figuring right, it was during the summer of 1999. That seems about right. Did lots of exciting and life changing events occur doing those few years? Nah, not really. I mean, we all grew a little older and maybe a little wiser, but just a little. Peter, naturally, grew the most, though.

Firstly and literally, he grew. By the time he turned eighteen, he'd grown something like five inches and was a strapping and devilishly handsome, six-two, slim and trim, young man. For the most part, he stayed on the directionally forward (see, I avoided that *straight* word, finally) and narrow path and rarely was in trouble either at home or in school. For that, we were grateful. So were the folks at Social Services. They commended us time and time again on how well we raised Peter. Honestly, I never really had any doubts. (Well, maybe just a few.) And, when Peter turned eighteen, he was legally considered an adult and the State no longer had any control over his or our lives.

Naturally, the first thing we did (surprise, surprise) was restock the bar in Sparkle's apartment. Not that we wanted Peter to take up drinking, mind you, but it was nice to be able to not have those pesky social workers watching over our shoulders for a change, and we wanted to celebrate. Besides, we trusted Peter. After all, he never gave us a reason not to. (Okay, mostly we just missed the damn bar.

Drinking in my tiny apartment was no fun at all, and the local watering holes, well, I think you know our opinion of those already.)

The next big change for Peter was when he graduated from high school. That truly was exciting. We went through two rolls of film and a box of Kleenex during the graduation ceremony. Peter, much to out delight, decided to stay on at the bookstore during the summer and then he would start school at San Francisco State in the fall. We all agreed, also, that he would stay at Sparkle's apartment while he was in college. It was certainly cheaper than getting his own place, and, just between you and me, we wanted to keep tabs on him. I think, by that time, we truly felt like his parents and we would've been heartbroken to see him move out.

Now on to the two of us. You know, I think you reach a certain point and then you just kind of coast. Basically, those three years went pretty much the same as the three years prior, except that we had the added responsibility of raising Peter. I think that that kept our lives rather routine and humdrum. No complaints, though, mind you; I wouldn't have changed a thing. Watching Peter grow up and mature before our very eyes was a wonderful experience. Honest.

Still, it would've been nice to have found a husband somewhere along the way. (Or at least a long-term boyfriend. Hell, I'd have settled for a steady fuck-buddy.) Sparkle, of course, was content with his boyfriends du jour, but I wanted something more than that. Unfortunately, between the store and Peter, there wasn't enough time left over for romance. Not to mention, the guys in San Francisco tend to be on the flaky side and could care less about a long-term monogamous relationship. Oh well, c'est la vie. The old bottle of lube got used from time to time, so who am I to complain?

Okay then, with all that out of the way, where were we? Oh, yeah, back to the summer of '99. It all started one fine morning at the bookstore. Peter, Sharon, and I had just opened up and were sitting down to our first cup of coffee. Oh, um, yeah, see, when Peter turned eighteen we let him start his first bad habit. We figured, what the heck, it was better than cigarettes or crack or something else that could kill you. And, besides, how could we tell him that it was bad for him and then go ahead and do it ourselves. (I couldn't wait for him to turn twenty-one, so I could see how Sparkle would try to convince him that drinking alcohol was bad for him. Maybe show the kid an x-ray of our livers, right?)

Anyway, we were shooting the shit when a very attractive young woman walked into the store and proceeded to look around. I could see immediately that Sharon's eyes were locked in on her. "Down, girl," I said, just under my breath.

"Woof," she responded in kind. The customer heard her and looked up from a book that she was holding. She caught Sharon's stare, a sly grin appearing on her beautiful face. Then, bold as she could be, the stranger set the book back on the shelf and proceeded to walk over to our table.

"Hi," she said, reaching out her hand to Sharon, "name's Betty."

Sharon reached up to shake Betty's hand and then introduced the three of us. Betty straddled the remaining chair at out table and sat down. She had some incredible sex appeal, I must say. I mean, you pretty much never see women straddle chairs like that anymore. I'm sure, had I any tendencies that way, it would've been erotic. In any case, it did at least have a very impressive air about it. And Sharon, well now, she was fairly mesmerized.

"So, Betty, what brings you into our little store?" I asked, breaking the ice.

"Oh, just passing by, and, since I'd been looking for a certain book on photography, I thought I'd check to see if you had it in stock. Here's the title and author," she said, handing me a little scrap of paper that she pulled out from her purse. I sent Peter off to look for the book as we got comfortable.

"Are you a photographer?" Sharon asked, once she got her wits back.

"Sometimes. At least I like to think of myself as one. It doesn't pay the bills, yet, but some day, maybe," she answered, not telling us what, exactly, did pay the bills. Not that we cared, really. See, Betty, whoever she was, was nothing if not fascinating. She had this, this certain, well, I guess you could say *aura* about her.

Peter came back and said that we didn't have the book in stock, but that we could order it for her. "Sure," she said and handed Peter a card. "Call me when it gets here."

Then she de-straddled herself, stood up, said that it was nice meeting all of us, but that she had to run. She then began to saunter out of the store, turning to wink at Sharon before she left. As soon as she was down the street a bit, Sharon and I, naturally, both made a grab for the card.

"Damn," she said, reaching it a split second before I did, "all it says is her name and number. I can't believe I've never seen her before. This town is just way too small to miss someone like that," she said, looking clearly perplexed. "Peter, you let me know as soon as that book comes in and let me call her, okay?" Peter nodded as we both stood there smiling at her. "What?" she asked.

"Oh, nothing," I taunted and then sing-songed, "Just that… Sharon's got a girlfriend, Sharon's got a girlfriend."

"Real mature, Bruce? How old are you, anyway? Shouldn't you be setting and example for Peter?" she said, hands on hips.

"I am," I responded, "watch." And I pointed to Peter, who then mimicked me with, "Sharon's got a girlfriend, Sharon's got a girlfriend."

"See," I said, proudly, "chip off the old block."

Peter and I laughed. Sharon merely shook her head and went back to the office.

"Bruce," Peter started, when she was out of earshot (he rarely, if ever, called me Secret), "I think I know where Betty works, and I don't think Sharon's going to like it."

"Ooh, you better tell your Uncle Bruce right this minute," I commanded and sat back down in my chair. Peter knew far too much for his own good, but I was never one to miss a chance to dish before, so why start now. Anyway, I always liked to have something over on Sharon, as she was forever one step ahead of me and almost dead even with Sparkle. And, heck, that was hard to do, seeing as Sparkle had his feelers practically everywhere. In any case, I was glad to be the first (almost) on something for a change.

"Well," he began, "I may be wrong. I mean, I've never actually been in the place, but I'm pretty sure it's her picture out in front."

"Out front of what? Where?" Fuck, I couldn't wait to find out.

"Er, oh, um…," Peter turned red and looked down. "The, uh, The Snatch."

"The Snatch!" I nearly shouted. "Are you sure?"

"Pretty sure. It looks just like her, but, like I said, I've never been in, so I can't be totally sure."

"Well, I should say not," I said, not because he was underage so much as that it was a straight tittie club along Polk Street and I would hope that he wouldn't want to be in such a vile establishment. (Yuck.)

"Should we tell her?" he asked.

Probably, yes, but I had a better idea. "No, I want to make sure first. Let me handle it, but thanks for telling me. It's always good to be honest." Sometimes I almost believed the stuff I was trying to impress upon Peter. See, honesty, though not wrong in its purest sense, is not nearly as fun or as easy as, say, underhanded trickery. Yes, my friends, Sparkle at long last had turned me over to the dark side. Plus, I was leaning a tad toward the wicked that day and wanted to have some fun for a change.

"Secret," Peter said, looking down at me as I stared into the abyss, "you have that same look on your face that Sparkle sometimes gets. Are you planning something?"

"Moi? Never. I was just… just… thinking about…hey, go order that book for Betty and let me enjoy my coffee in peace, please."

"Fine, but I've been around long enough to know when something is up. Can't kid a kidder, ya know," he said. "But shouldn't you let Sparkle come up with the bad ideas? At least then we'd know that a professional is handling it." We *had* raised him well; he truly was daddy's little boy.

"Peter, nothing is up. Now stop using that vivid imagination of yours and go order that book, okay?" I knew better than to fill him in. He may have been an adult in the strictest sense of the word, but he still had a big mouth, and I, for one, wanted this to be Secret's little secret for the time being."

"Fine, fine," he said and then added, "but when you play with fire…"

"That reminds me, never take up arson. Now go." Nope, it's never enjoyable to be lectured by someone much younger than yourself. Especially when they're probably right. Besides, the game was already underfoot, the match already lit.

***

The next night, just before closing, I casually mentioned to Sparkle and Sharon that the three of us hadn't gone out to dinner, just the three of us, in, like, forever. They agreed and started making suggestions, when I told them that there was this fabulous, little Thai place on Polk and that we should try it out. No, I had no idea if there really was a Thai restaurant anywhere near The Snatch, but, this being San Francisco, there's a fabulous, little Thai restaurant on almost every corner in every neighborhood, so, I figured, my odds were better than good.

"What's it called?" Sharon asked, after we told Peter to close up for the night and started out the door.

"What? Oh, I forget, but I'll know it when I see it," I lied.

"Sounds like a winner," Sparkle sarcastically added.

"There's a bar nearby," I threw in. Naturally, that perked him up right quick.

Sure enough, not a half a block from my true destination, there was a cozy Thai restaurant on the corner. Go figure. Anyway, we went in and ordered. And, like most restaurants in the city, it was pretty good. The added bonus was watching all the prostitutes walk by, both male and female and all points in between. It was like our own personal floorshow. See, Polk Street has always had something for every liking. In fact, it was the gay place to be long before The Castro ever was.

We ate up fast, as we were all in the mood for a drink or two. Of course, I steered our trio in the right direction as we left. Then it was time for some creative thinking. I mean, how do you get a gay man and a mostly gay woman into a straight strip club?

"I hear they make a good drink in there," I said, pointing at the sign that was glowing in hot-pink neon: *Snatch… Snatch… Snatch.* (When in doubt, shoot for the booze.) At least by looking up, no one was looking at the sign out in front. I caught a quick glance at it, and it may or may not have been Betty printed on top. For one, Betty was fully clothed when I met her, and the woman in the picture was, for the most part, naked and just barely concealing herself with her arms and hands. I was having second thoughts when, out of nowhere, Sharon replied, "I'm game."

"You are?" Sparkle and I asked in unison.

"Sure, why not? I've never been to a place like this before. Could be fun," she said, with a shrug, surprising the hell out of me. I mean, I didn't think a woman, even a bisexual woman, would want to go into a straight, male strip club.

"Well, maybe not," I backpedaled.

"But it was your idea," Sparkle said, suddenly taking her side. And, with arms akimbo, he added, "What's the matter? Chicken?"

"No, it's just…" I tried, causing them both to start cackling at me. "Fine! Before you both lay an egg or some poultry-fucker happens by (hey, what's the hanky color for that one?), let's go in." Damn, I'd heard of reverse psychology, but that was ridiculous. There I was, trying to trick them into going in and seeing Betty, and they had to coerce me into doing it myself. I was pissed off until I realized that I'd actually gotten away with it. And then, of course, I was scared shitless, because I suddenly realized that I was going into a tittie-bar. (Can they revoke you're gay membership card for that?)

First thing, it was cold in there. Second, there were lights, but only above the several stages scattered throughout. Third, and this explains the other two, there was a naked or nearly naked woman on each of the stages, and, yes, in evidence of the frigid air, their nips were on high-beam. Needless to say, we practically ran to the nearest available bartender.

"Three gin and tonics," Sharon ordered.

"It's free for you, pretty, little miss. Ladies night," he informed.

Now then, every other time, Sharon was your typical woman's libber: she never let us get the door for her; she thought we were crazy when we let her do anything first, simply because she was a girl; she hated the whole Miss vs. Mrs. thing; but as soon as someone was offering her a free drink, well then, that missing Y chromosome was certainly a big-time bonus. So I'm here to say, as long as there are ladies nights, there will never be equality between the sexes! (Okay, I was jealous. I wanted a free drink and, unless they had a former drag queen night, I was clearly shit out of luck.)

The bartender came back with our drinks, adding, "And it's amateur night. If you get up there and win, you get a hundred bucks plus all the tips you earn. Wanna enter?"

"I'll just start with the drink, thanks." Sharon blushed and took a swig of her gin.

"*Bock, bock, bock,*" I clucked in her ear.

"Only idiots fall for that one, Secret," Sparkle said and pulled us all to one of the stages.

"Fucker," I responded, staring up at the gyrating redhead now two feet above us. I had never been so close to a naked lady before and I felt slightly nauseous. (Could've been the cheap gin, though, but doubtful.)

"Here!" Sharon shouted above the music as she grabbed our hands to lead us to an empty table.

The three of us took our seats to the right of the stage, and, as my eyes grew accustomed to the lighting, I started to observe the goings on around me. I didn't see Betty, but there were, like, four or five other naked or nearly naked women dancing, strutting, swinging, and otherwise exposing their privates for the clusters of admiring men. It was an amazing site to behold, really. These guys, who I took for your typical working, married types, were all sitting there completely absorbed in the action before them. And, every minute or so, one of them would stand up and hand one of the women a bill. I couldn't tell the denominations, but these chicks were obviously raking it in, the men seeming only too happy to oblige. (Meanwhile, their wives were probably sitting at home trying to make ends meet. Sad, really.)

I guess, if I have to admit it, though, it wasn't nearly as disgusting or uncomfortable as I thought it was going to be. It was interesting to observe the control that these women had over their admirers. Plus, from what I could tell, they were making a great deal of money for doing very little. Still, I should've known not to get too comfortable, because, while I was looking around, I felt a tap on my shoulder. When I turned around, lo and behold, there was Betty.

"Table dance?" she asked, not yet recognizing me.

"A what?" I asked, stunned that it was actually her.

"You know. A table dance. You sit at the table, I dance, get a little undressed, you tip. Get it?" she explained, with a devilish smirk on her face.

Just then, Sharon noticed the interaction and spoke up. "Betty?" she blurted out, surprised that it was the same person that had been in the store earlier that day. Of course, Betty looked even more shocked. She didn't immediately recognize us, but hearing her real name and not whatever name she went by in the bar seemed to give her a jolt. Still, she relaxed a bit once she figured out who we were.

"Well, hi," she said, "did you guys find my book or something?"

"No," Sharon explained, "we were just passing by and decided to stop in and check the place out."

Betty sat down and joined us at our table. "Well? What do you think?" she asked, motioning with her hand around the place.

"Well… uh… it's different." Poor Sharon. I don't think she knew just how to react.

"Hey now, you don't have to put on an act for me. I know it stinks, but the pay is amazing and I have time for my photography during the day," she explained, gently slapping Sharon on the shoulder. "Besides," she added, "I have a whole showroom full of lovely ladies who are only to happy to pose naked for me."

"I can see where that would be a job perk," Sharon admitted, leaning in closer to Betty. Obviously, our new friend's choice of profession was not a turn off to our old friend, Sharon.

"So, how 'bout it?" Betty asked, standing up and shaking her stuff. "Care for a little show?"

That's when Sparkle, who had been sitting quietly in the background for a change, threw in his two cents. "Take it off!" he shouted. Naturally, I gulped. I mean, it's one thing to watch a naked chick dancing from a distance, after all, but it's something entirely different when they're right in front of you and you sort of, kind of, know them already. That didn't stop Betty, however; Sparkle's encouragement was all she needed.

She waited for the next song to start, which, thank goodness, was *Hit Me with Your Best Shot*. See, I felt safer knowing that Pat was going to be with me during the ordeal. And that's when Betty started to gyrate in front of us. She looked at all three of us, but concentrated on Sharon, who, from what I could see, had died and gone to heaven.

Naturally, the top was the first thing to go. One minute there's Betty; the next minute, there's Betty and her boobs. *Poof,* just like that. Honestly, I could've used a little more time to get used to the idea. Like when you're about to go into a cold pool and you gingerly put your toe in, and then your foot, and then you slowly, ever so slowly, slide the rest of your body in, until you hardly notice the cold water anymore. Well, with Betty, it felt like someone had thrown me into the pool. Head first. Into the deep, *deep* end.

Sparkle, to my amazement, was cheering her on. (How Sparkle manages to surprise me anymore is a mystery.) He got up and put a dollar in her garter belt. She thanked him with a wink and toss of her hair. I thanked him by kicking him under the table. Then Sharon joined in the festivities and seductively added to Sparkles dollar with one of her own. Sadly, that's when Betty looked over at me.

Well, what was a gay boy to do? I reached for my wallet and pulled out a dollar. (When in Rome...) But before I could reach for the garter, Betty turned around, bent over, and pulled down her shiny, pink panties. I was at a loss (to say the least). Now what?

"Put it between her cheeks!" Sparkle shouted at me. I shook my head no, in shock at the very thought.

"Do it!" Sharon joined in.

"Do it!" shouted the guy at the table next to me.

"Do it!" Betty commanded from her precarious position. "I can't stand here like this forever."

So I did it. I neatly folded my one-dollar bill in half and gently placed it between her round, upturned cheeks. Then Betty stood up, reached for the dollar, and stuck it in her garter. (Hey, I could've done that myself.) My table erupted into applause after that. Even I got into it and gleefully clapped. (Funny, basically she mooned me and I paid her a buck. Why that was cause for merriment, I have no idea.)

Of course, the show wasn't over yet. Completely naked except for the garter belt and a pair of, from what I could see, very nice heels, Betty swung and strutted her body and then plopped right down on my lap. Yikes. *Get it off me, get it off me*, I scream in my head. Sharon and Sparkle nearly fell off their chairs with laughter as all the blood in my body rushed to my head. Then, straddling me, Betty shook her chest right in my face and bumped and grinded her ass on my lap. That's when the whole chair thing back at the store that morning dawned on me. No wonder she sat down like that when she joined us: force of habit.

Realizing that I'd had enough, Betty jumped up, put her outfit back on, and took a bow. (Heck, I would've paid her to keep her clothes on if I had known what was going to happen.)

"That, my dear friend, is a table dance," she said and kissed me on the cheek. "Did ya like it?"

"Oh... yeah, sure... um, thanks," I stuttered.

"That's the closest Secret's been to pussy since we were down at the ASPCA last month," Sparkle shouted, and I, naturally, winced. (I'd almost bought a cat, until I realized that Sparkle and Peter were handfuls enough.)

We all laughed, while Betty moved on to another table. I hoped that her next customer would be more appreciative of her talents. Sharon shouted at her that she would give her a call when the book came in, to which Betty replied, "Why wait until then?"

"Sharon's got a girlfriend, Sharon's got a girlfriend," Sparkle chided, echoing my joke from that morning.

This time, Sharon smiled and replied, "I could do worse."

"You have," Sparkle returned. "Now let's vamoose before this place has any lasting effects on us."

"Yeah," I said as we stood up to leave, "what's next, Monday night football?"

"Heaven forbid," Sparkle answered, in mock horror.

We were outside in a flash. That, I must say, was enough machismo for one lifetime, and I, for one, was glad to be out of there. But, as they say, out of the frying pan and into the fire. We were barely two steps down the sidewalk when I noticed someone that looked like Peter standing across the street talking to another boy who also looked vaguely familiar..

I shouted "Peter!" to whoever it was, and that's when I knew that I'd been correct. Peter froze when he saw the three of us crossing the street to where he was standing. Of course, none of us looked happy to see him there. It was neither the right place nor the right time for a boy like him to be. After all, there was only one kind of person his age that was on Polk Street at that time of night. I prayed for a much better reason as we approached.

"Hey, guys. What are you all doing here?" he asked, nervously.

"I think I should be asking you the same..." Sparkle started to answer, until I interrupted him with, "Sam!"

"Hi, Cousin Bruce," Sam said as I stood there in shock. He looked horrible. As a matter of fact, he looked much like Peter did when he first came into our lives, and I knew that could mean only one thing: trouble.

"Okay," Sparkle barked, "what the fuck is going on?" He was mighty pissed. As far as he knew, Peter had never gone behind his back before and, obviously, he was doing just that right at that very moment.

"It's my fault," Sam said, looking down at the sidewalk. "I made him promise not to tell you. I didn't want my mother to know where I was. She'd send my miserable uncle out to get me, and I knew you'd call her if you knew I was here. I just wanted to get a job and a place to live before I told you guys that I left home and came here to live."

"Doesn't look like you've had much luck, Sam," Sparkle said, with some bitterness, but I could tell he was softening fast. Poor Sam looked pitiful. But he was right; I would've called home just so they wouldn't worry about him. Stupid kids.

"Where are you staying?" Sharon asked, concerned for my cousin.

"Right here," he said, pointing to a rundown hotel.

Immediately, I felt sick to my stomach. "How long have you been here?" I asked, barely wanting to hear the answer.

"Just a few days, but it took me a week to get here. I only got in touch with Peter two days ago, I swear, and he wanted to take me to you guys right away, but I wouldn't let him. Please don't be mad at him," he pleaded, all hound-dog-puppy looking.

Of course, we invented that look. "Too late," Sparkle said. "Now you," he commanded Sam, "get in that rat-trap, get your things, and get your skinny ass back out here in five minutes. And you," he added, now talking to Peter, "you get over to my car and sit yourself down in the back seat and don't say one word until I tell you too." Both boys did as they were told. Honestly, I'd never seen Sparkle so angry before. Usually, everything rolled right off his back.

Minutes later, Sam came running out with his meager possessions and followed us to Sparkle's car. Of course, fitting five in a Corvette is no easy task, but we managed. Then it was time for some answers.

"Okay," Sparkle began, "start at the beginning, please, Sam." I could tell that he was fuming beneath his relatively calm exterior.

"Well, you guys were there at that horrible dinner three years ago. Unfortunately for me, things went downhill after that night. My mother just couldn't deal, and Grandma and Grandpa lived too far away to have any real influence on her. Though Grandpa Jesse tried his hardest, my mom freaked out every time the subject of my being gay came up. And then some kids at school found out about me, and pretty soon I was getting regularly beat up ... (Sam started to sob, which meant that Sparkle and I immediately forgave him for anything he might've done.)... and, of course, the school had to keep calling my mom to come down and get me, which she hated doing. And then she hated *me* for being the cause of it all."

"Oh, Sam," I said, "I'm so sorry. Your mom always was anxious that way. But you're here now and, by my calculations, you must be at least eighteen, so, even if I do call home to say that you're here, there's nothing she can do about it. And you can stay with me until we figure something out. How does that sound?"

Through his tears, he said, "Oh, Cousin Bruce, thank you... thank you so much. I should've called you from the beginning. I'm sorry for making Peter go behind your back that way. I'd love to stay with you. I mean, that hotel was way scary. Heck, they don't have places like that back in Iowa."

They probably didn't, but there was something about Sam that gave me reason to pause. Oh, I was sure he was telling the truth about his mother; she always was a bitch. But the way he looked and sounded made me think that there were more things going on than met the eye.

Still, that wasn't the time or place to go into it, and I had a feeling that my mother could add something to his story anyway. I'd just have to wait until I got home to give her a call.

"It's okay, Sam. We'll straighten this whole thing out. At least you had the sense to call Peter," I began, and Peter started to smile, thinking he was out of trouble.

"No, Mister," I corrected him. "You should've known better. I don't care what Sam made you promise; you should've told Sparkle and me what was going on from the start. Sam is my family, after all, and you're *our* family. That means sometimes having to do things that we don't like in order to protect each other. So you're still in trouble." That wiped the smirk off his face. Of course, when you start preaching all high and mighty like that, there's always something that brings you down a notch. For me, it was my big mouth. "Well, at least now I know how you knew that Betty worked at The Snatch," added I, realizing right away what I'd just said and praying that no one else caught on.

"Excuse me?" Sharon coughed out, turning around to look at me cowering in the back seat. She had, apparently, caught on. "What do you mean Peter knew that Betty worked at The Snatch? And since when did you know that Betty worked there, Mister *Let's try that place out, I hear they make a good drink*? You fucking tricked us." Uh-oh, she had me.

"Not tricked, exactly. I mean, really, you guys sort of made me go in there in the first place." I made a hopeless attempt to save myself.

"Give it up," Sparkle said. "You tried to pull something over on Sharon and you got caught. Really, Secret, you should leave the underhanded trickery up to me."

"Told you so," Peter whispered in my ear.

"Shut up," I whispered right back. "You're still in trouble."

Sharon heard me and added, "Not as much as you are." (*Gulp.*)

Peter nudged me. I nudged him back. Sometimes I forgot that I wasn't that much older than him, but I should've known better. Still, I couldn't help but start to laugh.

"What's so fucking funny?" Sharon fumed.

"Well, I did get you. I mean, you were surprised, and she obviously likes you, so..."

"So what?" she said, but with a little less edge to her voice.

"So let the baby have this one," Sparkle interceded. "But he better not let it happen again," he said to Sharon, though he was clearly talking to me.

"Cross my heart," I said and crossed my heart. "I promise to leave the deceitful, conniving, manipulative, and otherwise evil behavior up to Sparkle."

"Well, okay then," Sparkle said. "And if Peter promises that from now on he'll never go behind our backs, no matter what, then he's forgiven as well."

"I promise," Peter promised and crossed his heart. I leaned over and kissed him on the cheek and ruffled his hair. I don't think I could ever stay mad at him for more than five minutes, anyhow.

"And if Sam wants to be a part of this family, he has to promise it, too," I added, but Sam was already sound asleep in the back seat. "I guess Sam will have to promise it in the morning then," I whispered. Still, I had my doubts that Sam wanted to be part of our family, or he would've called me when he got to San Francisco and not Peter. That, you see, was what was really nagging at me.

***

That night, Sparkle dropped Sam and me off at my place and he went to his apartment with Peter. I had to wait until the next morning to phone my mother, as it was way too late by the time we got home. Needless to say, I was nervous calling her, and I had good reason to be.

As it turned out, she had no idea that Sam was even missing. That was surprise number one. Surprise number two was that my mother got off the phone with me to call her brother to find out what he knew, and, it so happened, he didn't know that Sam was missing either. Well, as I said before, bad news comes in threes, seeing as that Uncle Jesse called Cousin Tess, and she did, in fact, know that Sam was missing and simply didn't care.

But, and this is a big old but, while Sam was telling the truth about the beatings and everything, what he neglected to tell us was that the school was calling Tess mostly because her son was caught smoking crack several times. They only let him graduate to get him out of their hair. My mother said that he was lucky not to be in jail or worse. She also said that it was the first she'd heard about any of it and apologized to me for having it thrown in my lap. I thanked her for the information, told her that that was what family was for, also told her to tell the rest of the family that I would look after Sam and not to worry, and then I hung up. All while a pit the size of a watermelon formed in my churning belly.

I knew something was off about Sam, as I'd mentioned, and now I knew what it was. But what was I to do about it? And did I really want him living in my home? First thing I did was call Sparkle, who, through Peter, already knew the whole story. He told me that he was sending Peter over to look after my cousin so that I could go to work. Meanwhile, said cousin was still fast asleep in the living room. I sighed and scratched my head. Did I really owe him anything? Did I need the aggravation? Did I have a choice?

When Peter arrived, he pulled me in the hallway to apologize again for what he'd done. Then he explained how he was trying his best to get Sam in a shelter or a drug clinic, but that he wasn't having any luck. Also, when we'd caught them the night before, he was there to tell Sam that he was going to tell me and Sparkle about him, when we just appeared out of nowhere and the whole mess was suddenly out in the open. I could tell that Peter was relieved now that we, too, knew about the drugs and everything.

"The only reason I didn't tell you guys from the very beginning was that I was afraid that Sam would split, and he needs help. Badly. I've seen his kind before, in case you've forgotten. (I hadn't.) But don't worry, go to work; I'll keep an eye on him." Peter was convincing enough, but I was still worried. Sam, after all, had too much Sparkle in him and not enough Secret, and I was afraid that Peter would be too naïve to see it. I was right, of course, but hindsight, as I always say, is twenty/twenty.

Anyway, what could I do? I went to work and was greeted by a forgiving Sharon and a not-too-concerned Sparkle.

"Let me guess," I guessed, "you've taken something little and blue, right?"

"No, Miss Smarty-Pants," he responded and stuck his tongue out at me. "It's merely that I trust Peter to watch your cousin, and, just as soon as we can, we'll call our old friend, Dan, and get Sam some help. Okay? Stop you're worrying; you'll get frown-lines. More of them."

"It was the little yellow one, wasn't it?" I tried again, choosing to ignore the backhanded comment as it slapped me in the face.

He shrugged. "Fine. Yes, it was the little yellow one, but I still trust Peter, and there's nothing we can do about it right this second. So sit down, have some coffee, and help me pick out a tattoo from this magazine."

"Oh, God, why do you make me face multiple problems simultaneously?" I asked, raising my hands up to the Almighty. "What on earth are you talking about now?" I then shouted at Sparkle, and gladly took the pill from his hand that he had waiting for me. (Judge not, lest ye be judged.)

Sharon yelled from the back, "He wants a tattoo. Haven't you been listening these past three weeks? It's all he can talk about." Actually, I had been listening, but I didn't want to encourage him. I knew that if he got one… well, you can guess what would happen, and I was scared to death about getting a tattoo. (Secretly, I really did want one, but it's those damn needles and all that pain that worried me.)

"You know," I shouted back, "he rants about so many things that I can hardly keep up."

"Hardy, har, har," Sparkle mock-laughed. "Now shut up and start looking at these magazines; and for once, I'm not going to force you to do something just because I'm doing it."

"You're not?" Of course, he would pick the one time to turn noble, just when I wanted him to force me to do something.

"No, I'm not, but you still need to help me pick one out." Damn that reverse psychology. Now I really wanted one and was just too chicken to admit it.

Just then, who should walk into the store but our friendly neighborhood stripper, Betty. She looked different with her clothes on. (By different, I mean better than naked.) Still, it was all I could do to not picture her undressed as she waltzed into the shop and again straddled the chair next to mine. Sparkle thanked her for the prior evening's entertainment and then excused himself. He went to the back to call Dan, which immediately made me feel better. See, if anyone could help Sam, it was going to be Dan. At least I prayed as much.

"Yes, Betty, thank you for… an enlightening evening," I added to Sparkle's parting sentiments.

"You're quite welcome," she said and then asked for Sharon.

"Sharon," I bellowed, "you're friend, Betty, is out here to see you." Man oh man, I never saw Sharon move so fast. She was sitting down with us before I could even blink an eyelash. She also gave me a warning look that said, *Look Buster, I've forgiven you for last night, but you better behave yourself.* Which, of course, I did, seeing as how Sharon was almost as dangerous as Sparkle, and I really didn't want her getting even with me. I may have been a bad liar and an awful sneak, but I knew how to save my own skin, at the very least.

"Hi, Betty," she said, practically panting.

"Hi, Sharon. I just wanted to come by to make sure that you guys were okay with, well, you know, *last night*. I mean, I don't know you all from Adam, but I hope I didn't shock you or anything."

"Well...," I started, but Sharon stopped me.

"No, not at all. We had a lovely evening. Thanks for your concern," she said and kicked me under the table. *Ouch.*

"Oh, good, because I was hoping that you might like to go out sometime," Betty professed.

And before Betty could even finish the word *sometime*, Sharon was spitting out a "yes". (There's a fine line between obvious and desperate. One that I'd crossed on numerous occasions. So I know of what I speak.)

"How's tonight grab you?" Betty offered.

"Grabs me fine!" Sharon accepted. (And then replace desperate with easy.)

"Great, I see that you guys close at eight. I'll be by to pick you up then, okay?" she asked as she stood up to leave.

"Great. Yes. I'll see you then." Sharon was positively beaming.

"Okay then. See you at eight," Betty said, then waved and walked out the front door.

"Sharon's got a girlfriend, Sharon's got a girlfriend," Sharon sang to herself. (How quickly they change their tune, right?)

Soon after Betty left, Sparkle returned from his phone conversation with Dan. Turned out, we were in luck. Dan knew of a halfway house not far from my apartment that specialized in young people with drug problems. He said that he would put a call in to a friend of his and then would get back to us as soon as possible. I felt better, but skeptical. See, Sam didn't strike me as the type that thought that he needed help. Obviously, if he were, he would've phoned way before he ever left for San Francisco.

"I think we're gonna need Peter to help us out on this one," I suggested.

"Agreed. Let's give him a call and tell him the plan and see if he can convince your cousin that it's in his best interest," Sparkle suggested. Seeing as there really was no better alternative, I prayed that Peter could do the job.

I called him right away and filled him in. He agreed to our plan whole-heartedly and said that he would spend the day with Sam trying to convince him to check himself in. Considering that he had ample firsthand experience with living on the streets and all that that entailed, I doubted it would be a hard sell. But I also knew that drugs severely interfered with one's better judgment and that Sam could very easily not see things our way. Thank goodness Peter was young and handsome, of course. If nothing else, it was hard to say no to such a pretty face. (Jeez, did I just describe my relationship with Sparkle in a nutshell or what?)

So then, all we could do was wait. Wait, that is, for Dan and his connection and then see if Peter could convince Sam to go along with it. Naturally, Sparkle had something for us to do while we wiled away the hours. (Besides the fact that I had a store to run.) Within minutes of hanging up the phone with Peter, Sparkle had me looking through one tattoo magazine after another.

Having never given much thought to getting a tattoo before, it never dawned on me how major a decision it was to pick one out. After all, it was something that was going to be on his body for the rest of his life. And I seriously doubted that when I was eighty I'd want a Tasmanian devil on my ass. Still, the thought of a tattoo did intrigue me. (The pain of getting one, however, was a definite turnoff.)

"You know, Sparkle, I think that whatever you get should come out of your own head and not from one of these magazines," I offered.

"Is this your tattoo? I think not. Keep looking," said he, rejecting my proposal. His demeanor, sadly, made me want one even more. Just to show him who was boss. What a fucking trip. I mean, either he was the slyest asshole ever or I was the biggest idiot. (Shut up. I know what you're thinking.) In either case, we spent most of the next couple of hours pouring through a dozen or so tattoo magazines, until I couldn't bear to see one more black panther with its claws ripping across some stranger's arm or one more Celtic pictogram just below someone's neck or just above someone's ass. Are people really that unimaginative?

Thank goodness Dan called back when he did, as I was quite over our little project by then. Fortunately, the news was good. There was room for Sam at the house, but only if he took it immediately.

Space, like any other room in San Francisco, was at a premium. So it was now all in Peter's capable hands.

Suffice it to say, between Sharon anxiously awaiting her date, Sparkle laboring over the tattoo decision, and all of us biting our nails thinking about Sam, it was a tense day, to say the least. I for one was glad when it was time to close up shop and head on home for the evening. We let Sharon lock up so she could be alone with Betty. Actually, she made us leave. I half expected to find some funky smelling towels in the morning in retaliation for my years-earlier sexcapade.

What I wasn't expecting was to find just that when I got home, with Sparkle in tow. There was no sign of Peter or Sam, but I recognized the smell of sex just the same. (After all, it was rare that I got to smell it much around my home. *Sob.*)

"Um, Sparkle?" I asked, after retrieving the dirty come-rags from the bottom of my hamper, "do you think it might not have been a good idea to leave two attractive and, more than likely, horny teenagers alone in the apartment all day without any adult supervision?"

"Well, when you put it that way...," he responded.

Just then, the culprits sauntered in. They took one look at us, noticed the soiled evidence, and turned beet red.

"Young man, may I see you in the bedroom?" I said, pointing at Peter. "You apparently already know the way." He tried not to grin as he made his way there, but I could make out the suppressed smile just the same.

He didn't look very repentant, either, as he stood there before me and I closed the door behind us. Still, I couldn't really be that mad at him. After all, if the shoe had been on the other foot, I'd have probably done the same. And Sparkle, well I think we know how that scenario would've played out.

Peter explained what had happened, nonetheless. "Actually, it was easy to convince him to go once I walked him through The Castro and showed him the alternatives," he told me. "Then we had nothing else to do the rest of the day and..."

"...and I can guess the rest. Well, at least you're keeping it in the family," I joked.

"That's gross, Secret. Besides, he is awfully cute, even if he is your cousin." He giggled and then jabbed me in the arm. "I guess your side of the family got the brains."

"Ha, ha. That's enough now. What say we pack Cousin Sam up and go show him his new digs? I'd say the sooner we get you two apart, the easier my life will be."

"Hey, no problemo. I'll know where to find him, anyway," he said and opened the door. Sparkle and Sam were sitting there waiting for us as we exited my bedroom.

"Okay then, Sam, you know I would love to have you stay with me," I lied, "but right now I think it's best if we get you some help first. Once the drugs are out of your life, we'll work on getting you a place to live."

Peter broke in with, "And then we can enroll him in college with me."

"Um... what?" I asked, with trepidation. The men in my life sure as hell had this awful way of throwing curve balls at me.

"Well," Peter continued, "I sort of promised Sam that if he checked himself into the home that we would put him through college with me. You know, after the first year, it's less than twenty bucks a semester per class."

"Who's this *we* you're referring to, Peter?" Sparkle asked, knowing exactly who the we was.

"Never mind," I spoke up. "We'll worry about that later. Let's just get Sam over there." There was no sense arguing about it. If we backed out of Peter's promise, Lord only knows what would happen to my cousin. Plus, I wanted him out of my home and quick. Blood may be thicker than water, but it's a bitch to get out of the carpeting. So we packed Sam up and drove him over to the address that Dan had given us.

They were expecting him and gave us all a tour of the place. In fact, it was a hell of a lot nicer than my apartment. Hurray for my tax dollars doing some good. Maybe I should become a crackhead so that I can increase my standard of living. Truly, I eyed the place with jealousy. Sam seemed just fine to be there, too, so it was easy to leave him. We kissed him goodbye, Peter a might too long for my liking, and got our asses out of there. I knew he was in good hands, and I, for one, was glad they weren't mine. One problem down, one to go: namely Sparkle's tattoo. Oh, and I had an idea on that front, but I was saving it, for the time being.

***

215

The next morning, Peter went into work with me, where we were greeted by a downright blissful Sharon. Sparkle appeared five minutes later. He didn't want to miss out on the dish, after all. For once, I couldn't blame him. I mean, dating an exotic-dancer was just about the most exciting thing to happen to our trio in quite some time. (Sexually-speaking, I mean. And, uh, if you left Sparkle out of the equation, of course.)

"Well?" Sparkle asked, practically jumping on Sharon.

"Well what?" she responded, coyly.

"You know what. Spill it, bitch." Blunt and to the point.

Sharon hesitated, then with a huge smile, shouted, "Oh... my... God! The earth shook."

"Um, Sharon?" I interrupted, "was this about eleven last night?"

"Yeah, why?" She looked puzzled.

"Then the earth *literally* did shake. There was a five-point-one earthquake last night at exactly eleven," I explained. (The hazards of living in San Francisco.)

"Oh," she mumbled, slightly deflated. Still, she quickly rebounded. "Well, let's say that I saw God, then. Okay?"

"That would work. No reported sightings of him at that time." I hated to rain on her pride parade. She could've seen Him, I suppose. Maybe He was in town for an Almighty convention or something.

"Anyway," she continued, "the woman is phenomenal; and not only in bed. Well, that was pretty incredible, too. She's got a tongue like a fucking snake. I think she licked my kidney."

"T.M.I.!" Sparkle and I shouted in unison. (Too Much Information, if you're acronym impaired.)

"Get over it," Sharon responded. "That's not half as bad the crap you two, well, Sparkle, anyhow, come in here with. (Ouch.) Anyway, we talked all night after we had the incredible sex. There was, like, this total connection between the two of us. There's just this one, little problem... well, not a problem, per se..."

"Oh, God, here comes that big *but* again," Sparkle interjected.

"No, no big buts, just a little something I wasn't expecting." She hesitated as we sat there anxiously awaiting the dilemma.

"Please, Mary, I have enough in my life to worry about. Spill it!" What Sparkle had to worry about, I have no idea, but I wasn't about to argue. Seriously, I couldn't wait to hear what was troubling Sharon, and I could tell that she was itching to share it with us.

"Promise not to laugh?" she asked, before telling us.

"Um, Sharon," I responded, "look who you're making that request to. Let's just say that we'll try to keep it down to a low roar."

She hesitated again, biting her lower lip, before blurting out, "She wants me to pose nude for her."

To our credit, we didn't start laughing for a full fifteen seconds. Then we couldn't hold it in any longer. It wasn't that Sharon wasn't, well, for whatever it's worth coming from me, attractive enough. It was just so completely out of character that it was unexpectedly very funny. Sharon, however, was not the least bit amused.

"Fine. Laugh. Never mind. I knew it was silly. I'll just tell her I won't do it. It's not like I wanted to anyway." She was pouting and looked quite pitiful sitting there. Sparkle stopped laughing just long enough to force out a, "Don't be silly. We're not laughing at you; we're laughing with you."

"I'm not laughing, Fuckhead," she coldly said to him.

"Oh, then I guess we're not laughing with you. Okay, then let's just say it's not something we can picture you doing," he amended with.

"I agree. Let's just forget that I brought it up. It was a silly idea." She looked profoundly disappointed.

"No, Sharon," I stood up and put my arm over her shoulder. "You should do it. Don't listen to him. You've got a great... you've got great... well, you know... you've got it." I wasn't in the habit of complementing women on their attributes, and was plainly bad at it.

"What he's trying, unsuccessfully I might add, to say is that you've got a nice rack," Sparkle clarified.

"Yeah, that's it," I agreed, glad to not have to actually say it myself.

"Thanks, Sparkle. That's the nicest thing you've ever said to me." She was being sarcastic and was starting to look mighty pissed at us. "And it will be a cold day in hell before you ever get to see them!"

"Hey, it was a complement," he insisted.

"Stick to being an asshole, Sweetie. You're much better at it." Uh-oh, the gloves were coming off.

"Okay now. Let's just calm down. (I was scheming a plan... yippy!) Do you want to pose naked for Betty or not?" I asked her.

"Not!" she shouted at me.

"Well, I have a distinct feeling that you do want to, but that you also know that it's out of character for you and so you won't do it. Am I right?" I knew I was.

"Well... maybe. So what?" She was looking less pissed and more piqued.

"Well... what if I did something equally out of character at the same time that you do?" (I bet you know what's coming up, but I don't think they did.)

"Oh no. You're not going to pose naked, too, are you?" Sparkle said, in mock terror.

"Sharon's right. You are an asshole. And, no, I am not going to pose naked, but I will go get a tattoo with you if Sharon poses naked for Betty first." They both immediately lit up.

"You will?" she shouted first.

"You will?" he shouted next. "No fucking way!"

"Okay then," Sharon said and finally cracked a smile. "It's a deal! If you, King Chicken-Shit, can get a tattoo, then I can get undressed in front of a camera."

"Hey, I'm on your side. Keep picking on the asshole (gross, that didn't come out right) and leave me out of it," I objected.

"Hey, enough with the asshole stuff," Sparkle complained, "besides, we still have a big problem."

"Now what?" Sharon asked, though I already knew what he was going to say.

"Like, duh, first we had one queen with no idea what to get etched on his body and now we have two." Yep, that's what I was expecting. Could I, Bruce Miller, finally have one scheme work out?

"No, we don't," I calmly objected.

"We don't?" he asked.

"Nope," I answered.

"Well, don't just sit there, fill us all in, if you please."

I was all atwitter as they sat there staring at me. "You're gonna love it," I promised.

"Let me be the judge of that," he said, skeptically.

"Okay... ready?" I stalled for effect.

"I'm gonna slap you..."

"Okay, okay... here goes... you get Sparkle across your upper back and I get Secret!" I shouted and jumped up.

He sat there with no expression on his face. For a second, I thought I'd figured it out wrong. Then he slowly stood up and, with a completely monotone voice, said, "I love it."

"What?" I asked, not sure that I heard him right.

Then he burst about with, "I love it! I fucking love it!"

"Good job, Secret," Sharon said and patted me on the back. Then she went back to the office. It was obvious that she was ecstatic that I gave her that added little push to do what she had wanted to do all along. I was glad for that, too. But I was selfishly even happier that I got to get a tattoo and that Sparkle didn't trick me or cajole me into getting one. *Score one for the Bruce-man*, I thought.

Then Sparkle and I were left alone sitting there drinking our coffee. When I looked up at him, he had just the slightest smirk on his face.

"What?" I asked, nervously.

"What, what?" he said, returning the question.

"What's with the grin?" I tried to be more specific that time.

"What grin?" But he wasn't playing along. (Or was he?)

"You know what grin, fucker. Why are you grinning?"

"I was not grinning," he said, adamantly, but was grinning even wider by that point.

"Okay, look, we both know you're grinning about something, so you might as well tell me."

"It's nothing. It's just..." He paused.

"*Just...*," I echoed.

"Well, come on now, Secret; I know and you know that you came up with that one way too fast. You wanted that tattoo all along, didn't you?"

Fuck. Fuck, fuck, fuck. I honestly though I won that one. I either needed stupider friends or better plans. In other words, I was crestfallen.

"Oh, stop looking so sullen," he commanded. "It's still a great idea for a tattoo. Just, next time, leave the deceit to the master, okay?" He stood up and came over to hug me.

"Okay," I agreed.

"Besides," he said, whispering in my ear. "We both knew all along that you were gonna get a tattoo with me. Who did you think you were kidding?"

"Sparkle?" I whispered to him and hugged him back. "You're such an asshole. You know that?"

"Yeah, Secret, so I've heard. And thank goodness for that."
Thank goodness indeed.

***

Right about now, I suppose your asking yourself, "But, Secret, where are the death threats? Isn't that the purpose of these endless stories you keep telling us? What gives?" Well, I guess you're right; though, to tell you the truth, not everyone wanted to see Sparkle dead. Most people did, yes, but not everyone. And I can't even begin to imagine all the times that people threatened Sparkle's life when I wasn't around. Remember, we weren't attached at the hip; Sparkle does have a life outside of mine. Still, I don't want to disappoint you. I mean, you have made it this far, and I give you credit for that. Well, fear not; there's a big whopper of a threat coming up, and it's got quite an unusual twist to it. But first, let me tell you about the day we went to get our tattoos.

Seeing as you're either gay or gay-friendly, or else hating every minute of all this, there's a good chance that you already have a tattoo. They seem as commonplace these days as earrings and nail polish: just another thing to slap on your body. But, just in case you haven't lived through the ordeal, I'd like to set the record, if you'll pardon the expression yet again, *straight*. They hurt. They hurt real bad. There's no real difference between getting a tattoo and having a sewing machine run rampant over your body. Is that vivid enough for you? Of course, I had to find that out the hard way.

Yes, Sharon did indeed pose nude for Betty first. That was the deal, after all. And she loved it. She claimed it was the most freeing and exhilarating experience of her life. As a matter of fact, she did it three days in a row. At the time, I didn't fully see how strange a request it was to have Sharon continue posing nude for Betty. Once, okay. Twice, maybe. But three times? I mean, really, how many different angles do you need of someone's tits and ass? And Sharon loved the attention, too. To a point. But I'm getting ahead of myself here.

In any case, once Sharon posed for the first time, I made Sparkle and I dual appointments at a local tattoo parlor. Tattoo parlors in San Francisco, by the way, are getting to be like grocery stores: there's one in nearly every neighborhood. And so, a week later, we were on our way to permanent body scarification. If you're catching the dread in my tone, it's on purpose, because, with each passing day before our scheduled rendezvous, I grew more and more freaked out by what I was about to do to myself. It wasn't just the thought of the pain that was scaring me, either; it was the thought that I would have the damn thing forever, whether I liked it or not. That's what really scared me the most. (Okay, it was the pain, but you get my drift.)

That day, I can honestly say, I was truly glad to have a walking pharmacy for a best friend. They don't let you get tattooed if you're drunk, you see, it thins the blood and makes for a messier experience. Plus, it pays to be alert while you're getting it done. One slide down the chair and you have a line that's not supposed to be there. However, they don't ask you if you've taken every pill in the book to calm you down and to stifle the pain. Needless to say, by the time we arrived for our appointments, I was giddy as a schoolgirl. (Though I would hope that not may schoolgirls chase Vicodin down with a shot of Xanax.)

I made sure that Sparkle and I got our tattoos simultaneously, too. I didn't want him to trick me like he did with the whole nipple thing. Plus, I really didn't want to watch him get his tattoo, either. There's something about watching your friends sit there and bleed that I find disquieting, you see.

Now, the first scary thing about getting a tattoo, generally, are the people that actually give you the damn things. Our artists were no exception. Mine was tall and lanky, pasty white and completely covered with old and faded tattoos that I wouldn't be caught dead with on my body. I thought it was just a cliché that people had words printed across their knuckles. Judas, as he was called, had *ANGEL* across one set of fingers and *DEVIL* across the other. Everything in between was certainly not quite human, and so I think he was leaning towards the latter. I felt fortunate that he worked with the hand of the former. Why, I have no idea. Superstition, I suppose.

Lucky, that was the other one's name, worked on Sparkle. Lucky had only four fingers on the hand he drew with. When we asked him why they called him Lucky, he raised his other hand and showed us that he had only three fingers on that one. And that's why they called him Lucky. I prayed that his tattooing skills were better than his logic.

And these two guys came highly recommended to us, too. I'd hate to see the bad tattoo artists. I casually asked Judas, before he started dragging the needles across my body, how someone gets training to do what he did. He answered that he'd practiced on potatoes and homeless people. I didn't feel in good company, needless

221

to say. That alone should've sent me running, but I knew that neither Sparkle nor Sharon would ever have let me live it down, so I removed my shirt and sat down on the rickety chair before me.

The first thing that Judas did was he wiped some rubbing alcohol across the area that he was going to be working on. Rather than make me feel safe and secure, I felt like I was being prepped for surgery by a disbarred doctor. My heart, though highly medicated, was beating fast. Then he took the design that I had given him, ran it through a machine that made a wet, purple, carbon copy, and pressed it to the area of my back just below the neck and between my shoulder blades. He then had me inspect the results in the mirror to my left. Seeing as it's near to impossible to look at ones back in a mirror with any degree of precision, Sparkle and I proofed each other. That calmed us down a bit. We both agreed that at least our temporary tattoos looked fabulous. Now all Lucky and Judas had to do was fill in the lines. (Which any fifth grader could reasonably do. Then again, I had to wonder if these two guys made it that far.)

When Judas turned on the tattooing device for the first time, my stomach lurched and my heart skipped a beat. True, it may have stopped due to the large amount of prescription medications I had taken, but I was more inclined to believe that it was the jarring noise the tool made while it was running. It drowned out the sound of the awful music playing in the background, though. Honestly, I didn't know which was more unnerving. Should I have asked how long the session would take? Probably. Should I have brought one of my own CDs to listen to? Definitely. It had been years since I listened to AC/DC, and I had thought my life rid of them. As it turned out, I was sadly mistaken.

But nothing, I repeat, *nothing* could've prepared me for the touch of the needles to my skin those first few seconds. There's simply nothing to compare the sensation to, so I won't even try. I can say, however, that every muscle in my body tensed at once. And for the next hour and a half, that's how they remained.

Judas outlined the letters first. Slowly and methodically, he worked his way across my back. The only saving grace to the experience was that he frequently had to stop his work to fill the needles up with ink. I relished those brief moments in between the shocking bouts of pain. The rest of the time, I tried to concentrate on other things: the stains in the carpet, the stains on the ceiling, the stains on Judas' pants. But the pain was so intense that it became the only thing I could think about. Thankfully, when he was done with the outline, he gave me a five-minute break while he smoked a cigarette. (Inside!)

As *SPARKLE* has one more letter than *SECRET*, my break came before my friend's. I slowly made my way over to the area were Lucky worked and watched the progress from behind. It was intriguing to witness the results unfold. See, he had amazing dexterity with just the four fingers, and his pen flowed through Sparkle's once-unblemished skin like a skater's blades through the cold, hard ice. Mere trickles of blood emerged from under his skin, but that was enough to turn my stomach queasy, and, after a few minutes, I stopped watching and walked around the chair to face the victim.

Sparkle's face was a crimson red and his jaw was locked tightly in a grimace. He blinked his eyes open when he realized that I was standing before him, and I gave him a look that said that I knew what he was going through. I was sure glad that we had short nicknames at that moment. Just think what it would've been like if we'd been calling each other *Moonbeam* and *Sassafras* all those years. I mean, I couldn't even begin to image sitting in that chair for an additional half-hour. And people have tattoos that take multiple sittings. The fools!

"How's it going?" I asked, knowing full well what he was experiencing.

"Why are we doing this again?" he pondered, out loud.

"Beats me." By then, I had forgotten my motivation. But I did remember that all Sharon had to do was lie around naked for a few hours. Guess I should've set my sites a little lower. Next time, I thought, I'd just paint my toenails.

"Okay, take a fiver," Lucky said, putting down his instrument of torture.

"No problem, Boss." Sparkle breathed easily for the first time since we got there.

"Pretty bad, huh?" I whispered. I didn't want our new friends to think we were sissies. Why? I have no earthly idea, as we were, after all, two of the biggest sissies on the face of the planet. But eighteen year old girls all over the country were getting butterflies tattooed on their butts, so, I figured, I could tough it out for the brief period of time it would take.

"I had no idea," Sparkle confessed, while I nodded in full agreement.

And then, all too soon, we were back in our chairs and the needles were once again pressed deep into our flesh. Now it was time for the fill in work. If it was at all possible, this hurt even worse than the outline. Where Judas practically glided across my back during the first part of the ordeal, he then began to slowly, and with a much heavier hand, start to etch in the filler. Multiply *ouch* by a thousand and you'd be coming close to the searing pain I was feeling at that very moment. I had visions of what it must've been like at the dentist's before someone had graciously invented Novocain.

In what seamed like hours, but in reality could only have been forty-five minutes or so, Judas finished up his work. I had never in my whole life been more anxious for something to be over and done with. But Judas had one more surprise for me. When he was through, and I thought the pain to be finished, he whipped out a spray bottle and told me that he had to clean the wound. Strange wording, I thought, and couldn't begin to imagine what he was preparing me for. I was glad, however, that he didn't tell me, as the bottle was full of rubbing alcohol, and, with each spray, it felt like a thousand little daggers were stabbing into my back.

Thankfully (?), that part only took a few moments. When he was satisfied that it was clean, he put some kind of ointment on my new piece of body art and then wrapped my wound in a dressing. Done! Thank God! I couldn't believe people came back and did that over and over again. Once was, by far, enough (or at least I thought, at the time). Then I got to watch Lucky finish up on Sparkle.

I wasn't about to tell my friend how it all would end. Why add insult to injury? What I did do, however, was hold Sparkle's hand just before Lucky sprayed the bottle on him. I was rewarded with a death-grip as Sparkle shook all the life out of my hand as the spray ravaged his sore back.

"Finished?" he asked, a bead of sweat dripped from his brow.

"All done, Champ," I answered, gladly.

"Thank God."

"Amen, Brother. Let's never do that again."

"Agreed."

***

Well, as any of you in the same position can attest, those damn tattoos become habit-forming. And, just like when a woman gives birth and swears that she'll never go through the pain and agony again, and then goes through it at least once if not twice or thrice more, Sparkle and I weren't quite done adorning our bodies, either. Up to the time of this unfortunate coma thing, we were both up to three and were planning our fourths. The best explanation I can give is that you simply forget how painful it really is. It's not until you sit down to get another one that you remember, and by then it's entirely too late. Oh well, no one ever accused us of being the brightest bulbs on the tree, right?

In any case, two weeks after our joint adventure, our tattoos were healing nicely. We were done bathing them in Bacitracin and were rubbing Lubriderm over them daily. There was still some itching and flaking, but, for the most part, they were looking fairly spectacular. At least that's what I told Sparkle and he told me. After all, we couldn't see our own tattoos very well at all. Truth be told, I for one was feeling butcher by the moment. Tattooed and pierced. I couldn't begin to imagine what we would do to our bodies next. (No, getting shot through the chest doesn't count.)

Also, over those two weeks, Sharon continued seeing Betty. As a matter of fact, when Betty wasn't at The Snatch, she was at Classics II. At first, we all found it kind of endearing, but after a few days of her presence, it became, well, sort of creepy. And then, as they frequently do, the bomb dropped.

"Oh my God, Sharon, where's Betty today?" I asked her one morning, when Betty was noticeably missing from the shop and our lives.

"She had a photo shoot at the beach and needed to catch the early rays," she said, and I caught just a glimmer of relief in her voice.

"Really? I didn't know she was photographing anybody but you these days. Is the intrigue finally waning? Has she moved on to the next pretty face?" I may have been joking, but deep down I'd hoped that it was true. Our trio simply wasn't meant to be a quartet. Besides, when Betty was around, she barely paid any attention to anybody but Sharon. Plus, Sparkle couldn't really stand her and took to avoiding the shop during the day in order to maintain his distance. Still, I tried to support Sharon, as it'd been forever since she had dated anyone seriously, and my horizons, needless to say, looked fairly bleak.

"No, she's as enamored of me as ever, but since I can't get away during the day, Betty still takes pictures of the girls from the club. Anyway, it's not like she's here every day, you know," she said,

225

defensively. And I knew something was up. See, Sharon rarely took that tone with me.

"No, no, I know that. It's just that, well, she is here most of the time." I tried to be as non-judgmental as possible in the hope of avoiding any potential conflict.

"Do you have a problem with that?" Sharon asked and looked up from what she was doing in order to face me. Since I was into it up to my ears, I decided to take it all the way through.

"Do *you*?" I tried.

She paused for a moment, started to say something, and stopped. Then she sat down at a table and rested her head in her hands before answering my rather pointed question. "Secret, I really like this woman, but there are a few things that bother me."

"Such as?" I asked and sat down with her at the table. See, I knew all was not right on the Western front.

"Such as this whole wanting to be with me every spare minute thing, for one. I'm not sure it's exactly healthy. Do you?"

"Well I..."

"I mean, I barely know her and she's already talking about maybe moving in with me. (Danger, Will Robinson. Danger, danger, danger.) She's great and everything, but I'm not ready for that. Maybe in a month or two, but not right now. Right?"

"Well, of course, but..."

"No, you're right, Secret, it's crazy. We've only known each other a couple of weeks. She doesn't even know the real me yet. She's only seen the good side so far. Next week is my you know what time of the month. Wait until she meets *that* side of Sharon. Whoa, that should change her mind, right?"

"Actually, I don't..."

"I know what you're going to say, and keep it to yourself, Funny Man. I'm just saying that I don't think we really know each other enough yet. Take for instance that morning she happened in here to look for that book on photography. Do you want to know the truth, Bruce?"

"Well, sure..."

"I know, I should've told you guys sooner, but I didn't want any lectures. Anyway, it seems like that was just a ruse. Betty told me that she'd been walking by here for days trying to get the nerve to come in and meet me. Me! I mean, really. What's that about? Look at her. She could have anybody she wants. Since when am I so special?"

"Now I…"

"I know, thanks, Secret. That's not exactly what I meant. I just meant that this whole fascination with me is kind of, well, *unnerving*. Did you know that she calls me at least twice a night and meets me almost every morning to walk me to work?"

"Well, no, I…"

"Of course you didn't, Secret. And did you know that she told her parents all about me after just a week. My parents don't even know that I have a cat, and I've had Blacky for nearly three years. I seriously doubt that I would tell them about Betty after just under three weeks. That's some scary shit. I just don't know what to do about all this. Should I break up with her? Should I tell her to back off a little? I think she might freak if I tried that."

"Well, I would…"

"No, you're right, Secret. I'm gonna put my foot down and tell her that I need some space. And if she doesn't think that she can do that, then I'm gonna have to tell her that it's over. You know, Secret, I was a little apprehensive talking to you about this stuff, but you've really helped me decide what I need to do. Thanks for the great advice."

"Well, it was no…"

"Oops, customer. Thanks, Secret. I'll get it. You've been enough help already. You just sit there and take a break."

"Glad I could help," I said to myself.

Well, that was easy. Maybe I should've been a relationship counselor. After all, those who can't, teach. I hoped that whatever it was I said, or didn't say, would actually do some good. At least Sharon realized that there was a problem, because I was beginning to worry. Which brings me to Gay Rule #11. Ready? Got a pencil? Okay, here it is: never point your friend's problems out to them when you already have enough of your own to worry about. You know, most people know they're fucked up without other people calling attention to it.

The next morning, as it turned out, I found that I had good reason to be worried.

Sharon looked like she hadn't slept a wink and the hopeful face that I'd left the night before had been replaced by a miserable one. She attacked me as soon as the door to the shop shut behind me.

"Well, Mister Advice Man, that was a horrible idea! Betty freaked out when I told her that it was either back off or get out. She was hysterical for nearly the entire night, and I had to swear up and

227

down this morning that everything was alright before she'd let me leave to come in here this morning. I've never met a more obsessed person in my entire life. I should've known better than to take advice from someone whose longest relationship was with the milk carton in his refrigerator," she hollered at me.

And I knew better than to argue. She was obviously working her brain cells and her mouth on nearly no sleep. So I did the only smart thing I knew that I could do in the circumstance. The situation, after all, called for someone sneaky and deceitful; it needed someone who was accustomed to breaking hearts and distancing themselves from unwanted paramours. Honesty wasn't going to work with someone who was already clearly off the deep end. In other words, I got Sparkle to come down to the shop immediately. I probably should've done that the night before, though. The straightforward path hadn't worked in any relationship that I or any of my friends had been in so far; why should this one have been any different? (Are you being judgmental up there? Well stop it! Most people are, at best, unstable, mentally and emotionally, and shouldn't be treated like intelligent, rational human beings. Especially when dealing with relationships.)

And so, Sparkle swooped in for the rescue. Sharon filled him in on the details, blaming me for nearly everything. Naturally, I let her. Look, why make the situation worse, I figured. I told Sparkle later on, and in private, what really happened. He'd already figured as much, as it seemed extremely unlikely that I would offer up any advice that involved being honest or mature. (What great friends I have.) Thankfully, he had a better solution. And it was a doozie.

That night, before we closed up for the evening, Betty came by on her way to work. The three of us were there waiting for her and we were well-rehearsed.

"Hey, guys," she said, with a wave and a smile, as she walked into the shop.

We all said hello back to her, but were obviously a bit standoffish. She caught on immediately. Pulling up a chair, she asked, "Everything okay?"

"Not exactly," Sparkle responded. Sharon and I stood behind him and off to his sides. We figured we would look more formidable that way.

"What does that mean?" she asked, looking tense and, at the same time, ready to pounce. I could see why Sharon was afraid to face her alone; she was obviously a tad off kilter. I think working under those lights night after night might have made her loopy. You know what they say, after all, about the need for natural lighting.

"Well, Betty, it's like this," he started, keeping to the script, "I'm sure that Sharon told you that she's bisexual, right?"

"What's that got to do with the fucking price of tea in China?" she spat out. "Yeah, I know she's bi. So what?" Now she was showing signs of anger, and Sharon and I were fidgeting in the background, nervous for what might happen. Sparkle, as usual, was cool, calm, and collected. He had dealt with his share of lunatics before, after all.

"Did she tell you that I was a bisexual as well?" he asked, with a straight (bi?) face.

"What? No fucking way. You're as queer as Liberace at a gay pride parade. Maybe even more so." She gave a small chuckle, making her seem even more menacing. I couldn't begin to imagine how she'd react to what we'd cooked up.

"Be that as it may," he continued, unperturbed, "I am. And, what's more, Sharon and I have been seeing each other regularly for the last three years." That did it. Betty rose up and threw the chair she was sitting on off to the side. The three of us gave a little jump backward, fearing that more furniture would soon follow.

"Bullshit!" she shouted at us. "Why is this the first I'm hearing about it then?"

"Because," Sparkle began to explain, "Sharon and I have an arrangement. She experiments on the side and I experiment on the side, but we don't officially date anybody except for each other. It's how we keep our relationship, well, *fresh*. Unfortunately, this thing between the two of you has gotten a little beyond our agreement, and I'm afraid that it's going to have to end. Sorry."

"Sorry my ass!" she hollered and moved toward us. "I don't believe a word of it. Is this true, Sharon?"

With a quiver in her voice, Sharon answered, meekly, "I'm afraid so, Betty, and I'm so sorry. I should've told you sooner."

Now Betty was livid. We could see the rage in her eyes as she stood there, fists clenched and eyes staring right through us like two hot pokers. "Damned straight you should've told me. I can't believe this is happening. I thought we had something special. You're killing me here, Sharon." Now her voice was shaking, and for a second I felt a twinge of guilt, but just for a second, because then she really let go. "Fine!" she raged, and moved to within inches of Sparkle. "I guess I have no choice in the matter." Then she raised her fist in front of

Sparkle's face. "But I'll tell you this, you three have made one big, fucking enemy here, especially you, you fucking, little fruit. (She was talking to Sparkle, of course). You better pray that you don't run into me in some dark, deserted alley in the middle of the night because you're gonna regret treating me like this some day. That I promise. Got it?" And she punched Sparkle on his chest to drive home the point. It sounded like it hurt, but my friend took it in stride and just stood there staring right back at her. Honestly, I had to give him credit; I would've beaten the shit out of her. (If I were a violent man, which I'm not, of course.)

With nothing else to say or do, Betty stormed out of the store and slammed the door behind her. The three of us let out an audible sigh and then reached for each other for a much needed group hug.

"Crazy bitch," Sparkle chuckled.

"Told ya so," Sharon agreed. "And thanks."

"No sweat," he said as we stood there hugging. "Guess I'm gonna have to avoid those alleys from now on, though."

"Wow," I piped in, "how will you ever meet any potential new boyfriends then?"

"The old fashioned way," he replied. "Men's bathrooms."

"And locker rooms. Don't forget those." Sharon offered, regaining her composure and her sense of humor.

"Oh, definitely. And of course there's always The Castro," I added.

Sparkle shuddered. "No, let's not get drastic here. I'd rather take my chances with the alleys. Anyway, let's pray that's the last time we ever see our nice stripper friend there. She packs quite a hard wallop," he said, rubbing his chest.

"Amen," Sharon and I chorused.

"By the way," Sharon added as we all de-embraced, "now that we're officially dating, Sparkle, I like irises, not roses, gin, not vodka, and I prefer Verdi to Wagner."

"Get a grip, Mary," he chuckled. "I prefer men to anything and that was my one foray into Straightsville. Got it?"

"Got it, Lover," she said and gave him a peck on the cheek.

"Good, now let's get the fuck out of here and get us some booze," he said, practically running for the door.

"Hey, I know a bar that serves great drinks," I proclaimed.

"Forget it, Secret!" Sparkle shouted as he opened the door and stepped out into the cold, crisp evening. "You've forever lost the right to suggest places to imbibe. From now on, we'll wing it without your troublesome help. Now let's go. My liver is shouting up at me to feed it, and, you know, it's never a good idea to argue with your internal organs."

I, for one, couldn't argue with that.

CHAPTER NINE
QUEER AND PRESENT DANGER

Okay, that didn't help at all. Here I sit, yapping away, and Sparkle just lies there. And do you want to know something really sick? He looks fabulous. Even the gaunt look works for him. Anyway, it's really no fun recounting a fairly riotous tale and having no one around to laugh at all the funny parts. (Present company excepted.) Peter, God love him, stops by every chance he gets, but it's very lonely here without my Sparkle. I mean, yes, he's here, in the bodily sense, but that's not what counts. Not really. I have to say, even with all his many, many bad traits and severe character flaws, I miss him more than words can express. I'd give anything to hear a *Mary* or a *Miss Thing* right about now. But listen to me, all maudlin and sappy. If Sparkle can hear me, I'm sure he's quite over my bitching and whining.

Well then, let's try a different approach. The preceding recounting was one that Sparkle had already heard. Hell, he's told it a million times himself. It's not every day that you get threatened by a lesbian stripper, after all. So, let's try a tale he hasn't heard before. And while we're at it, let's go hog-wild and talk about the one event that everyone has been sworn to secrecy on. Sparkle would kill us if he found out, so, if he's listening, it's sure to bring him around.

Wow, I never thought I'd be talking about this with him only a few inches away, but here goes...

It all started about three months after the whole Betty episode. Luckily for us, or Sparkle at least, we never did run into her again. Of course, we pretty much stay clear of Polk Street these days, just in case. Why tempt fate? That's the funny thing about San Francisco: people flow in and out of your life so easily until they're nothing but a distant memory. Unfortunately, just when you think you've seen the last of them, they float right back in. (Yep, there's that nasty foreshadowing again.)

Such was not the case with Cousin Sam. We were expecting him to come awaftin' back. In fact, we dreaded it. That is, Sparkle, Sharon, and I dreaded it; Peter was counting down the days. See, he was the only one that ever visited my cousin, try as we might to dissuade him against his frequent trips to the shelter. Fortunately, visiting hours were only during the day, while we worked, and only Peter had the time to pop in on him. Sparkle would've just as soon swallowed tonic without the gin before he would step foot in that place. I mean, he'd never quite forgiven Sam for getting Peter to go behind our backs. (Yes, it's childish, but I think I've clearly pointed out that Sparkle is petty, unfair, and callous, so why be surprised?)

Peter gave us periodic updates on Sam's condition, promising us time and time again that he was getting better and that when he got out of the half-way house, he would be a new man. (Of course, new doesn't necessarily equate to better.) And whenever we'd try to convince Peter that he shouldn't get his hopes up, he would remind us that if we had had that same attitude with him, we wouldn't have been together all these years later. Which is true, without a doubt, but we did have Peter's best interests in mind when we lectured him about the pitfalls he had to look forward to. We freely admitted that we were simply being over protective. Still, Peter got pissed whenever we talked badly about Sam. And even though we knew it was pushing the two of them even closer together, we couldn't help ourselves. It simply wasn't in our nature to feign tolerance.

That's why, when Sam was released with a clean bill of health, we weren't surprised that the two of them decided to get an apartment together. And, for our part, as promised, we enrolled Sam in summer school right along with Peter. We weren't the least bit happy in doing so, but we figured that it would keep the two of them busy and, hopefully, out of trouble. Plus, I knew it would make my family happy. I supposed I owed them that much. (Always the martyr. Or is that always the bridesmaid? Whichever, we let them have their way. They would've managed it without us, anyway, so at least, this way, we could hold it over their heads.)

As I've repeatedly mentioned, available apartments in San Francisco are about as rare as an honest politician, so, like it or not,

Sam checked himself out of the shelter and into Chez Sparkle. (Yes, yes, I know; what were we thinking?) But we knew that if we separated them, they would find a way to be with each other anyway. This way, with Sparkle home most days, one of us could keep an eye on them. And let me tell you, Sparkle was none too happy for the company. The morning after Sam arrived, the three of them were already out of the house and off looking for small, relatively cheap apartments to move into.

Okay, you guessed it, that was about as easy as finding a straight man working in a... in a... (and that's when we got the answer to our problem)... a beauty salon. After three days of looking and turning up no leads (who, after all, would want to rent a place to two college students with no references and no signs of support other than Sparkle?), we remembered that Kiki and Larry had a spare garage apartment. Meaning, it was finally time to cash in on the favor of working that drag show all those years earlier. Granted, the drag show was our way of returning the favor for them bailing Sparkle out of jail, but far be it from us to point out the obvious.

Anyway, we did it the smart way: we surprised them. On a beautiful Sunday morning, knowing they'd be home, the four of us showed up at their doorstep, feigning a post-brunch outing. They were thrilled to see us. (Suckers.) And I almost felt guilty for what we had in mind for them.

Kiki and Larry greeted us like long-lost family. Seeing as they rarely got to spend any time with Peter, and had never even met my cousin, they fairly rolled out the red carpet. Drinks were served (martinis for the adults, lemonade for the kiddies), snacks were rustled up (though we did actually come from brunch, that part was true), and we had no problem convincing them for a grand tour of their home. See, only I had been over before. Sparkle and Kiki had become, and I use the term loosely, *friends*, but Sparkle drew the line at making house calls. (To Kiki's great relief.)

Larry led the excursion, with Kiki as our pointer-outer of interesting tidbits: what was new, what had been recently repainted, what was original to the house, and what had been added on, etc. He was busting with glee at having the chance to show it all off. I gathered that they rarely had company, and so we *oohed* and *ahed* our way through each room in order to keep them in good spirits before we reached our final destination: the basement.

It was to our good fortune that the bottom of the house was, shall we say, less manicured than the upper floors. Kiki quickly explained that they simply hadn't had the time or energy to bother with the apartment beneath them, but they eventually hoped to make it rentable sometime in the near future. Why waste the space, as they put it. And that, of course, was my cue.

"Why wait?" I suggested. Their grins were replaced by puzzled expressions and, in turn, by ghastly looks of horror as they each realized what I had in mind. It didn't take a brain surgeon (Larry was an Orthopedist) to figure it out. After all, Sam and Peter's eager faces said more than mere words ever could.

"Now wait a minute," Kiki tried as he looked from face to shining, young face. "I didn't mean..."

I jumped in before he could finish. "Well, you just said that you planned on renting it out as soon as you got it fixed up. Now you don't have to fix it up; the kids can do it for you." The kids in question looked less than enthused all of a sudden, but knew better than to voice their opinions.

"But we...," Kiki tried again.

"Oh, come on now. They're two young men just starting out, and, besides, they'll be in school or studying most of the time, and you'll barely even notice that they're here," I argued.

"Please, Kiki," Peter pleaded, all doe-eyed and pitiful.

"Yes, please, sir," Sam joined in. I knew the sir part wouldn't earn them many points, but at least my cousin was making an effort.

"Okay." Larry caved first. "We'll give it a shot." And then he whispered into Sparkle's ear, "And this makes us even, and then some, for that drag show." Sparkle nodded in order to seal the deal. Sam and Peter caught on and jumped up and down with youthful exuberance. I, on the other hand, breathed a sigh of relief. I mean, I wasn't the least bit happy having my cousin and Peter living together, but at least now we had two responsible adults to watch out for them. (Okay, one responsible adult and one hairdresser, but beggars couldn't be choosers.)

And so, with the few personal belongings they owned, plus some crap Sparkle and I threw in, Peter and Sam moved in with Kiki and Larry the very next day. Try as I might, I couldn't help but feel just a twinge of jealousy for them. After all, I couldn't get a boyfriend to save my life, and here they were, dead broke, clueless, and ever so young, but still, they had each other. Plus an apartment twice the size as mine and just outside of The Castro. I could kick myself for never having the bright idea to move down there myself.

Our victory was bittersweet, however. True, we had Sam out of our hair, or at least out of our respective neighborhoods, but we had lost our shared roomie and virtual son, Peter. Those first few nights, Sparkle and I felt like the loneliest two people on the face of the planet. No amount of booze or pills could cheer us up. (Okay, you know us better than that. We were perked up a little by the booze and the pills, but just a little.) We did, however, put on a brave front when Peter would call one of us or drop by the store. We did want him to be happy, you know.

And he was. Or at least he said as much. Also, we called Kiki and Larry just about every day to check up on them behind their backs. We were told that they were the perfect tenants: barely home and helpful when asked. As a matter of fact, they were painting the place within days after moving in. I guess that I worried for nothing. So I had little else to do but get on with my life.

That's just what I did, too. Now, I know that what I'm about to say may sound a bit pitiful, but remember, I work all the time and the bars suck around here. Okay, so what I did was... sigh... I ran a personal ad in one of the local gay rags. It sounded so easy, so foolproof, so... well, *sexy*.

I mean, really, I imagined having my pick of the litter. Little did I know how prophetic that little turn of a phrase would be. I suppose that I should start by telling you exactly what my ad said. It was, for the most part, truthful. At least truthful enough to land me a man. Or at least I hoped (dreamed, prayed, offered my soul to the Devil) for that much. So here goes:

GWM, young, fun-loving, attractive and educated (so far so good, huh?), *seeks same for long-term committed relationship. Must be honest, caring, open, and sincere.* (Sort of like Sparkle in reverse.) *Not into the bar scene, heavy drugs, or partying the night away. You shouldn't be either.* (That's where I stretched it a bit.) *I love snuggling by the fire* (if I had one) *and long walks along the beach.* (I would if I had a car and could drive there.) *If you're looking for that special someone, give me a call.* (Please, dear God, send me a man!)

That was it. Short, sweet, and to the point. Well, that's what I thought, anyway. I left out a little something about *your recent picture gets mine* or something to that effect. Apparently, attractive is a subjective term, you see. As is educated, honest, and, most definitely, fun-loving. I also left out the part (I mean to you) that I neglected to let Sparkle in on my adventures in *PersonalAdLand*. I figured that I would tell him if and when I found a suitable man. I mean, I just didn't want to deal with the harassment or embarrassment that would inevitably ensue should I tell him. Probably not a wise decision, but live and learn. (Okay, live, anyway.)

To my utmost surprise, within three day, I had over sixty responses. Most of them were purporting exactly what I'd been searching for. I had little reason to doubt the veracity of the claims that were being made, figuring that there had to be eligible, successful men like myself all over the city who had no time or desire to meet other men at bars and who were desperate enough to look for them in the back of a newspaper. (Fine, saying it out loud, it seems ridiculous, but, at the time, it appeared plausible.)

And so, I had a burgeoning project on my hands. For this I needed help, and turned to the logical choice, besides the obvious, and that was Sharon. As Sharon was almost always as desperate for love and affection as I was, I figured she'd be a compassionate aide de camp. I was right, thankfully. She was eager to help and immediately started rummaging through the growing list of responses I was getting. Certainly, there had to be one suitable boyfriend in the stack, right?

We quickly dwindled down the list to the top ten. Men over thirty-five, heavier than one hundred eighty pounds, and taller than six feet, were tossed out. (No offense to all the tall, heavy, older men out there, but I had a type and I was sticking with it.) Those requests with numerous typos and/or bad grammar made it to the trashcan as well. Men who sent photos were given priority. Men with attractive-looking photos zoomed to the top.

Fine, that sounds shallow, but let me say this: the shallow end is *sooo* much easier to swim around in. Besides, all that treading water down in the deep end gets to be tiresome, and you don't need a lifeguard in the shallows. Plus, you can hop right on out of the pool whenever you like when you're in the shallow end. Anyway, rather than tagging myself as shallow, I like to think of myself more like an onion: thinly veiled, but deeply layered. Of course, once you get below the top layers there is a certain stink, but it does add flavor to the mix. Okay, enough with the analogies. On with the hunt!

Even I was smart enough to realize that it would be better to make a coffee date first, rather than get caught in a restaurant with a complete dud for two hours. That way, I could at least sample the merchandise and not waste my time or my money. Sharon came up with the routine: one man per day at precisely three (when Sparkle was usually at the gym), coffee and a scone served, on the house (hey, it was the least I could do), conversation for thirty minutes, and, if I didn't like him, I would make the secret gesture to Sharon to come over and rescue me. Little fuss and no mess; I was ready to begin.

Blind date number one was Ed. Ed was one of the few prospects who had no accompanying picture with his response, and that's why he was at the bottom of my short list. He did, however, appear reasonably qualified. He was thirty-two, but claimed to look years younger, my size, gainfully employed, and sounded quite witty in the few paragraphs he wrote to me. He had the added bonus of being both tattooed and pierced, which I'd grown to find sexy. Funny how your tastes change over the years. I prayed that, down the line, I wouldn't be into scat or anything so vulgar, but I knew better than to hold out for a miracle. Life has so many funny ways of surprising us, don't you know.

Well, Ed was nothing if not prompt. He arrived exactly at three. He was also completely honest in his description of himself. (Two for two, but I walked him just the same.) Yes, indeed, he looked younger than his thirty-two years. As a matter of fact, he looked eighteen. I actually carded him, just to make sure that I wouldn't be committing any felonies should we do anything beyond the coffee. And, yes, he was tattooed. Besides his face, the only patches of skin that were inkless were, he informed me, his ass and prick. Those he saved for his piercings, which, besides his nipples and ears, totaled nine. I imagined taking a vacation with him and going through the metal detectors at the airport. Yikes. Thanks, Ed, but unless you got some eighteen carat gold or platinum rings running though those holes, I'm afraid I'll have to pass.

Of course, I didn't say that to his face. I played by my rules and chitchatted for the full half-hour before I signaled for my accomplice. Sharon saved me with some drummed up, back-room emergency, and I told Ed I'd give him a call sometime. I didn't say exactly when, and he didn't press it. No harm, no foul, and nine prospects to go. I hoped to not have to take it that far, but again, I wasn't holding out for that miracle. I figured that God was busy enough, what with war, famine, and pestilence, and had little time to worry about my social life.

Number two, bless his heart, did send a picture. And, for what it's worth, he was exactly my type. Too bad the picture was at least ten years old. Norman apologized immediately and claimed that he rarely took photos of himself. Guess why? Apparently, years of working as a restaurant manager had taken its toll. He had had one too many turfs and clearly not enough surfs. I felt sorry for the guy and doubled up on the scones before summoning for help. I politely excused myself, and when I came back out of the office, Norman was gone. He seemed really sweet and I did feel a twinge of guilt, but I wasn't fooling myself; I knew what I was looking for, and sweet/roly-poly was simply not it.

Now, number three seemed promising. He sent a recent picture, was clearly attractive, young, and had a beautiful smile on him. An added bonus, he sent a picture of himself shirtless from the waist up. Neil had pecs of death and a sexy-ass smattering of chest hair. The single nipple piercing was icing on the cake. In his letter, he said that he was a down to earth romantic who just didn't have the time to find Mister Right and was constantly forced into dating whatever he could find at the bars, those few times he could make it out to one. The reason he was seventh on the list? I didn't want to date anyone that was even busier than I was. Still, I couldn't wait to meet him.

At three o'clock, he walked in the shop, and my heart promptly sank. When he wrote *down to earth*, he was being literal. He couldn't have been more than five-foot-three, and that was in boots. He was devilishly cute, though, with a perfectly cut Vandyke on his chin and hair cut short in a near Caesar. I could see the pert nipples popping out of his tight tee, and he had just about the cutest little ass I'd ever seen. I kept picturing him bouncing on my knee. (Or, better yet, my lap.) I asked him to take a seat, quickly following suit so as not to call attention to the obvious differences in height. Honestly, I don't think his toes even came close to touching the floor. It took every ounce of restraint I had to not ruffle his hair and pinch his cheeks, he was that adorable.

What he lacked in size, however, he made up for in conversation. He was quick and witty and obviously well-educated. There was immediate chemistry in those first few minutes and no need for Sharon to come to my rescue. We made a dinner date for that very night. I planned on wearing sandals to lessen the difference in height, though. But short of him wearing stilts, I would surely be towering over him. Naturally and unfortunately, I was correct.

I met him at The Metro for a before-dinner drink. They have high stools there, and I figured every little bit would help. But when I got there and he hugged me hello, I knew we were in trouble. He barely came up to my chin, and, what was worse, he wore a really cheap smelling hair gel. Meaning, I ordered a double and hoped for the best.

Two doubles later, we still had barely broken the ice. That's when Neil shattered it.

"Um, Bruce, you seem like an awfully nice guy, but… (I sat up straight and waited for the but)… but you're just too tall for me." (I hunched back over.)

"Oh, come on now. No I'm not," I protested, though I have no earthly idea why. I guess I just hate rejection, even when I'm practically begging for it.

"Really? Well, then I'm game if you are." Damn my mouth. I was that close. (Picture me holding my fingers barely a few centimeters apart.) So I had no choice, and suggested that we head on out to dinner. Then it was time for some chicanery.

During the entire six-block walk, I intentionally stood very erect and talked straight ahead and somewhat whisperish. The effect? I had to keep leaning down and repeating myself. It didn't take long before Neil repeated his objection, and, this time, I fully agreed with him. I know, it was a mean, low-down, dirty trick. Sparkle would've been so proud; I, however, was not. That's why I paid for dinner and a cab home. And… er… well, had sex with him. Guilt can do strange things to a man. Guilt and three double gin and tonics. (Fine, guilt, four double gin and tonics, and no sex for the last month and a half.)

Besides, when you're lying down, height makes very little difference. And, it figured, the sex was fantastic. He was short, yes, but he was spry and limber as all hell. The little guy completely wore me out. We agreed, when it was all over, that it had been nice, but it simply would never work out. I almost objected, but he hugged me again and I knew to keep my mouth shut. Shame really. I know it seems like such a minor inconvenience, but I was looking for that perfect somebody, and that perfect somebody isn't able to shop in the boy's department at Macy's. So full steam ahead I went.

Number four?… see number five. Seems they were lovers, both of them ad-dating behind the other's back. I guess they figured that it was easier to break up with someone if there was someone else waiting in the wings. Needless to say, I was a bit shocked to be driven back to the same apartment two nights in a row. Not shocked enough to not have sex with both of them, but shocked enough to not make a second date with either. I'd let them work out their own problems; I had enough of my own to worry about.

So there I was, five down and five to go. Granted, I was having more sex then I was use to, but it seemed like a hollow victory. Partly because it wasn't getting me anywhere on the boyfriend front, and partly because I couldn't gloat to Sparkle. I couldn't even tell Peter. The two young lovebirds were keeping themselves busy studying and fixing up their apartment. Well, at least that was working out. I was glad to not have to worry about Peter's love life on top of my own. Yes, I realized that ignorance was bliss, but I was only up for opening one can of worms at a time. Luckily, Sparkle took to dropping in on them unexpectedly, and that kept the boys on their toes and Sparkle out of my hair.

I took a day's rest and then moved on to number six. Sadly, that one was a closet case. True, he was cute and successful. And it didn't bother me so much that he was in the closet at work. I mean, it's difficult to be out in the business world sometimes. And it didn't bother me all that much that he was closeted in public either. After all, not everyone likes to show affection in front of others. No, what really bothered me was that he was closeted with his wife. Granted, that didn't stop me from having sex with him, but, after the third date, I put my foot down. (Better late than never, right?) And, I hate to admit it, but I kind of liked having sex with a nearly straight guy. Talk about your novelty items.

Well, after six failed attempts, Sharon and I decided to retool. It was time to come up with a more practical, less ideal personal ad, and throw away the responses from what could only have been more disasters. The new ad was blunt, honest, and as foolproof as possible. After all, I was getting awfully tired of the false starts and was eager for a real relationship. This is what we came up with:

GWM, tired of the bar scene, liars, losers, and letches. Looking for that special someone to wile away the hours. You MUST be between 25 and 35, slim, trim, and moderately cute to handsome. Please be well-educated, financially secure, and emotionally stable. (I'd have settled for best two out of three.) *Wackos, winos, and wedded need not respond. I'm worth it, please be the same. Recent picture only for consideration.* (Bitter, yes, but I wasn't taking any chances.)

Well, my plan backfired. I'd left a very narrow window open, and only a handful of men responded. I suppose it was for the best, though; at least I could be reasonably sure to be getting what I asked for. Still, it would've been nice to have a ton of choices like from my first attempt. What I was left with, when all was said and done, were only two candidates.

241

Both seemed ideal. Both were young, my age exactly, and had decent jobs and educations. Both were bright and witty and charming, too. But only one sent me a photo. The one who didn't send a pic signed his letter, *Looking For Love,* and said that he hadn't taken a good picture in years, but promised me that I wouldn't be disappointed. The other, who did send a picture, was cute, but looked a little too Sweet Polly Purebread for my liking. So, against my better judgment and Sharon's numerous objections, *Looking* was the one I chose. I figured that if he was ballsy enough to send a guarantee, he was at least worth a shot. Plus, he said that he had three tattoos and a nipple piercing. As Goldilocks would've said, *Juuust right.* (If you're thinking that it was Sparkle that I was responding too, you're wrong. True, that would've made for a funny story, but real life doesn't work out that way. Real life, as it turns out, is stranger than fiction.)

On the day of our coffee date, I was in my office on the phone when Sharon came back and mouthed that my mystery date was waiting for me in the front of the store. I mouthed, *Is he cute?* Thankfully, she nodded in the affirmative and gave me a two-thumbs up. Needless to say, I quickly got off the phone, prettied myself up in the mirror, and hurried out to greet him.

He was, absolutely, positively adorable. He also looked vaguely familiar. As I approached, his face went from polite and inquisitive to outright beaming. And that's when I placed him.

"Chuck!" I screamed.

"Bruce!" he screamed back.

"Chuck!" I screamed again and drew closer.

"Bruce!" he volleyed back and stood within inches of me.

"Chuck," I said in a normal tone, not wanting to shout in his face. And then I hugged him, long and hard and with gusto.

It'd been years since I'd laid eyes on him, and I hadn't even heard his name mentioned in all that time, owing much to the fact that Sparkle was no longer on speaking terms with anybody in Chuck's circle. As a matter of fact, I'd completely written off all hope of ever seeing him again, and, yet, here he was, firmly in my grasp. This time, I wasn't about to let go.

"Oh my God," I said, pulling back after the longest hug of my life. "You look terrific." And I meant it. He did. His boyish good looks had matured into adult sexy. His beautifully hairy, golden arms were now ripped with hard, little muscles and his strawberry blond goatee was flecked with gray. In other words, he was all man and, if I had anything to say about it, he was all mine.

"Oh my God," he said, echoing my sentiment, "you look great, too. It's been forever. I can't believe we haven't even so much as bumped into each other... oh, wait... are you still hanging around with William?"

"Uh huh," I grimaced.

"Then I *can* believe it. None of my friends will go near him anymore after our last run-in. Shame really, I always liked him. True, he's a mean, twisted fuck, but he's never far off the mark. How is he anyway?" he asked as we took a seat.

Actually, I had to sit down. Seeing Chuck like that made me all weak in the knees. "Same. Mean. Twisted. Fuck. Whatever, you name it, he hasn't changed one iota. As a matter of fact, if we can keep the how-tos of our meeting up again a secret, I would really appreciate it."

"Understood. Besides, I'm just glad that we did. Meet up again that is," he said and sat there grinning and staring at me. I did the same in return. It was just so damn good to see him again that I didn't know what to say.

Luckily, I didn't have to say anything. As we sat there, staring into each other's eyes, our faces drew nearer and, before I knew it, we were kissing. A warm flush ran through my body as I remembered that night, so many years earlier, when we'd crossed paths in the bathroom at Badlands. I was thrilled that those paths had finally run full circle. (Jeez, did that sound like it came right out of a soap opera or what? Sorry, I'll try to keep the schmaltz to a smidge.)

I stopped kissing Chuck long enough to introduce him to Sharon, who, bless her heart, told me to go take an extended break. I gave her a peck on the cheek, grabbed my jacket, and tore on out of there with Chuck in tow. Walking down the street, arm in arm, I couldn't have been any happier.

First thing we did was catch up. Funny how you think your life is just rolling along, uneventful and boring, but when you start to recap, it suddenly sounds so lively and full. Least that's how I made it sound. Anyway, we also found out another reason why Chuck and I never ran into each other. See, after finishing his biochemistry degree, he started working nights in a hospital lab and rarely had the energy to go out on weekends or during the day. He'd finally switched to a day shift when, as luck would have it, he spotted my ad. And, voila, there we were. (It only took ten minutes to get back to my house, two to undress, fifteen to do the nasty, and ten more to lay there in complete and utter bliss.)

***

We started seeing each other from that moment on. He was the first guy I'd dated in years that I had any real fondness for. I think I was just going through the motions with everyone else, but I could've taken or left any one of them. I wouldn't say that I was finally in love, but I was head over heels in something with the guy, and I could tell that the feeling was mutual. Sparkle, not surprisingly, was less than ecstatic.

I mean, don't get me wrong, he liked Chuck. It was awfully hard not to. It was just that we were spending every spare moment together. I did try to include Sparkle in most everything we did, but he felt like a third wheel and usually declined our offers. And, try as I might, I just couldn't feel guilty about that. After all, I'd waited so long for Chuck to come along that I wasn't about to feel miserable over it. On the contrary, I was walking on Cloud Nine. Heck, Ten and Eleven, too. I mean, Chuck was so full of life, just a bundle of energy when we were together, and it completely wore off on me. Truth be told, I felt like running a marathon whenever I was with him.

But, since I had flat feet, I settled for painting my home instead. I enlisted the help of the boys, who had already finished painting their own apartment. Chuck helped out most every night we painted, and even Sparkle wet the brush a few times. It was a real family project. Between the five of us, it only took a week. I did have to run the store as well, and I felt bad asking anybody to paint without me, otherwise, it would've only taken a couple of days, as Chuck painted twice as fast as anybody I'd ever seen. As a result, we took to calling him Whirlwind. Lucky for me, he wasn't so fast at *other* assorted tasks.

It was sweet, actually, how we all meshed together. I would frequently come home to find Chuck waiting for me, and one of the boys would be with him, and supper would already be on the table and a glass of wine would be poured and waiting for me. Or, on the weekends, when I would be at work, one or two or all three of them would pop in to keep me company. If Sparkle was already there, he would leave with them, and Sharon and I would catch up with the group sometime later in the evening.

244

Most times, we would all go over to The Castro and hang out at Kiki and Larry's. Seeing as they had the most room for company (and the best stocked bar), it was the logical choice. And they loved to entertain. Kiki was the ultimate hostess, with Larry playing bartender. One night, to our great surprise, we discovered that Sharon had towed all of our drag gear over to the house and surprised us with it after dinner. It was drag central from there on out. Before long, Sam and Peter knew every Joni Mitchell, Stevie Nicks, and Grace Jones song that we could lip-synch to. Needless to say, we were so proud.

Chuck and my cousin, Sam, had become inseparable during that first month of our dating, too. They were like kindred spirits. Apparently, Chuck also had a fairly bad time of it as a teen. Personally, I was thrilled. Sam had really come around during the short amount of time he had been with us, gaining back some much-needed weight and looking and acting like a young man ought to. He cooked and cleaned and did chores around our house, and, by all accounts, was doing well in summer school.

Sparkle, however, was still apprehensive. "I don't like it," he said, on numerous occasions, when we would be out and about or sitting around Kiki and Larry's, and we would look over and see Sam and Chuck sitting in a corner somewhere, giggling about something. They rarely filled us in on the joke, though. Peter blew it off, but Sparkle was always put off by it. Even I, on those rare times I felt like being immature, would feel hurt by the exclusion of the rest of us in their little gab sessions. Still, if I said anything, Chuck would come over and peck me on the cheek and tousle my hair, and Sam would go over to Peter and give him a hug. It would always be over in a few seconds and we would go back to being one big, happy family. Sparkle, unfortunately, always remained weary, though he never said anything to anybody but me about it.

"Just seems odd, is all," he would explain to me later on. "Those two are always together. What can they possibly have to discuss? They have almost nothing in common, besides a lousy childhood, and, by the way they're always laughing and carrying on, I doubt that's what they're talking about. I smell a rat, Secret. A big, stinking rat."

"Come on now," I would respond, "you just don't like not being the center of attention. I would think you'd be happy that Sam's keeping out of trouble. He hasn't given us one, single, solitary reason to give us cause for alarm, and Chuck is just being like a big brother to him. I think it's sweet."

"Sweet, shmeet. Something's rotten in Denmark, and I, for one, don't like it," he would harrumph and cross his arms in protest.

"You know, you haven't liked anything Scandinavian since Sven took up with that go-go boy and stopped sleeping with you." I attempted joking with Sparkle to try and get him to lighten up. And he would, in fact, drop it for a time, but I could tell that he never felt easy around the two of them. Thankfully, everyone else was oblivious to his misgivings, Sam and Chuck especially. If they did know how Sparkle felt, they certainly didn't appear to pay any attention to it. And so I blew it off as well. I mean, what choice did I have? My boat was finally sailing smoothly; why start rocking it again?

Anyway, besides Sparkle's petty jealousies, all was happy in my gay, little world. I had everything I could wish for and then some. Fate had thrown me my share of lemons and I was finely drinking the lemonade. Corny, but true. And then... and then... well, you just have to guess that something God-awful was about to happen. Nobody remains that happy for very long. I'm sure even Santa Claus steps in some reindeer shit from time to time. Or chokes on a lemon pit.

The first sign of things to come happened one afternoon while Peter was spending the afternoon working at the shop. I could tell that he was preoccupied with something, and, after a few hours of watching him brood, I finally asked him if everything was all right. Honestly, I felt like being selfish for a change and let him live his life and make his own mistakes, but then those maternal genes kicked in and I butted my nose in just the same.

"What's up, Peter?" I asked, sitting down at a table and inviting him over with a wave of my hand.

"Probably nothing," he answered, but not nearly with as much conviction as I would've liked.

"Probably nothing or probably something, Peter?" I tried again. My heart was racing, though I hadn't a clue as to what he was worrying about.

"Well, I know I'm just being silly, but... but...," he hesitated, and I nearly fell off my seat in anticipation of him finishing the sentence.

"Jesus Christ, Peter, what is the but?" I practically shouted.

"*But*, I think something is up between my boyfriend and yours." Yikes, I wasn't expecting that one.

"What?" This time I did shout it, which caused Peter to jump in his seat. I patted his shoulder and apologized. Whatever was happening, it clearly wasn't his doing, and I didn't want to cause him any more discomfort than he was already experiencing. Still, the admission had thrown me for a loop. "Let's try that again," I said, regaining my composure, but just barely. "What makes you think something is going on between Sam and Chuck?"

"You know, I'm sure it's nothing; probably just an overactive imagination." He tried to sound reassuring, but I wasn't buying it.

"Spill," I commanded.

"Okay, fine, but I really doubt it's anything to worry about. It's just, well, there have been a few times when I've come home and, as soon as I walk in the door, they stop talking about whatever it is they were talking about, and when I ask them to continue with their conversation, they say they weren't really saying anything worth continuing. Now that alone wouldn't make me worry, but there have also been a couple of times when I've walked in and I can tell right away that they were doing something they didn't want me to see, and they look and act just a bit, well, guilty. It's completely subtle, but just enough so I get this hunch that something's up."

"But you haven't actually caught them messing around, right?" I asked.

"Well, no," he answered.

"Then I say that we give them the benefit of the doubt. From what I can tell, they're just friends. Besides, I seriously doubt that they would cheat on us right under our noses." Even as I said it, I knew that it was a distinct possibility. Straight, gay, bi or otherwise, men are all pigs. I never forgot Sparkle's first lesson. And, though I wanted to believe with all my heart that Peter was mistaken, I knew that there was the outside chance that he was right.

"That's fine with me. Like I said, I'm sure it was just my imagination." Peter didn't sound too convincing either, but he smiled as he got up and gave me a hug just the same. I felt awful and went back to work. Needless to say, the thoughts that were going around in my twisted, little head were none too pretty.

As a matter of fact, the whole thing was giving me the biggest headache ever. I asked Sharon if she would close up for me and I left work an hour early in the hope that my bed and a pretty, blue pill would help alleviate the pain. Halfway home, I remembered that I'd left my prescription bottle at Chuck's. So I veered off my intended route and headed for the comfort of my boyfriend's bed.

When I got to Chuck's, the door was unlocked, and so I walked right on in. But no Chuck. Strange, I thought, that the door was unlocked and he didn't seem to be at home. I checked the kitchen, the living room, and the bathroom, but no sign of him. Then, realizing what room was left, I suddenly felt a rush of panic. If he was home, he must've been in the bedroom. I prayed that he was alone. Honestly, I got down on my knees, folded my hands in prayer, closed my eyes, and prayed to the dear Lord that Chuck was alone in his bedroom.

Then I stood up, inched closer to the door, which was slightly ajar, and held my breath as I grabbed for the knob. But, just as I was about to walk in, I heard voices. I knew instantly who they belonged to. Clearly, it was Chuck and Sam. My stomach sank and I nearly started to cry as I stood there, trying to draw the strength to walk into the bedroom and confront them. Man, I wished Sparkle was with me at that moment. (Even more so, I wished that the prescription bottle was with me at that moment.)

With little choice, I again grabbed for the knob, swung the door open, and walked into the room. It was worse than what I was expecting, sad to say. Oh, yes, Chuck and Sam were in there on the bed, all right. And, yes, they were as shocked to see me as I was to see them. But they weren't having sex, though I would've preferred that, truth be told. As a matter of fact, they were fully dressed. Fully dressed with a mirror between their laps and a large heap of something white and powdery piled upon it. Chuck was so surprised to see me that he neglected to move the straw away from his nose.

I stood there in shock. Honestly, I didn't have the faintest idea what to say. I wanted to scream at them, to hit them and smash the mirror over their stupid heads, to… to…

"Told you so," Sparkle weakly mumbled from his bed.

"Well, fuck you… Wait, what did you say? WHAT DID YOU SAY?! SAY IT AGAIN! SAY IT AGAIN!

"Stop shouting. I said, told you so. You were a schmuck not to believe me." Five seconds out of a coma and he was already being an asshole. "Now, would you mind telling me where I am and why does my head feel like an axe just ran through it?"

"Where, I can tell you, but why, well, you're gonna have to fill me in on that one, good buddy."

248

CHAPTER TEN
AND THE ANSWER IS...

Well, I suppose you want to know who shot Sparkle, right? I mean, you did make it all the way here and listened to my rantings and ravings along the way for something. Unless you really do care about my lack of sex, my uneventful job, and my tiny, little apartment. Do you? No? I didn't think so. Well, okay then, I'll fill you in on how Sparkle managed to have a bullet ruin his otherwise perfect chest.

But first...

(Now, you didn't think that I was just gonna come right out and say it, did you?)

***

Six months have past since Sparkle snapped out of his coma and back into our lives. And let me tell you, they have not been the most pleasant six months of my life. Or any of our lives, for that matter. Recuperation is a bitch, you see. And Sparkle was a none-to-eager-to-cooperate patient. Such a shock, right? In any case, rehab has been slow but steady. Sparkle is walking with a cane and has nearly all his facilities back. He's still an asshole, but I think the whole experience has mellowed him a bit. Well, that and losing all those brain cells, probably. Still, I'm glad to have him back. Man, I'm *really* glad. Life would've been pretty boring without him, sad but true.

Well, I guess all that's left to do is to fill you in on what happened to our little troupe since that fateful evening when I burst in on Chuck and Sam. It does, after all, play a major role in the shooting. So, let's go back to that horrible night...

The shock of catching my boyfriend snorting coke with my recently-out-of-rehab cousin was quickly replaced by rage. In all my years of hanging around Sparkle, I'd never seen anything that selfish, that destructive, or that moronic. I couldn't imagine how the two of them could justify their behavior. I felt a deep, unending pain in my chest at the thought that Chuck, the man I was falling in love with, and Sam, my own flesh and blood and the person I'd bent over backward to help, were going behind all of our backs in such a foolish way.

"What the fuck are you doing?" I screamed at the two of them.

That broke the shock. They immediately dropped the mirror and jumped off the bed. Chuck tried everything he could to hug me or to even come within a foot of me, but every time he tried, I angrily pushed him away. He was lucky that I wasn't a violent person by nature, because I would've certainly killed him if I thought it would solve anything.

Not knowing what to do, I called Sparkle. No answer. He was obviously not at home. By that time, Chuck and Sam were in near hysterics and cowering in the corner of the living room. In all honesty, I wished they were both dead at that very moment. With my rage growing even more intense, I called Peter's to see if Sparkle was there. Nope. But Peter, hearing the obvious agitation in my voice, pressed me until I told him what I'd discovered. He begged me to wait until he got there before I did anything else. Knowing that this was just as painful for him, I agreed and locked myself in the bathroom. See, I couldn't face the two shitheads in the other room. Instead, I screamed through the door and told them that Peter was on his way and to stay in the living room and not move from there. They meekly agreed.

I sat in that bathroom for twenty minutes, trembling and crying until Peter arrived. It was the worst twenty minutes of my life. God, I wished that Sparkle were there right then. I mean, I desperately needed someone I could count on. And, apparently, Sparkle was it. The only one. (No, my dear friend, the irony was not lost on me either.)

Hearing Peter storm into the apartment and immediately start in on Sam and Chuck woke me from my daze and I emerged from the bathroom to join him. Seeing me in the state I was in, he stopped shouting and ran over to hug me and to apologize.

"I knew something was up, Secret. I just knew it." He sobbed on my shoulder. "I should've confronted them weeks ago."

"Come on now, Peter. There was no way for any of us to imagine this," I said, rubbing Peter's back and shooting angry leers at Chuck and Sam. "Trust me, if I'd had even a clue about this, I would've ended it weeks ago, too. Don't blame yourself. Blame the two pricks over there." I pointed at said pricks and started shouting at them myself. Having no excuse for their behavior, they stood there and took it all. I screamed until I was hoarse and still didn't feel any better or any less angry.

After ten minutes of this, Peter stopped me and had us all sit down. By then, I was exhausted and only too glad to oblige.

"Okay," he began, "I've been standing here for the last ten minutes thinking about what you two bozos have done, and this is what I've come up with. Firstly, you're both obviously very sick. (I nodded in full agreement.) There's no way a sane, thinking person could do what you two were doing and even begin to imagine that it was right or fair to the people around you or to yourselves." Chuck and Sam bowed their heads down in shame. Fuck, I wanted to go over there and smack them.

"Secondly, you both need a lot of help. (Again, I nodded my head vigorously.) Whatever drug habits you might have, you're both headed down a road that can only lead to trouble. Obviously, you both need to be in counseling immediately. What you did is nearly unforgivable. I hope you both realize that." They nodded that they did. (Nearly? Uh-oh. I stopped nodding my head and waited for the bomb to drop)

"Lastly, I can't speak for Chuck or Secret here, but I can speak for myself, Sam. What you did was awful and underhanded and unimaginably unhealthy. For someone whose life was taking such good turns for the better, I can't even begin to imagine why you chose to use drugs again." Sam's face was red, with tears streaming down his cheeks. Peter continued. "But I do know this, I love you very much. And I know that I have two choices right now. I can either throw your ass back on the street and let you go ruin your life again (oh, Lord, I knew what the *or* was and I didn't like it one bit), or I can get you some help and try to keep you from fucking up your life even worse. What's it going to be?"

Sam looked up at Peter for the first time since the harangue began, wiped the tears from his eyes, and slowly walked over to where he was standing.

"Oh, God, Peter, I'm so sorry," he cried, and they wrapped their arms around each other and started bawling together. I, for one, was sick. I was all for voting on Plan A. We should've left Sam in the street where we found him. I should've trusted my first instincts all those months ago. Now, I was left with this mess and none too happy about it.

Chuck, seeing the way the two lovebirds were making up, looked up at me with hope in his eyes. He carefully made his way toward me as well, and lifted up his arms for a conciliatory hug. (Yeah, right. As if.)

"Get the fuck out!" I shouted.

"But...," he jumped back, surprised.

"Now. Get the fuck out!" I shouted again and pushed his tired ass toward the door.

"Bu... but... this is my apartment," he whined.

"Fine, Peter and Asshole Number Two, stop that wretched hugging and get your asses out of this rat's nest immediately." I pushed Chuck out of the way, opened the front door, and motioned for the boys to hurry on out. They obeyed and were in the hallway in seconds. "And you," I said, with a finger in Chuck's face, "stay away from me and my family, or else!" By *or else*, I meant Sparkle. He would know what to do with the jerk. I, for one, was finished with Chuck and all men forever. (Yeah, yeah, I know. Whatever.) I slammed the door behind me and ran down to the street. I desperately needed some fresh air and a good hundred yards distance from that place by then.

Once I made it far enough way, I sat down on the curb and buried my head in my lap. And, Lord only knows why, I actually, for a split second, thought about going back up there and forgiving him. Damn it, I loved him. I knew I did, but I also knew that what he did to me was inexcusable. If he loved me even half as much as I loved him, there was no way he could've done what he had done. No amount of drugs (and as you've seen, I've taken quite a few) could justify his actions. I stood up and started to walk down the street, with the boys following a few feet behind. I had to put the temptation safely out of reach, I figured.

After a bit of walking, and with my head clearing up a bit, I slowed down and let the boys catch up with me. I punched my cousin on the arm first; it made me feel better. Peter punched him as well. That made us both feel better. Too bad anything more would've been illegal. Plus, we were in the street where there would've been witnesses.

"Where are we walking to, Bruce?" Peter asked me, knowing full well the answer to that question.

"Please, we all know where we're headed," I answered, firmly.

"Um, Bruce." He stopped walking and grabbed my arm for me to stop, too. "I have a favor to ask."

"Oh no," I cried.

"Now listen just a second, Bruce. I know what you're thinking. What Sam did was stupid and underhanded. (I nodded a yes.) And I know that you think I'm an idiot for taking him back. (Again a yes.) But you also know that if I turn my back on him now, he'll end up alone, unloved, and in the street. Or worse. Do you want that?" (Somewhere, deep, deep down, I think I did, but I nodded a no. Why should I have been the bad guy?)

"What's your point?" I asked him.

"Oh, you know my point. You know that if we tell Sparkle about what just happened there would be no chance in hell for Sam. There's no way he will let us stay boyfriends. There's no way he'll continue to pay for Sam's education. There's no way he'll let us live together, because he'll go tell Kiki and Larry about it and they'll kick us out. You know all of this, Bruce."

"So what you're saying is…"

"No telling Sparkle the truth," he finished my sentence. "We have to keep this a secret if we're going to get help for Sam and try and keep us all together. You took a chance on me all those years ago, and I'm asking you to take a chance again." He looked at me with his soulful eyes, and I knew the answer. So, as hard as it was going to be, I promised them that I wouldn't tell Sparkle. That is, so long as Sam stayed off the drugs and never lied to us again. If he dared try anything even almost resembling a repeat performance of that evening, not only would I tell Sparkle the whole story, but also, I'd turn Sam into the police myself. They gleefully agreed and hugged me. I wasn't the least bit happy about the arrangement, but I knew that the alternative would surely hurt Peter a great deal. That I could not do.

***

And that was that. The next day, Peter and Sam signed up for drug counseling through their school. And, though my heart wasn't into it, I went along with the plan. What did I tell Sparkle in terms of me no longer seeing Chuck? Well, I told him that I left work early to go home the night before and decided instead to go over to Chuck's, and that's when I found him with another man. It was short and simple. I screamed and shouted at him and then dumped his cheating ass. Sparkle, though furious at Chuck, was obviously thrilled at having me back as a fulltime best friend. It seemed, alas, that I was the biggest loser in all this mess. Typical.

Life went on pretty much as normal, thereafter. The only difference was that we almost never went over to Peter and Sam's anymore; I just couldn't sit there and enjoy myself. It was hard enough to lie to Sparkle, but doubly difficult to do it in front of the people who asked me to lie in the first place. Sparkle was just as happy with that arrangement, as he never much cared for my cousin's company anyway. I just let Peter worry about him and Sam; I didn't want to invest any more energy into it. Whatever was going to happen, I'd let the two of them work it out.

Pretty much it quickly became Sharon, Sparkle, and myself once again. The Three Queerskateers. And, for better or worse, that's the way it stayed up until the coma. Am I bitter? Oh, please, if you have to ask that question, you haven't been paying attention. Do I have any regrets? Thousands. Doesn't everybody? But I have my friends and my family. And they love me, pretty much unconditionally. Peter is still in our lives, but he's growing up and has his own responsibilities and his own life to live.

And, for the most part, I'm fairly happy. I have more than most. Maybe some day I'll have a lover and a home with a white picket fence. Maybe I won't. But I'll keep trying for it, nonetheless. Nobody likes a quitter, after all. In the meantime, I have what I have, and that makes me happy. Lord only knows what adventures will befall Sparkle and me, and I'm looking forward to all of them. I can't say that it's ever been dull around here, that's for sure. So, I guess I'll let you get back to doing whatever it is you were doing before all of this started. You've been a great listener. It's been a real pleasure and....

What?

What was that?

Oh, yeah, I nearly forgot to tell you who shot Sparkle. Couldn't let you leave without that little piece of information, could I?

***

254

A few days after Sparkle woke up, I came by for my daily visit, and he seemed more lucid than he'd been the first couple of days. Now was as good a time as any to find out the truth. Though I had a feeling that I would've been better off not knowing. I was right, of course. Too bad for me.

I pulled a chair up close to his bed, held his weakened hand in my own, looked him in his eyes, and asked, "Baby, who shot you?"

He closed his lids for a second before answering. I gathered he was gaining the strength to talk about it. Still, I wasn't expecting what came next.

"I know the real reason you and Chuck broke up," he spoke, still in a whisper, which was all he could muster at the time.

"But how?" I gulped.

"He came by to see me just after that night. Wanted to explain himself and asked if I would talk to you. Try to get you to see him. Fix things up for him. That kind of stuff. He was pretty pathetic." My friend paused and gulped. "I almost agreed."

"But you obviously didn't, seeing as this is the first I'm hearing about it. Why?" I knew why because I knew Sparkle.

"Well, I knew he was no good for you. Oh, yes, I knew he loved you and that you loved him. That, of course, was the worst part. But no one that did what he did could possibly be worth it. So I told him to save his breath; I wouldn't help him." A tear slipped from Sparkle's eye. I brushed it away for him. "Did I do the right thing?"

I squeezed his hand. "Yeah, Buddy, you did the right thing. How could I have ever trusted him again? As it was, I could barely trust Sam again. And that I did only for Peter's sake. But why didn't you say anything all this time. Why would it matter?"

"I don't know. It seemed easier not to say anything. It wouldn't have made losing Chuck any easier on you, and the boys seemed to be getting along okay. I never cared much for Sam, but at least I knew to keep an eye out for any more problems. And time went by and I just let it go. I shouldn't have, though. I should've said something. I should have... I should have..." More tears interrupted his admission. I wiped them off and held a glass of water up to his lips so he could take a drink. My heart was breaking seeing him so weak like that. I was, as you now well know, used to him being the strong one.

"Do I really want to hear the rest of this?" I asked.

"No," he whispered and looked away. We sat there like that for some time. I didn't want to press him. What energy he had was dripping into him from a bag to his left. He would, I figured, tell me when he was ready.

The nurse came in after a time to check on his vitals. They were coming in a lot more now that he was out of the coma. This one was a male nurse and quite the looker. Needless to say, the fact didn't go unnoticed by my friend.

"Sponge bath? Sparkle asked, a barely noticeable grin spreading across his chapped lips. And that's when I knew he'd be okay.

"In a bit, Mister Astan. Just coming in to check on your vital signs here," the nurse said, monitoring the instruments and then writing notes down on Sparkle's chart. "I'll be back soon for your bath. You'll be okay until then?"

"I'm not going anywhere," Sparkle joked. I laughed, for the first time in a while. "And call me Sparkle. Not Mister Astan."

"Fine, Sparkle, I'll be back in an hour. You enjoy your visitor's company until then." He winked at me and left.

"He wants me," Sparkle moaned as he tried to shift his tired body. I fluffed up his pillows and maneuvered him around until he was comfortable enough.

"I'm sure," I laughed again. "Think you can get it up?"

He gave me a sly look and coughed out a "Bitch." Oh, that word had never sounded so beautiful before. "I suppose I'll have to tell you how I got here eventually. May as well do it now, so we can figure what to tell the police," he said, with a noticeable frown. I didn't like the way he said it, of course. It sounded like more lying was needed, and I, for a change, had had my full. And then some.

"It can wait. You need your rest." I tried to stop him, but more because I didn't think I was ready for the answer than for his wellbeing.

"No. It won't take long to tell you. I'll feel better once I get it out. Just give me a second." He closed his eyes and lay there very still. My heart and my mind were racing. It felt like an eternity before he finally opened them again and started to tell me the rest of the story. "Once I knew the truth, I took to visiting Peter and Sam while you were at work. Peter was always happy to see me. Sam, however, showed an obviously forced courtesy toward me. Fuck it, though, I didn't care. Peter was seeing through a boy's lovesick eyes, and I needed to see for myself that Sam was sticking to his promise to stay clear of the drugs. It was a charade I felt I had to put on. Since neither boy knew that I knew their secret, it was the prefect plan." Another rest before he continued. The strain was showing.

"There was one obvious drawback, however. If I did see anything out of the ordinary, I couldn't say anything. Also, I just couldn't hurt Peter. And saying anything bad about Sam would most certainly hurt. Luckily, I never noticed anything amiss. I owe this less to Sam's willpower and more to the fact that Peter seemed never to let Sam out of his sight. This, thank God, worked to our advantage."

"How's that?" I asked, now just a tad curious. See, I just loved it when Sparkle was being sneaky.

"Well, it was immediately obvious that Sam was resentful of my uninvited company. And he couldn't say anything while I was there, because he knew that if I knew their little secret, he would most certainly be back on the street. In other words, I made sure that I was around a lot. And then I enlisted Kiki's help."

"You did what?" I suppressed a laugh as I jumped up. "Kiki knew about all this and didn't say a word to me?" The thought of Sparkle and Kiki teaming up was so absurd and the image of them plotting together so riotous, that I began to laugh, despite myself. Even Sparkle let out what I assumed was a laugh. In his present state, it was hard to tell.

"Yup. And it worked, too. I told Kiki everything I knew and then I made him promise not to tell anybody, not even Larry. The plan was simple: never let Sam have a moment to himself. I learned the boys' school hours, knowing that, while they were in class, Peter was keeping a watchful eye on his boyfriend. When they were at home, during the day, I would pop in. And, at night, Kiki would unexpectedly come acallin'. Peter loved seeing both of us. Sam was obviously miserable, and since I was paying his way and since Kiki was providing a roof over his head, he couldn't say a thing."

"So that's why...," I was putting the pieces together, but Sparkle shushed me so that he could continue. Even weak from the coma, a good story could still perk him up.

"Anyway, within a few days of putting our plan into effect, Kiki reported good results. He said that he could hear the boys arguing through the floor. And, as the weeks progressed, the arguing became more frequent. Until..." This time, as Sparkle was catching his breath, I cut in.

"Until that day we all came over to find Peter alone in his apartment with that note and most of their belongings suddenly missing."

"Exactly." Sparkle managed a smile, though I could tell it hurt to do so.

"God, I wondered what caused him to pick up and move out. You guys must've been truly awful to make him leave like that." I stood up and bowed before him. "Bravo, Sparkle, I tip my hat to you. I know it was crushing to Peter, but that was one of the happiest days of my life."

"Ain't that the truth. Goodbye to bad rubbish. That boy was no good from the get go, and I was damned if I was gonna see him drag our Peter down with him, if I had any say in the matter. And, even though I knew that Peter was hurting badly, I could still detect just a hint of relief on his part to finally be rid of him. That's when I knew that I'd done the right thing."

Sparkle stopped there to rest again. I needed a break as well. That was the most excitement I'd faced since Sparkle uttered his first words just a few days earlier.

Anyway, I should've seen the signs earlier. It was just too perfect an ending to a bad situation. I should've known that we couldn't have been so lucky without a little help from our friend, Tom Foolery. I guess I was just so happy for the whole thing to be over with that I didn't even stop to think that Sparkle was the cause of it all. Now it all made sense.

Of course, that didn't answer the original question of who shot him. For that, I would have to wait another day. Sparkle, you see, was suddenly fast asleep. He didn't even wake up for his sponge bath, and he was going to be mad at me for that. But I'll take mad over dead any day. I did, needless to say, stay around to flirt with his nurse, Justin, though. I had to take advantage of Sparkle's weakness while I could. You know, strike while the getting's good. After all, I had little to no chance once my friend regained his strength. Thankfully, yummy Justin was quite receptive.

That night, I went over to visit Kiki and Larry. Kiki was surprised to see me and even more surprised when I rushed in and gave him a big, old hug. I pulled him off to the kitchen so that Larry couldn't hear us, and then I told him that I knew about his and Sparkle's little arrangement. He was thrilled to not have to keep it a secret anymore. At least from Larry and me. We would never be able to tell Peter, though. He'd be furious if he knew.

"I already know about it," came a voice from the wall vent.

"Hey," Kiki shouted as he crouched down to get closer to the vent. "I didn't know that you could hear us up here!"

"Um, well, sorry, I can," came the voice again.

"Stay there," I shouted into the vent. "We're coming down."

"No problemo," Peter shouted back up. Damn kids!

"What do you mean you already knew?" Kiki shouted at Peter as we stormed into the apartment below. Did you overhear Sparkle and I planning it or something?"

"No, not really, Kiki. I mean, please, you were both so incredibly obvious about it. For starters, I know that Sparkle would rather have been anywhere else than hanging out with Sam and me practically every afternoon. Up until Sam got caught, he'd never so much as visited us without Secret, not even once. Then, like clockwork, he was here as soon as we got home from school every day. And you, Kiki, were down here every single night. I thought Larry was going to break up with you long before Sam broke up with me." He started laughing.

"What's so funny?" It was Peter's lover Mitch, coming out of the bathroom. Oh, yeah, Mitch quickly replaced Sam in Peter's life. So much for young love. The head may have a memory, but the heart rolls merrily along. Thank God.

"The truth is finally out," Peter said to Mitch.

"Oh, that." Mitch giggled and plopped down on the sofa. He was tall and goofy and completely irresistible. We loved him dearly. Of course, anybody would've been better than Sam. Luckily for us, Mitch wasn't just anybody.

"Yes, oh that," Kiki echoed. Then we all started to crack up. It was pretty funny, after all. We were all, except me, of course, too quick to have the wool pulled over our eyes for very long. Naturally, I was in darkness throughout the ordeal. If ignorance really is bliss, it wasn't doing a hell of a lot of good for me.

"But you never complained," Kiki said to Peter, once the laughing subsided.

"No, but Sam sure did. Every night, in fact. I guess that I was secretly glad that you guys were trying to get him to leave. I suppose I wasn't brave enough to end it myself. And I did love him. Or at least I thought I did. But I realized that I could never trust him. Once I figured that out, it was pretty much over between the two of us. Then it was just a matter of waiting for him to move out on his own. Fortunately, you guys were so persistent. It felt like a million pounds had been lifted off my shoulders when I found that note of his."

"Amen," I agreed.

"Amen," Kiki agreed.

"Amen," Peter joined in.

"I think we know my opinion," said Mitch from the couch.

We had a big group hug and agreed that we all needed a drink. Kiki went upstairs and got Larry. Once we filled him in on the details of Kiki and Sparkle's scheme, we were off to pick up Sharon from work and then on to a nice family dinner. Well, almost family. But we all knew it wouldn't be long before you-know-who could join us. We said grace for the first time ever and thanked God for bringing Sparkle back to us. In all honesty, I was sure that the good Lord was glad to get rid of him. I could only imagine the havoc Sparkle was wrecking up there.

I recounted the day's events to my friends after the wine was poured. They were all thrilled at Sparkle's noticeable recovery. Then the conversation turned to who we each thought shot him. We went through one scenario after another, pretty much touching upon all the stories I've already told you, but none of them sounded too likely. True, all those people hated Sparkle, but I was sure that they had other things in their lives more pressing than knocking him off.

We would just have to wait until I spoke to Sparkle the next day to find out. Seeing as how we'd waited that long, what was another day? And so, with a rousing toast to our dear incapacitated but mending friend, we ate and drank and enjoyed ourselves like any family would. I knew how lucky I really was to be blessed with such wonderful people in my life, and right there and then I told them all that.

The whole thing with Sparkle taught me that you never know when something crazy will happen, and that you should count your blessings before it's too late. No, there's no Gay Rule for that one. But, word to the wise, don't wait too long to tell those around you that you love them. After all, you never know when you'll get that call in the middle of the night telling you to come down to the hospital. (Last preachy thing I say. Promise.)

***

The next afternoon, I showed up in Sparkle's room and was greeted by a pleasant surprise. Sparkle was propped up in his bed and watching *Oprah*. Meaning, the long road to recovery had finally begun. I sat down and watched it with him. I almost never get a chance to watch it, as I'm always at the shop. Funny, very little can make me cry. Not movies, not real life tragedies, not family deaths, but five minutes into *Oprah* and I'm balling like a baby. Sparkle, too, and he has even less of a heart than I do.

An hour later, we both knew what had to be said. I was dreading it, but *Oprah* had me prepared for anything. Whatever happened, it couldn't be any worse than the shit she has going on during her show. (Yes, yes, I was wrong as usual.)

"I suppose I fell asleep yesterday before I could finish my story," he began.

"Yup. That's okay. Justin and I had a fine time with you," I kidded.

"Who's Just…. oh… you're being awfully mean to a man who, until recently, was very close to death, aren't you?"

"Please, Mary, look who taught me. If the situation was reversed, I'm sure I would've woken up this morning with some dried up something in my hair, and it wouldn't have been mine," I said. And it was probably true.

"I'll give you that one," he agreed. Justin, after all, is rather pretty to look at. It was everything I could do to behave. Sparkle, however, would've gone hog-wild. That would've been just my luck, too. My first three-way and I'd have been fast asleep.

"Anyway," he started again, "I feel better today. Let's get it over with."

"Fine," I said, bracing myself.

"Fine," he said, obviously stalling.

"Sparkle, just say it already. You're killing me here," I commanded.

"Bad choice of words, but okay," he said and took a breath. "First, well, I guess you should know that this whole mess is partially my fault."

"No shock there. Isn't it usually?" I commented. It really wasn't a big surprise. I said all along that he probably had it coming to him somehow.

"Fucker. Be nice. I'm in pain here," he said, wincing. That I did doubted, as he was hopped up on every painkiller and medication in the book. I suspected, actually, that he wasn't feeling much of anything, but I kissed him on the forehead for good measure and bade him to continue, and that he did.

"Okay, well, Sam did take whatever he could lay his grubby, little hands on and he did leave that note for Peter. That much you know. That's what all of you know, by now. What you don't know, however, is that he wasn't completely out of our lives after that."

"Oh Lord, here we go," I lamented.

"Be quiet, Secret, and let me finish. So, anyway, about a week after the vanishing act, he shows up at my door. For a split second, I had forgotten what he had done and took pity on him. He did look horrible, and I'm nothing if not merciful."

"Ahem." I cleared my throat while he shot me a menacing look. I let him continue.

"He sat down and got right to the point. Basically, he came to extort money from me. He threatened that if I didn't cooperate, he would reappear in Peter's life, begging forgiveness. He pointed out that he was sure to succeed and that I alone had the means to prevent him from doing so. Meaning, I relented, and quickly. I figured that it was worth it for Peter's sake. And I knew that he was right. Peter would have let him right back in." (Huh, Sparkle was actually wrong in this instance; Peter wouldn't have let him return, as I had come to find out, but far be it from me to rub salt in the wound. Tempting though it was.)

"He returned to my doorstep three more times. Each time, he looked worse than the time before. Each time, he threw the same threat at me, but we both knew that he had gone way beyond what Peter would've ever taken back. What he didn't know was that Peter had already started seeing Mitch. See, I never told him." Sparkle paused. I could tell that this was wearing him out.

"Why?" I asked.

"Don't rightly know. I guess I felt responsible. Their break up, after all, was somewhat through my own doing." He looked remorseful. First time for everything, I guess.

"Sparkle, you are so not responsible in any way for his condition. He was snorting coke with my boyfriend behind all of our backs. Remember?" I get angry every time I think of that, but I tried to be gentle with my weakened friend.

"I know, I know. But you should've seen him. He was so pitiful. And, anyway, he wasn't even asking for that much money. I think he was there to be around the normalcy more than anything else. (Strange thought that.) I assumed he'd really hit rock bottom by that point. I even offered to get him back into a treatment program, but he refused. So I would give him money and lunch, and then he would leave. I never even knew if I would see him again each time. And then, of course, I didn't. Not until that night." Long pause followed by a sigh.

"My cousin shot you, Sparkle?" I choked out, barely in a whisper. That scenario had never played out in my head, and an incredible sense of guilt enveloped me.

He paused a moment before he answered. He was obviously having a hard time in the retelling. "Not exactly. And not intentionally," he offered.

"Um, did he shoot you or didn't he? Seems like a pretty cut and dried situation." I was getting sort of frantic by then. How awful that my own flesh and blood shot the person that meant the most to me in the whole entire world.

"Not on purpose, no. Let me explain... Secret, sit down, you're making me nervous... Okay, the night I was shot, I came home early from the gym..."

"Slow night in the sauna?" I broke in.

"And we are friends *why*?"

"Sorry, couldn't resist. Continue."

"Fine. And, yes, it was. Fucker. Anyway, I came home from the gym and my front door was unlocked. *That* I never do. I entered slowly and saw nothing unusual. Not until I walked into the bedroom. Then I saw your cousin going through my dresser drawers. My best guess is that he got the key while he was living with Peter. My door wasn't forced, so it's the only way he could've gotten in. He'd already found my jewelry and some medication by the time I walked in on him. He also had my gun in his hospital-gloved hands. It was all very bad timing." He sat there, shaking his head.

"Bad timing that he was robbing you or that you caught him?" I asked.

"Yes and yes, but mostly that I had just happened in when the gun was in his hand. He was obviously strung out on something and he wasn't thinking clearly, I would guess. I surprised him and he pointed the gun straight at me. He was shaking as he did it. That made me even more nervous, because I keep my gun loaded. And, before you say anything, hindsight is twenty/twenty, as you so often say. Besides, I never expected for that gun to be in anybody else's hands but my own."

"And that's when he shot you?" I asked, anxiously.

"Man, pay attention. Your cousin didn't actually shoot me. Per se. I guess," he answered, vaguely.

"Well, you were shot, you know." I was getting a bit tired of this game by then, as I'm sure you are too. (Fret not, friend, it's almost over.)

"Duh. Let me finish. Anyway, as I stood there, with that gun pointing straight at me and with Sam sweating and shaking, I did what seemed like the logical thing to do. I pulled that old TV trick, the one where you slowly walk up to the person with the gun and calmly say, 'You know you don't want to do that. Just put the gun down slowly and place it on the dresser.' I said this as I approached him, but he just stood there, frozen. Then I grabbed my gun and tried to wrench it from his hand. Still, he wouldn't give it up. I'm not even sure he heard me talking to him. I can't even begin to imagine what he was on. Truth be told, he looked completely zonked out. And that's what really scared me, that I couldn't rationalize with him.

"And then, the gun went off. I'm not sure if he pulled the trigger, or I, in my attempt to get the gun out of his hand, pushed his finger myself. I do know that everything after that went in slow motion. At least the gunshot had one good result, though; it woke Sam up from his stupor. As soon as realized what he'd done, he dropped the gun. Too little, too late, of course. With the blood pouring out of my chest and with Sam growing hysterical, I slowly and painfully dialed 911 and reported that I'd been shot. Then I told Sam to put everything back where he had found it and to get the hell out, fast. He complied, mechanically, and then ran out the door. Next thing I knew, I woke up here."

"I'm sorry," I sobbed, grabbing for his hand.

"Why? You didn't shoot me."

"But he's my cousin, and… and…"

"And nothing. We blame Sam and no one else. Least, just between us, we admit that it was your cousin," Sparkle said, looking me in the eyes so I knew he meant it.

"How come?" I asked, sitting back down. I was ready to call the cops right there and then, I mean. Cousin or not, he was a menace and should've been behind bars. At least that's what I thought. Sparkle, suffice it to say, had a different take on it.

"Look," he reasoned, "what good would it do? Fine, they arrest Sam. Then what? He goes to jail, where he becomes a hardened criminal? And you know your entire family will blame themselves. Not to mention, so will Peter. So why bother? I just don't see what good can come from it. It was, for the most part, an accident. Sam never meant to shoot me. The best we can hope for is that this whole mess will make him realize that he needs help. At least, that's what I would like to see happen. Do you think we can do that? Please?"

I had to think about it for a second, but I already knew that it would be useless to argue. If Sparkle didn't want to press it, why should I? And so, that's how we left it. Sparkle told the police that he answered the door, the robber pushed his way in, held a gun on him, and then robbed him. When the robber wasn't paying attention, Sparkle made a rush for the gun, and the robber shot him. He gave the police a very nondescript description, and that was the end of it. The police, for their part, seemed like they couldn't care less and, after a few weeks, we stopped hearing from them. Case over.

And with case over, my dear friend, so is this story. Sad? Gonna miss me? I think you will. Check back from time to time. Who knows what mischief will follow once Sparkle is fully recuperated? I do know this much, though: no more lies. Least not from me. I've learned my lesson the hard way. Cross my heart and hope to… well, let's not go that far. One near fatal death is all I can endure. Until then… oh, just forget what I said. We all know it will never work out that way. Just pray for me, okay? For us, I mean. Me and my whole crazy family, every last one of them.

If you enjoyed *Sparkle: The Queerest Book You'll Ever Love*, please check out my other novels:

Divas Las Vegas
Hot Lava
And my erotica collection: *Good & Hot*

And feel free to visit my website for more on me, my work, and my life: www.therobrosen.com

Or drop me an email at: robrosen@therobrosen.com

Much Love,

Rob